U0077393

力得文化
Leader Culture

Lead your way, be your own leader!

力得文化
Leader Culture

Lead your way, be your own leader!

英文文法超圖解 精裝修訂版

Diagramming English Grammar

30天攻略本

圖解式英文文法

邏輯式有效學習

文法恐懼症救星

必備文法
概念圖解 X20

必學實戰
句型會話 X30

必閃常見
誤用陷阱 X40

擊敗陌陌長文法
必殺密技

有計畫
30天文法KO進度表,讓你
有系統性規劃學習進度

高效率 圖解式核心文法觀念,刺激大腦記憶,讓你
快速掌握文法大綱

全方位 本書獨創20-30-40邏輯式學習,提升你的
Globish,從文法到對話樣樣行

朱懿婷◎著　羅展明◎審定

PREFACE
作者序

關於英語

　　有一陣子，我相當羨慕可以出國遊學或是留學的人。因為工作上常常遇到具有「什麼都不管，只要有喝過洋墨水就是好人才」這種偏執的上司。

　　但是在社會上歷練了五、六年之後，漸漸地也可以辨認出喝過洋墨水這件事背後帶來的具體意義，及老闆看不到的「致命盲點」。後來，我就不再太過於羨慕這種人，甚至有不需出國英文也可以說得比他們更溜的信心。

　　這絕對不是老王賣瓜心態喔！在與國外客戶溝通 Meeting 的經驗中，我發現外國人在口語交談上真的不是那麼注重文法能力，重點是談吐的氣度和話題的深度。談吐的氣度來自於個人的自信心，而話題的深度則來自於個人的素養和字彙的能力了。

　　這就是我開始對英語教學有興趣的起源。

　　我希望可以透過自身的經驗，搭配一些在職場上學習到的科學方法，讓學英文這件事不用非得花大錢不可。我絕對認同到國外遊學或留學可以增進英語能力，但我認為，與其說「國外留學」這件事增強了英語能力，不如說是增強了個人「開口說話的勇氣」及「了解西方文化的程度」，讓你更能夠得心應手地與外國人交談。

　　說到底，那文法到底重不重要呢？我覺得這件事就像每個學生都想問的：「學歷到底重不重要？」這件事一模一樣。「文法和學歷，都是要等你懂了、拿到了，才可以說不重要。」這就是我對文法重要程度的概念。

朱懿婷

PREFACE
編者序

關於文法

在學習英語的過程中，難免對所謂「文法」懷抱著或多或少的恐懼感；每到必須開口，或是難得有機會開口說英語的時候，更總是戰戰兢兢，深怕說得不夠完美！

但可別忘了，英語本來就是種「溝通工具」，只要能夠完整地表達自己的想法，即可和談話對象相互理解、交流，沒人會幫你打分數！換句話說，掌握基本文法架構便能築出你的英語力，別讓文法完美與否成了你跨越國界、展現自我的絆腳石。

既然如此，為什麼我們還需要《圖解式英文文法》這一本書呢？那是因為這本書打破了一般文法的藩籬，不需死背一條又一條的規則，而是進階式地引導你理解文法的道理及邏輯，幫助你舉一反三；另搭配上貼近日常生活、社交的活潑例句，讓你一看就懂，現學現用！

無論你的目標是外派出差、搞定英文簡報，或是想要自助旅行，還是單純想和外國朋友聊天、搏感情，《圖解式英文文法》都能成為你的加分利器。它提供日常必備英文文法的全方位導覽，將焦點放在「理解」與「應用」；不在單點上過度鑽研，深入淺出的說明讓你輕鬆吸收、零負擔。

《圖解式英文文法》還為你規劃了 30 天的衝刺學習日程，帶你迅速達陣！對於需求並沒有那麼急迫的讀者，也可以利用進度表了解自己的學習進度，從容排程以達到更好的效果。

想要學好一門語言，就怕你「開不了口」。實際嘗試表達，是檢視學習進度的最佳方式；除了每天乖乖按照進度「紙上談兵」之外，也別放過任何現學現用的機會，秀出你的英語力！你懂文法嗎？能夠倒背如流不等於懂文法；懂得怎麼「用」文法才是最高境界！

倍斯特編輯部

文法 KO 進度表

請依照以下的進度表，填上你的預定學習日期，一口氣 KO 你的文法惡夢吧！
完成進度的當天記得劃上大叉叉，可以刺激學習欲望喔！

學習天數	01	02	03	04	05	06	07
預定學習日							
學習內容	文法概念 1～3	文法概念 4～6	文法概念 7~9	文法概念 10～12	文法概念 13~15	文法概念 16～18	文法概念 19～20

學習天數	08	09	10	11	12	13	14
預定學習日							
學習內容	必學句型 1～2	必學句型 3～4	必學句型 5～6	必學句型 7～8	必學句型 9～10	必學句型 11～12	必學句型 13～14

學習天數	15	16	17	18	19	20	21
預定學習日							
學習內容	必學句型 15～16	必學句型 17～18	必學句型 19～20	必學句型 21～22	必學句型 23～24	必學句型 25～26	必學句型 27～28

學習天數	22	23	24	25	26	27	28
預定學習日							
學習內容	必學句型 29～30	文法陷阱 1～5	文法陷阱 6～10	文法陷阱 11～15	文法陷阱 16～20	文法陷阱 21～25	文法陷阱 26～30

學習天數	29	30					
預定學習日							
學習內容	文法陷阱 31～35	文法陷阱 36～40					

CONTENTS
目次

第一階段：Day 01~07
20 個一定要知道的文法概念

Step 1
先搞懂概念與時態

Step 2
了解英文中關鍵的關鍵一字詞

Step 3
該如何使用進階的句子？

第二階段：Day 08~22
30 個一定要學的句型

Level 1
基礎觀念馬上建立！（程度分級：國中英語）

He is so sick that he can't go to work today.
└ 延伸 so... that...

Let's go to see Transformer 4 today!
└ 句型 05 Let's; Let us...
Why not go for a walk after dinner?
└ 延伸 Why not; Why don't we...?

Not everybody like you want Federer to win, ok?
└ 句型 06 Not everybody / both / all / every...

It is no wonder you always feel sleepy during the class.
└ 句型 07 (It is) no wonder (that)...

It will take 7 working days to finish the project.
└ 句型 08 It takes (sb.)... + to do sth.

What do you think of/about the ending of the Harry Porter?
└ 句型 09 What do you think of / about...?

My mother asks me to go home as soon as the class is over.
└ 句型 10 ... as soon as...

Level 2
可以開始簡單英語會話囉！（程度分級：高中第一～二冊）

I won't go to a movie with your brother unless you go with us.
└ 句型 11 unless...
I won't leave here until you give me the money.
└ 延伸 until...

We don't know whether big screen iPhones will be released or not.
└ 句型 12 whether... or...

第三階段：Day 23~30
40 個不能不閃的文法**陷阱**

Trap 1
單字陷阱・類義單字辨析篇

單字陷阱‧
一字多義使用篇

單字陷阱‧
類義單字辨析篇

Day 23~30
個不能不
閃的文法 陷阱

‥or‥

‥t/Can't/Won't‥) + sb.‥?

‥w‥!

‥d you mind‥?

‥but also‥

‥ of/for sb. + to do‥

‥es not think/suppose/believe that‥

‥for sb.) to do sth.‥

可以開始簡單
英語會話囉！

基礎觀念馬上建立！

看到阿豆仔
也不用怕！

第二階段：Day 08~22
30 個一定
要學的 句型

先搞懂概念與時態

第一階段：Day 01~07
20 個一定要知道的文法概念

了解英文中
關鍵的關鍵一字詞

該如何使用
進階的句子？

01 圖解文法，一看就會！
Grammar Mind Mapping

1. 單字
- 1-1 名詞
- 1-2 代名詞
- 1-3 形容詞
- 1-4 動詞
- 1-5 副詞
- 1-6 介系詞
- 1-7 連接詞
- 1-8 感嘆詞

3. 句型
- 3-1 主詞＋不及物動詞
- 3-2 主詞＋動詞＋主詞補語
- 3-3 主詞＋及物動詞＋受詞
- 3-4 主詞＋授與動詞＋間接受詞＋直接受詞
- 3-5 主詞＋及物動詞＋受詞＋受詞補語

英文文法概論

2. 片語
- 2-1 名詞片語
- 2-2 副詞片語
- 2-3 動詞片語
- 2-4 介系詞片語

4. 文法
- 4-1 動詞不能連用
- 4-2 兩個動詞用 to / -ing
- 4-3 第三人稱動詞加 s
- 4-4 否定句不可直接加 not
- 4-5 to ＋ V 原形
- 4-6 助動詞
- 4-7 問句要用助動詞
- 4-8 動詞隨主詞變化形式

英文文法是針對英語語言的文法進行的研究，指英語中語言的結構規律，主要包括「單字、片語、句型和文法」四個要素。以下就根據這四個要素做細節說明：

1. 單字

單字英文依據在句子中的功能，共可分為八大詞類，分別為名詞、代名詞、形容詞、動詞、副詞、介系詞、連接詞和感嘆詞。以下為詳細說明：

- **1-1. 名詞**：表示人、地、事、物等名詞的字。名詞分為可數名詞和不可數名詞，可數名詞要加冠詞 a / an，不可數名詞要加定冠詞 the，例如：a book, an apple, the air。

- **1-2. 代名詞**：表示代替名詞或名詞短語的形式用詞。代名詞可以分為：

01 人稱代名詞	I, you, his...
02 指示代名詞	this, that, those...
03 不定代名詞	some, any, one, other, another, all, every...
04 疑問代名詞	what, who, why, which...
05 關係代名詞	that, which, who, whose...

- **1-3. 形容詞**：用來修飾「名詞」或「代名詞」的字。形容詞可分為：

01 性狀形容詞	表示物品的狀態或是性質。 a **good** student（一位好學生） 3 **young** people（三個年輕人） an **American** movie（一部美國電影）
02 代名詞形容詞	具有代名詞功能，後面需接名詞。並可細分為：指示形容詞、不定形容詞、所有格形容詞、疑問形容詞及關係形容詞。
2-1 指示形容詞	**These** 2 girls are from Canada.（這兩個女孩來自加拿大。）
2-2 不定形容詞	I need **some** new ideas.（我需要一些新想法。）
2-3 所有格形容詞	**Your** dress is so elegant.（妳的洋裝好優雅。）
2-4 疑問形容詞	**Whose** pen is this?（這是誰的筆？）

2-5 關係形容詞	I have a classmate **whose** sister is a famous singer. （我有個同學的姊姊是知名歌手。）
03 數量形容詞	用來表示數目和份量的形容詞。 可分為：不定數量形容詞、基數數詞、序數數詞、倍數數詞。
3-1 不定數量形容詞	Linda has so **many** friends to play with. （琳達有很多可以玩在一起的朋友。）
3-2 基數數詞	My mother has **five** younger sisters.（我媽媽有五個妹妹。）
3-3 序數數詞	This is my **first** time to travel alone. （這是我第一次獨自旅行。）
3-4 倍數數詞	**Half** of my clothes are black. （我有一半以上的衣服都是黑色。）

- **1-4. 動詞**：是用以表示動作或狀態的字，例如：be, go, get, have, run, send 等。另外，動詞在使用上，要特別注意時態和語態的變化。

時態	
簡單式	現在簡單式
	過去簡單式
	未來簡單式
進行式	現在進行式
	過去進行式
	未來進行式
完成式	現在完成式
	過去完成式
	未來完成式
完成進行式	現在完成進行式
	過去完成進行式
	未來完成進行式

語態	
主動語態	S+V...
被動語態	S+be+P.P. ...

- **1-5. 副詞**：可用來修飾動詞、形容詞和其他副詞，也可以用來修飾片語。副詞分為：

情狀副詞	carefully, successfully, slowly...
地方副詞	here, there, home, abroad, south, outside...
時間副詞	now, yesterday, today, ago...
頻率副詞	sometimes, barely, hardly, once, daily, twice...
程度副詞	entirely, much, many, almost, very...
疑問副詞	where, when, why...
連接副詞	however, meanwhile, besides...

- **1-6. 介系詞**：又叫前置詞，通常放在名詞和代名詞之前，用來表示名詞或代名詞和其前面字的關係。介系詞從形式上來分有四種：

簡單介系詞	只有一個單字	at, before, from, under...
合成介系詞	由兩個字合成	into, upon, outside, without...
雙重介系詞	由兩個介系詞組成	from behind, till after...
片語介系詞	由兩個或多個單字組成	at the end of, according to, because of...

- **1-7. 連接詞**：用來連接單字、片語、子句和句子的字。連接詞分為：

對等連接詞	連接同等地位的單字、片語及子句	(both)... and..., (not only)... but (also)..., as well as...
從屬連接詞	引導從屬子句	so... that..., such... that...

- **1-8. 感嘆詞**：用以表示強烈的情緒和感情的一種聲音或叫喊。例如：Hello! Hurrah! Hi! Oh! 等等。

2. 片語

片語是由兩個或兩個以上的英文單字所組合的詞語，不包含主詞和動詞，可以構成句子的一部分，也可以用來當名詞、形容詞和副詞使用。片語主要分為以下五大種類：

01 名詞片語	**To tell a lie** is wrong.（說謊是錯的。）
02 形容詞片語	**The best way** to lose weight is to exercise more!（減肥最好的方法就是多運動。）
03 副詞片語	I can't finish this book **without Linda's help**.（沒有琳達的幫助我不可能完成這本書。）
04 動詞片語	She **takes care** of the children.（她照顧她的小孩。）
05 介系詞片語	He stood **in front of** the door.（他站在門前面。）

3. 句型

句型結構是按照一定的文法規律組成的，表達一個完整的意義。一個句子一般由兩部分構成，即主詞部分和動詞部分，這兩部分也是句子中最主要的成分。而句子的次要成分包括受詞、形容詞、副詞、主詞補語等。首先來介紹一下在一般文法說明中較常使用到的字詞縮寫：

- S   Subject   ＝主詞
- V   Verb   ＝動詞
- Vt   Transitive Verb   ＝及物動詞
- Vi   Intransitive Verb   ＝不及物動詞
- O   Object   ＝受詞
- DO   Direct Object   ＝直接受詞
- IO   Indirect Object   ＝間接受詞
- C   Complement   ＝補語
- SC   Subject Complement   ＝主詞補語
- OC   Object Complement   ＝受詞補語

以下為英文基本五大句型：

句型 01：S ＋ V（主詞＋不及物動詞）

Everybody laughed.（大家都笑了。）
S 　　　V

句型 02：S ＋ V ＋ SC（主詞＋動詞＋主詞補語）

此結構中的動詞常為連綴動詞，例如：look, seem, appear, prove, become, turn, sound, taste, keep, stay... 等。

The girl in the red dress looks cute.（那個穿紅色洋裝的女孩看起來好可愛。）
　　　　S 　　　　　　　　V 　SC

句型 03：S ＋ V ＋ O（主詞＋及物動詞＋受詞）

Nobody answered the question.（沒有人回答這個問題。）
S 　　　V 　　　　O

句型 04：S ＋ V ＋ IO ＋ DO（主詞＋授與動詞＋間接受詞＋直接受詞）

間接受詞通常會是「人」，直接受詞通常會是「物品」。

Mary lent me her car.（瑪莉借我她的車。）
S 　V 　IO 　DO

句型 05：S ＋ V ＋ O ＋ O.C.（主詞＋及物動詞＋受詞＋受詞補語）

They named this cat "Tiger".（他們把這隻貓命名為「老虎」。）
S 　V 　　O 　　OC

4. 文法

凡語言皆有一定的文法規則，它是客觀存在的，並不是語言學家規定的。語言學家只是對其進行歸納、整理，並選擇恰當的方式把它們敘述出來。學習英文文法得注意如下基本規則：

規則 01：兩個動詞是不能連在一起的。例如：
　　❌ I like play the piano.（我喜歡彈鋼琴。）
　　⭕ I like **to play the** piano.

規則 02：如果一定要同時用兩個動詞，第二個動詞的前面必須加「to」，或是加上「-ing」。例如：
　　❌ I like swim.（我喜歡游泳。）
　　⭕ I like **to swim**. / I like **swimming**.

規則 03：現在簡單式中，主詞如果是第三人稱單數，動詞必須加「s」，例如：
　　❌ She sing very well.（她歌唱得很好。）
　　⭕ She **sings** very well.

規則 04：絕大多數的否定的句子，不能直接加 not，必須加上助動詞或使役動詞。例如：
　　❌ I not want to go.（我不想離開。）
　　⭕ I **don't** want to go.

規則 05：在不定詞「to」的後面，必須用原形動詞，例如：
　　❌ She wants to becomes a good teacher.（她想要變成一位好老師。）
　　⭕ She wants **to become** a good teacher.

規則 06：英文中有很多助動詞，除了 do 外，can, may, might, would, will, must 也都是助動詞，助動詞後須接原形動詞。例如：
　　❌ You must practiced your English every day.（你必須每天練習英語。）
　　⭕ You **must practice** your English every day.

規則 07：有動詞的完整問句，都要加上助動詞，例如：
　　Do you like playing basketball?（你喜歡打籃球嗎？）
　　How many books **do** you have?（你有多少本書？）

規則 08：動詞除了會隨時態不同而做變化之外，也會因主詞的不同而有所變形，像是 be 動詞。例如：
　　I **am** a good student.（我是一位好學生。）
　　She **has** a big heart.（她有寬大的胸襟。）
　　Leon **has** been to Paris.（里昂曾經去過巴黎。）

Step 1 先搞懂概念與時態

02 現在簡單式 vs. 過去簡單式

01 圖解文法，一看就會！
Grammar Mind Mapping

- 1.1 現在時刻發生的動作或狀態
- 1.2 經常性或習慣性的動作
- 1.3 主詞具備的性格、能力和本質特徵等
- 1.4 客觀事實、普遍真理、名言、警句或諺語等
- 1.5 按規定、時刻表、計畫或安排要發生的動作
- 1.6 與時間副詞連用可表未來的動作
- 1.7 以 here、there 引導之倒裝句表正在發生之事

1. 現在簡單式使用時機

現在簡單式 vs. 過去簡單式

2. 過去簡單式使用時機

- 2.1 表示過去特定時間發生的動作或狀態
- 2.2 表示過去經常或反覆發生的動作或狀態

現在簡單式表示經常性、習慣性發生的的動作、行為或者現在的某種狀況；過去簡單式表示過去某時間內發生的動作或存在的狀態，常與表示過去的時間副詞連用，例如：yesterday, last night / week, a month ago, in 1990's 等。

1. 現在簡單式使用時機

與現在式動詞連用，依照使用時機分為：

- **1-1. 表示現在時刻發生的動作或狀態。**
  It's five o'clock now.（現在五點鐘了。）

- **1-2. 經常性或習慣性的動作，常與 always, usually, often, sometimes 等頻率副詞連用。**
  We have three meals every day.（我們每天吃三餐。）

- **1-3. 主詞具備的性格、能力和本質特徵等。**
  He likes playing soccer.（他喜歡踢足球。）

- **1-4. 客觀事實、普遍真理、名言、警句或諺語等。**
  The earth goes round the sun.（地球繞著太陽轉。）

- **1-5. 按規定、時刻表、計畫或安排要發生的動作。**
  通常會用簡單現在式表示將來的狀態。常用的動詞有：begin, start, stop, arrive, come, go, leave, return, open, close, be 等。例如：
  School begins the day after tomorrow.（學校後天開學。）

- **1-6. 在由 when, before, after, until, as soon as 等連接的時間副詞子句和 if 引導的條件副詞子句，以現在簡單式表示將來的動作。**
  Remember to turn off the lights before you leave.（離開之前記得關上電燈。）

- **1-7. 在由 here、there 引導的倒裝句中，表示此刻正在發生的動作。**
  There goes the bell.（鈴在響。）

2. 過去簡單式使用時機

- **2-1. 表示過去特定時間發生的動作或狀態。**
  My dad won a music award last year.（我爸去年贏得了一座音樂獎。）

- **2-2. 表示過去經常或反覆發生的動作。**
  She often came to help me when I was in trouble.
  （我遇到麻煩的時候她總是來幫助我。）

另外若是要表示過去的「習慣性」動作，可用 would, used to, 來表達，例如：
He used to go to school by bus. （他過去經常坐公車去上課。）

02 延伸用法，事半功倍！
Learning Plus!

1. 現在簡單式 vs. 過去簡單式的「相同點」

兩者均可表示人的性格、特徵、愛好以及習慣，時常與頻率副詞 usually, often, sometimes, seldom, always, once a week 等連用。

I often play basketball. （我常常打籃球。）
I often played basketball when I was at school.
（我以前在念書的時候常常打籃球。）

2. 現在簡單式 vs. 過去簡單式的「不同點」

- 1. 現在簡單式表示現階段發生的動作或狀態，以及永恆不變的事實、自然規律，常與時間副詞 today, every day, every morning, on Sunday 等連用。

  I ride a bike to school every day. （我每天都騎腳踏車上學。）
  Spring returns in March. （春天會在三月回來。）

- 2. 過去簡單式表示過去階段發生的動作或狀態，常與時間副詞 yesterday, last year, last night, the day before yesterday, this morning, two days ago 等連用。

  I lost my cellphone yesterday. （我昨天弄丟了我的手機。）
  She ran into her ex-boyfriend on the street the day before yesterday.
  （她前天在路上遇到了她的前男友。）

03 文法觀念例句示範
Grammar Demonstration

01. Shelly is my best friend since I was 10.
    雪莉從我 10 歲時開始就是我最好的朋友。

02. I get up at seven every day.
我每天都七點鐘起床。

03. She speaks English very well.
她英語說得很好。

04. We lived in Thailand ten years ago.
我們十年前住在泰國。

05. It was very hot yesterday.
昨天天氣很熱。

06. When I was a child, I often read comic books.
我小的時候經常看漫畫書。

07. Did you have a good time last night?
你昨天晚上玩得開心嗎？

08. She stayed in Paris for almost a month.
她在巴黎待了將近一個月。

09. Wendy lives in Canada and speaks good French.
溫蒂住在加拿大，而且說得一口好法語。

10. Mandy doesn't know how to read the map.
曼蒂不會看地圖。

04 文法觀念辨析練習
Grammar Practice

請填入正確時態的動詞。

01. I often _____ (go) to school by bus.

02. He _____ (play) basketball every day.

03. I _____ (be) hungry now.

04. They _____ (go) to the Ocean Park yesterday.

05. Mr. Smith _____ (come) to Hong Kong last Sunday.

06. His mother _____ (watch) TV for 8 hours last night.

07. There _____ (be) a shop not long ago.

08. I _____ (need) a glass of wine by the end of the night.

09. She _____ (be) a student two years ago.

10. The river _____ (run) to the ocean.

正確答案及題目中譯：

01. go	我經常坐公車去上學。
02. plays	他每天都打籃球。
03. am	我現在很餓。
04. went	他們昨天去了海洋公園。
05. came	史密斯先生上個星期天到香港的。
06. watched	他媽媽昨天晚上看了八個小時的電視。
07. was	不久前這有個商店。
08. need	在這個夜晚結束以前我需要一杯酒。
09. was	她兩年前是一個學生。
10. runs	河水流向大海。

Day01

03 未來式

---

01 圖解文法，一看就會！
Grammar Mind Mapping

- 1.1 基本句型：S + will / shall + V 原形
- 1.2 否定句：S + will / shall + not + V 原形
- 1.3 疑問句：Will / Shall + S + V 原形？

1. 句型構成

未來式

2. 使用時機

- 2.1 表示未來某個時間點要發生的事
- 2.2 表示將來會經常或重複發生的事
- 2.3 表示不受人意志影響而將自然發生的事
- 2.4 徵詢對方意圖或願望時
- 2.5 表示即將要做的動作或決定

未來式表示將來某個時間要發生的動作或存在的狀態，也表示將來經常或者重複發生的動作，常與表示將來的時間副詞連用，例如：tomorrow, soon, next week, this afternoon... 等。

We will graduate next year.
我們明年畢業。

1. 未來式的句型構成

- **1-1. 基本句型：S ＋ will / shall ＋ V 原形**
  第一人稱 I, we 用 shall 或 will，其餘人稱都用 will。
  I will call you this afternoon.（我下午會打電話給你。）
  He believes that he will win the Best Sales of the Year.
  （他深信他會贏得年度最佳業務員獎。）

- **1-2. 否定式：S ＋ will / shall ＋ not ＋ V 原形**
  Because John failed his final exam, his parents will not let him join the band.
  （約翰的父母不會讓他參加樂團，因為他的期末考沒有及格。）

- **1-3. 疑問式：Will / Shall ＋ S ＋ V 原形？**
  Shall we dance?（我們來跳舞吧？）

2. 未來式使用時機

- **2-1. 表示未來某個時間點要發生的事**
  She will go to visit the British Museum tomorrow.（她明天會去參觀大英博物館。）

- **2-2. 示將來會經常或重複發生的事。**
  She'll come to work here from now on. (她從現在開始將在這裡工作。)

- **2-3. 表示不以人意志為轉移的自然發展的事。**
  Jack will be 20 next year.（傑克明年將滿 20 歲。）

- **2-4. 在疑問句中用來徵詢聽話人意圖或願望。**
  Will you go shopping with me?（你要和我一起逛街嗎？）

- **2-5. 表示說話時馬上要做的事，也就是臨時決定要做的動作。**
  A：Tom is in hospital now; he is seriously ill.（湯姆現在在醫院，他病得很嚴重。）
  B：Oh, I'm sorry to hear that, I will go and see him.
  （我很遺憾聽到這個消息，我馬上就去探望他。）

02 延伸用法，事半功倍！
Learning Plus!

1. 用「be going to ＋ 動詞原形」表示未來

- **1. 表示打算或計畫在最近或將來要做的事。**
  My friend and I are going to travel together this summer.
  （我和我朋友打算今年夏天一起去旅遊。）

- **2. 表示根據某種跡象，在最近或將來將要發生的事情。**
  Dark clouds are gathering. It is going to rain.
  （烏雲在聚集，看來要下雨了。）

2. 用「be to ＋動詞原形」表示未來

- **1. 表示按計畫、安排要做的事，具有「必要」的強制性意義。**
  The meeting is to take place tonight.（今晚要召開會議。）

- **2. 表示約定、責任、命令或註定要發生的動作。**
  Your job is to proofread all the articles.（你的工作就是要校閱所有文章。）

- **3. 官方計畫或決定（常見於報紙或廣播）。**
  The President is to visit US next week.（總統下個星期將出訪美國。）

- **4. 用「be about to ＋動詞原形」表示未來**。表示（按計畫）即將發生的動作或狀況。
  My father is about to retire.（我父親就要退休了。）
  She was about to go out when I arrived.（我來的時候她正準備出門。）

3. 用「一般現在式」表示未來

表示按規定、計畫而將發生的情況，句中會述及未來時間；若主句時態為未來簡單式，則在 after, when, while, if 等字引導的子句中以現在簡單式表未來。
The train leaves at three this afternoon.（火車將在下午 3 點出發。）
The film begins in ten minutes.（電影十分鐘後開始放映。）

TIPS!

時間副詞、條件副詞子句中，子句一般用現在式表示未來，而主句則用未來式。
I will go shopping when I am free.
（我空閒的時候就去逛街。）

4. 用「現在進行式」表示未來

表示即將發生的將來，常與表示移動的動詞 come, go, arrive, leave, start, take off 等連用。表達的是在說話之前就安排好，或已可預期的事情。

The doctor is coming to check you in 5 minutes.
（醫生 5 分鐘後就會來察看你了。）
The train is leaving.（火車要離開了。）

5. 用「There will be」表示未來將有

There will be ＋名詞＋其他補語，表示未來將有某事物或將存在某狀況，be 動詞必須用原形。此句型常被誤用，千萬別說成 "There will have..."！
There will be a conference call at 3 p.m. tomorrow.
（明天下午 3 點有個電話會議。）

6. 祈使句＋未來式

句型：祈使句＋ and / or ＋未來式＋（will）
Work hard or you will fail.（努力工作否則你就會失敗。）
Work hard and you will succeed.（努力工作你就會成功。）

03 文法觀念例句示範
Grammar Demonstration

01. My sister will go on a vacation In Paris .
我姐姐要去巴黎度假。

02. I'll be a good teacher as long as I can pass this test.
只要我能通過這個測驗，我就能成為一名優秀的教師。

03. He is going to play tennis next week.
下星期他要去打網球。

04. I am going to have a picnic with my co-workers in a few weeks.
幾星期後我要和我的同事們一起野餐。

05. Will you leave for Hong Kong tomorrow?
你明天要去香港嗎？

06. He will come to see me at four this afternoon.
他今天下午 4 點會來見我。

07. I will meet you at 10 a.m. in the airport tomorrow, ok?
我們明天早上 10 點在機場見面，好嗎？

08. She was about to leave when the phone rang.
她正準備出門的時候，電話響了。

09. We are about to finish this project, don't give up now.
我們快要完成這項專案了，千萬不要現在放棄！

10. If it rains tomorrow, the picnic will postpone to next weekend.
如果明天下雨，野餐就延到下個週末舉行。

04 文法觀念辨析練習
Grammar Practice

請選出題目中最適合的選項。

01. He will write to his father as soon as he _____ Italy.
    A arrived   **B** arrives
    C is arriving   **D** will arrive

02. My father _____ fifty years old next year.
    A is going to be   **B** shall be
    C is to be   **D** will be

03. Look at these black clouds. _____.
    A It is to rain   **B** It'll be raining
    C It's going to rain **D** It'll raining

04. I hope that you _____ a good time this evening.
    A going to have   **B** are having
    C will have   **D** has

05. ingThere _____ a basketball match this afternoon.
    A will have   **B** will be
    C has   **D** have

06. We _____ to the park if the weather is nice tomorrow.
　　A will go　　　　　　　　　**B** went
　　C goes　　　　　　　　　　**D** to go

07. Don't be late, Lily. The test _____ at 10 a.m.
　　A will starting　　　　　　**B** has started
　　C would start　　　　　　 **D** starts

08. I don't know if it _____ or not tomorrow.
　　A will snow　　　　　　　 **B** snows
　　C has snowed　　　　　　　**D** to snow

09. She has bought some fabric and she _____ herself a cocktail dress.
　　A makes　　　　　　　　　 **B** is going to make
　　C would make　　　　　　　**D** is to making

10. There _____ a birthday party for Kevin this Sunday.
　　A it to　　　　　　　　　　**B** will be
　　C shall going to be　　　 **D** will going to be

正確答案及題目中譯：

01. **B**	他一抵達義大利就會寫信給他爸爸。	
02. **A**	我爸爸明年就要 50 歲了。	
03. **C**	看看那些烏雲。就快要下雨了。	
04. **C**	我希望你今天晚上玩得愉快。	
05. **B**	今天下午會有一場籃球比賽。	
06. **A**	如果明天天氣好的話，我們就會去公園。	
07. **D**	莉莉，不要遲到。考試早上 10 點鐘就會開始。	
08. **A**	我不知道明天會不會下雪。	
09. **B**	她買了一些布料而且她想替自己做一件小禮服。	
10. **B**	這個禮拜天將有一場為凱文舉辦的生日派對。	

Day02

04 現在進行式 vs. 過去進行式 vs. 未來進行式

01 圖解文法，一看就會！
Grammar Mind Mapping

進行式的句型構成

1. 現在進行式句型構成

- 1.1 一般式：S ＋ be（is / am /are）＋現在分詞（V-ing）
- 1.2 否定句：S ＋ be（is / am /are）＋ not ＋現在分詞（V-ing）
- 1.3 疑問句：be（is / am /are）＋ S ＋現在分詞（V-ing）？

3. 未來進行式句型構成

- 3.1 一般式：S ＋ will be ＋現在分詞（V-ing）
- 3.2 否定句：S ＋ will be ＋ not ＋現在分詞（V-ing）
- 3.3 疑問句：Will ＋ S ＋ be ＋現在分詞（V-ing）？

2. 過去進行式句型構成

- 2.1 一般式：S ＋ be（was / were）＋現在分詞（V-ing）
- 2.2 否定句：S ＋ be（was / were）＋ not ＋現在分詞（V-ing）
- 2.3 疑問句：be（was / were）＋ S ＋現在分詞（V-ing）？

Part 1 完成式的句型構成

1. 現在進行式

- **1-1. 一般句型：S ＋ be（is / am /are）＋現在分詞（V-ing）**
  I am playing piano with my brother now.（我和我哥哥正在一起彈鋼琴。）

- **1-2. 否定句型：S ＋ be（is / am /are）＋ not ＋現在分詞（V-ing）**
  Tony is totally not listening.（湯尼根本就沒在聽。）

- **1-3. 疑問句型：be（is / am /are）＋ S ＋現在分詞（V-ing）？**
  Where are you going?（你正要去哪裡？）

2. 過去進行式

- **2-1. 一般句型：Sere ＋ be（was / were）＋現在分詞（V-ing）**
  She was trying on a new dress when her phone rang.
  （電話響時候她正在試穿一件新洋裝。）

- **2-2. 否定句型：S ＋ be（was / were）＋ not ＋現在分詞（V-ing）**
  I was not speeding!（我當時並沒有超速！）

- **2-3. 疑問句型：be（was / were）＋ S ＋現在分詞（V-ing）？**
  Were you talking to Tom on the phone at 8 p.m. last night?
  （你昨晚八點是否正在跟湯姆講電話？）

3. 未來進行式

- **3-1. 一般句型：S ＋ will be ＋現在分詞（V-ing）**
  If I continue to go out with you, I will soon be pissing off my mom.
  （如果我繼續跟你出去的話，我很快就會把我媽給惹毛。）

- **3-2. 否定句型：S ＋ will be ＋ not ＋現在分詞（V-ing）**
  I hope it won't still be raining when I have to go to work.
  （我希望我要上班的時候不要還在下雨。）

- **3-3. 疑問句型：Will ＋ S ＋ be ＋現在分詞（V-ing）？**
  Will you be working on Christmas Day?
  （你聖誕節還要上班嗎？）

- 1.1 表示現階段正在進行的動作
- 1.2 表示一個在最近按計畫要進行的動作
- 1.3 表示反覆發生或持續存在的狀態
- 1.4 表示強調逐漸變化或改變的過程

1. 現在進行式

進行式的使用時機

3. 未來進行式

- 3.1 表示在將來某個時間正在進行的動作
- 3.2 表示按計畫或安排，未來要發生的動作
- 3.3 表示不含意圖，又未發生的動作
- 3.4 委婉語氣

2. 過去進行式

- 2.1 表示過去的某個時刻或時間正在進行的動作
- 2.2 表示某種強烈感情
- 2.3 表示過去某個事件發生時，另一個正在進行的動作
- 2.4 委婉語氣
- 2.5 表示過去某個時間日認為「將來」要發生的事

Part 2 進行式的使用時機

1. 現在進行式

- **1-1. 表示現階段正在進行的動作**。常與 now, right now, at present, at the moment, for the time being 等時間副詞連用，例如：
I am looking for someone to talk with now.（我現在想找個人來說說話。）

- **1-2. 表示一個在最近按計畫要進行的動作**。常與一個表示將來的時間副詞連用，這種情況僅限於少數動詞，如 go, come, leave, start, arrive, work, have, stay, play, return 等。
  I am coming to pick you up.（我馬上就來接你。）

- **1-3. 表示反覆發生或持續存在的狀態**。常與 always, constantly, forever 等詞連用，往往帶有發話人的主觀色彩，多含抱怨意味。
  You are always changing your mind with no reason.
  （你老是毫無理由的改變主意。）

- **1-4. 表示強調逐漸變化或改變的過程**，常與 get, grow, change, become, turn, go, run, begin 等動詞搭配。
  My parents are getting old.（我的父母越來越老了。）

2. 過去進行式

- **2-1. 表示過去的某個時刻或時間正在進行的動作**。常與表示過去的時間副詞 then, at that time, this time yesterday, at six yesterday 等連用。
  I was reading a novel this morning.（早上我在看小說。）

- **2-2. 表示某種強烈感情**。常與 always, constantly, forever 等副詞連用。
  She was always complaining.（她老是在抱怨。）

- **2-3. 表示過去某個事件發生時，另一個正在進行的動作**。此時，延續性動作用過去進行式，瞬間動作用過去簡單式。
  I ran into Ann when I was shopping this evening.（我晚上逛街時遇到了安。）

TIPS!

如果表示的是兩個延續性的動作，都用過去進行式。
Some students were playing football,
while others were running around the track.
（一些學生在踢足球，其他一些學生在跑道上跑步。）

- **2-4. 用過去進行式可以表委婉語氣**，例如：
  I was wondering if you can give me a lift.（不知我可否順便搭你的車。）

- **2-5. 表示過去某個時間日認為「將來」要發生的事。**
  When his son arrived, the old man is dying.
  （當他的兒子抵達的時候，這位老人已經奄奄一息。）

3. 未來進行式

· **3-1. 表示在將來某個時間正在進行的動作。**
At this time tomorrow, I will be sleeping at home.
（明天這個時候我將會在家睡覺。）

· **3-2. 表示按計畫或安排，未來要發生的動作。**
We will be spending our summer vacation in Hawaii.（我們將在夏威夷過暑假。）

· **3-3. 表示不含意圖又未發生的動作。**
Lucy won't pay this bill.（露西不肯付這筆錢。）→表意願
Lucy won't be paying this bill.（不會是露西來付這筆錢的。）→單純談未來情況

· **3-4. 表示委婉語氣。**
Will you be having a cup of coffee?（要來杯咖啡嗎？）

02 延伸用法，事半功倍！
Learning Plus!

表示狀態或感覺的動詞，如果指現在的情況的話，一般不用進行時，而要用現在簡單式，這樣的動詞有：love, like, hate, want, hope, need, wish, know, understand, remember, belong, hear, see, seem, have, sound, taste 等，但如果他們的詞義改變，便也可以用進行時態。

She looks pale. What's wrong with her?（她看起來很蒼白。她怎麼了嗎？）
→ look 在此為連綴動詞，意為「看起來，顯得」。

She is looking for her books.（她在找她的書。）
→ look 在此為實義動詞，look for 意為「尋找」。

03 文法觀念例句示範
Grammar Demonstration

01. I was reading the newspaper when the doorbell rang.
門鈴響的時候我正在看報。

02. I'll be taking holidays soon.
不久後我就會休假了。

03. It's raining outside now.
現在外面在下雨。

04. We are having a meeting now.
我們現在正在開會。

05. I was doing my homework while she was listening to music.
我在做作業的時候，她正在聽音樂。

06. I will be lying on the beach this time next week.
下個星期的這個時候我將會躺在沙灘上了。

07. When I got to the top of the mountain, the sun was just rising.
當我到達山頂的時候，太陽剛好升起來。

08. The train is leaving soon.
火車很快就要開了。

09. She will be coming home soon.
她不久後就會回家了。

10. The leaves are turning yellow.
樹葉變黃了。

04 文法觀念辨析練習
Grammar Practice

用所給動詞的正確形式填空。

01. I _____ (clean) my room now.

02. Jessie _____ (do) her homework when I called her last night.

03. What _____ you _____ (do) now? I _____ (sing).

04. My father _____ (read) newspaper at ten yesterday.

05. It _____ (rain) when I went out yesterday.

06. David _____ (play) chess with his grandfather right now.

07. He _____ (mend) a car when someone broke in.

08. They _____ (sit) in the cinema this time tomorrow.

09. I _____ (have) a meeting at 3 o'clock tomorrow afternoon.

10. What do you think you _____ (do) at this time next year?

正確答案及題目中譯：

01. am cleaning	我現在正在打掃我的房間。
02. was doing	我昨晚給潔西打電話的時候她正在做作業。
03. are, doing, am singing	你現在正在幹嘛？我在唱歌。
04. was reading	我爸爸昨天十點在看報紙。
05. was raining	我昨天出去的時候正在下大雨。
06. is playing	大衛正在和他的祖父下棋。
07. was mending	當有人闖入的時候他正在修車。
08. will be sitting	明天的這個時候他們將坐在電影院裡。
09. will be having	我明天下午三點將有一個會要開。
10. will be doing	你認為你明年的這個時候將在幹嘛呢？

Day02

05　現在完成式 vs. 過去完成式 vs. 未來完成式

01 圖解文法，一看就會！
Grammar Mind Mapping

- 1.1 一般式：S ＋ has / have ＋過去分詞（p.p.）
- 1.2 否定句：S ＋ has / have ＋ not ＋過去分詞（p.p.）
- 1.3 疑問句：Has / Have ＋ S ＋過去分詞（p.p.）？

1. 現在完成式

完成式的句型構成

2. 過去完成式

- 2.1 一般式：S ＋ had ＋過去分詞（p.p.）
- 2.2 否定句：S ＋ had ＋ not ＋過去分詞（p.p.）
- 2.3 疑問句：Had ＋ S ＋過去分詞（p.p.）？

3. 未來完成式

- 3.1 一般式：S ＋ shall / will ＋ have ＋過去分詞（p.p.）
- 3.2 否定句：S ＋ shall / will ＋ have ＋ not ＋過去分詞（p.p.）
- 3.3 疑問句：Shall / Will ＋ S ＋ have ＋過去分詞（p.p.）？

Part 1 完成式的句型構成

1. 現在完成式

- **1-1. 基本句型**：S ＋ has / have ＋過去分詞（p.p.）
  I have already finished my homework.（我已經完成了我的作業。）

- **1-2. 否定句型**：S ＋ has / have ＋ not ＋過去分詞（p.p.）
  Sandy has not been a nurse in this hospital for 15 years.
  （珊蒂已經不在這間醫院擔任護士長達 15 年了。）

- **1-3. 疑問句型**：Has / Have ＋ S ＋過去分詞（p.p.）？
  Have you seen Peter in past 3 months?
  （過去 3 個月當中你有看見過彼得嗎？）

2. 過去完成式

- **2-1. 基本句型**：S ＋ had ＋過去分詞（p.p.）
  This proposal had been delivered by Eva before Aaron finished it.
  （這個計畫在艾倫完成以前，伊娃就已經提交出去了。）

- **2-2. 否定句型**：S ＋ had ＋ not ＋過去分詞（p.p.）
  I had not been to Tokyo before I met you.
  （在我遇見你之前，我從未去過東京。）

- **2-3. 疑問句型**：Had ＋ S ＋過去分詞（p.p.）？
  Had you ever been to a blind date before?
  （妳曾經相過親嗎？）

3. 未來完成式

- **3-1. 基本句型**：S ＋ shall / will ＋ have ＋過去分詞（p.p.）
  They will have finished the meeting by noon.（他們將會在中午前開完會。）

- **3-2. 否定句型**：S ＋ shall/will ＋ not ＋ have ＋過去分詞（p.p.）
  We won't have made 10 apple pies by the end of today.
  （我們在今天結束之前無法完成 10 個蘋果派。）

- **3-3. 疑問句型**：Shall / Will ＋ S ＋ have ＋過去分詞（p.p.）？
  Will they have already left by the time we get there?
  （我們到的時候，他們會不會已經離開了？）

— 1.1 表示過去發生的動作對現在所造成的影響
— 1.2 表示從過去某一時刻開始一直延續到現在的動作或狀態
— 1.3 表示從過去到現在，不斷重複發生且會持續或結束的動作或情況
— 1.4 可用於時間或條件副詞子句中代替一般現在式

1. 現在完成式

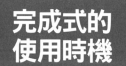

3. 未來完成式

— 3.1 表示在未來某一時刻或某一時刻之前已經完成的動作
— 3.2 表示一種推測

2. 過去完成式

— 2.1 表示在過去某一時刻或某一動作之前已經完成的動作
— 2.2 表示從過去某一時刻開始一直延續到另一過去時刻的動作或狀態
— 2.3 表示未曾實現的希望或打算

Part 2 完成式的使用時機

1. 現在完成式

- **1-1 表示過去發生的動作對現在所造成的影響。**常與 just, already, yet, recently, before, twice, three times 等時間副詞連用，例如：
  Luckily, I have seen the questions before.
  （很幸運地，我之前就已經看過這些問題。）

- **1-2 表示從過去某一時刻開始一直延續到現在的動作或狀態**，常與「since ＋時間點」、「for ＋時間段」，及 how long, (ever) since, ever, before, so far, in the last / past few years, up to now, till now 等時間副詞連用。例如：
  She has been a PE teacher for five years.
  （她已經當了 5 年的體育老師了。）

- **1-3 表示從過去某個時間直到現在的這個時間範圍內，不斷重複發生的動作或情況，並且這個不斷重複的動作可能繼續下去，也可能到現在就結束。**
  He has always gone to school by bus.（他總是坐公車上學。）

- **1-4 有時可用於時間或條件副詞子句中代替現在簡單式，表將來意義。**例如：
  You can have a rest if you have finished your work.
  （如果你完成了工作就可以休息一下。）

2. 過去完成式

- **2-1 表示在過去某一時刻或某一動作之前已經完成了的動作，即「過去的過去」。**例如：
  The train had left before she got to the station.
  （在她抵達車站之前，火車已經開走了。）

- **2-2 表示從過去某一時刻開始一直延續到另一過去時刻的動作或狀態。**常與 how long, for three days, before 等表示一段時間的狀語連用。例如：
  By twelve o'clock, I had worked for ten hours.
  （到 12 點鐘時我已經工作了 10 個小時。）

- **2-3 表示未曾實現的希望或打算，即「本來希望或打算做某事（但卻沒有做）」，**常與 wish, hope, want, expect, think, suppose, plan, mean, intend, desire 等動詞連用，例如：
  I had meant to take a good holiday this year, but I wasn't able to get away from this job.（本來打算今年好好度假的，但還是沒辦法從工作中脫身。）

3. 未來完成式

- **3-1 表示在未來某一時刻或某一時刻之前已經完成的動作，往往對未來某一時間產生影響，常與表示未來的時間副詞及條件或時間副詞子句連用。**例如：
  They should have arrived by now.（她們現在應該已經到了。）
  If you come at six o'clock, I shall not have finished dinner yet.
  （你若六點鐘可以到，我應該還沒吃完晚飯。）
  When we get there, he will have gone to work.
  （我們到那裡時，他應該已經去上班了。）

- **3-2 表示一種推測，主詞要用第二、第三人稱**。例如：

You should have finished your homework by now.（這時候你應該已經完成你的作業了。）

She might have watched this film already.（她恐怕已經看過這場電影了。）

02 延伸用法，事半功倍！
Learning Plus!

- **1. 主句與子句中完成式的運用：**

　如果主句中的動詞為現在簡單式，子句中動詞就用現在完成式；如果主句中動詞是過去簡單式，子句動詞用過去完成式。例如：

It is the first time that I have gone to beach.（這是我第一次去海邊。）
　現在簡單式　　　　　　　現在完成式

This is the last bread that we have left.（這是我們剩下的最後一個麵包。）
　現在簡單式　　　　　　　　現在完成式

That was the most expensive clothes that I had ever bought.
　過去簡單式　　　　　　　　　　　　　　過去完成式
（這是我買過最貴的衣服。）

- **2. 過去完成式常用於以下固定句型：**

(a) hardly, scarcely, barely ＋過去完成式＋ when ＋簡單過去式
Hardly had I got on the bus when it started to move.
（公車開駛前，我差一點就趕不上了。）

(b) no sooner ＋過去完成式＋ than ＋簡單過去式
No sooner had I got in the office than the manager started to yell at me.
（我一到辦公室，經理就開始對我吼叫。）

(c) by (the end of) ＋過去時間→主詞的謂語動詞用過去完成式
The experiment had been finished by 4 o'clock yesterday afternoon.
（這個實驗在昨天下午四點結束。）

03 文法觀念例句示範
Grammar Demonstration

01. I have just received a letter from my mother.
我才剛收到一封來自我媽媽的信。

02. As soon as the sun had set, we returned to our hotel.
太陽一下山我們就回到了旅館。

03. I had not understood the problem until she explained it.
直到她向我解釋後我才理解這個問題。

04. They have seen the film several times.
這部電影他們已經看了好幾次。

05. I have lived here for ten years.
我已經在這裡住了十年了。

06. Next Monday, I shall have been in this company for a year.
到下週一，我到這間公司就滿一年了。

07. He must have gone back to Paris.
他想必已經回巴黎去了。

08. I had meant to go to your party, but something happened.
我本打算去你的派對，但突然發生了一點事。

04 文法觀念辨析練習
Grammar Practice

請選出題目中最適合的選項。

01. No sooner _____ than the accident happened.
　　A he had gone　　　　　　　**B** had he gone
　　C his going　　　　　　　　**D** he went.

02. We have been friends for over _____.
　　A ten year　　　　　　　　**B** ten years

C ten years ago　　　　　　**D** ten years before

03. You _____ that question three times.
A already asked　　　　　　**B** have already asked
C have asked already　　　　**D** asked already

04. All the machines _____ by the end of next week.
A were repaired　　　　　　**B** will repaired
C been repaired　　　　　　**D** will have been repaired

05. His grandfather _____ for thirty years.
A dead　　　　　　　　　　**B** was died
C has been dead　　　　　　**D** has been died

06. A: Are Alice and Tom still living in London?
B: No, they _____ to New York.
A are just moved　　　　　　**B** have just moved
C had just moved　　　　　　**D** will just move

07. I lost the dictionary I _____.
A have bought　　　　　　　**B** bought
C had bought　　　　　　　**D** had been bought

08. I _____ 800 English words by the time I was ten.
A learned　　　　　　　　　**B** was learning
C had learned　　　　　　　**D** learnt

正確答案及題目中譯：

01. **B**	意外一發生他就不見了。
02. **B**	我們已經是十幾年的朋友了。
03. **B**	這個問題你已經問過三次了。
04. **D**	全部的機器在接下來這個禮拜都會修好。
05. **C**	他的祖父已經去世 30 年了。
06. **B**	A：愛麗絲跟湯姆還住在倫敦嗎？　B：不，他們已經搬到紐約去了。
07. **C**	我買的那本字典不見了。
08. **C**	我 10 歲的時候就已經學會了 800 個英文單字。

Day02

06 完成進行式
（現在 vs. 過去 vs. 未來）

01 圖解文法，一看就會！
Grammar Mind Mapping

- 1.1 基本句型：S ＋ has / have ＋ been ＋ V-ing
- 1.2 否定句型：S ＋ has / have ＋ not ＋ been ＋ V-ing
- 1.3 疑問句型：Has / Have ＋ S ＋ been ＋ V-ing？

1. 現在完成進行式

完成進行式的句型構成

2. 過去完成進行式

- 2.1 基本句型：S ＋ had been ＋ V-ing
- 2.2 否定句型：S ＋ had not ＋ been ＋ V-ing
- 2.3 疑問句型：Had ＋ S ＋ been ＋ V-ing？

3. 未來完成進行式

- 3.1 基本句型：S ＋ will / shall ＋ have been ＋ V-ing
- 3.2 否定句型：S ＋ will / shall ＋ not ＋ have been ＋ V-ing
- 3.3 疑問句型：Will / Shall ＋ S ＋ have been ＋ V-ing？

Part 1 完成式的句型構成

1. 現在完成進行式

- **1-1. 基本句型：S + has / have + been + V-ing**
  The Smith Family has been making sport cars for 200 years.
  （史密斯家族有 200 年製作跑車的歷史。）

- **1-2. 否定句型：S + has / have + not + been + V-ing**
  I have not been dancing for 3 months.（我已經三個月沒跳舞了。）

- **1-3. 疑問句型：Has / Have + S + been + V-ing ?**
  Has Enzo been learning English since last year?
  （恩佐從去年開始就在學英語了嗎？）

2. 過去完成進行式

- **2-1. 基本句型：S + had been + V-ing**
  Eli had been playing Wii before you got home.
  （伊萊在你回家之前一直都在玩 Wii。）

- **2-2. 否定句型：S + had not + been + V-ing**
  Amy had not been working for 10 years before I met her.
  （愛咪在我遇到她以前就已經有 10 年沒在工作了。）

- **2-3. 疑問句型：Had + S + been + V-ing ?**
  Had your father been driving all day before he went to sleep?
  （你爸爸在睡覺之前開了一整天的車嗎？）

3. 未來完成進行式

- **3-1. 基本句型：S + will / shall + have been + V-ing**
  When Mrs. Wang retires next month, she will have been teaching for 40 years.
  （當王太太下個月退休時，她就已經教書教了 40 年。）

- **3-2. 否定句型：S + will / shall + not + have been + V-ing**
  I won't have been waiting for you if you kept on treating me like this.
  （如果你繼續這樣對待我的話，我就不會一直等著你的。）

- **3-3. 疑問句型：Will / Shall + S + have been + V-ing ?**
  Will it have been raining when Leo goes out tonight?
  （當李歐今晚出門時，是否有可能就已經在下雨了？）

1.1 表示從過去某個時候開始一直延續到現在的動作
1.2 表示根據直接或間接的證據得出的結論

1. 現在完成進行式

完成進行式的使用時機

2. 過去完成進行式

2.1 表示從過去某一時間開始一直延續到另外一個過去時間的動作
2.2 持續性動詞不可用於過去完成進行式

3. 未來完成進行式

3.1 表示在將來某一時刻之前開始的一個動作或狀態一直延續到將來某一時刻
3.2 表示一種經常性反覆進行的持續性動作

Part 2 完成進行式的使用時機

- 完成進行式特別強調動作的持續，分為現在完成進行式、過去完成進行式及將來完成進行式。
- 現在完成進行式表示從過去某個時候開始一直延續到現在的動作，強調現在仍然在進行，並還可能繼續延續下去；
- 過去完成進行式表示從過去某一時間開始一直延續到另外一個過去時間的動作，這個動作在當時仍在進行並可能繼續延續下去；
- 未來完成進行式表示在未來某一時間以前已經完成，或可能一直持續的動作。

1. 現在完成進行式

- **1-1 表示從過去某個時候開始一直延續到現在的動作**。強調現在依然在進行，並還可能繼續延續下去。例如：
  I have been looking for my lost book for two days, but I still haven't found it.
  （我已經找我弄丟的書找了兩天了，但我仍然沒有找到。）

- **1-2 表示根據直接或間接的證據得出的結論。**
  Her eyes are red. She has been crying.（她眼睛紅了。她已經哭過一陣子了。）

2. 過去完成進行式

- **2-1 表示從過去某一時間開始一直延續到另外一個過去時間的動作，這個動作在當時仍在進行並可能繼續延續下去**，例如：
  We had been waiting for her before she came in.
  （在她進來之前，我們就在等她。）

- **2-2 持續性動詞不可用於過去完成進行式**。例如：know, belong。但 wish 和 want 除外。
  The little girl was delighted with her new toy. She had been wishing one for a long time.（這個小女孩很高興擁有她的新玩具，她早就想要一個了。）

3. 未來完成進行式

- **3-1 表示在將來某一時刻之前開始的一個動作或狀態一直延續到將來某一時刻**，常與一個以 by 開頭的時間片語連用。例如：
  By the end of this month, she will have been learning piano for half a year.
  （到這個月底，她就學鋼琴半年了。）

- **3-2 表示一種經常性反覆進行的持續性動作**。例如：
  By the end of this month, he will have been mountain climbing for ten years
  （到了這個月底他的登山資歷就滿 10 年了。）

02 文法觀念例句示範
Grammar Demonstration

01. We have been living here since 2000.
從 2000 年起我們就住這裡了。

---

02. He was out of breath. He had been running.
他氣喘吁吁。直到剛剛為止他一直在跑步。

03. I heard you had been looking for me.
我聽說你一直在找我。

04. I have been looking forward to meeting you.
我一直盼望著見到你。

05. By the end of this year, she will have been teaching for five years.
到今年年底，她就教書滿 5 年了。

06. You have been working very hard without any doubt.
毫無疑問地，你工作一向非常努力。

07. Joe will have been working for thirty years by the end of nest month.
到下個月底，喬便工作滿三十年了。

08. She had been suffering from a bad cold when she took the exam.
她在考試之前一直在重感冒。

09. By the time you arrive tomorrow, she will have been typing for hours.
到明天你抵達的時候，她將已經打了數小時的字。

10. He had been mentioning your name to me.
他老是向我提起你的名字。

03 文法觀念辨析練習
Grammar Practice

請填入正確時態的動詞。

01. We _____ (wait) for her for two hours. I don't think she's coming.

02. They _____ (build) the bridge for six months and will finish next year.

03. He _____ (study) abroad for one year since last April.

04. By the end of this month, I _____ (work) here for three months.

05. He _____ (prepare) his exam till one o'clock last night.

06. Up to that time he _____ (live) there and he was known to all the old residents.

07. I wanted to know what _____ (go) on.

08. She _____ (have) treatment for 3 months by tomorrow.

09. By this time next year, we _____ (do) business with each other for 20 years.

10. He quit up smoking last year. He _____ (smoke) for thirty years.

正確答案及題目中譯：

01. have been waiting	我們已經等了她兩個小時了。我不認為她會來了。
02. have been building	他們建這橋已經建了六個月了，而且會在明年完工。
03. has been studying	從去年四月開始，他已經在國外學習一年了。
04. will have been working	到這個月月底，我就已經在這工作三個月了。
05. had been preparing	他直到昨晚一點還一直在準備他的考試。
06. had been living	直到那個時候他還住在那裡並和所有的老住戶都認識。
07. had been going	我想知道一直在發生什麼事。
08. will have been having	到明天為止，她就已經接受治療滿三個月了。
09. will have been doing	到明年這時候，我們的業務往來就滿 20 年了。
10. had been smoking	他去年戒菸，他已經抽了 30 年菸。

Day03

07 形容詞（含比較級 & 最高級）

01 圖解文法，一看就會！
Grammar Mind Mapping

- 1.1 定語形容詞：置於修飾詞之前
- 1.2 主詞補語：置於連綴動詞或感官動詞之後
- 1.3 受詞補語：修飾句中受詞
- 1.4 副詞子句：成為形容詞片語子句以修飾主句

1. 使用時機及用法

形容詞用法

2. 使用規則及要點

- 2.1 修飾不定代名詞時置於其後
- 2.2 兩個以上的形容詞的順序
- 2.3 The ＋形容詞可表示特定族群的人／物
- 2.4 兩個以上形容詞當定語置於最後
- 2.5 修飾長寬高深及年齡置於名詞之後

Part 1
形容詞的用法

形容詞主要用來修飾名詞或不定代名詞，表示人或事物的性質、狀態和特徵的詞。形容詞在句中作定語、補語及修飾子句等。例如：

She is a pretty girl.（她是一個漂亮的女孩。）
He looks very happy.（他看起來很開心。）

1. 使用時機及用法

・ **1-1. 定語形容詞：一般放在所修飾詞的前面。**

Prague is a romantic city.（布拉格是一座浪漫的城市。）

・ **1-2. 主詞補語：放在連綴動詞後面。**

The leaves of maple turn red in fall.（楓樹的葉子在秋天變紅。）

・ **1-3. 受詞補語：修飾句中受詞。**

We must keep the classroom clean.（我們應該保持教室乾淨。）

・ **1-4. 副詞子句：成為形容詞片語子句，修飾主句。**

He arrived home, hungry and tired.（他又累又餓地回到家裡。）

2. 使用規則及要點

・ **2-1. 修飾不定代名詞時置於其後：**
當形容詞修飾由 some-, any-, no-, every- 這些字首所構成的不定代名詞時，形容詞要放在這些不定代名詞之後。例如：

There must be something wrong with my computer.（我的電腦出了點問題。）

・ **2-2. 兩個以上的形容詞的順序：**
當一個句子中，有兩個以上的形容詞用來修飾同一個名詞時，其先後順序為：（冠詞＋序數＋基數＋性質＋大小＋形狀＋新舊＋顏色＋國籍＋材料）＋名詞。各位可背誦以下的例句輔助記憶：

I have a beautiful little new white Chinese wooden table.
（我有一張漂亮小巧的嶄新的白色中國木製桌子。）

- **2-3. the ＋形容詞可表示特定族群的人 / 物：**
  用「the ＋形容詞」可用來表示特定族群的人或物，例如：the rich（富人）、the young（年輕人）、the elderly（老人）等等。後面需接複數動詞。

  The elderly are a formidable force in any election.
  （老年人在各種選舉當中都是一股不可小覷的力量。）

- **2-4. 兩個以上字詞組成的形容詞片語當定語要置於最後：**
  用 and 或 or 連接起來的兩個形容詞做定語，或以形容詞為首的形容詞片語做定語時，一般都放在所修飾的名詞後面，以進一步產生修飾作用。

  The director has finally found an actress suitable for the role.
  （導演終於找到一位適合這角色的女演員。）

- **2-5. 修飾長寬高深及年齡置於名詞之後：**
  表示長、寬、高、深、厚度及年齡的形容詞，應放在相應的名詞之後。

  The river is about two hundred meters long.（這條河大約兩百公尺長。）

Part 2 形容詞的比較級、最高級

1. 規則變化

- **1-1. 單音節在字尾加 -er / -est：**
  單音節形容詞在轉變為比較級和最高級時，規則是在字尾加 -er 和 -est。例如：clean → cleaner → cleanest。

- **1-2. 單音節以 -e 結尾在字尾加 -r / -st：**
  以 -e 結尾的單音節形容詞，轉變為比較級和最高級時，規則是在字尾加 -r 和 -st。例如：wide → wider → widest。

- **1-3. 雙音節以 -y ,-er, -ow, -ble 結尾字尾加 -er / -est：**
  少數以 -y , -er, -ow, -ble 結尾的雙音節形容詞，在轉變為比較級和最高級時，規則是在字尾加 -er 和 -est。例如：tender → tenderer → tenderest。

- **1-4. 形容詞以 -y 結尾字尾去 -y 加 -ier / -iest：**
  以 -y 結尾，但 -y 前是子音字母的形容詞的比較級和最高級是把 -y 去掉，加上 -ier 和 -iest。例如：lonely → lonelier → loneliest。

- **1-5. 形容詞字尾「子母子」重覆字尾再加 -er / -est：**
  當形容詞或其字尾出現「子音＋母音＋子音」現象，也就是最後三個字母和音標的排列是「子母子」，在轉變為比較級和最高級時，規則是要重覆字尾，再加 -er /

1.1 單音節在字尾加 -er / -est

1.2 單音節以 -e 結尾在字尾加 -r / -st

1.3 雙音節以 -y , -er, -ow, -ble 結尾字尾加 -er / -est

1.4 形容詞以 -y 結尾字尾去 -y 加 -ier / -iest

1.5 形容詞字尾「子母子」重覆字尾再加 -er / -est

1.6 三音節以上及部分雙音節，以 more / most 修飾

1. 規則變化

形容詞的比較級、最高級

2. 不規則變化

2.1 good / well → better → best

3. 比較級與最高級用法

3.1 兩個人或兩種事物比較時，用比較級

3.2 三個或以上的人事物比較，其中有一個超過其他幾個時，用最高級

3.3 表示雙方程度相等時→ as...as...，不相等→ not so... as

3.4 越……就越……→ the ＋比較級 , the ＋比較級

3.5 程度越來越強→比較級＋ and ＋比較級 / more and more ＋形容詞原級

3.6 most ＋形容詞原級→極 / 很 / 非常～

3.7 副詞＋比較級→強調

3.8 兩者中哪一個更……→ which / who ＋ is ＋比較級 , ...or...?

3.9 最……之一→ one of ＋ the ＋最高級

-est。例如：big → bigger → biggest。

- **1-6. 三音節以上及部分雙音節，以 more / most 修飾：**
  兩個音節以上的形容詞，則在其前加 more / most，以形成比較級及最高級。
  另外，注意 more / most 後的形容詞是須用原級。例如：beautiful → more beautiful → most beautiful。

2. 不規則變化

原級	比較級	最高級
good / well	better	best
many / much	more	most
bad / ill	worse	worst
old	older / elder	oldest / eldest
little	littler / less or lesser	littlest / least
far	farther / further	farthest / furthest
late	later / latter	latest / last

3. 比較級與最高級用法

- **3-1. 兩個人或兩種事物比較時，用比較級。**
  句型為「比較級＋ than...」例如：
  Bob is taller than Jack.（鮑伯比傑克高。）

- **3-2. 三個或三個以上的人或事物比較，其中有一個在某一方面超過其他幾個時，用最高級。**
  句型為「the ＋最高級＋ ...in / of...」。例如：
  Bob is the tallest in his class.（鮑伯是他班上最高的。）

- **3-3. 欲表示雙方程度相等時，可使用「…as + 形容詞原級 + as…」句型**，中譯為「……和……一樣……」；表示雙方程度不相等則用「…not so / as + 形容詞原級 +as…」句型，可譯為「……不像……那麼……」或「……和……不一樣」，例如：
  This box is as big as mine.（這個盒子和我的一樣大。）
  You are not so smart as I am.（你沒有我聰明。）

- **3-4.**「**The ＋形容詞比較級……, the ＋形容詞比較級**」可表「**越……就越……**」。例如：
  The more you study, the more you know. （你學習得越多，你就知道越多。）

- **3-5. 表示程度越來越強，用「比較級＋ and ＋比較級」句型**，可譯為「越來越……」。例如：
  It is getting hotter and hotter. （天氣變得越來越熱。）

- **3-6. Most 同形容詞連用，前面不需 the，可表示「極～，很～，非常～，十分～」。**例如：
  It's most dangerous to be here. （在這兒實在很危險。）

- **3-7. 比較級前可以加副詞修飾，以加強程度。**例如：much, far, still, even, a lot, a little, a bit 等等。例如：
  The rope is much longer than that one. （這條繩子比那條長。）

- **3-8. 兩者之間選擇「哪一個更……」時，用句型「Which / Who ＋ is ＋比較級，...or...?」**例如：
  Which is bigger, the sun or the moon? （太陽和月亮，哪一個更大？）

- **3-9. 表示「最……之一」時，用「one of ＋ the ＋最高級」。**例如：
  The light bulb is one of the most helpful inventions.
  （電燈泡是最有用的發明之一。）

02 文法觀念例句示範
Grammar Demonstration

01. The sunset was so beautiful.
    日落好美。

02. He is the happiest man on earth.
    他是地球上最快樂的人。

03. The film is boring.
    那個電影很無趣。

04. It's an utter mystery.
    這完全是個謎。

05. She looked embarrassed.
    她好像很尷尬。

06. He is one of the greatest composers.
他是最偉大的作曲家之一。

07. It's foolish of her to go alone.
她單獨出去太傻了。

08. The black one is the more expensive of the two boxes.
黑色的是這兩個盒子當中最貴的。

09. The more careful you are, the fewer mistakes you will make.
你越仔細，犯的錯誤越少。

10. Mountain climbing is one of the most dangerous sports.
爬山是最危險的運動之一。

03 文法觀念辨析練習
Grammar Practice

請最適合的題目的選項答案。

01. The writer died before finishing his _____ book.
A late
B later
C last
D latest.

02. She got _____ that she couldn't dance anymore.
A very angrily
B too angrily
C too angry
D so angry

03. The sweater is very beautiful, but it's _____ small.
A too much
B much too
C many
D more

04. She looks very _____. I think she needs rest.
A tired
B hard
C well
D hardly.

05. Lots of visitors come to visit Hamburg because she's _____ city.
A very a beautiful
B quite a beautiful

   C so a beautiful　　　　　　　　**D** a quite beautiful

06. A: Which is _____, the sun, the moon or the earth?
　　B: Of course the moon is.
　　A small　　　　　　　　**B** smaller
　　C smallest　　　　　　　　**D** the smallest

07. She isn't so _____ at math as you are.
　　A well　　　　　　　　**B** good
　　C better　　　　　　　　**D** best

08. I have _____ to do today.
　　A anything important　　　　　　**B** something important
　　C important nothing　　　　　　**D** important something

09. Mary writes _____ of the three.
　　A better　　　　　　　　**B** best
　　C good　　　　　　　　**D** well

10. My _____ brother is _____ than I.
　　A elder, three years older　　　　**B** older, older
　　C older, three years elder　　　　**D** elder, elder

正確答案及題目中譯：

01. **C**	這位作者在完成他最新的作品之前就過世了。	
02. **D**	她氣到再也無法跳舞。	
03. **B**	這件毛衣很漂亮，但是真的太小了。	
04. **A**	她看起來非常累。我想她需要好好休息。	
05. **B**	很多遊客都來參訪漢堡，因為她真的是一個非常美麗的城市。	
06. **D**	那一個是最小的，太陽、月亮還是地球？當然是月亮。	
07. **B**	她不像你數學那麼好。	
08. **B**	我今天有些重要的事要處理。	
09. **B**	瑪莉在這三個人之中寫作寫得最好。	
10. **A**	我的哥哥比我年長三歲。	

Day03

Step 2　了解英文中關鍵的關鍵─字詞

08　副詞（含比較級 & 最高級）

01 圖解文法，一看就會！
Grammar Mind Mapping

- 1.1 修飾形容詞→置於前方
- 1.2 修飾動詞用→置於前方
- 1.3 修飾副詞用→置於前方
- 1.4 修飾介系詞片語用→置於前方
- 1.5 使用 enough 修飾形容詞或其他副詞時→置於後方。
- 1.6 頻率副詞→置於行為動詞前；使役動詞、助動詞或 be 動詞之後。
- 1.7 副詞排序，先地點再時間
- 1.8 某些副詞有兩種形式，一種與形容詞同形，一種以 -ly 結尾，字義不同

1. 使用時機及用法

副詞用法

2. 副詞的比較級與最高級

- 2.1 同級副詞的比較→ as ＋原級＋ as
- 2.2 比較級副詞的比較→副詞比較級＋ than
- 2.3 最高級副詞的比較→同形容詞用法但不加 the
- 2.4 副詞的比較級與最高級規則變化→同形容詞
- 2.5 副詞的比較級與最高級常見之不規則變化→同形容詞

副詞主要用來修飾動詞、形容詞、其他副詞或全句，說明時間、地點、程度、方式等概念，副詞在句中主要作修飾語。副詞可以分為時間副詞、地點副詞、方式副詞、程度副詞、頻率副詞等。

She speaks English quite well.（她英語說得相當好。）
They live frugally.（他們生活很節儉。）

1. 使用時機及用法

• 1-1. 置於形容詞前方，修飾形容詞用。例如：

He works very hard.（他工作很努力。）

• 1-2. 置於動詞前方，修飾動詞用。例如：

I always like to dance by myself.（我總是喜歡一個人跳舞。）

• 1-3. 置於副詞前方，修飾副詞用。例如：

He plays piano quite well.（他鋼琴彈得很好。）

• 1-4. 置於介系詞片語前方，修飾介系詞片語用。例如：

Danny was absolutely out of control last night.（丹尼昨晚徹底地失控了。）

• 1-5. 使用 enough 修飾形容詞或其他副詞時，置於被修飾詞後方。例如：

The boy isn't old enough to enter the club.（這男孩年紀不足，還不能進夜店。）

• 1-6. 頻率副詞，例如：usually , always, often, never 等，一般放在行為動詞前，或是使役動詞、助動詞或 be 動詞之後。例如：

I always get up late.（我經常起得晚。）

You can always call me anytime.（你隨時都可以打電話給我。）

- 1-7. 句中同時出現時間、地點的副詞時，先地點再時間。

He arrived here yesterday.（他昨天抵達這裡。）
　　　　　　地點　　時間

- 1-8. 某些副詞有兩種形式，一種與形容詞同形，一種以 -ly 結尾，但要注意，兩種形式的字義略有不同。例如：

close 接近地；合身地；塞滿地 ←→ closely 接近地；仔細地；密切地
wide 廣泛地；張得很大 ←→ widely 廣泛地；大大地

2. 副詞的比較級、最高級

副詞和形容詞一樣有比較級和最高級，但大多數僅限於情狀副詞和少數時間副詞和程度副詞。

- 2-1. 同級副詞的比較→ as ＋原級＋ as：

My mother drives **as fast as** my father (does).（我媽車開得跟我爸一樣快。）

- 2-2. 比較級副詞的比較→副詞比較級＋ than：

Peter sings **better than** John.（彼得歌唱得比約翰好。）

- 2-3. 最高級副詞的比較→同形容詞用法，但不可加 the：

Who runs (the) **fastest** in your class?（你們班上誰跑得最快？）

- 2-4. 副詞的比較級與最高級規則變化：
  同形容詞，單音節在字尾加 -er / -est、以 -y 結尾字尾去 -y 加 -ier / -iest 等等。

（速度）快地：fast → faster → fastest
（時間）快地：soon → sooner → soonest
（時間）提早：early → earlier → earliest

- 2-5. 副詞的比較級與最高級常見之不規則變化：

（程度）良好地：well → better → best
（程度）不好地：badly → worse → worst
（距離）遠地：far → farther / further → farthest / furthest
（時間）遲地：late → later → last
（數量、程度）多地：much → more → most
（數量、程度）少地：little → less → least
（程度）糟糕地：poorly → worse → worst
（程度）邪惡地：ill → worse → worst

02 文法觀念例句示範
Grammar Demonstration

01. He knew London very well.
   他對倫敦很熟悉。

02. You need to form the habit of reading carefully.
   你需要養成仔細閱讀的習慣。

03. Please listen to me carefully.
   請認真聽我說。

04. Her pronunciation is very good.
   她的發音很棒。

05. He didn't study hard enough.
   他學習不夠認真。

06. Tom looked at me suspiciously.
   湯姆懷疑的看著我。

07. I sometimes stay up all night.
我有時候會熬夜。

03 文法觀念辨析練習
Grammar Practice

請填入正確時態的副詞。

01. My purse was stolen on the bus yesterday. _____ (Fortunate), there was no money in it.

02. He put on his coat and went out _____ (quick).

03. It's snowing hard. You must drive _____ (careful).

04. I used to smoke _____ (heavy) but I give it up three years ago.

05. What have you been doing _____ (late)?

06. He thinks _____ (high) of my opinion.

07. He is _____ (strong) enough to carry the heavy box.

08. These oranges taste _____ (good).

正確答案及題目中譯：

01. Fortunately	我錢包昨天在公車上被偷了，幸運的是裡面沒有錢。
02. quickly	他穿上衣服然後很快地出門了。
03. carefully	下很大的雪，你應該小心駕駛。
04. heavily	我以前抽煙抽得很凶，但我三年前戒掉了。
05. lately	你最近在幹嘛？
06. highly	他對我的想法評價很高。
07. strong	他壯得足以提起那個重箱子。
08. good	這些柳橙嚐起來很美味。

09 動詞片語（不可分離 vs. 可分離）

01 圖解文法，一看就會！
Grammar Mind Mapping

- 1.1 句型結構：（不及物）動詞＋介系詞＋受詞
- 1.2 常見動詞片語：look after, search for, ask for...

1. 不可分離動詞片語

動詞片語

2. 可分離動詞片語

- 2.1 句型結構 ─┬─ 2.1.1（及物）動詞＋受詞＋介副詞
  └─ 2.1.2（及物）動詞＋介副詞＋受詞
- 2.2 介副詞改變原動詞字意
- 2.3 常見動詞片語：give up, find out, think over...
- 2.4 名詞放介副詞之前或之後
- 2.5 人稱代名詞、反身代詞放介副詞之前

所謂的動詞片語，是指由動詞加上介系詞／副詞／介副詞所組成的片語。其片語意義有時與原先單獨動詞之字意不同，並且有多種字意。英語中的動詞片語依照結構分為兩種：不可分離的動詞片語（動詞＋介系詞），及可分離的動詞片語（動詞＋介副詞）。

1. 不可分離動詞片語

- **1-1. 句型結構：（不及物）動詞＋介系詞＋受詞**
  不可分離動詞片語中，常常是不及物動詞連接介系詞，受詞必須接在後面。

- **1-2. 此類常見的動詞片語有 look after, look for, ask for, care about, laugh at, hear of** 等，所組成之動詞片語字意通常不變。

  Don't laugh at others.（不要嘲笑別人。）
  They didn't look after the children properly.（她們沒有好好地照顧孩子們。）

2. 可分離動詞片語

- **2-1. 句型結構：**

  a)（及物）動詞＋受詞＋介副詞

  b)（及物）動詞＋介副詞＋受詞

  可分離動詞片語是及物動詞與介系詞可以被分開，並在中間加入人稱代名詞或反身受詞，也可以接在介副詞後面。

- **2-2. 介副詞改變原動詞字意：**
  可分離動詞片語中的介系詞，常常當作副詞使用，因此稱為介副詞。可置於動詞後修飾動詞，使得動詞改變原本的意思，而產生新的字意。

- **2-3. 此類常見的動詞片語有：**
  give up, find out, think over, pick up, point out, hand in 等。

- **2-4. 名詞放介副詞之前或之後：**
  可分離動詞片語中，如果受詞是名詞，既可放在介副詞前面，又可放在介副詞後面。

  He is taking off his clothes and going to bed.（他正脫掉衣服，準備睡覺。）

  　動詞　介副詞　（名詞）受詞

= He is taking his clothes off and going to bed.

動詞　　受詞　　介副詞

• 2-5. **人稱代名詞、反身代詞放介副詞之前**：
可分離動詞片語中，如果受詞是人稱代名詞或反身代詞，則只能放在介副詞前面。

Put them away, please.（請把它們收拾好。）

動詞　人稱代名詞　介副詞

02 文法觀念例句示範
Grammar Demonstration

01. The police are looking into the case.
員警們在調查那件案子。

02. They turned down my offer.
他們拒絕了我的提議。

03. Something unexpected has turned up.
出現了令人意外的情況。

04. This paper comes out once a week.
這份報紙每星期出版一次。

05. The meeting has been called off.
會議被取消了。

06. I filled in an application form.
我填寫了申請表。

07. Mr. Ericsson, please put it down.
艾瑞克森先生，請把東西放下來。

08. Please don't forget to hand it in.
請不要忘了把它交上來。

09. I can't figure out why you said that.
我不能理解你為什麼那麼說。

10. I won't let him down in any way.
無論如何我是不會讓他失望的。

03 文法觀念辨析練習
Grammar Practice

請使用提示的動詞片語，翻譯出正確的英文句子。

01. 沒有人能夠解釋他的怪異行為。（account for）

02. 火車被大霧阻擋而誤點了。（hold up）

03. 我在公園等了她很長時間，但是她沒有出現。（turn up）

04. 請勿踐踏草坪！（keep off）

05. 如果我這次饒恕了你，你就能保證下次不會怎麼做了嗎？（let off）

06. 不要把今天的事情拖到明天做。（pull off）

07. **別受騙上當**。（take in）

08. **請關門**。（shut off）

09. **妳昨天買的這條裙子很漂亮，快穿上吧**。（put on）

10. **明天早上記得叫我起床**。（wake up）

正確答案：

01. Nobody could account for his extraordinary behavior.

02. The train was held up by fog and arrived late.

03. I waited for her in the park for a long time but she didn't turn up.

04. Keep off the grass, please!

05. If I let you off this time, will you promise never to do it again?

06. Never pull off till tomorrow what you can do today.

07. Don't be taken in.

08. Please shut off the door.

09. The skirt you bought yesterday is beautiful. Please put it on.

10. Don't forget to wake me up tomorrow morning.

10 連綴動詞 vs. 感官動詞

01 圖解文法，一看就會！
Grammar Mind Mapping

```
                    ┌─────────────┐
                    │   1. 本質    │
                    └─────────────┘
                         └─ 1.1 是在主詞和補語之間起連接功能的動詞

        ┌──────────────────┐
        │    連綴動詞       │
        └──────────────────┘

┌──────────────────────┐      ┌──────────────────┐
│ 2. 補語特性及句型結構 │      │  3. 狀態的改變   │
└──────────────────────┘      └──────────────────┘
  └ 2.1 連綴動詞＋形容詞         └ 3.1 become, get, grow
  └ 2.2 連綴動詞＋ like ＋名詞
```

連綴動詞是用來補充描述和指明事物的，常用形
容詞來補充說明主詞的不足，使得整句意思更完
整，常用的連綴動詞有 seem, appear, look, feel,
sound, taste, become, get, turn, smell, grow 等；
感官動詞是表示人的感覺的動詞，常見的感官動詞
有 feel, hear, sound, see, taste, smell, look at 等。

Part 1 連綴動詞

1. 本質

連綴動詞是在主詞和補語之間起連接功能的動詞

2. 補語特性及句型結構

- 2-1. **連綴動詞＋形容詞**
- 2-2. **連綴動詞＋ like ＋名詞**

連綴動詞所連接的主詞補語多半為形容詞。若要連接名詞時可以在連綴動詞後加「like」，例如：

The story sounds **interesting**. （這個故事聽起來很有趣。）
It sounds **like an interesting story**. （這聽起來是個有趣的故事。）

3. 狀態的改變

狀態的改變：become, get, grow

become, get, grow 等連綴動詞可用來表示「從一種狀態變為另一種狀態」，並且可以搭配使用進行式。

I am getting more and more tired. （我變得越來越累。）

Part 2 感官動詞

1. 本質

表達人類感受的動詞。

感官動詞是表示人類感覺、感受的動詞，故稱為感官動詞。可作完全及物動詞或不完全及物動詞，例如：listen to, hear, watch, see, feel 等。

I feel sick today. （我今天覺得不舒服。）

2. 句型結構及特性

- 2-1. **不完全及物動詞＋受詞＋動詞原形**→表示全部過程
- 2-2. **不完全及物動詞＋受詞＋現在分詞**→強調正在進行的動作

I saw the old lady cross the road.（我看到老太太過馬路。）
I saw the old lady crossing the road.（我看見老太太正在過馬路。）

3. 被動語態

感官動詞用於被動語態，**「V 原形」改為「to + V」或「V-ing」：**

感官動詞用於被動語態，後面原有動詞原形要改為不定詞或動名詞，例如：

I hear the boy sing every day. ⟷ The boy is heard **to sing** every day.
（我每天都聽到那個男孩唱歌。）
I saw the man entering a bar. ⟷ The man was seen **entering** a bar.
（我看到那個男人進了酒吧。）

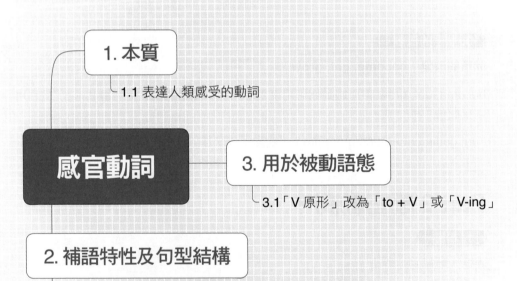

02 文法觀念例句示範
Grammar Demonstration

01. His suggestion sounds ridiculous.
他的建議聽起來很可笑。

---

02. The soup tastes good.
這湯的味道嚐起來不錯。

---

03. He becomes lazy.
他變懶了。

---

04. She feels nervous before the exam.
考試前她很緊張。

---

05. It sounds like a good idea.
聽起來是個不錯的主意。

---

06. The weather usually turns cold in the end of September.
天氣通常在九月底開始變冷。

---

07. You get fat again.
你又變胖了。

---

08. The weather is getting hotter every day.
天氣一天天變熱了。

04 文法觀念辨析練習
Grammar Practice

請將以下句子翻譯為英文。

01. 我聽到有人在唱歌。

---

02. 我昨天晚上覺得牙齒很痛。

_____

03. 我看他進房間了。

_____

04. 她長得像她媽媽。

_____

05. 那時候他很開心。

_____

06. 這件布料很柔順。

_____

07. 比賽越來越精彩了。

_____

正確答案：

01. I hear someone singing.

02. I felt toothache last night.

03. I saw him get in the room.

04. She looks like her mother very much.

05. He looked happy at that time.

06. This cloth feels so soft.

07. The game is getting more exciting.

Step 2 了解英文中關鍵的關鍵一字詞

11 動名詞與不定詞

01 圖解文法，一看就會！
Grammar Mind Mapping

- 1.1 作為主詞使用→置於句首
- 1.2 主詞為動作→使用動名詞
- 1.3 動名詞作補語使用，句子的主詞通常為無生命的名詞
- 1.4 作為受詞使用 ── 1.4.1 動詞受詞
　　　　　　　　　　 1.4.2 介系詞的受詞
- 1.5 作形容詞使用→置於名詞之前

1. 使用時機

動名詞

2. 時態

- 2.1 簡單式動名詞→所表時間與主要動詞時間一致或未來
- 2.2 完成式動名詞→所表時間比主要動詞時間更早

動詞除原形以外，也常以下列兩種形式出現。

一、**動名詞**：**動詞＋ ing** →具有動詞及名詞的特性，在句子中作為名詞使用。

二、**不定詞**：**to ＋原形動詞**→具有名詞、形容詞和副詞的特性，在句子中可當主語、補語及副詞使用。

Part 1 動名詞

1. 使用時機

- **1-1. 作為主詞使用→置於句首：**
  當動名詞作為主詞時，通常位於句首，例如：
  Seeing is believing.（眼見為憑。）（= To see is to believe.）

- **1-2. 主詞為動作→使用動名詞：**
  在英文語法中，若句子的主詞為動作時，通常必須轉化為動名詞形式。例如：
  Walking to office is the best way to lose weight.（走路上班是減肥的最好方法。）

- 1-3. 動名詞作補語使用，句子的主詞通常為無生命的名詞。例如：
  My favorite sport is playing tennis.（我最喜歡的運動是打網球。）
  The national personality of Chinese is peace-loving.
  （中國人的民族性是愛好和平的。）

- **1-4. 作為受詞使用→可當動詞受詞或介系詞的受詞：**
  a) **動詞受詞：**
  英語中有些動詞後面，只能使用動名詞作為受詞。這類動詞常見的有：admit, advice, anticipate, appreciate, avoid, consider, delay, deny, dislike, enjoy, escape, excuse, fancy, favor, finish, imagine, include, keep, mind, miss, postpone, practice, prevent, propose, resist, risk, suggest 等。例如：

  Please pardon my disturbing you.（請原諒我打擾您了。）
  I suggest doing it in a different way.（我建議用不同的方法做。）

TIPS!　連接在 need, require, want 之後的動詞，需以動名詞呈現，此類動名詞的表示被動意義。例如：
The car needs repairing.（這輛車需要被修理。）

b) **介系詞的受詞**：

連接在介詞後面的動詞，需要以動名詞的形式呈現。例如：

She is worring about discussing the new proposal with sales manager tomorrow very much.（她現在非常擔心明天要跟業務經理討論新提案。）

TIPS!　例外：kind of 和 sort of 都表示「稍微」、「有一點」，兩者皆當副詞使用，並不影響動詞，故動詞隨主句上下文變化即可。例如：I kind of expected it would happen.

- 1-5. **作形容詞使用→置於名詞之前**：

動名詞放在名詞之前可作為形容詞使用，例如：

This is a sleeping car.（這是臥舖車。）
動名詞→形容詞　名詞

2. 時態

- 2-1. **簡單式動名詞→所表時間與主要動詞時間一致或未來**：

簡單式動名詞所表示的時間，與句中動詞所表示的時間「一致或是表示未來」。例如：

I am sure of his qutting. ＝ I am sure he will quit.
（我很肯定他會辭職。）

- 2-2. **完成式動名詞→所表時間比主要動詞時間更早**：

完成式動名詞所表示的時間，比句中動詞所表示的時間「更早發生」。例如：

I am sure of his having done so. ＝ I am sure that he has done so.
（我很肯定他曾經這樣做過。）

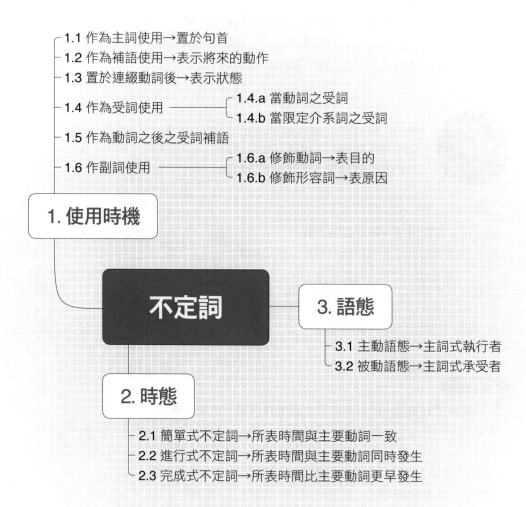

Part 2 不定詞

1. 使用時機

- 1-1. **作為主詞使用→置於句首**：
  不定詞做為主詞使用時，一般表示具體的動作，常置於句首。例如：

  To save time is to lengthen life.（節約時間就等於延長生命。）

- 1-2. **作為補語使用→表示將來的動作**：
  不定詞作補語使用時，常表示將來的動作。而句中主詞常常是表示意向、打算、或計畫的詞，例如 wish, idea, task, purpose, duty, job 等。

  My work is to clean the classroom every day. （我的工作是每天打掃教室。）

- 1-3. **置於連綴動詞後→表示狀態**：
  不定詞置於連綴動詞 seem, appear, prove 等連綴動詞後面時，表示狀態，例如：

  This plan seems to be possible. （這個計畫似乎是可行的。）

- 1-4. **作為受詞使用→可當動詞受詞或限定介系詞的受詞**：
  a) **動詞受詞**：
  作受詞動詞不定詞常在下列動詞後做受詞，例如 afford, agree, apply, arrange, ask, attempt, beg, begin, care, choose, claim, consent, demand, decide, desire, determine, expect, fail, hope, hesitate, hate, intend, learn, like, manage, mean, neglect, offer, plan, prepare, pretend, promise, refuse, resolve, seek, tend, threaten, want 等。

  He promises to keep my secret. （他答應替我保守秘密。）

  b) **限定介系詞之受詞**：
  動詞不定詞通常不做介系詞的受詞。但是遇到 but, except, besides, than, instead of, about 這幾個特殊介系詞，不定詞可連接在後面。例如：

  We have nothing to do but wait. （除了等，我們什麼也做不了。）

- 1-5. **作為動詞之後之受詞補語**
  不定詞常跟在下列動詞之後作受詞補語：ask, advise, allow, beg, cause, compel, command, enable, encourage, expect, feel, force, find, hear, have, inform, invite, let, make, mean, notice, order, permit, persuade, remind, require, request, teach, tell, urge, watch, warn, watch 等。

  The teacher asked her to answer the question. （老師叫她回答問題。）

TIPS!

不定詞在下列動詞的後面做受詞補語時，需要省略 to，例如 feel, hear, listen to, let, have, make, look at, see, watch, notice, observe, help 等，但是變成被動語態時，省略的 to 必須再補上。
Whenever something is wrong with you, please do let me know. （無論你什麼時候有問題，請務必告訴我。）

- 1-6. **作副詞使用**

a) **修飾動詞→表目的：**

不定詞做副詞修飾動詞時，通常表示特定目的，或是表示出乎意料的結果。

He woke up to find everybody gone.
（他起來後發現所有人都不見了。）→**不定詞表結果**

b) **修飾形容詞→表原因：**

不定詞做副詞修飾形容詞時，通常表示原因。並且通常與以下表示感情的形容詞連用：glad, sorry, proud, angry, ashamed, excited, disappointed, interested...

I am sorry to hear this information.（我很遺憾聽到這個消息。）→**不定詞表原因**

2. 時態

- 2-1. **簡單式不定詞→所表時間與主要動詞一致**
I like to read newspapers.（我喜歡看報紙。）

- 2-2. **進行式不定詞→所表時間與主要動詞同時發生**
I am very glad to work with you.（我很高興能與妳一同工作。）

- 2-3. **完成式不定詞→所表時間比主要動詞更早發生**
I am sorry to have kept you waiting so long.（我很抱歉讓你等這麼久。）

3. 語態

- 3-1. **主動語態→主詞式執行者**
句中不定詞使用主動語態時，通常代表主詞是該動作的執行者。例如：

I am glad to attend your wedding.（我很高興能出席你的婚禮。）

- 3-2. **被動語態→主詞式承受者**
句中不定詞使用被動語態時，通常代表主詞是該動作的承受者。例如：

He didn't like to be laughed at.（他不喜歡被別人嘲笑。）

02 延伸用法，事半功倍！
Learning Plus!

- 1. 動名詞和不定詞都可以做主詞。不定詞做主詞表示具體的動作，動名詞做主詞則可以表示抽象或一般性的動作或情況。例如：

To play with fire will be dangerous.（玩火是非常危險的。）
→指特定的人之具體動作

Playing with fire is dangerous.（玩火是非常危險的。）
→泛指玩火

- 2. 在 allow, advise, forbid, permit 等動詞後，以另一個動詞作受詞時，要用動名詞形式。但如果後面有名詞、代名詞作受詞時，需連接不定詞。例如：

We don't allow cheating to be unpunished.（我們不允許作弊不受處罰。）
I don't allow you to smoke here.（我不允許你在這裡抽煙。）

03 文法觀念例句示範
Grammar Demonstration

01. Smoking may cause cancer.
吸煙會致癌。

02. It's useless arguing about it.
爭論這件事沒有意義。

03. Her hobby is painting.
她的愛好是繪畫。

04. Remember to tell him the news.
記得告訴他這個消息。

05. I don't feel like going to the movies.
我不想去看電影。

06. To master a foreign language is really important nowadays.
在現今，學好一門外語真的很重要。

07. It's kind of you to think so much of us.
你為我們設想這麼多真是太好了。

08. To see is to believe.
眼見為憑。

09. You must learn to look after yourself.
你必須自己學會照顧自己。

10. I don't know what to do next.
我不知道接下來該怎麼做。

04 文法觀念辨析練習
Grammar Practice

請最適合的題目的選項答案。

01. She can't help _____ the house because her guests is about to come.
- Ⓐ to cleaning
- Ⓑ cleaning
- Ⓒ cleaned
- Ⓓ being cleaned

02. It is difficult to get used _____ on the sofa.
- Ⓐ sleep
- Ⓑ to sleeping
- Ⓒ slept
- Ⓓ to sleep

03. Though _____ money, his parents managed to send him to university.
- Ⓐ lacked
- Ⓑ lacking of
- Ⓒ lacking
- Ⓓ lacked in

04. She pretended _____ me when I passed by.
- Ⓐ not to see
- Ⓑ not seeing
- Ⓒ to not see
- Ⓓ have not seen

05. It's no use _____ to get a bargain in the department store.
- Ⓐ to except
- Ⓑ excepting
- Ⓒ crying
- Ⓓ you excepting

06. After _____ for the job, you will be required to take a language test.
- Ⓐ being interviewed
- Ⓑ interviewed
- Ⓒ interviewing
- Ⓓ having interviewed

07. It was unbelievable that the fans waited outside the gym for three hours just _____ a look at the sports stars.
   A had
   B having
   C to have
   D have

08. I saw him _____ out of the room.
   A go
   B had gone
   C has gone
   D goes

09. No one can avoid _____ by advertisements.
   A to be influenced
   B being influenced
   C influencing
   D having influence

10. It was impolite of him _____ without _____ good-bye.
   A to leave ; saying
   B leaving ; to say
   C to leave ; to say
   D leaving ; saying

正確答案及題目中譯：

01. **B**	她忍不住打掃房子，因為她的客人快到了。	
02. **B**	要適應在沙發上睡覺是很困難的。	
03. **C**	就算沒有錢，他的父母還是安排讓他出國唸大學。	
04. **A**	當我經過的時候，她假裝沒有看到我。	
05. **B**	期望在百貨公司中找到便宜是沒有用的。	
06. **A**	工作面試結束後，你將會被要求參加語言能力測試。	
07. **C**	粉絲們在體育館外面枯等三個小時，僅是為了見運動明星一面，這件事真是難以置信。	
08. **A**	我看到他走出這間房間。	
09. **B**	沒有人可以避免被廣告所影響。	
10. **A**	他沒有說再見就離開，真是沒禮貌。	

12 連接詞

01 圖解文法，一看就會！
Grammar Mind Mapping

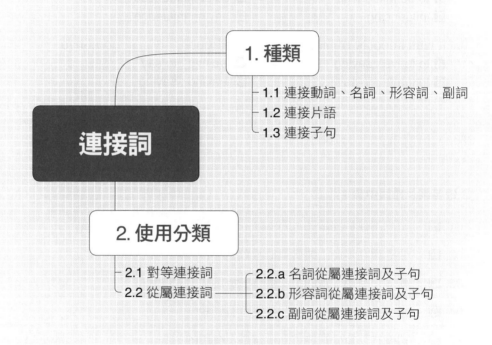

1. 種類

- 1.1 連接動詞、名詞、形容詞、副詞
- 1.2 連接片語
- 1.3 連接子句

連接詞

2. 使用分類

- 2.1 對等連接詞
- 2.2 從屬連接詞
  - 2.2.a 名詞從屬連接詞及子句
  - 2.2.b 形容詞從屬連接詞及子句
  - 2.2.c 副詞從屬連接詞及子句

1. 種類

- 1-1. **連接動詞、名詞、形容詞、副詞**
  love and hate（愛和恨）
  a difficult but worthy life（一個困難卻值得的人生）
  neither the teacher nor his student（不是那位老師也不是他的學生）

- 1-2. **連接片語**
  ready to start and easy to finish（準備出發和容易完成）

・1-3. **連接子句**

Johnny has not smoke since his daughter was born.（自從強尼的女兒出生後，他就沒有抽過煙了。）

2. 使用分類

・2-1. **對等連接詞**

此類連接詞有 **and, but, so, yet, still, either, or, neither, nor, than, either…or, neither...nor, not only...but also, as well as** 等。例如：

I will do it right away and do it well.（我現在就做，而且我會把這件事做好。）

She agreed with Martin's proposal, but she didn't want to join his team.（她同意馬丁的提案，但是她不想加入馬丁的團隊。）

・2-2. **從屬連接詞**

a) **名詞從屬連接詞及子句**

可用來當主詞和受詞，此類連接詞有 **whoever, whatever, who, whom, which, that, when, where, how, what, why, whether** 等。

What they said has nothing to do with my decision.
（他們說什麼話與我的決定無關。）→**名詞子句當主詞**

Micheal joined the team which is led by his father.
（麥可加入了由他爸爸領軍的團隊。）→**名詞子句當受詞**

b) **形容詞從屬連接詞及子句**

可用來當主詞補語和形容詞，此類連接詞有 **who, whom, whose, which, that, when, where** 等。

The point is who did this.（重點是誰完成了這件事。）→**形容詞子句當主詞補語**

The old lady who has 5 dogs is my mother-in-law.
（有五隻狗的老太太是我的岳母。）→**形容詞子句當形容詞**

c) **副詞從屬連接詞及子句**

可用當副詞使用或是引出副詞子句，此類連接詞有 **after, as, although, because, before, if, since, though, until, when, whenever, while, wherever** 等。

She woke up after I left home.（我一出家門她就醒了。）→**連接詞帶出副詞子句**

02 文法觀念例句示範
Grammar Demonstration

01. Air and water are indispensible for human beings.
空氣和水對人類來説是不可或缺的。

02. You may go, only if you come back early.
你可以去，只是要早點回來。

03. We should strike while the iron is hot.
我們要打鐵趁熱。

04. Where there is a will, there is a way.
有志者，事竟成。

05. We wouldn't lose heart even if we should fail then times.
我們就是失敗十次也不灰心。

06. Now that you are all back, we'd better start the work right now.
你們既然都回來了，我們最好馬上就開始工作。

07. Wherever you are, I will be with you.
不管你到哪，我都會在你身邊。

03 文法觀念辨析練習
Grammar Practice

請圈選最適合的題目的選項答案。

01 I was reading the newspapers _____ he came in.
　A as soon as　　　　B since
　C while　　　　　　D when

02. Hurry up, _____ you'll be late for school.
　A and　　　　　　B but
　C so　　　　　　　D or

03. Excuse me for breaking in, _____ I have some news for you.
 A so
 B and
 C but
 D yet

04. _____ you've got a chance, you might as well make full use of it.
 A Now that
 B After
 C Although
 D As soon as

05. The old man _____ lives in that old house is my uncle.
 A who
 B which
 C where
 D how

06. One can't learn a foreign language well _____ he studies hard.
 A because
 B though
 C unless
 D if

07 _____ you decide to take this job, you should try to make it a success.
 A Once
 B Unless
 C Whenever
 D If only

08. I'll accept any job _____ I don't have to get up early.
 A lest
 B as long as
 C in case
 D though

正確答案及題目中譯：

01. D	當他走進來時，我正在看報紙。
02. D	快一點，不然你上學就要遲到了。
03. C	很抱歉打斷你，但是我有消息要帶給你。
04. A	你現在有個機會，同樣地你可以善加利用。
05. A	住在那間房子裡的老人是我叔叔。
06. C	沒有人可以不努力用功就把一門外語學好。
07. A	一旦你決定接受這份工作，你就應該下決心把它做好。
08. B	只要可以讓我睡晚一點，我可以接受任何職缺。

Day05

13 介系詞

01 圖解文法，一看就會！
Grammar Mind Mapping

介系詞

1. 種類
- 1.1 簡單介系詞→只有一個單字
- 1.2 複合介系詞→兩個以上字根組成
- 1.3 雙重介系詞→由兩個介系詞組成
- 1.4 介系詞片語→由兩個或以上的單字組成

2. 使用時機
- 2.1 表示時間→ at, on, in, by, for, during, from
- 2.2 表示地點→ at, in, on
- 2.3 表示方位→ above, over, below, under, in front of, in the front of
- 2.4 表示運動方向→ along, across, through
- 2.5 表示在～之間→ between, among
- 2.6 表示方法、手段、工具→ by, with, in
- 2.7 表示原因→ because, as, for

介系詞，是介於中間。用以表明名詞與其他詞間各種關係的詞，主要是用來引出具有名詞作用的單字，例如名詞、動名詞、代名詞及名詞子句。

1. 種類

- 1-1. **簡單介系詞**→只有一個單字：
  簡單介系詞是指只有一個單字的介系詞。例如：**at, before, for, from, in, next, of, over, since, to, under, with** 等。

- 1-2. **複合介系詞**→兩個以上字根組成：
  複合介系詞是指由兩個字根所合成的介系詞。例如：**inside, into, out of, outside, upon, within, without** 等。

- 1-3. **雙重介系詞**→由兩個介系詞組成：
  雙重介系詞是指，由兩個介系詞所組成的介系詞。例如：**according to**（根據）、**from behind**（從……後面）、**along with**（與……一起）等等。

- 1-4. **介系詞片語**→由兩個或以上的單字組成：
  介系詞片語是指，由兩個或以上的單字組成的片語。例如：**at the end of**（在……最後）、**because of**（由於）、**by means of**（以……為手段）、**in case of**（萬一）、**in need of**（需要）、**in front of**（在……之前）、**in spite of**（儘管……還是）、**instead of**（代替）、**owing to**（由於）。

2. 使用時機

- 2-1. **表示時間**→ **at, on, in, by, for, during, from**
  a) **at：用來表示特定的時間點或短時間、節日、年齡等**。例如：
  at night（在晚上）、at 5 p.m.（在下午五點）。（in the night 亦可，文雅但極罕用。）
  I will meet you at 10 a.m. tomorrow morning.（明天早上 10 點見。）

  b) **on：用來表示某一天或星期幾，放在特定日子、節日或星期幾前面**。例如：
  on Friday（在禮拜五）、on the date your were born（在你出生的那天）
  Sarah's birthday this year is on Saturday.（莎拉今年的生日是禮拜六。）

  c) **in：用來表示較長的某段時間，如天、週次、月、季節、年等。**
  例如：in the morning（在早上）、in summer（在夏天）、in 2014（在 2014 年）
  I always like to go the beach in summer.（每天夏天我都喜歡去海邊。）

  d) **by：表示「……的時候、到～、等到～，已經～」，用在日期、時間的前面**，例如：by 5 o'clock（到五點截止）。
  Please wait for my information. I will come back by 7 p.m.
  （請等待我的消息。我會在七點的時候回來。）

e) **for：表示一段不明確的時間，指時間的長度，動作是斷斷續續的**。例如：
I have been living here for ten years.（我已經住在這裡 10 年了。）

f) **since：表示從過去某一時間點開始，到現在的一個時間點**。例如：
I have been living here since 2000.（我從 2000 年開始就住在這裡了。）

g) **during**：在～期間。**表示一段從開始到結束，相當分明的時間片段**。動作是規律性的持續，例如：
He swims every day during this summer.（在今年夏天，他每天都會游泳。）

h) **from**：自從～。**僅說明從什麼時候開始，不說明某動作或情況持續多久**，例如：
I began to work from this morning.（我從今天早上就開始工作。）

i) **after：表示在～之後**。如果後面接「一段不明確的時間」，就表示從過去某一段時間以後；如果後面接「一個精確的時間點」，表示從「某一時刻以後」。例如：

My mother was exhausted after 3 hours' housework.
（媽媽在做完三個小時的家事之後整個累翻了。）

We'll go out for a walk after dinner.（我們晚餐之後會出去散步。）

- **2-2. 表示地點→ at, in, on**
  a) **at：在一個精確的點（point）**，表示地點、地方、位置，指範圍較小的地方，或是特定的地點。例如：

  at the school's front gate（在學校的前門）、
  at the same restaurant（在同一間餐廳）。
  Tommy has been waiting for you at the bus stop for almost 3 hours!
  （湯米一直在公車站等你，等了快三個小時！）

  b) **in：表示在某個特定，有明顯區域範圍的空間之內（enclosed space）**，例如：
  in London（在倫敦）、in the garden（在花園裡面）、in my bag（在我的包包裡）。

  Iris has an important meeting at the World Trade Center in Bangkok.
  　　　　　　　　　　　　　　　　　↑　　　　　　　　↑
  　　　　　　　　　　　　　　　　特定地點　　　特定範圍內

  （艾瑞斯在曼谷的世界貿易中心有一個重要的會議。）

c) **on：表示在一個位置、地點或某個表面的上方**，例如：
on the wall（在牆上）、on the floor（在地板上）、on a page of the book（在這本書的頁面上）。
I live on the 6th floor at Wall Street in New York.（我住在紐約華爾街的 6 樓。）

- **2-3. 表示方位→ above, over, below, under, in front of, in the front of**
  a) **above：指在⋯⋯上方**，即水平位置較高，於 below 相反，例如：
  The moon is now above the pine tree.（月亮現在在松樹的上方。）

  b) **over：指「垂直」的上方**，與 under 相對，但通常是指上方的物體從一邊移動到另一邊時經過的情況，或意味著居於並未觸及所指物件的上方處。例如：
  The bird is flying over my head.（這隻鳥飛過了我的頭上。）

  c) **below, under：都表示在～下面**，但 under 在正下方，below 不一定在正下方。
  There is a ball under the chair.（有顆球在椅子下面。）
  My new skirt came below my ankles.（我的新裙子比我的腳踝還低。）

  d) **in front of / in the front of：都表示在～前面**，但 in front of 指甲物在乙物之前，兩個物體為各自獨立的物體，反義詞是 behind（在～後面）；in the front of 指甲物在乙物的「內部的前方」，即乙物包含了甲物在內，反義詞為 at the back of（在～範圍內的後面）。

  There is a river in front of my house.
  （我家門前有一條小河。）→**我家跟小河各自獨立，沒有接觸**

  Our teacher stands in the front of the classroom.
  （我們老師站在教室的前面。）→**老師在教室裡面，但是站在教室的前面**

- **2-4. 表示運動方向→ along, across, through**
  a) **along：表示「沿著～」**，例如：along the river（沿著這條河）。
  Just walk along the street and you will find the bus stop.
  （只要沿著這條街一直走，你就會看到公車站了。）

  b) **across：表示「橫過～」**，通常與「道路、河川、平原」等地點連用，例如：
  across the road（橫越馬路）。
  The Wangs just live across the street.（王氏一家人就住在這條街的對面。）

  c) **through：表示「穿過～、穿越～」**，指從物體內部穿過，例如：
  through the door（穿過門）。
  I saw Sandy through the window.（我透過玻璃窗看到了珊蒂。）

- **2-5. 表示在～之間→ between, among**
  a) **between：指在「兩個」人或事物之間**，例如：
  between you and me（在你跟我之間。）→ It's between you and me.（這要保密。）
  My boss devided all the profit between John and him.
  （我老闆把所有的營利分給了他自己和約翰。）

  b) **among：指在「三個或以上」的人或物之間**，例如：among all of us.
  My boss divided all the profit among all of us.
  （我老闆把所有的營利分給了我們所有人。）

- **2-6. 表示方法、手段、工具→ by, with, in**
  a) **by：表示以～方法、手段或泛指某種交通工具**。例如：
  I go to school by bus every day.（我每天都搭公車上學。）

  b) **with：表示用～工具、手段**，一般接具體的工具和手段，如：
  I cut the apple with a knife.（我用刀子切開蘋果。）

  c) **in：表示用～方式，用～語言（語調、筆墨、顏色）等**，例如：
  He talks with me in English for 15 minutes every day.（他每天都用英文跟我說話 15 分鐘。）

- **2-7. 表示原因→ because, as, for**
  a) **because：表示直接的、明確的原因**，用來回答 why 的問句。例如：
  He was late for school, because he didn't catch the bus.
  （他上學遲到，因為他沒有趕上公車。）

  b) **as：表示由於～，鑒於～**，指一種顯而易見、談話雙方已知的理由如：
  She stayed at home as she was ill.（她待在家因為她生病了。）

  c) **for：表示由於、因為**，指一種間接原因，甚至只是一種附帶的說明。例如：
  It must have rained last night, for the road is wet.
  （昨天晚上一定有下雨，因為路是溼的。）

02 文法觀念例句示範
Grammar Demonstration

01. He is intent on winning.
　　他一心只想著要贏。

02. Joe was very disappointed at not finding her at home.
喬發現她不在家很失望。

03. I shall prevail on him to make the attempt.
我將說服他試一試。

04. We concentrated on doing one job at a time.
我們專心一次做一份工作。

05. I don't mean to break in your thoughts.
我無意打斷你的思緒的。

06. He achieved his aim by force of sheer determination.
他完全憑著十足的決心達成他的目標。

07. Such irresponsible conduct can only cause to the prejudice of our work.
這種不負責任的行為只會有損於我們的事業。

08. He is working hard now with an eye to the future.
他為了前途而現在努力工作。

09. In the event of an accident, the police must be called at once.
如果出了事故，應該立刻叫員警。

10. She was cheated out of 1,000 dollars by the young man.
她被一個年輕男人騙了 1000 美元。

03 文法觀念辨析練習
Grammar Practice

請填入適合題目句中底線的介系詞。

01. Please don't get mad _____ me. I was only trying to help.

02. Fruit is rich _____ vitamins.

03. John was impatient _____ his daughter.

04. Cathy was particular _____ the jewelry she wore.

05. The jury decided that Susan was guilty _____ murder.

06. The word derives _____ Latin.

07. Everyone blamed you _____ a certain mistake; you need to say something.

08. This water taste _____ salt.

09. It's rude to point _____ someone.

10. I'll find someone to fill in this form _____ you.

正確答案及題目中譯：

01. at	請不要對我生氣。我只是想要幫忙。	
02. in	水果富有維他命。	
03. with	約翰對他的女兒失去耐性。	
04. about	凱西對於她配戴的珠寶特別講究。	
05. of	陪審團認定蘇珊謀殺罪成立。	
06. from	這個字是從拉丁語過來的。	
07. for	每個人都因為一項錯誤而責怪你，你一定要説些什麼才行。	
08. of	水嚐起來有鹽的味道。	
09. at	用手指著別人是很沒禮貌的。	
10. for	我會找人來幫你填寫這份表格。	

Day05

Step 2　了解英文中關鍵的關鍵一字詞

14 片語

01 圖解文法，一看就會！
Grammar Mind Mapping

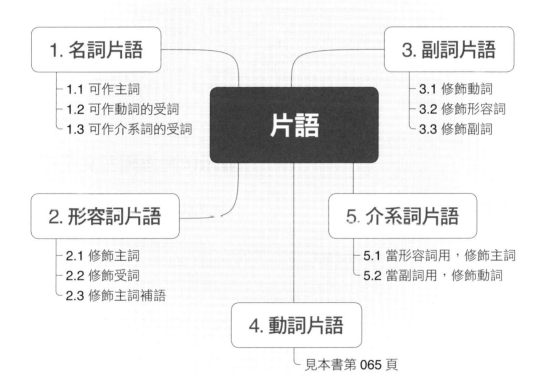

片語

1. 名詞片語
- 1.1 可作主詞
- 1.2 可作動詞的受詞
- 1.3 可作介系詞的受詞

2. 形容詞片語
- 2.1 修飾主詞
- 2.2 修飾受詞
- 2.3 修飾主詞補語

3. 副詞片語
- 3.1 修飾動詞
- 3.2 修飾形容詞
- 3.3 修飾副詞

5. 介系詞片語
- 5.1 當形容詞用，修飾主詞
- 5.2 當副詞用，修飾動詞

4. 動詞片語
- 見本書第 065 頁

片語是指由兩個或兩個以上的英文單字所組合的詞語，（其中不包含主詞和動詞），連在一起具有類似一種詞類作用的字群。

1. 名詞片語

名詞片語如同名詞，可做句子中的：

- 1-1. **主詞**

  Let me down is the most terrible thing you've ever done.
  名詞片語→當主詞

  （讓我失望是你做過最糟糕的事情。）

- 1-2. **及物動詞的受詞**

  I don't know how to deal with it.（我不知道該如何處理它。）
  　　　　　　名詞片語→當動詞的受詞

- 1-3. **介系詞的受詞**

  She is a huge fan of rock music.（她是超級搖滾樂迷。）
  　　　　　　名詞片語→當介系詞的受詞

2. 形容詞片語

形容詞片語如同形容詞，用以修飾句中的名詞，置於所修飾的名詞之後，由於形容詞能修飾名詞，而名詞又能做句子的主詞、受詞等，所以形容詞片語也有同樣的功能。

- 2-1. **修飾主詞**

  The girl sitting behind you is my best friend.

  （坐在你身後的女孩是我最好的朋友。）

- 2-2. **修飾受詞**

  The company offered the job to the person with the best experience.

  （公司把工作交給最有經驗的人。）

・ 2-3. **修飾主詞補語**

This is a book of many interesting stories.

（這是一本有許多有趣故事的書。）

3. 副詞片語

副詞片語如同副詞，用來修飾句中的動詞、形容詞、副詞和整句。

・ 3-1. **修飾動詞**

He spoke loudly and clearly.（他説話很清晰洪亮。）

・ 3-2. **修飾形容詞**

We are sorry to have kept you waiting so long.

（很抱歉要你等這麼久的時間。）

・ 3-3. **修飾副詞**

He is too young to go to school.（他太小還不能上學。）

4. 動詞片語

動詞片語是由動詞加上副詞所形成，這些副詞常見的有 up, down, in, out, on, off...。而這些副詞同時也可當介系詞使用，因此也被稱為「介副詞」。詳細説明可見本書第 065 頁。

・ 4-1. **受詞為名詞時→放在片語之後或是中間**，例如：
take off the coat 或 take the coat off。
・ 4-2. **受詞為代名詞時→放在片語中間**，例如：put it up。

5. 介系詞片語

介系詞片語就是介詞和受詞連在一起，當形容詞或副詞用。

• 5-1. 當形容詞用，修飾主詞：

The boy with blonde hair is playing soccer there.

（金色頭髮的男孩正在那兒踢足球。）

• 5-2. 當副詞用，修飾動詞：

You may come to my living room anytime.（你隨時都可以來到我的客廳。）

02 文法觀念例句示範
Grammar Demonstration

01. I will call on you next Sunday.
我下個星期天會去拜訪你。

02. I want to run some errands.
我要去辦點雜事。

03. There is a bunch of books in my living room.
我的客廳裡有一堆書。

04. He pulled an all-nighter last night.
他昨晚熬夜了。

05. They hang out a lot.
他們常在一起。

06. Above all, we must finish the work at hand.
最重要的是，我們必須把手上的工作完成。

07. As a matter of fact, I'm a very efficient worker.
事實上，我是個做事非常有效率的員工。

08. I will go with the chicken noodle soup.
我會選擇雞肉湯麵。

09. Take a little more money with you, just in case.
多帶一點錢在身上，以備不時之需。

10. You've said a lot, but nothing was to the point.
你說了很多，但都沒有說到重點。

03 文法觀念辨析練習
Grammar Practice

請將題目句翻譯成英文。

01. 我們為何不停車，下車一會兒呢？

_____

02. 在你出門前把帽子帶上。

_____

03. 請打開燈，這裡太暗了。

_____

04. 我只能一天又一天的等待奇蹟的發生。

_____

05. 關於那份新的工作，你接到公司的通知了嗎？

_____

06. 我相信這個產品會非常暢銷。

_____

07. 你必須準時趕到約定的地方。

08. 請千萬小心，別讓小孩靠近馬路。

09. 員警正在調查電腦失竊的案件。

10. 沒有證據可以證明我是被陷害的。

正確答案：

01. Why don't we stop and get out of the car for a while?

02. Put your hat on before you leave the house.

03. Please turn on the light; it's too dark in here.

04. I can only wait day by day for miracles to happen.

05. Have you heard from the company about that new job?

06. I would count on this product becoming a bestseller.

07. You must make it to the appointed place on time.

08. Please be sure to keep the children away from the street!

09. The police are looking into the matter of the stolen computers.

10. There was no evidence to prove that I was being set up.

Step 3　該如何使用進階的句子？

15　假設語氣

01 圖解文法，一看就會！
Grammar Mind Mapping

1. 與現在事實相反
　1.1 If ＋過去簡單 , 主句 would ＋原形 V

假設語氣

2. 與過去事實相反
　2.1 If ＋過去完成 , 主句 would ＋ have p.p.

3. 與未來事實相反
　3.1 純屬臆測或假設
　3.2 有「萬一」的含意→ If ＋ should ＋原形 V, 主句＋ should ＋原形 V

> 假設語氣用來表示說的話不是事實，或者是不可能發生的情況，
> 而是一種願望、建議、假設的語氣。假設語氣有三種基本類型：
> 與現在事實相反，與過去事實相反，與將來事實相反。

1. 與現在事實相反

- **If ＋過去簡單 , 主句 would ＋原形 V**
  表示與現在事實相反的假設時，句型為「If ＋過去簡單，主要句子用 should /
  would / might / could ＋原形 V」

要特別注意的是，與現在事實相反時 If 句中的動詞為過去式，而所使用的 Be 動詞不論人稱為何，「一律用 were」。例如：

If I were you, I would accept his suggestions.
（如果我是你，我就會接受他的建議。）

2. 與過去事實相反

・ **If ＋過去完成 , 主句 would ＋ have p.p.**
表示與過去的事實相反的假設時，句型為「If ＋ had ＋ p.p., 主要子句用 should / would / might / could ＋ have ＋ p.p.」例如：

If you had been here yesterday, you would have seen her.
（如果你昨天在這裡，就能見到她了。）

3. 與未來事實相反

・ **3-1. 對未來的假設、臆測**
句型為「If ＋ 過去簡單式，主要子句用 should / would / might / could ＋ 原形 V」或「If ＋ 現在簡單式，主要子句用現在簡單式或 will ＋ 原形 V」。例如：

If the sun were to disappear, you would win the jackpot.（如果太陽消失不見，那你就會贏得大獎。）**→你沒有贏得大獎，因為太陽並不會消失不見。**

If it rains heavily, the river nearby floods / will flood.
（若下大雨，附近河流就會氾濫。）

・ **3-2. 有「萬一」的含意→ If ＋ should ＋原形 V, 主句＋ should ＋原形 V**
如果與未來事實相反的假設句中，帶有「萬一」或「可能發生」的含意，那麼句型請使用「If ＋ should ＋原形 V，主要句子用 should (shall) / would (will) / might (may) / could (can) ＋原形 V」。例如：

If Mike would come tomorrow, I will bring him to the best resataurant I have ever been.（如果麥克明天來的話，那我就會帶他去我去過最好的餐廳。）
→麥克明天可能會來，所以我可能會帶他去最好的餐廳

02 延伸用法，事半功倍！
Learning Plus!

假設語氣的其他形式：
・ 1. 省略 if 的假設法

句型 1「Were ＋主詞 , ...」
Were I young, I would learn English well.
（如果我還年輕，我要好好學英語。）

句型 2「Had ＋主詞 P.P., ...」
Had you been here earlier, you would have seen him.
（你要是早點到這兒，你就見到他了。）

句型 3「Should ＋主詞＋原形 V, ...」
Should that be true, the contract would be canceled.
（如果那是真的，合約就該取消。）

• 2. 表示「但願」的假設法
常使用「I wish (that) / If only / Would that」等開頭，後面接

a) were 或者過去式假設語氣，以表示「目前無法實現的願望」。
b) 過去完成式，表示「過去不能實現的願望」。

I wish that I didn't have to go to work today.（我今天要能不上班就好了。）
→目前無法實現的願望

Would that she could see her son now!
（要是她現在能看到她的兒子就好了！）→目前無法實現的願望

If only I knew her address.（我當時要是知道她的地址就好了。）
→現在無法實現的願望

I wish I hadn't said that.（真希望我當時沒有說那話。）
→過去無法實現的願望

03 文法觀念例句示範
Grammar Demonstration

01. If you should happen to see him, please give him my regards.
如果你萬一見到他，請代我向他致意。

02. If the sun were to disappear, what would the earth be like?
萬一太陽消失了，地球會變成什麼樣呢？

03. If I were free now, I might to call on him.
如果我有時間，我可能去看他了。

04. If you were in my shoes, what would you do?
如果你站在我的立場，你會怎麼做？

05. If only she came here earlier.
如果她可以早點來就好了。

06. I could have finished the task if I had had more time.
如果當時我有多一點時間，我就能完成這項任務。

07. Had he not apologized to her, she would not have forgiven him.
要不是他道歉，她那時是不會原諒他的。

08. If I had worked hard when young, I would be well off now.
如果我年輕時多努力一點，現在就能過得舒服些。

04 文法觀念辨析練習
Grammar Practice

請圈選最適合的題目的選項答案。

01. He described the town as if he _____ it himself.
A had seen
B has seen
C saw
D sees

02. He's working hard for fear that he _____.
A should fall behind
B fell behind
C may fall behind
D must fall behind

03. _____ I young, I would learn German also.
A Am
B Were
C Was
D Be

04. "Only if I know her address." That means:
A I know her address.
B I don't know her address.
C I didn't know her address
D I've forgotten her addressd

05. He was very busy yesterday, otherwise he _____ to the meeting.
    A would come   **B** came
    C would have come   **D** had come

06. If you had told me this information, I _____ some suggestion to you.
    A might make   **B** would have made
    C may have made   **D** had made

07. I hadn't expected James to apologize but I had hoped _____.
    A him calling me   **B** that he would call me
    C him to call me   **D** that he call me

08. It's high time they _____ this road.
    A mend   **B** mended
    C must have mended   **D** will mend

15
假設語氣

正確答案及題目中譯：

01. **A**	他描述這個城鎮，彷彿他親眼見過一般。
02. **A**	他努力工作，擔心自己進度落後。
03. **B**	如果我還年輕，我會也學學德文。
04. **B**	"要是我現在知道她的地址就好了。" 意思為：我不知道她的地址。
05. **C**	他昨天非常地忙碌，否則他會來開會。
06. **B**	如果你早點讓我知道這個消息，我就可以給你一點建議。
07. **B**	我沒有期待詹姆士跟我道歉，但是我希望他可以打電話給我。
08. **B**	也該是他們修補這條路的時候了。

Step 3 該如何使用進階的句子？

16 被動語態

---

01 圖解文法，一看就會！
Grammar Mind Mapping

- 1.1 及物動詞→ be+p.p.
- 1.2 助動詞→助動詞＋ be ＋ p.p.
- 1.3 授與動詞→其中一個受詞變主詞時，另一個受詞仍為句中受詞
- 1.4 受詞＋受詞補語→主動式的受詞變成被動式的主詞，受詞補語不變

1. 被動語態的構成

被動語態

2. 被動語態的基本用法

- 2.1 動作的執行者沒必要提出，可被省略時
- 2.2 出於禮貌或婉轉，希望省略執行者時
- 2.3 強調動作的承受者時
- 2.4 為了文章通順
- 2.5 正式的通告

英語中有兩種語態：主動語態和被動語態。主動語態表示主詞是動作的執行者。被動語態表示主詞是動作的承受者。

1. 被動語態的構成

- 1-1. **及物動詞**→ **be+p.p.**

英文文法中僅有及物動詞有被動形式。其句型結構為「be ＋及物動詞的過去分詞」。另外，被動語態可以使用於各種時態，例如：

現在式：My mother is not easily **deceived**. （我媽媽不是容易上當受騙的。）

過去式：A new house was **built** in this town. （有一棟新房子蓋在這個城市裡。）

過去完成式：She had been **accepted** by the team 2 years ago.
（她兩年前就被這團隊接納為一員了。）

過去未來式：Somebody said that this museum would be **built** in 5 months.
（有人說這棟博物館五個月後可以蓋完。）

過去進行式：All the injured visitors were being **taken** care of by the nurses.
（所有受傷的遊客當時都有護士在照顧著。）

現在進行式：This subject is being **discussed** by all the department directors in company now. （所有的公司部門主管都在討論這個話題。）

現在完成式：The laundry has been **done**. （衣服已經都洗好了。）

- 1-2. **助動詞**→**助動詞＋ be ＋ p.p.**

當句中動詞為助動詞型態時，轉變為被動語態的句型結構為「助動詞＋ be ＋ p.p.」，例如：

All the players could be found in the gym.
（所有的選手都可以在體育館中被找到。）

- 1-3. **授與動詞**→**其中一個受詞變主詞時，另一個受詞仍為句中受詞**

授與動詞的句型結構中可以存在兩個受詞，而需將句中的動詞改為被動語態時，通常是將直接受詞往前拉作主詞，間接受詞仍保留為句中受詞。如果主動結構中的直接受詞變為被動結構中的主詞，這時在間接受詞前要加介系詞 to 或 for。例如：

The doctor gave me a prescription.
= I was given a prescription by the doctor.
= A prescription was given to me by the doctor.
（醫生幫我開了一張處方籤。）

Mickey brought me a gift.
= I was brought a gift by Mickey.
= A gift was brought for me by Mickey.
（米奇帶了一份禮物給我。）

- **1-4. 受詞＋受詞補語→主動式的受詞變成被動式的主詞，受詞補語不變：**
  當句型中含有「受詞和受詞補語」的結構時，要轉換為被動語態時，只需將主動結構中的受詞變為被動結構中的主詞，受詞補語不變。例如：

  I painted all the wall purple.
  = All the walls were painted purple by me.（所有的牆壁都被我漆成紫色）

2. 被動語態的基本用法

- **2-1. 動作的執行者沒必要提出，可被省略時**
  This plan will be finished next week.（這項計畫下週就會被完成。）

  Father told us that a swimming pool is being built in our town.
  （爸爸告訴我們鎮上正在建造一座游泳池。）

- **2-2. 出於禮貌或婉轉希望省略執行者時**
  Johnny was considered to be a natural leader.
  （強尼被認為是一個天生的領導者。）

  My brother is said to be a super star in the future.
  （有人說我弟弟日後會成為一個大明星。）

- **2-3. 強調動作的承受者時**
  All the desks were cleaned by me this morning.
  （所有的桌子我今天早上都打掃過了。）

  Some of the people in your office are asked to speak with lower voice.
  （你們辦公室有些人被要求說話小聲一點。）

- **2-4. 為了文章通順**
  The president appeared, and was warmly applauded by the citizens.
  （當總統出現時，市民們給予熱烈的掌聲。）

- 2-5. 正式的通告：
Passengers are requested to remain seated until the aircraft comes to a complete stop.（飛機停妥前，請乘客不要離開座位。）

02 文法觀念例句示範
Grammar Demonstration

01. Paper was first made in China.
紙張首先在中國被製作出來。

02. He was laughed at by all people.
他被所有人嘲笑。

03. It's said that this book has been translated into several languages.
據說這本書被翻譯成多種語言。

04. Such questions are settled by us.
這樣的問題被我們解決了。

05. I was frightened by his ghost story.
我被他的鬼故事嚇到了。

06. A new public school will be built up in this town.
一座新的公立學校將被建在這座城鎮裡。

07. Plastic bags full of rubbish have been piled in streets.
人們把裝滿垃圾的塑膠袋子堆放在街上。

08. You will be asked a lot of strange questions.
他們將會問你許多怪問題。

09. It is generally considered impolite to ask one's age, salary, marriage, etc.
問別人的年齡、薪水、婚姻狀況等，通常被認為是不禮貌的。

10. I was given ten minutes to decide whether I should accept the offer.
我有十分鐘的時間來決定是否接受這項提議。

03 文法觀念辨析練習
Grammar Practice

請把下列句子改寫成被動語態。

01. A car knocked him down yesterday.

_____

02. Two doctors and ten nurses make up the medical team.

_____

03. Everybody likes this song.

_____

04. They have sold out all the red lanterns.

_____

05. He made the poor girl work for 12 hours a day.

_____

06. Children saw the movie last week.

_____

07. We shouldn't allow young children to drive.

_____

08. It is thought that he is coming.

_____

09. It is supposed that the ship has been sunk.

_____

10. You mustn't throw away the old books.

正確答案及題目中譯：

01. He was knocked down by a car yesterday. 昨天有輛車撞到他了。

02. The medical team is made up of by two doctors and ten nurses.
2 位醫生和 10 位護士組成這個醫療團隊。

03. This song is liked by everybody. 大家都喜歡這一首歌。

04. All the red lanterns have been sold out. 他們將所有的燈籠都賣完了。

05. The poor girl was made to work for 12 hours a day.
他逼這個可憐的女孩每天工作 12 個小時。

06. The movie was seen by children last week. 孩子們上星期看過這部電影。

07. Young children should not be allowed to drive. 我們不應該讓孩童開車。

08. He is thought to be coming. 以為他會過來。

09. The ship is supposed to have been sunk. 一般認為這艘船已經沉了。

10. The old books must not be thrown away. 你不能將這些舊書丟掉。

Step 3 該如何使用進階的句子？

17 附加問句

---

01 圖解文法，一看就會！
Grammar Mind Mapping

1. 語調
- 1-1 上升→確認
- 1-2 下降→強調

3. 一致性
- 3-1 前後主詞需一致
- 3-2 前後動詞需一致

附加問句

2. 否定要縮寫

4. 依目的決定肯定或否定
- 4-1 肯定＋否定→希望得到肯定答案
- 4-2 否定＋肯定→希望得到否定答案

---

1. 語調

附加用句為接在敘述句後的簡短問句，用意在加強語意或確認訊息內容。

- 1-1. **語調上升→確認訊息**→表示發話者不確定訊息內容，希望對方給予意見。

> Mandy will come here today, won't she?（曼蒂今天會過來，對吧？）
> → 希望「確認」曼蒂今天「會」過來這裡。

- 1-2. **語調下降→強調訊息**→用於發話者意圖強調說明之訊息。

Sandy is such a nice girl, isn't she? 珊蒂真是個好女孩，不是嗎？

→表示「強調」珊蒂「是」個好女孩。

2. 否定要縮寫

附加問句若為否定句（含有 not），則通常以縮寫形式出現。

- ✗ Sam is a student, is not he?
- ○ Sam is a student, **isn't** he?

3. 一致性

- 3-1. **前後主詞需一致**
  附加問句的主詞需與前敘述句中的主詞一致，且附加問句中的主詞需使用敘述句中相符之「人稱代名詞」。

  Michael is your brother, isn't **he**? 麥可是你哥哥，對嗎？

- 3-2. **前後動詞需一致**
  附加問句中的時態需與敘述句保持一致。
  敘述句使用 **be 動詞**，附加問句則使用 **am / are / is、am not / aren't / isn't**；
  敘述句使用**一般動詞**，附加問句則使用 **do, did, does**；
  敘述句使用**過去動詞**，附加問句則使用 **did**；
  敘述句使用**完成式**，附加問句則使用 **have / has、haven't / hasn't**；

  Grandpa **likes** gardening, **doesn't** he? 爺爺喜歡園藝，不是嗎？

  Ms. Jackson **has** been to Paris, **hasn't** she? 傑克森小姐去過巴黎，不是嗎？

4. 依目的決定肯定或否定

說話者可以依其目的，來決定敘述句為肯定句或否定句。

- 4-1. **肯定**（敘述句）＋否定（附加問句）→希望得到**肯定**答案
  You **love** your children, **don't** you? 你**愛**你的孩子，**不是**嗎？
  Yes, I **do**. 是的，我愛。

• 4-2. **否定**（敘述句）＋肯定（附加問句）→希望得到**否定**的答案。

Your teacher **didn't** tell you to cheat, **did** she?（老師**沒**叫你作弊，**對**吧？）

No, she **didn't**.（對的，她**沒有**。）

02 延伸用法，事半功倍！
Learning Plus!

1. 祈使句

• 1-1. 建議或請求：

Let's go to the movies, shall we?（我們一起去看電影，好嗎？）

Let's not talk about it, all right?（別再談這件事了，好嗎？）

Let me take a look at this, will you?（讓我看看，可以嗎？）

• 1-2. 命令：

Keep quiet, **will you?**（保持安靜，好嗎？）

• 1-3. 邀請：

Have a seat, **won't you?**（坐下來，好嗎？）

2. there 為首的敘述句

There are many Japanese restaurants near here, aren't there?

（這附近有許多日本餐館，不是嗎？）

03 文法觀念例句示範
Grammar Demonstration

01. Steven is the smartest boy in your class, **isn't he?**

史蒂芬是你班上最聰明的男生，對嗎？

02. You will not invite him to the party, **will you?**

你不會邀請他來派對，對吧？

03. I don't have to go with you, **do I?**

我不必跟你一起去，對吧？

04. Joanna can babysit the kids tonight, **can't she?**
喬安娜今晚可以幫忙帶小孩，對不對？

05. You have done your homework, **haven't you?**
你們已經把作業做完了，不是嗎？

06. Peter was a pilot, **wasn't he?**
彼得曾經是個飛行員，對不對？

07. I am the most beautiful woman in the world, **am I not?**
我是世上最美麗的女人，對不對？

08. We must do it by ourselves, **mustn't we?**
我們必須自己做這件事，不是嗎？

09. Calm down, **will you?**
冷靜下來，好嗎？

10. There isn't too much water left in the reservoir, **is there?**
水庫裡沒有剩下多少水了，是嗎？

04 文法觀念辨析練習
Grammar Practice

請圈選出題目句中底線「附加問句」中相對應的標準答案。

01. They hadn't have chance to talk, had they ?
　Ⓐ No, they hadn't.　　　　Ⓑ Yes, they did.

02. You don't have to work late today, do you ?
　Ⓐ No, I don't.　　　　Ⓑ Yes, we have.

03. Sit down, _____ ?
　Ⓐ will you　　　　Ⓑ won't you

04. They didn't recognize who you are, did they ?
　Ⓐ No, they didn't.　　　　Ⓑ No, you aren't.

05. He will never cheat on me, will he ?
　　A No, he won't.　　　　　　**B** Yes, he won't.

06. Michael didn't call me, _____ ?
　　A did him　　　　　　　　**B** did he

07. She can hardly move the stone, _____ ?
　　A can she　　　　　　　　**B** can't she

08. Everyone should come tomorrow, _____ ?
　　A they shouldn't.　　　　　**B** shouldn't they

09. That's Marie, _____ ?
　　A isn't it　　　　　　　　**B** is it

10. Let's have a coffee break, _____ ?
　　A won't you　　　　　　　**B** shall we

正確答案及題目中譯：

01. **A**	他們沒有任何機會談話，對嗎？／是的，他們沒有。	
02. **A**	你今天不用加班，對吧？／是的，我不用。	
03. **B**	坐下，好嗎？	
04. **A**	他們沒認出來你是誰，對嗎？／是的，他們沒有。	
05. **A**	他永遠不會欺騙我，對嗎？／是的，他不會。	
06. **B**	麥可沒有打電話給我，對嗎？	
07. **A**	她搬不動那塊石頭，對嗎？	
08. **B**	每個人明天都要來，對嗎？	
09. **A**	那是瑪莉，對嗎？	
10. **B**	讓我們休息一下喝杯咖啡，好嗎？	

Day06

Step 3 該如何使用進階的句子？

18 關係代名詞

01 圖解文法，一看就會！
Grammar Mind Mapping

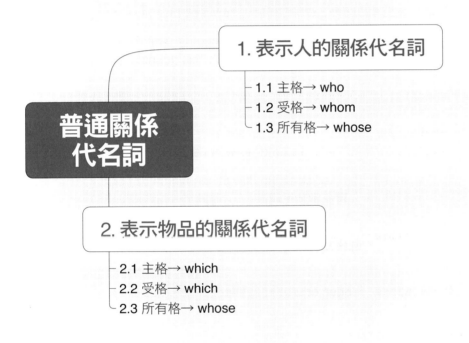

關係代名詞是指兼具代名詞與連接詞雙重作用的代名詞，常簡稱為「關代」。關係代名詞所代表的名詞或代名詞就做「先行詞」，句中該用何種代名詞視先行詞的種類而定。關係代名詞的數、性、格應該與先行詞一致。

Part 1. 普通關係代名詞

1. 表示人的代名詞

表示人的關係代名詞有 who, whom ,whose，除非前面有介系詞時要用受格 whom 之外，who 與其餘情況的 whom 均可用 that 代替。

- 1-1. **主格→ who**
  關係代名詞 who 是人的主格，通常後面會直接接一個動作。例如：

  The boy who lives near the park is my new classmate.

  （住在公園旁邊的那個男孩是我新同學。）

- 1-2. **受格→ whom**
  關係代名詞 whom 是人的受格，通常後面會接主詞＋動詞，有時會有介系詞，要視情況而定。例如：

  I don't know the man whom you met at the gate this morning.

  （我不認識你早上在門口遇到的那個人。）

  The new student whom I talked to in class was very shy.

  （和我在教室交談的那位新同學非常害羞。）

- 1-3. **所有格→ whose**
  關係代名詞 whose 是人的所有格，通常後面接名詞。

  That is the professor whose course I am taking this semester.

  （就是那個教授，我這個學期要上他的課。）

2. 表示物品的代名詞

表示物的關係代名詞有 which, whose。其中 which 可用 that 代替，但 which 前面有介系詞時除外。

- 2-1. **主格→ which**
  關係代名詞 which 是用來代替沒有生命的先行詞，如果 which 後面接的是動詞，它就是主格；

The jacket which is on the desk is mine.（桌上的那件夾克是我的。）→主格

- 2-2. **受格**→ **which**
  如果 which 後面接的是主詞＋動詞，它就是該動詞的受格。

The information which I found on the Internet helped me a lot.

（我在網上找的那些資訊幫了我很多。）→受格

- 2-3. **所有格**→ **whose**
  關係代名詞 whose 也可以表示事物的所有格，當 whose 前面的先行詞是事物或動物，後面接名詞，可用「of which」代替，但不可用 that。

The house whose door is red is mine.（門是紅色的那棟房子是我的。）
The house of which the roof was painted red is my mother's.
（那棟屋頂漆成紅色的屋子是我媽媽的。）

Part 2 表示人和物品的關係代名詞 — that

關係代名詞 that 既可以表示人又可以表示物，可當主格或受格，但不能當所有格。
有些場合關係代名詞只能用 that，有的場合則不能用 that。

1. 只能用關係代名詞 that 的場合

- 1-1. **先行詞同時有人和事物時**，例如：
  I know the man and his dog that were dead in the accident.
  （我認識在事故中逝去的那個人和他的狗。）

- 1-2. **先行詞前有限定字**，如最高級，序數詞，the only, the same, the very, any, no, all, every 等等。
  This is the greatest invention that I've ever seen.（這是我見過的最偉大的發明。）

He is the first student that goes into the classroom every day.
（他是每天第一個到教室的學生。）

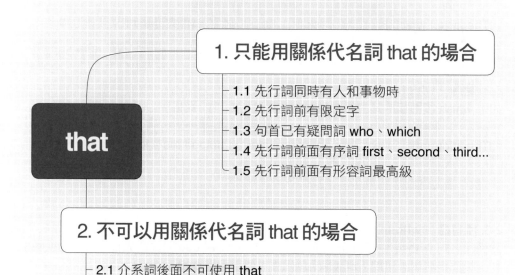

- 1-3. **句首已有疑問詞 who、which**，避免重複。
  Who is the boy that is standing over there?（站在那兒的那個男生是誰。）

- 1-4. **先行詞前面有序詞**，例如：
  The first man that stepped on the moon was Armstrong.
  （第一個登陸月球的人是阿姆斯壯。）

- 1-5. **先行詞前面有形容詞最高級**，例如：
  The meanest man that was absent hit the jackpot.（那個缺席的機車男中了頭彩。）

2. 不能用關係代名詞 that 的場合

- 2-1. **介系詞後面不可使用關係代名詞 that**，例如：
  This is the house in which he lives.（這是他住的房子。）

- 2-2. **逗號後面不可使用關係代名詞 that**，例如：
  My elder sister, who is in Paris, will come back tomorrow.
  （我那個住在巴黎的姊姊，明天就會回來。）**→我只有一個姐姐**，而且住在巴黎。

關係代名詞與先行詞之間有逗號,表示先行詞具有唯一性;關係代名詞和先行詞之間無逗號,表示不止一個。

My elder sister who is in Paris will come back tomorrow.(我住在巴黎的姊姊,明天就會回來。)→**我不止有一個姐姐**,其他姐姐可能在其他地方。

02 文法觀念例句示範
Grammar Demonstration

01. The toy which belongs to me disappeared.
那個屬於我的玩具不見了。

02. I have a friend whose father is an artist.
我有一位朋友,他的爸爸是藝術家。

03. The lady whom you talked to is my teacher.
跟你說話的那個女士是我老師。

04. Amy enjoys the food which her mother cooks.
艾米喜歡她媽媽做的食物。

05. I like the boy who has short hair.
我喜歡留短髮的那位男孩。

06. The man about whom you were talking is my husband.
你在談論的那個人是我的丈夫。

07. The book of which the cover is green is mine.
那本封面是綠色的書是我的。

08. Take any book that you like.
帶走任何一本你喜歡的書。

09. He is the first boy that came this morning.
他是今天早上最先到的男孩。

10. He borrowed a book whose author is a young lady.
他借了一本作者是一位年輕小姐的書。

03 文法觀念辨析練習
Grammar Practice

請以適當的關係代名詞填入題目空格中。

01. The kid and his cat _____ are in the garden are cute.

02. That is the house in _____ they live.

03. Do you know the girl _____ is crossing the street?

04. This is the boy _____ I met at the station yesterday

05. These are the photographs _____ I took last month.

06. I've become a good friend with several of the people _____ I met in my English class.

07. The package _____ I mailed to my sister was heavy.

08. The man _____ answered the phone was polite.

正確答案及題目中譯：

01. that	花園裡的小孩和他的貓很可愛。
02. which	那是他們住的房子。
03. who	你知道那個正在過馬路的女孩是誰嗎？
04. whom	這是我昨天在車站遇到的那個男孩。
05. which	這是我上個月拍的照片。
06. whom	我與在英語課堂遇到的幾個人成了好朋友。
07. which	我寄給我妹妹的包裹很重。
08. who	接電話的那個人很有禮貌。

Step 3 該如何使用進階的句子？

19 子句（名詞子句、形容詞子句、
副詞子句……）

01 圖解文法，一看就會！
Grammar Mind Mapping

┌─ 1.1 名詞子句→可做主詞、受詞或補語用
├─ 1.2 形容詞子句→用以形容先行詞
└─ 1.3 副詞子句→由連接詞引導之子句

┌─ 2.1 以 that 引導之子句
├─ 2.2 以疑問詞引導之子句
└─ 2.3 以 if / whether 引導之子句

1. 種類

2. 名詞子句的用法

子句

3. 形容詞子句的用法

4. 副詞子句

└─ 3.1 以關係代名詞引導之子句

└─ 4.1 以連接詞引導之具有
副詞功能的子句

1. 子句的種類

・ 1-1. **名詞子句→可做主詞、受詞或補語用**

> What you eat is what you are.（人如其食。）
> 　主詞　　　　主詞補語

He said that he is the only boy in his class.（他說他是班上唯一的男生。）
　　　　　　受詞

- 1-2. **形容詞子句→用以形容先行詞**

I like the man who cares about his family.（我喜歡在乎家庭的男人。）

- 1-3. **副詞子句→由連接詞引導之子句**。有表示時間、地點、原因等副詞功能。

Although you are young, you still need to show respect to others.
（就算你還年輕，你還是得尊重別人。）

2. 名詞子句的用法

- 2-1. **以 that 引導之子句**：
  一個完整句子前面加上 that 使其成為另一個句子的主詞、受詞或補語。以「他已婚這件事是真的。」來當例句，有以下三個寫法。

  that 子句當**主詞**：That he is married is true.
  that 子句當**補語**：It is true that he is married.
  that 子句當**受詞**：I found out yesterday that he is married.

- 2-2. **以疑問詞（who / where / how / when / what）引導之子句**：
  通常以動詞的受詞形式出現，例如：I'll tell you where he is.（我會告訴你他在哪裡。）→ Where is he? 作為 tell 的受詞，以間接問句方式出現。

- 2-3. **以 if / whether 引導之子句**：
  亦常以動詞的受詞形式出現，例如：
  Do you know if / whether he's available now?（你知道他現在是否有空嗎？）
  → if / whether... 子句作為 know 的受詞，以間接問句方式出現。

3. 形容詞子句的用法

- 3-1. **以關係代名詞（who / which / that / whom / whose）引導之子句**：
  The woman who is on the phone is my supervisor.
  （那個正在講電話的女人是我的主管。）

關係代名詞 who 引導出的子句用來修飾前面的名詞 the woman。

4. 副詞子句的用法

- **4-1. 以連接詞引導之具有副詞功能的子句：**

We were shocked when he told us the truth.（當他告訴我們實情時，我們很震驚。）→連接詞 when 引導出「表示時間」的副詞子句。

He doesn't like school because he has no friends there.（他因為沒有朋友而不喜歡上學。）→連接詞 because 引導出「表示原因」之副詞子句。

02 文法觀念例句示範
Grammar Demonstration

01. That Jack passed all his exams is unbelievable.
傑克通過所有的考試真是令人無法相信。

02. I didn't know that you two are friends.
我不知道你們兩個是朋友。

03. It is exciting that we're going to have dinner with the super star.
我們將要跟那位巨星共進晚餐，真是令人興奮。

04. He didn't tell me whom he will invite to the party.
他沒跟我說會邀請誰來參加派對。

05. I don't know what you are talking about.
我不知道你在講什麼。

06. No one cares whether he's coming or not.
沒人在乎他要不要來。

07. The car which he is driving was a gift from his parents.
他現在開的那台車是他父母送的禮物。

03 文法觀念辨析練習
Grammar Practice

依文意填入正確的連接詞
（that、which、where、how、what、who、whether、before 等）。

01. _____ he wants to be a woman terrified his parents.

02. The man _____ is talking to Andy is an old friend of mine.

03. I have no idea _____ I should believe him or not.

04. We are all curious about _____ Mr. and Mrs. Brown met each other.

05. The farm _____ we're visiting tomorrow is a famous tourist spot.

06. It is incredible _____ a man like him would be the hero of his country.

07. Please show me the pictures _____ you took during your trip to London.

08. You are lucky to find out _____ he is nothing but a liar before you marry him.

正確答案及題目中譯：

01. That	他想要變成女人這件事嚇壞了他的父母。	
02. who	在跟安迪講話的那個人是我的一個老朋友。	
03. whether	我不知道我究竟該不該相信他。	
04. how	我們都很好奇，究竟布朗夫婦是怎麼認識的。	
05. which	我們明天要去參觀的農場，是這裡非常有名的景點。	
06. that	一個像他這樣的男人會成為國民英雄，真是一件令人難以置信的事。	
07. which / that	請讓我看看你去倫敦旅遊時拍的照片。	
08. that	妳非常幸運能在嫁給他之前，就發現他只不過是個騙子。	

Step 3 該如何使用進階的句子？

20 倒裝句

01 圖解文法，一看就會！
Grammar Mind Mapping

```
1. 句型構成 ──┬─ 1.1 將整個主詞修飾語提到主詞之前

        完全倒裝

        2. 使用時機 ──┬─ 2.1 以 here, there, now, then, out, in, up, down, off, away
                       │      等方向性副詞開頭的句子
                       ├─ 2.2 句首為表示地點的介系詞片語
                       ├─ 2.3 主詞補語拉到句首時，須用全部倒裝
                       └─ 2.4 以 so, nor, neither 開頭的句子
```

英語句子通常有兩種語序：一種是陳述語序，一種是倒裝語序。將主詞修飾語的一部分或全部置於主詞之前的語序叫做倒裝語序。

倒裝時，變動的部分通常為：

……主詞 + 動詞……→……動詞 + 主詞……

Part 1 完全倒裝

1. 句型構成

- 1-1 **將整個主詞修飾語提到主詞之前**。例如：

You must <u>on no condition</u> go to Italy alone.
→ <u>On no condition</u> must you go Italy alone.
（不管怎樣，你都不能自己去義大利。）

2. 使用時機

- 2-1. **以 here, there, now, then, out, in, up, down, off, away 等方向性副詞開頭的句子，且句子主詞是名詞時，句子用完全倒裝**。例如：

Here comes the bus.（公共汽車來了。）

TIPS!
> 但如果主詞是**代詞**時，不能用倒裝。
> 例如：Here it is. / Here you are.（你要的東西在這。）

- 2-2. **當表示地點的介系詞片語放在句首，要倒裝**。用來強調語氣，例如：on the wall, under the tree, in front of the house, in the middle of the room 等。

At the foot of the hill lies a small river.（山腳下有一條小河。）

- 2-3. **主詞補語拉到句首時，須用全部倒裝**。此句型常常是因為主詞有較長修飾語，故以倒裝呈現。

Among the goods are flowers, candies, toys.（這些商品中有花，糖果，玩具。）

- 2-4. **以 so, nor, neither 開頭的句子**。以 so, nor, neither 開頭的句子使用倒裝，用來表示前句所說的內容也適合另外的人或物。

He has been to London, and so have I.（他去倫敦了，我也是。）

┌ 1.1 將 be 動詞 / 使役動詞 / 助動詞放在主詞之前

1. 句型構成

部份倒裝

2. 使用時機

┌ 2.1 疑問句
├ 2.2 否定詞 / 部分否定詞 / 不定詞片語 / 頻率副詞為句首
├ 2.3 在 so / such...that... 的句子
├ 2.4 假設語氣的條件句
└ 2.5 以 as / though 引導的副詞子句

Part 2 部份倒裝

1. 句型構成

- 1-1. **將 be 動詞 / 使役動詞 / 助動詞放在主詞之前**

Not until last night did Sammy changed her mind.
（直到昨天晚上，珊米才改變了主意。）

2. 使用時機

- 2-1. **疑問句**：疑問句中，一般須用部分倒裝，例如：

What do you think about the movie?（你認為這場電影怎麼樣？）

TIPS!

但當對句子的主詞提問時，一般不用倒裝語序。例如：
What happened last night? / Who lost the cellphone?
（昨天晚上發生了什麼事？）/（誰遺失了手機？）

- **2-2. 否定詞 / 部分否定詞 / 不定詞片語 / 頻率副詞為句首：**
  句中若以下字詞為句首時，一般須用部分倒裝。

  a) **否定詞**，例如：no, none, neither, nor, nobody, nothing, never
  b) **半否定詞**，例如：hardly, seldom, scarcely, barely, little, few
  c) **否定詞片語**，例如：not until, by no means, not only... but also..., neither... nor..., in no time, no sooner... than..., hardly... when...
  d) **頻率副詞**，例如：every day, every other day, many a time, often

  Never shall I do this again. （我再也不那麼做了。）
  Hardly does she have time to listen to music. （她幾乎沒時間聽音樂。）
  No sooner had I got home than it began to rain. （我一到家就開始下雨了。）
  Often have I heard it said that he is not to be trusted.
  （我常常聽說他是不可信的。）

- **2-3. 在 so / such... that... 為首的句子：**
  在 so / such... that... 的句子中，so 修飾形容詞、副詞或 such 修飾名詞放句首時，句子需半倒裝。

  So easy was the work that they finished it in a few days.
  （這個工作太容易了，所以他們在幾天內就完成了。）

- **2-4. 假設語氣的條件句：**
  當假設語氣的條件句含有 were, should, had 時，可省略 if 並將 were, should, had 置於句首。例如：

  Were I you, I would take the job. （我要是你，就接受那份工作。）

- **2-5. 以 as / though 引導的副詞子句：**
  在以連詞 as / though 引導的讓步副詞子句中，要用倒裝。

  Try as he would, he might fall again. （儘管他非常努力，但還是再次失敗了。）

02 文法觀念例句示範
Grammar Demonstration

01. There goes the bell.
響鈴了。

02. Behind the counter she stood.
她站在櫃檯後。

03. Only in this way can you do it well.
只有這樣你才能做好。

04. Not only did he speak more correctly, but he spoke more easily.
不僅他講得更正確，也講得更不費勁了。

05. Never shall I forgive him.
我永遠不會寬恕他。

06. So fast does light travel that we can hardly imagine its speed.
光速很快，我們幾乎沒法想像它的速度。

07. May you have a good journey.
祝你旅途愉快。

08. Child as he is, he knows more than you.
雖然他是孩子，但他懂的比你多。

09. Were I in school again, I would work harder.
如果我重新回到學校，我會加倍努力學習。

10. Every other day did he go to the hospital to see his father.
每隔一天他就去醫院看望他父親。

03 文法觀念辨析練習
Grammar Practice

請圈選最適合的題目的選項答案。

01. No sooner _____ than it started to rain heavily.
   Ⓐ the game began   Ⓑ has the game begun
   Ⓒ did the game begin   Ⓓ had the game begun

02. A: Do you know Jim quarreled with his brother?
    B: don't know _____.
   Ⓐ nor don't I care   Ⓑ nor do I care
   Ⓒ I don't care neither   Ⓓ I don't care also

03. Not only _____ he refuse the gift, he also severely criticized the sender.
   Ⓐ does   Ⓑ has
   Ⓒ did   Ⓓ didn't

04. Only when you have finished your homework _____ go home.
   Ⓐ can you   Ⓑ would you
   Ⓒ you will   Ⓓ you can

05. There _____ .
   Ⓐ come they   Ⓑ they come
   Ⓒ they are come   Ⓓ they will come

06. A: It was careless of me to leave the door open all night long.
    B: My God! _____.
   Ⓐ So did I   Ⓑ So I did
   Ⓒ So were you   Ⓓ So did you

07. Look! There _____.
   Ⓐ comes the bus   Ⓑ the bus comes
   Ⓒ bus comes there   Ⓓ does the bus come

08. They thought that somewhere in the desert _____ an ancient city.
   Ⓐ being   Ⓑ lay
   Ⓒ was there   Ⓓ lay there

09. _____ the plane.
  A Flew down　　　　　　**B** Down flew
  C Down was flying　　　**D** Down fly

10. Now _____ your turn to recite the text.
  A there is　　　　　　　**B** has come
  C comes　　　　　　　　**D** will come

正確答案及題目中譯：

01. **D**	比賽開始沒多久就下起滂沱大雨。
02. **B**	A：你知道吉姆跟他哥哥吵架了嗎？　B：我不知道也不在乎。
03. **C**	他不僅沒有收下這份禮物，還嚴厲地譴責送禮的人。
04. **A**	除非你完成你的作業，否則你不能回家。
05. **B**	他們來了。
06. **A**	A：我一整晚都忘了關門真是太不小心了！　B：天啊！我也是耶！
07. **A**	看！巴士來了！
08. **B**	他們認為沙漠中的某處有一個古老城市。
09. **B**	飛機飛下來了。
10. **C**	現在輪到你背課文了。

單字陷阱‧
一字多義使用篇

單字陷阱‧
類義單字辨析篇

Day 23~30
個不能不
閃的文法 陷阱

先搞懂概念與時態

該如何使用
進階的句子？

第一階段：Day 01~07
20 個一定
要學的 句型

了解英文中
關鍵的關鍵一字詞

基礎觀念馬上建立！

第二階段：Day 08~22
30 個一定要學的句型

看到阿豆仔也不用怕！

可以開始簡單英語會話囉！

Day08

01 那裡有正妹！
There is a hottie.

句型 **There be (not) ...**

01 文法句型常用情境說明
Sentence Patterns Introduction

There be 句型用來表達「某時／某處有某人／某物）」的語意，也就是「存在」的語意，需特別注意的是，這個句型並不是用來表示「某地／人／物／時『擁有』某物／人。」其基本句型是 there be ＋主語＋補語。There 在此句型結構中的作用為「引導語」，本身並無詞義，be 動詞是修飾語，包含時態變化，也可與情態動詞連用。be 動詞要和後面的主詞取得單複數的一致。

02 文法句型示範情境會話
Dialogue Practice

情境 1

David : I am hungry, Mom. Can you give me some bread and milk?

Mom : Oh, Honey. I am so sorry. **There isn't any milk in the fridge. I will buy some this afternoon.** Do you want cookies? I have some left here.

David : Thanks, Mom. Cookies would be just fine.

大衛：媽媽，我好餓呀，可以給我點麵包和牛奶嗎？

媽媽：噢，寶貝，抱歉。冰箱裡已經沒有牛奶了。我今天下午會去買。你想吃餅乾嗎？我這邊還有一些。

大衛：謝謝媽媽。餅乾就可以了。

情境 2

Charles : How many students are there in your class, Ann?

Ann : **There are fifty-six students in my class.** There are thirty girls and twenty-six boys.

查爾斯：安，你們班有多少位學生呀？

安：我們班一共有 56 位學生。分別有 30 位女生和 26 位男生。

情境 3

Robert : Do you know I am a huge fan of Beyoncé?

Amy : Really? I love her, too! And you know what? I think **there are hundreds and thousands of Beyoncé fans in the world.**

Robert : Oh, it's so true.

羅伯特：你知道嗎我是碧昂斯的超級粉絲嗎？

艾咪：真的嗎？我也非常喜歡她。而且你知道嗎？我覺得這個世界上有成千上萬的碧昂絲粉絲。

羅伯特：噢！確實如此呀！

情境 4

Tom : Good afternoon, Mr. Johnson. May I ask you a question?

Mr. Johnson : Of course, Tom.

Tom : Do you know **how many books are there in our library?**

Mr. Johnson : We have the best library in this state. I think **there might be over ten million books in our library.**

湯姆：強森老師，午安。我可以問您一個問題嗎？

強森先生：當然可以，湯姆。

湯姆：您知道我們的圖書館總共有多少藏書嗎？

強森先生：我們的圖書館是本州最好的圖書館。我想我們的圖書館應該有超過一千萬冊的藏書吧！

情境 5

Mike : Hi, Stephen. Have I told you that **there is a beautiful lake just in front of my grandparents' house?** And I always swim in that lake during summer vacations.

Stephen： Wow! That sounds great. I want to swim in that lake, too.
　　Mike： Really? Would you like to visit my grandparents with me this summer vacation?
Stephen： Awesome! Thanks very much for inviting me. I think we will have a good summer vacation.

　　麥克： 嗨，史蒂芬！我有沒有告訴你，我的祖父母家門前有一座很美的小湖？暑假期間我經常去那座湖裡游泳。
　史蒂芬： 哇！聽起來好棒。我也很想在那座小湖裡游泳。
　　麥克： 真的嗎？那你願意我一起去拜訪我祖父母，並且一起過暑假嗎？
　史蒂芬： 太棒了！非常謝謝你邀請我。我想我們這個暑假一定會很愉快。

03 文法句型翻譯練習
Sentence Patterns Exercise

請運用上面學到的句型，試著寫出完整的英文句子吧！

01. 有很多人出席了會議。

_____

02. 天上沒有一絲雲彩。

_____

03. 一年有十二個月。

_____

04. 我的家族裡一共有十五位女性。

_____

05. 瓶子裡面沒有水了。

_____

04 延伸句型加分學習
Learning Plus!

There is (not) + enough... + to do... 有（沒有）足夠的……來做……

There is (not) + enough... + to do... 這個句型表示「有（沒有）足夠的……來做……」。enough 後面通常接名詞，例如：

There is enough food for all of us.
有足夠的食物給我們所有人。

There is not enough time to do so many things.
沒有足夠多的時間做這麼多的事。

There is enough money to buy that car.
有足夠的錢買那輛車。

翻譯練習正確答案：

01. There were a lot of people present at the meeting.

02. There is not a single cloud in the sky.

03. There are twelve months in a year.

04. There are fifteen females in my family.

05. There is not any water in the bottle.

02 要不要喝點水啊？
Would you like some water?

句型 **Would you like ...?**

01 文法句型常用情境說明
Sentence Patterns Introduction

Would you like...? 句型是用來禮貌詢問對方的意願、委婉地提出請求、建議或陳述個人的想法。肯定回答可以説 "Yes, please."，否定回答可以説 "No, thanks."。Would you like...? 句型的回答也可以很靈活的，要根據説話雙方及不同的語境來決定。

02 文法句型示範情境會話
Dialogue Practice

情境 1

Charles : Hi, Rose. **Would you like to go to the cinema tonight?**
Rose : I'd like to. But I am sorry. I have to prepare for my English exam tomorrow.
Charles : That's O.K. We can go some other time.

查爾斯：嗨，蘿絲，妳今晚要不要一起去看電影呀？
蘿絲：我很想去。但是很抱歉。我得準備明天的英語考試。
查爾斯：沒關係的，我們改天再去也可以。

情境 2

Waiter : **Would you like another cup of coffee, sir?**
Mr. Green : Yes, please. Thank you.
Waiter : It's my pleasure!

服務生：先生，要不要再來一杯咖啡？
格林先生：好的，來一杯吧，謝謝。
服務生：這是我的榮幸！

情境 3

Jessie： **Would you mind turning down the TV,** Ann? I am preparing for a test and need to concentrate.
Ann： Sure, I am sorry for disturbing you.
Jessie： It's O.K. Thanks for your understanding.

潔西：安，妳介意把電視音量調小一點嗎？我在準備一個考試，需要專心一點。
　安：沒問題，對不起吵到妳了。
潔西：沒關係。謝謝妳的體諒。

情境 4

Mom： Honey. **Would you like some desserts?**
Wendy： No, thank you, Mom. I am on a diet.
Mom： No problem, dear.

媽媽：親愛的，要不要吃點心啊？
溫蒂：不要了，謝謝媽媽。我正在減肥呢！
媽媽：沒關係，親愛的。

03 文法句型翻譯練習
Sentence Patterns Exercise

請運用上面學到的句型，試著寫出完整的英文句子吧！

01. 你要不要四處看看？

02. 你要不要和我們一起去海邊？

03. 你晚上要不要和我一起吃飯？

04. 你要不要來我們公司工作？

05. 你要不要喝點什麼？

04 延伸句型加分學習
Learning Plus!

How about... / What about...?　那……如何？／要不要……呢？

How about... / What about...? 那……如何？／要不要……呢？
How about... / What about...? 都用來表示詢問意見、情況或提出建議，
其中的 about 是介系詞，後面常接名詞、代名詞或動名詞。例如：

How about / What about another cup of tea?
要不要再喝一杯茶？
How about / What about going for a walk?
要不要出去散散步？
How about / What about going to the zoo with us?
要不要和我們一起去動物園？

翻譯練習正確答案：

01. Would you like to look around?

02. Would you like to go to the beach with us?

03. Would you like to have dinner with me tonight?

04. Would you like to work in our company?

05. Would you like something to drink?

03 從捷運站走回家要花多久時間？

How long does it take to walk home
from the MRT station?

句型 **How long / soon / often...?**

01 文法句型常用情境說明
Sentence Patterns Introduction

- 1. How long...? 是用來提問「時間多長？」，主要是指「一段時間的長短，例如：
three days（三天）、two weeks（兩週），常與連續性動詞連用。

- 2. How soon...? 則表示「多久以後、還要多久？」，主要是強調從事件開始到結束
有多久，例如：in two minutes（兩分鐘後）。

- 3. How often...? 則是用來提問某動作或狀態發生的頻率，回答通常是 always（總
是）、usually（通常）、often（時常）、sometimes（有時候）、never（從不）、
once a day（一天一次）、twice a month（一個月兩次）等時間副詞或片語。

02 文法句型示範情境會話
Dialogue Practice

情境 1

Mike： Did you watch the NBA last night, Jack?
Jack： Of course. I never miss any NBA games.
Mike： But I missed the one last night. **How long did the game last?**
Jack： About two hours.

麥克：傑克，你有看昨晚的 NBA 籃球嗎？
傑克：當然啦。我從來不錯過任何一場 NBA 比賽 。
麥克：但是我昨晚錯過一場了。那場比賽打了多久呢？
傑克：大約兩個小時。

情境 2

Stephen : The 31st Olympic Games will be held in Rio in 2016.
　　Bill : Yeah, I know.
Stephen : But **how often are the Olympic Games be held?**
　　Bill : Every four years.

　史蒂芬：第三十一屆奧運會將於 2016 年在里約熱內盧舉行。
　　比爾：沒錯，我知道。
　史蒂芬：但是奧運會多久舉行一次？
　　比爾：每四年。

情境 3

Manager : **How soon will you finish the work, Peter?**
　Peter : At least in two days.
Manager : Please try to make it shorter, ok?
　Peter : I will try my best to finish it ahead of time.
Manager : Thank you.

　經理：彼得，你要多久才能完成這項工作？
　彼得：至少要 2 天後。
　經理：請試著用更短的時間完成，好嗎？
　彼得：我將盡力提前完成工作。
　經理：謝謝。

情境 4

Wendy : **How soon will your brother go to Hong Kong, Jessie?**
Jessie : He will go to Hong Kong in three days.

　溫蒂：潔西，妳哥哥還有多久要去香港呀？
　潔西：他三天後會去香港。

情境 5

Frank : What do you think about fast food?
　John : I think it is not good for our health, but it is very convenient.
Frank : **How often do you have it?**
　John : About twice a month.

法蘭克：你認為速食怎麼樣？
　約翰：我覺得它對身體沒有好處，但是很方便。
法蘭克：你多常吃一次呢？
　約翰：大約一個月兩次吧。

03 文法句型翻譯練習
Sentence Patterns Exercise

請運用上面學到的句型，試著寫出完整的英文句子吧！

01. 工人們還要多久才能建好大樓？

_____

02. 你多常拜訪你的祖父母？

_____

03. 你多常去電影院？

_____

04. 你在美國待了多久？

_____

05. 你要花多久時間才能解出那道數學題？

_____

翻譯練習正確答案：

01. How soon will the workers finish the building?

02. How often do you visit your grandparents?

03. How often do you go to the cinema?

04. How long did you stay in the United States?

05. How long will you spend working out that math question?

Day09

04 他太宅了，所以他不可能追到校花！
He is too indoorsy to get the school babe!

句型 too... + (for sb. / sth.) + to...

---

01 文法句型常用情境說明
Sentence Patterns Introduction

　　too... to... 句型表示「太……而不能……」的意思，其基本構詞順序是「too ＋形容詞／副詞＋ to ＋動詞原形」；如果需要強調動作所指的對象時，需要再加上一個邏輯主語 for sb. / sth.（對某人／某事而言），其構詞順序為「too ＋形容詞／副詞＋ for sb. / sth. ＋ to ＋動詞原形」，意思為「對某人或某物來說，太……而不能……」。

02 文法句型示範情境會話
Dialogue Practice

情境 1

　　　Clerk：May I help you, Ma'am?
Customer：I want to buy a hat.
　　　Clerk：What kind of hat do you want, Ma'am?
Customer：I like this one, but **it is too large to wear.**
　　　Clerk：**This hat is really too large for you to wear.** But I can find a smaller one for you.
Customer：Oh, really? Thank you very much.

　　售貨員：女士，我能為妳做點什麼嗎？
　　　顧客：我想要買一頂帽子。
　　售貨員：那妳喜歡什麼樣的帽子呢，女士？
　　　顧客：我喜歡這頂，但是這頂帽子太大了，戴不下。
　　售貨員：這頂帽子對於妳來說確實大了點，但我可以為妳找一頂尺寸較小的。
　　　顧客：噢，真的嗎？非常謝謝你。

情境 2

Alice： Jim, can you do me a favor?

Jim： Of course. I guess you want me to carry the box.

Alice： You are right. **This box is too heavy for me to carry.**

Jim： No problem.

愛麗絲：你能幫我一個忙嗎，吉姆？

吉姆：當然可以。我猜妳是要我幫妳提箱子吧。

愛麗絲：你說對了。這個箱子太重了，我提不動。

吉姆：沒問題。

情境 3

Mr. Benny： Why are you late again, Vicky?

Vicky： Sorry, Mr. Benny. **I got up too late to catch the bus.**

Mr. Benny： Get up early next time.

Vicky： Yes, sir.

班尼先生：薇琪，妳怎麼又遲到了？

薇琪：對不起，班尼先生。我太晚起床，所以沒趕上公車。

班尼先生：下次要早點起床。

薇琪：好的，先生。

情境 4

David： What are you doing, Tina?

Tina： I am trying to solve this math question, but **it is too difficult for me to figure out the answer.**

David： Maybe I can help you. Let me take a look.

Tina： Oh, thank you. Here you are.

大衛：蒂娜，妳在做什麼？

蒂娜：我在試著解這道數學題，但是這題對我來說太難了，我解不出來。

大衛：也許我可以幫妳。讓我看看。

蒂娜：噢。謝謝你，拿去吧。

情境 5

Stephen : Dad, I want to travel this summer.
Dad : Who are you going to travel with?
Stephen : I will go by myself.
Dad : **You are too young to travel alone, my son.**
Stephen : Please, Dad.
Dad : I will discuss this with your Mom.

史蒂芬：爸爸，這個夏天我想去旅行。
爸爸：你打算和誰一起去旅行呢？
史蒂芬：我自己去。
爸爸：兒子，你太小了，不能一個人去旅行。
史蒂芬：拜託你，爸爸
爸爸：這件事我要和你媽媽討論。

03 文法句型翻譯練習
Sentence Patterns Exercise

請運用上面學到的句型，試著寫出完整的英文句子吧！

01. 這男孩年紀太小，不能上學。

_____

02. 這個問題太難，我無法回答。

_____

03. 這輛汽車太貴，他買不起。

_____

04. 這杯牛奶太燙了，還不能喝。

_____

05. 外面天氣太冷了，不適合跑步。

_____

04 延伸句型加分學習
Learning Plus!

so... that...　如此⋯⋯以致於⋯⋯

- 1. so... that... 表示「如此⋯⋯以致於⋯⋯」，也強調兩個事件的因果關係，其後引導結果狀語子句，基本句型為「so ＋形容詞 / 副詞＋ that 從句」。例如：

  He is so sick that he can't go to work today.
  他病得很嚴重以致於他今天不能去上班。

  He was so angry that he couldn't say a word.
  他太生氣了以致於說不出話來。

- 2. too... to... 句型可以與 so... that... 句型相互轉換，只要將 too 改為 so，並將 too... to... 後的動詞不定詞改為否定式的子句，例如：

  I was too tired to go to the movies with you.
  ＝ I was so tired that I couldn't go to the movies with you.
  我太累了，不能跟你去看電影。

翻譯練習正確答案：

01. The boy is too young to go to school.

02. This question is too difficult for me to answer.

03. The car is too expensive for him to buy.

04. This cup of milk is too hot to drink.

05. It's too cold outside to go jogging.

05 今天我們去看變形金剛4吧！
Let's go to see Transformers 4 today!

句型 **Let's; Let us...**

01 文法句型常用情境說明
Sentence Patterns Introduction

- 1. Let's 是 Let us 的縮寫，用來表示「讓我們……」含有催促、建議或請對方一起行動的意思。
- 2. 兩者間有細微差別。由 Let's 引導的祈使句把談話雙方都包括在內，而 Let us 將對方排除在外，只限於説話的那方。例如：
  Let's go. = 讓我們（一起）走吧。→「你」也包括在所指的「我們」之中
  Let us go. =（請你）讓我們走吧。→所指的「我們」當中並不包括「你」
- 3. 在附加問句中，Let's 搭配的附加問句用是「shall we?」表示徵詢意見或者提建議。Let us 的附加問句用「will you?」表示較委婉、客氣的請求。

02 文法句型示範情境會話
Dialogue Practice

情境 1

Richard : **Let's go to the zoo, shall we?**
　　Bob : O.K. When will we go?
Richard : What about tomorrow afternoon?
　　Bob : Sure. I happen to be available tomorrow.
Richard : That is great.

　　理查：我們一起去動物園怎麼樣？
　　鮑伯：好，我們什麼時候去？
　　理查：明天下午怎麼樣？
　　鮑伯：當然好。我明天正好有空。
　　理查：那就太棒了。

情境 2

      Eric：This Sunday will be Linda's birthday. Will you go to her party?

Maggie：I can't be sure now.

      Eric：That's fine. **Just let us know if you can come.**

Maggie：O.K. I will call you if I can come.

艾瑞克：這個星期天是琳達的生日。妳會去她的派對嗎？

瑪姬：我現在還不能確定。

艾瑞克：沒關係。如果妳能來的話就讓我們知道。

瑪姬：好，如果我能去就打電話給你。

情境 3

   Sam：What about going to the Ocean Park this afternoon, John?

John：Good idea. When and where shall we meet?

   Sam：**Let's meet at the gate of the Ocean Park at 2 p.m.**

John：O.K. See you then.

   Sam：See you.

山姆：約翰，下午去海洋公園怎麼樣？

約翰：好主意，我們幾點在哪裡碰面呢？

山姆：那我們就下午兩點在海洋公園門口碰面吧。

約翰：好，到時候見。

山姆：待會見。

情境 4

Daughter：Mom, I want to have Chinese food tonight. **Let's dine out for a change, shall we?**

    Mom：Sure.

女兒：媽，我今天晚上想吃中國菜。我們出去吃，換換口味，好嗎？

媽媽：當然好。

情境 5

Cindy：Bella, why do you look so sad? Is there anything bothering you?

Bella：Hmm... Actually, there is one thing.

Cindy：**Let us help you, will you?**

Bella：That's fine. Thank you. But I want to deal with it by myself.
Cindy：O.K. **Just let me know if you need me.**

辛蒂：貝拉，妳為什麼看起來這麼難過？妳是不是在煩惱什麼呢？
貝拉：嗯……，事實上是有件事。
辛蒂：讓我幫助妳好嗎？
貝拉：沒關係。謝謝妳。但是我想自己解決。
辛蒂：好，如果妳需要我幫忙就讓我知道。

03 文法句型翻譯練習
Sentence Patterns Exercise

請運用上面學到的句型，試著寫出完整的英文句子吧！

01. 讓我們跳支舞吧。

_____

02. 讓我們為你唱首歌吧。

_____

03. 讓我們做好朋友，好嗎？

_____

04. 讓我們舉杯祝你健康。

_____

05. 我們在咖啡廳等你，好嗎？

_____

04 延伸句型加分學習
Learning Plus!

Why not; Why don't we...?

· 1. Why not / Why don't we...?「為什麼不……呢？」用來表示勸誘、建議或命令，只能接動詞原形，不能接句子。例如：

Why not go for a walk after dinner? 為什麼晚飯後不去散步呢？
Why not try once more? 為什麼不再試看看呢？

· 2. Why not 後面只能接原形動詞，不可以接句子，也不能用「why didn't + 原形動詞」。此外，why not 的句型只能指將來的情況，不能用於過去：

Why not start our work now?
＝ Why don't we start our work now?
為什麼我們現在不開始工作呢？

誤用例：Why not come when I called your name? → ✕
應改為：Why didn't you come when I called your name? → ○
（我叫你名字的時候，你為什麼不來呢？）

翻譯練習正確答案：

01. Let's dance.

02. Let us sing a song for you.

03. Let's be good friends, shall we?

04. Let us toast for your health.

05. Let us wait for you at the coffee shop, will you?

Day10

06　不是所有人都想要費德勒贏，好嗎？

Not everybody wants Federer to win, O.K.?

句型　**Not everybody / both / all / every...**

---

01 文法句型常用情境說明
Sentence Patterns Introduction

Not 與 both（兩者都）、all（全都）、every（每一）以及 every 的衍生詞，例如：everything（每件事）、everybody（每個人）、everywhere（每處）、everyone（每個人）連用時，表示部分否定。not 可置於這些詞的前後，意義不變。意思如下：

- They are not both good students.（他們兩個並非都是好學生。）
- Not all the girls like Kenny.（並非所有的女孩都喜歡肯尼。）
- Not every manager attended this meeting.（並非所有的經理都出席這次會議。）
- I don't know everything.（我並非知道每件事。）
- Jason didn't invite everybody to his party.（傑森並沒有邀每個人參加他的派對。）
- Not everywhere is as warm as home.（不是每個地方都像家一樣溫暖。）
- Not everyone enjoys ice cream.（不是每個人都喜歡吃冰淇淋。）

02 文法句型示範情境會話
Dialogue Practice

情境 1

Teacher : Excuse me, **not all your names are given to me.** Would you please introduce yourselves?
Student 1 : Sure. I am Mark. I am in Class 102.
Student 2 : I am Jack. I am in Class 102, too.
Student 3 : My name is Linda. I am in Class 203.
Teacher : Thank you so much.

老師：不好意思，並非你們所有人的名字都給了我。你們能自我介紹一下嗎？
學生 1：當然好，我是馬克。我在 102 班。
學生 2：我是傑克。我也在 102 班。
學生 3：我的名字是琳達。我在 203 班。
老師：非常謝謝你們。

情境 2

Joe : Do you know why Sophia didn't come to work today?
Vivian : Sorry, but I don't know. **I don't know everything about her.**
Joe : That's fine. I will call her later. Thank you anyway.
Vivian : You are welcome.

喬：妳知道為什麼蘇菲亞今天沒來上班嗎？
薇薇安：抱歉，但是我不知道。我並不都知道她的所有事情。
喬：沒關係。晚一點我再打電話給她。總之謝謝妳。
薇薇安：不客氣。

情境 3

Lucy : Wow! Susan, you look so lovely today.
Susan : Thank you. I think you mean my new dress.
Lucy : Where did you buy it?
Susan : It is limited in Hong Kong. **This kind of dress cannot be found everywhere.**
Lucy : Oh. No wonder it looks so special.

露西：哇！蘇珊，妳今天看起來真漂亮。
蘇珊：謝謝，我想妳是指我的新洋裝吧。
露西：妳在哪裡買的呀？
蘇珊：這是香港限定。這款洋裝並不是到處都可以找到的。
露西：噢，難怪看起來這麼特別。

情境 4

Chris : Hey, Kate. I heard you have a twin sister. Is that true?
Kate : Yes, her name is Ann.
Chris : You are so lucky.

Kate ： Err... maybe, but **not both of us have the same hobbies.** When I read book, she always listens to rock music. I really hate that.

克里斯： 嗨，凱特，我聽說妳有個雙胞胎妹妹。是真的嗎？
　凱特： 是的，她的名字叫安。
克里斯： 妳真是太幸運了。
　凱特： 哦……也許吧，但是我們並不是都有相同的愛好。我在看書的時候，她總是在聽搖滾樂。我真的很討厭這樣。

___

情境 5

Wendy ： Why did you refuse to work abroad, Sasha? **Not everybody has a chance like this.**
Sasha ： I know. But I don't want to leave my parents.
Wendy ： You are right. **Not everyone will make the same choice.**

溫蒂： 妳為什麼拒絕到國外工作呢，莎夏？並不是每個人都有像這樣的機會。
莎夏： 我知道。但是我不想離開我的父母。
溫蒂： 妳說得沒錯。並不是每個人都會做出一樣的選擇。

03 文法句型翻譯練習
Sentence Patterns Exercise

請運用上面學到的句型，試著寫出完整的英文句子吧！

01. 這兩種物質並不都能溶於水。

___

02. 並不是這裡所有的人都很友善。

___

03. 並非人人都喜歡這部電影。

___

04. 並非他所有的話都是對的。

___

05. 這種植物並不是隨處可見的。

___

04 延伸句型加分學習
Learning Plus!

　　若要在 all、both、every、always、entirely、altogether、quite 和 all the time 等詞上表達完全否定，則必須分別使用與之相對應的全否定詞，如 no、none、neither、no one、never、not (never)... at all 等。例如：

- Both are good. → Neither is good.
  兩個都好。 → 兩個都不好。

- Everyone likes it. → Nobody likes it.
  人人都喜歡它。 → 沒有人喜歡它。

- We don't trust him entirely. → We never trust him at all.
  我們並非完全信任他。 → 我們完全不信任他。

- All of them can do it. → None of them can do it.
  他們全部人都會做這件事。 → 他們之中沒有人做這件事。

- He has been here all the time. → He has never been here.
  他一直都在這裡。 → 他從來不在這裡。

翻譯練習正確答案：

01. Not both of the substances can be dissolved in water.

02. Not all people here are friendly.

03. Not everybody likes this film.

04. Not all his words are right.

05. The plant is not seen everywhere.

Level 1 基礎觀念馬上建立！（程度分級：國中英語）

07 難怪你上課時總是想睡覺！

It is no wonder (that) you always feel sleepy in class.

句型 **(It is) no wonder (that)...**

01 文法句型常用情境說明
Sentence Patterns Introduction

(It is) no wonder (that)... 意思為「難怪⋯⋯怪不得⋯⋯」，後面接名詞子句。It 是虛主詞，that 後的名詞子句才是真正的主詞。

02 文法句型示範情境會話
Dialogue Practice

情境 1

Stephen : Do you see Eric, Susan?
Susan : He is studying in the classroom.
Stephen : Wow. He studies very hard. **It is no wonder that he always gets the highest score.**
Susan : That's true.

史蒂芬：蘇珊，妳看到艾瑞克了嗎？
蘇珊：他正在教室裡念書。
史蒂芬：哇，他好用功。難怪他總是得最高分。
蘇珊：你説的沒錯。

情境 2

Joy : Why didn't Ann come to work today?
Tony : She has been ill for several days.
Joy : Oh, **it is no wonder that I didn't see her yesterday.**

喬伊：為什麼安今天沒來上班呢？
湯尼：她已經病了好幾天了。
喬伊：哦，難怪我昨天沒看到她。

情境 3

Michael： Could you give me a hand, Betty?
Betty： Sure. What can I do for you?
Michael： I don't understand this math question very well. Can you explain it to me?
Betty： No problem.
Michael： You are so kind, Betty. **It is no wonder that everyone loves you.**

麥可：貝蒂，妳可以幫我一個忙嗎？
貝蒂：當然啦，我能幫你什麼？
麥可：我不是很懂這題數學，妳可以解釋給我聽嗎？
貝蒂：沒問題。
麥可：貝蒂，妳真是太好了。怪不得每個人都喜歡妳。

情境 4

Daniel： Hi, this is Daniel speaking.
Sophia： Hi, Daniel. This is Sophia. I have called you for three times. Where have you been?
Daniel： Oh, really? I am so sorry. I was listening to music and didn't hear the phone ring.
Sophia： Hmm... **It is no wonder that you didn't answer it.**
Daniel： I am really sorry.
Sophia： It's O.K.

丹尼爾：喂，我是丹尼爾。
蘇菲亞：嗨，丹尼爾。我是蘇菲亞。我已經打過三次電話給你了。你去哪裡了？
丹尼爾：噢，真的嗎？真不好意思，我剛剛正在聽音樂，沒聽到電話鈴響。
蘇菲亞：嗯，難怪你沒有接電話。
丹尼爾：真是對不起。
蘇菲亞：沒關係。

03 文法句型翻譯練習
Sentence Patterns Exercise

請運用上面學到的句型，試著寫出完整的英文句子吧！

01. 難怪她拒絕你的邀請。

_____

02. 難怪他不想和你去看電影。

_____

03. 難怪我好像曾經在哪裡見過你。

_____

04. 難怪人們說世界越來越小。

_____

05. 難怪她這麼傷心。

_____

翻譯練習正確答案：

01. No wonder she turned down your invitation.

02. It is no wonder that he didn't want to go to the movies with you.

03. No wonder it seems that I have seen you somewhere.

04. No wonder people say that the world is getting smaller and smaller.

05. It is no wonder that she was so sad.

Level 1 **基礎觀念馬上建立！**（程度分級：國中英語）

08 完成這個專案得花上七個工作天呢！

It will take 7 working days to finish this project!

句型 **It takes (sb.)... + to do sth.**

01 文法句型常用情境說明
Sentence Patterns Introduction

- 1. It takes (sb.)... + to do sth.，這個句型表示「做某事花費了某人多少的時間、錢、心力」。這個句型的主詞是虛主詞 It，動詞為 take，其後接動詞不定詞。例如：

  It took Jason two hours to finish the report.（把這份報告做完花了傑森兩個小時。）

- 2. 如果以某人做主詞，動詞需改用 spend（某人花費多久時間、錢、心力做某事），其後接介系詞「on＋事物」或直接加動名詞。例如：

  Jason spent two hours finishing the report.（傑森花了兩小時把報告做完。）

- 3. 如果單指金錢的花費時，此句型可等同於 It cost sb. +（金錢）+ to + V。要注意 cost 的主詞並非執行動作的人。例如：

  It cost him five hundred dollars to buy the watch.
  =The watch cost him five hundred dollars.（這手錶花了他五百美元。）

02 文法句型示範情境會話
Dialogue Practice

情境 1

Steven：Johnson, I heard that you made great progress on this exam.
Johnson：Yes, **it took me two days to prepare it this time.**
Steven：That's really good. No pains, no gains. You deserve the high score.

Johnson： Thank you.

史蒂芬： 強森，我聽説你這次考試進步很多。
強森： 沒錯，我花了兩天準備這次的考試。
史蒂芬： 那真是太好了。一分辛勞，一分收穫。你應該得高分的。
強森： 謝謝你。

情境 2

Richard： Hi, Jack. What about your new job?
Jack： Not bad. **It took me several weeks to get used to the new job.**
Richard： That's great.

理查： 嗨，傑克。你的新工作怎麼樣啊？
傑克： 還不錯。我花了好幾個星期熟悉這份工作。
理查： 那很好。

情境 3

Cathy： What about going to the shopping mall this afternoon, Linda?
Linda： That sounds great. When are we going to meet?
Cathy： **It will take me two hours to go to the shopping mall.** So let's meet at 3 o'clock, shall we?
Linda： O.K. See you then.
Cathy： See you.

凱西： 今天下午去購物中心好不好啊，琳達？
琳達： 聽起來不錯。我們要什麼時候見面呢？
凱西： 到購物中心要花我 2 個小時。所以我們 3 點鐘見面，好嗎？
琳達： 沒問題。到時候見。
凱西： 拜拜。

情境 4

James： Oh, Tina, your English is very good. How long did you learn English?
Tina： **It took me years to learn English well.**
James： Can you tell me how to learn English well?
Tina： Practice more. As you know, practice makes perfect.
James： You are right.

詹姆斯：噢，蒂娜，妳英語非常好。妳學英文多久啊？
蒂娜：學好英語花了我好幾年。
詹姆斯：妳可以告訴我要怎麼學好英語嗎？
蒂娜：多練習。你知道的，熟能生巧。
詹姆斯：妳説的沒錯。

03 文法句型翻譯練習
Sentence Patterns Exercise

請運用上面學到的句型，試著寫出完整的英文句子吧！

01. 我花了 2 個小時才完成作業。

02. 我將花 2 天時間把這本書看完。

03. 他花了 1 個小時才到台北。

04. 為了講一口流利的英語，羅伯特花了好多年時間辛苦練習。

05. 我花了相當長的時間，才明白這幅畫的意思。

翻譯練習正確答案：

01. It took me two hours to finish my homework.

02. It will take me two days to finish reading this book.

03. It took him an hour to arrive in Taipei.

04. It took Robert many years of hard working to speak English fluently.

05. It took me quite a long time to understand the meaning of the painting.

08 完成這個專案得花上七個工作天呢！

Day12

Level 1　基礎觀念馬上建立！（程度分級：國中英語）

09 你覺得哈利波特的結局怎麼樣？
What do you think of / about the end of Harry Porter?

句型　**What do you think of / about...?**

---

01 文法句型常用情境說明
Sentence Patterns Introduction

What do you think of / about...? 表示「你認為……怎麼樣？」，用來詢問對方對某事的看法，也可以說「How do you like...?」。當然對這樣的問題不能簡單地用「Yes」或「No」來回答，要具體說明理由。

02 文法句型示範情境會話
Dialogue Practice

情境 1

Bob : **What do you think of the NBA game last night?**
Jimmy : It's amazing. I love it very much.
Bob : Me, too. I saw Kobe Bryant. He is my favorite player.
Jimmy : He is one of the best players. I also like LeBron James.
Bob : He is a great player, too. I am looking forward to their rivalry next season.
Jimmy : Me, too. That must be a great game.

鮑伯：你覺得昨晚的 NBA 籃球賽怎麼樣？
吉米：太棒了，我非常喜歡。
鮑伯：我也是，我看到了柯比・布萊恩。他是我最愛的球員。
吉米：柯比是最好的球員之一。我也喜歡勒布朗・詹姆斯。
鮑伯：他也是個很棒的球員。我很期待他們下一季的對決。
吉米：我也是。那一定會是很精采的一場比賽。

情境 2

Husband : I am considering moving to a bigger house. **What do you think of the house price now, honey?**

Wife : In my opinion, the house price will continue to rise. So it is not a good idea to change a house now.

Husband : Maybe you are right. I have to think more about it.

丈夫：我現在正在考慮搬到比較大的房子。親愛的，妳覺得現在房價怎麼樣？
妻子：在我看來，房價將會持續上漲。所以現在換房並不是一個好主意。
丈夫：也許妳是對的。我得再好好想想。

情境 3

Alice : **What do you think about the film, Noah?**

Sarah : It is an amazing film.

Alice : Do you think the plot of the film will be happened in the real life?

Sarah : I have no idea. But I think we human beings should learn to protect the environment.

Alice : I can't agree more.

愛麗絲：妳覺得挪亞方舟那部電影怎麼樣？
莎拉：那是一部很棒的電影。
愛麗絲：那妳認為電影中的情節是否會發生在現實生活中嗎？
莎拉：我不知道。但我認為我們人類應該要學會保護環境。
愛麗絲：我非常同意。

情境 4

Frank : **What do you think of your new English teacher, Cindy?**

Cindy : She is very pretty. And she can speak good American English. The most important thing is that she is very patient.

Frank : It seems that she is an excellent teacher.

Cindy : Yes, we all love her very much.

法蘭克：辛蒂，妳覺得妳新的英語老師怎麼樣啊？
辛蒂：她非常漂亮。而且她能說一口流利的美式英語。最重要的是她很有耐心。
法蘭克：看來她是一名優秀的老師。
辛蒂：是的，我們都很愛她。

03 文法句型翻譯練習
Sentence Patterns Exercise

請運用上面學到的句型，試著寫出完整的英文句子吧！

01. 你認為那部電影怎麼樣？

_____

02. 你覺得新市長怎麼樣？

_____

03. 你對這次學運有什麼看法？

_____

04. 你覺得他的演講怎麼樣？

_____

05. 您覺得我們的服務怎麼樣？

_____

翻譯練習正確答案：

01. What do you think of / about the movie?

02. What do you think of / about the new mayor?

03. What do you think of / about this student movement?

04. What do you think of / about his speech?

05. What do you think of / about our service?

Level 1 基礎觀念馬上建立！（程度分級：國中英語）

10 我媽叫我下課後就馬上回家。

My mother asks me to go home
as soon as the class is over.

句型　**... as soon as...**

---

01 文法句型常用情境說明
Sentence Patterns Introduction

- 1. ... as soon as... 用來表示「一……就……」，強調兩個連續發生或是幾乎同時進行的動作。其句型為主句＋ ... as soon as... ＋時間狀態子句。

- 2. 如果主句用未來式、情態動詞或祈使句，則時間狀態子句必須用現在式代替將來式。例如：

  Put on your raincoat as soon as it rains.（一下雨就把你的雨衣穿起來。）
  I will call you as soon as I am home.（我一回到家就會打電話給你。）

- 3. ... as soon as... 在句子中的位置比較靈活，可以置於句首、句中或句末。或與 possible（可能的）組合成片語「as soon as it is possible」，省略形式為「as soon as possible」，意為「儘快」。

02 文法句型示範情境會話
Dialogue Practice

情境 1

Linda： Hi, Lily. This is Linda. I have called you several times but you didn't answer.

　Lily： Sorry, Linda. I'm busy now. **I will call you back as soon as I can,** O.K.?

Linda： Sure. Waiting for your call.

琳達：嗨，莉莉，我是琳達。我打了好幾次電話給妳，妳都沒有接。

莉莉：抱歉，琳達。我現在很忙，我一有空就打電話給妳，好嗎？

琳達：當然好。我等妳電話。

情境 2

Stephen : Doctor, when can you start my uncle's operation?

Doctor : I am not sure. **But we will schedule the operation as soon as an operation room is available.**

Stephen : O.K. Please make it quick.

史蒂芬：醫生，我叔叔的手術什麼時候可以開始？

　醫生：我不是很確定。但一旦有空的手術室，我們就會立刻安排手術。

史蒂芬：好的，請儘快。

情境 3

Customer : Can you deliver this air-conditioner to my house?

Salesman : Yes, we can. Just fill out this form, please.

Customer : O.K.

Salesman : When do you want it to be delivered, Ma'am?

Customer : **As soon as possible.**

Salesman : Mmm... How about tomorrow?

Customer : Tomorrow will be fine.

　顧客：你們能把這台冷氣送到我家嗎？

售貨員：是的，我們可以的。只要請您先填完這張表。

　顧客：好的。

售貨員：您希望什麼時候送貨，女士？

　顧客：越快越好。

售貨員：嗯……明天怎麼樣？

　顧客：明天可以。

情境 4

Betty : Carl, do you know where Susan is? **I must find her as soon as possible.** It's urgent.

Carl : I didn't see her today. Did you call her?

Betty： Yes, of course. I have called her for three times. But she didn't answer it.
Carl： O.K. I will call her roommate, Tina. See if she knows where Susan is.
Betty： Thank you.
Carl： You're welcome.

貝蒂：卡爾，你知道蘇珊在哪裡嗎？我必須儘快找到她，有急事。
卡爾：我今天沒見到她。妳打電話給她了嗎？
貝蒂：當然有。我已經打了三次電話給她，她都沒接。
卡爾：好吧。我會打給她室友，蒂娜。看看她知不知道蘇珊在哪。
貝蒂：謝謝你。
卡爾：不客氣。

情境 5

Philip： Would you like to play soccer with me, Ricky?
Ricky： I'd love to. But I have to finish my homework. **I will go as soon as I finish it,** Okay?
Philip： O.K. See you later.

菲力普：瑞奇，要不要和我一起去踢足球呀？
瑞奇：我很樂意，但我必須先把作業做完。我一做完作業馬上就過去，好嗎？
菲力普：好。晚點見。

03 文法句型翻譯練習
Sentence Patterns Exercise

請運用上面學到的句型，試著寫出完整的英文句子吧！

01. 我要求她儘快與瑪麗聯繫。

02. 這項政策應該儘快付諸實踐。

03. 我一到就馬上打電話給你。

_____

04. 如果出了什麼事，儘快讓我知道。

_____

05. 我一睡醒就會忘記夢的大部分內容。

_____

翻譯練習正確答案：

01. I asked her to get in touch with Mary as soon as possible.

02. The policy should be brought into effect as soon as possible.

03. I will call you as soon as I arrive.

04. Let me know as soon as possible if anything happens.

05. I forgot most of my dreams as soon as I woke up.

11 除非你跟我們一起去，否則我是不會跟你哥去看電影的。

I won't go to a movie with your brother
unless you go with us.

句型 **unless...**

01 文法句型常用情境說明
Sentence Patterns Introduction

- 1. unless... 是從屬連接詞，意為「除非……否則……」，其後連接條件子句。
  例如：

  Jessica won't date you unless her mom asks her to.
  （潔西卡不會和你約會，除非她媽媽要求她。）

- 2. 由 unless... 引導的條件子句和 if（如果）後的條件子句，因為假設語氣，動詞都需用現在式代替將來式。例如：

  Unless it rains tomorrow, the show will still be on.
  （除非明天下雨，否則的話表演還是舉行。）

02 文法句型示範情境會話
Dialogue Practice

情境 1

Mother：Sam, **you will miss the bus unless you hurry up.**
　　Sam：I know, Mom. I am leaving now.
Mother：Don't forget to take your breakfast with you.
　　Sam：O.K. Don't worry, Mom. Bye.
Mother：Bye.

媽媽：山姆，如果你不快點，你會錯過公車。
山姆：我知道，媽媽。我現在就出發。
媽媽：不要忘記帶你的早餐。
山姆：好，別擔心。媽媽。再見。
媽媽：再見。

情境 2

　Boss：You made the same mistake again, Steven.
Steven：I am really sorry. I will be much more careful.
　Boss：**Unless you work harder, you will get the sack.**
Steven：Yes, I will keep that in mind.

　老闆：史蒂芬，你又犯同樣的錯誤了。
史蒂芬：我真的很抱歉。我會更加小心。
　老闆：除非你再努力點工作，否則你就要被解雇了。
史蒂芬：好，我會謹記在心的。

情境 3

John：I heard that you went to Beijing last week, Jack.
Jack：That's right. It's a very beautiful city.
John：Did you go to the Great Wall?
Jack：Of course I did. It is said, **"You are not a hero unless you climb up to the Great Wall."**
John：What's the scenery like on the Great Wall?
Jack：The scenery is beyond description. You must go there some other time.

約翰：傑克，我聽說你上個星期去北京了。
傑克：沒錯。那是個非常美麗的城市。
約翰：你去長城了嗎？
傑克：當然有。俗話說「不到長城非好漢。」
約翰：長城上風景如何？
傑克：風景美的難以形容。你一定要找時間也去一趟。

情境 4

Patient：Can I see Dr. Blair at 10:00 tomorrow morning?

Secretary：I'm sorry. **She can't see you until 10:30 unless there's a cancellation.**

Patient：How about 11:30?

Secretary：No problem. She's available then.

> 病人：我明天上午 10 點可以見布雷爾醫生嗎？
> 秘書：很抱歉。除非有取消預約，否則醫生在 10 點半之前都不能見你。
> 病人：那麼 11 點半怎麼樣呢？
> 秘書：沒問題。她那時有空。

情境 5

Jenny：Can I go mountain climbing with you this Sunday?

Alice：You are very welcome. **We will leave at 10 in the morning unless it rains.**

Jenny：O.K. I hope it will be sunny this Sunday. It must be great fun to go with you.

Alice：It must be. See you on Sunday.

> 珍妮：我這個星期天可以和妳們一起去爬山嗎？
> 愛麗絲：很歡迎妳。除非下雨，否則我們早上十點出發。
> 珍妮：好的。我希望星期天是晴天。和妳們去一定會很好玩的。
> 愛麗絲：一定會的。星期天見。

03 文法句型翻譯練習
Sentence Patterns Exercise

請運用上面學到的句型，試著寫出完整的英文句子吧！

01. 你要快點否則就會錯過公車。

---

02. 除非我們早點離開，否則不能準時到。

---

03. 除非我確定事實如此，否則我就不會這樣說了。

---

04. 除非你百分百確定，否則不要作任何的承諾。

05. 除非你更努力用功，否則考試永遠過不了。

04 延伸句型加分學習
Learning Plus!

until... 直到……

- 1. until...「直到……」，表示某一個動作一直持續到某一時間，後面可以接具體的時間，如 3 o'clock（三點鐘），也可以接一個時間副詞子句。例如：

  He has been here until now.（他一直待在這裡，直到現在。）

- 2. until... 可以用於肯定句與否定句中，但用法不同。在肯定句中，動詞必須是可延續性的，例如：

  The movie won't last until three o'clock.（這場電影不會一直放映到三點。）
  It may rain until Friday.（這雨可能要下到星期五。）

- 3. Not...until... 是否定形式，意指「直到……才……」，表示直到某一時間某一行為才發生，且之前該行為並沒有發生。否定句中的動詞可以是延續性或非延續性動詞。例如：

  I won't leave here until you give me the money.
  （直到你給我錢，我才會離開這裡。）

翻譯練習正確答案：

01. You will miss the bus unless you hurry up.

02. We won't get there on time unless we leave earlier.

03. I wouldn't be saying this unless I were sure of the facts.

04. Don't promise anything unless you're 100 percent sure.

05. You will never pass the exam unless you study harder.

12 我們不知道大螢幕 iPhone 是不是會被推出。

We don't know whether big screen iPhones will be released or not.

句型 **whether... or...**

01 文法句型常用情境說明
Sentence Patterns Introduction

• 1. whether... or... 強調在兩者之間的選擇，表示「是……還是……」或是「無論 / 不管……還是……」。

• 2. whether... or not 常用來強調「無論是不是 / 不管要不要……還是……」, or not 也可以省略。

02 文法句型示範情境會話
Dialogue Practice

情境 1

David : Eric, why don't you take part in the competition?

Eric : Hmm... I am afraid I might fail.

David : **It doesn't matter whether you fail or not.** Just try your best.

Eric : Well, I think you are right. I will give it a try.

David : Good for you.

大衛：艾瑞克，你為什麼不參加這次的比賽呢？

艾瑞克：嗯……我怕我可能會失敗。

大衛：無論你會不會失敗並不重要。只要你盡力就好。

艾瑞克：好吧，我想你說得對。我會試試看。

大衛：很好。

情境 2

Sarah： Will Mr. Smith come to your birthday party, Cindy?
Cindy： I don't know. **But it makes no difference to me whether Mr. Smith will come or not.**
Sarah： Anyway, I will come.
Cindy： Glad to hear that, Sarah. You are my best friend. I hope our friendship can last forever.
Sarah： I believe it will.

莎拉： 辛蒂，史密斯先生會參加妳的生日派對嗎？
辛蒂： 我不知道。但是對我來說，史密斯先生來或不來都無所謂。
莎拉： 不管怎樣，我會去的。
辛蒂： 很高興聽妳這樣說，莎拉。妳是我最好的朋友，我希望我們的友誼可以一直持續下去。
莎拉： 我相信我們會的。

情境 3

Joanna： Mary's wedding will take place next Sunday. Are you going?
Julie： **I am not sure whether I can go or not.** I have an appointment with my dentist on that day.
Joanna： That's too bad. Maybe you can come and join us later.
Julie： That's a good idea.

喬安娜： 瑪麗的婚禮是下個星期天。妳會去她的婚禮嗎？
茱麗： 我不確定我能不能去。我那天和牙醫有約。
喬安娜： 那太不巧了。或許妳可以晚點過來加入我們。
茱麗： 真是個好主意。

情境 4

Donna： Why do you look so confused, George?
George： **I am wondering whether I should play basketball or go to the movies this afternoon.**
Donna： That's quite an easy question. You can play basketball this afternoon, and then go to the movies later.
George： Would you like to see a movie tonight with me?

Donna： Yes, I'd love to.

唐娜： 喬治，你為什麼看起來這麼困惑呀？
喬治： 我在想我下午應該去打籃球，還是去看電影。
唐娜： 這是個相當簡單的問題。你可以下午打籃球，稍後再去看電影。
喬治： 妳今晚願意和我一起去看電影嗎？
唐娜： 是的，我很樂意。

情境 5

Student： Professor, do you have a minute? I have something I need to talk to you about.
Professor： Yes, I do.
Student： It's about my paper. I don't know how to make use of the information in my thesis.
Professor： **First, I think you should make sure whether the information is related to your topic or not.**
Student： I can't be sure about this...
Professor： That's fine. Just bring you paper to my office. Maybe I can give you some suggestions.

學生： 教授，您有空嗎？我有事想和您談一下。
教授： 好的。
學生： 是關於我的論文。我不知道如何在我的論文裡善加利用這些資料。
教授： 首先，我想你應該確定你找到的資料是不是與你的題目相關。
學生： 這點我不是很確定……
教授： 沒關係。你就帶你的論文來我辦公室。或許我可以給你一些建議。

03 文法句型翻譯練習
Sentence Patterns Exercise

請運用上面學到的句型，試著寫出完整的英文句子吧！

01. 我們要出去還是要待在家裡，都取決於天氣好壞。

02. 無論下不下雨，我們每個星期六都會去打網球。

___

03. 不管你喜不喜歡，我還是要做。

___

04. 我不能判斷她是對還是錯。

___

05. 不管你是否告訴她們，她們都會查明真相。

___

04 延伸句型加分學習
Learning Plus!

if... 是否……

- 1. if... 除了表示「如果……」引導條件子句外，還有「是否……」的意思，其後連接子句。

- 2. if... 做「如果……」解釋時，為假設語氣，其後子句需以現在式代替未來式。若為「是否……」意思時，則不需要。例如：

If it rains tomorrow, I won't go with you.
（如果明天下雨的話，我就不跟你們去了。）
I don't know if they will come to help us.
（我不知道他們是否來幫助我們。）

翻譯練習正確答案：

01. Whether we will go out or stay at home depends on the weather.

02. Whether it rains or not, we always play tennis on Saturdays.

03. Whether you like it or not, I'll still do it anyway.

04. I can't tell whether she is right or wrong.

05. They'll find out the truth, whether you tell them or not.

Level 2　可以開始簡單英語會話囉！（程度分級：高中第一～二冊）

13 你不想一起去嗎？
Don't you want to come along?

句型 **Isn't (Don't / Can't / Won't...) ＋ sb....?**

---

01 文法句型常用情境說明
Sentence Patterns Introduction

否定疑問句通常使用於表示驚異、失望、責難、反問、讚嘆、建議或有禮貌的邀請等語氣。這樣的疑問句比起一般疑問句，帶有濃厚的情感色彩。善用否定疑問句，可巧妙地向對方透露說話時的情緒。面對否定疑問句時，無論是否同意問話者的看法，只要答案是肯定的，即答 yes；若為否定，則答 no。例如：

A: Isn't Mary a beautiful bride?　B: Yes, she is.
（A：瑪莉不是個很美麗的新娘嗎？　B：是啊，她是。）

02 文法句型示範情境會話
Dialogue Practice

情境 1

Mom： Amy, your father and I are going to the supermarket.
　　　Don't you want to come along?
Amy： No, Mom. I think I'd better stay in and finish my homework.

媽媽：愛咪，妳爸跟我要去超市。妳不一起去嗎？
愛咪：不了，媽。我想我最好待在家裡把作業寫完。

情境 2

Nancy： How could you say that to hurt his feeling?
　　　　Aren't you his best friend?
Peter： I am. But I just want him to face the truth.

南西：你怎麼能說那些話傷害他呢？你不是他最好的朋友嗎？
彼得：我是啊。但我只是希望他面對現實而已。

情境 3

Vivian：Wow! Look! **Isn't this place beautiful?**
Larry：It sure is. I'm glad this is where we're going to spend our summer.

薇薇安：哇！你看！這個地方難道不美嗎？
賴瑞：真的好美！我很高興這是我們接下來要度過夏天的地方。

情境 4

Bill：Lucy? What are you guys talking about?
Jack：Huh? **Haven't you seen the movie yet?**
Steven：Are you kidding me? **Don't you know the film?** This is one of the most popular movies this summer.

比爾：Lucy？你們在講什麼呀？
傑克：咦？你還沒看過這部電影嗎？
史蒂文：你在開玩笑嗎？你不知道這部片？這是今年夏天最受歡迎的電影之一。

情境 5

Man：I'm afraid that I can't go to work today.
Woman：Why not? **Aren't you feeling well?**
Man：No. I feel nauseous. I think I need to see a doctor.

男子：我今天恐怕不能去上班了。
女子：怎麼了？你不舒服嗎？
男子：嗯，我覺得想吐。我想我得去看個醫生。

---

03 文法句型翻譯練習
Sentence Patterns Exercise

請運用上面學到的句型，試著寫出完整的英文句子吧！

01. 難道你不吃早餐的嗎？

02. 你不是跟我說你想吃漢堡嗎？

_____

03. 這不是你正在找的書嗎？

_____

04. 他們不是你的祖父母嗎？

_____

05. 你還沒讀過這本書嗎？

_____

04 延伸句型加分學習
Learning Plus!

附加問句

在直述句後加上一個附加問句，以反問的方式加強語氣或確認訊息內容。

例如：This is a beautiful place, isn't it?
　　　這是個美麗的地方，不是嗎？
　　　You have been to London, haven't you?
　　　你去過倫敦，不是嗎？

回答附加問句的方式與回答否定疑問句的方式相同。無論是否同意說話者的看法，只要答案是肯定的，即肯定答之；若為否定，則否定答之。

翻譯練習正確答案：

01. Don't you have breakfast?

02. Didn't you tell me that you want to eat hamburgers?

03. Isn't it the book that you are looking for?

04. Aren't they your grandparents?

05. Haven't you read this book yet?

Day14

14 這個包包真漂亮啊！
How beautiful this bag is!

句型 **What / How...!**

01 文法句型常用情境說明
Sentence Patterns Introduction

- 1. 感歎句通常由 what / how 引導，表示讚美、驚歎、喜悅、等感情。由 what / how 分別引導強調的名詞及形容詞，並將強調的部分移至句首，其後再接句子的主詞與動詞。句子的主詞與動詞，也可以省略。句型分別如下：

  What ＋名詞（＋主詞＋動詞）！→ What cute cats they are!
  How ＋形容詞（＋主詞＋動詞）！→ How cute those cats are! 　（真可愛的貓！）

- 2. what 修飾名詞，單數可數名詞前要加不定冠詞 a / an ，複數可數名詞和不可數名詞前不用冠詞。例如：

  What a beautiful girl (she is)！（她真是個漂亮的女孩！）

- 3. how 修飾形容詞、副詞或動詞，並將強調的部分移至句首。例如：
  How beautiful she is!（她真是漂亮！）
  How fast she can run!（她跑得真快！）

02 文法句型示範情境會話
Dialogue Practice

情境 1

Husband : **Oh, what a mess!** Why didn't you clean up the room today, honey?

Wife : Honey, I was really busy today, and I stayed up for work last night. So I really don't have time to do the housework today.

Husband : That's fine, sweet heart. Let's do it together tomorrow, O.K.?

丈夫：噢，真是一團糟呀！親愛的，妳今天怎麼沒打掃房間呀？

妻子：親愛的。我今天很忙，而且我昨天晚上熬夜工作。所以我今天真的沒有時間做家事。

丈夫：沒關係，甜心。我們明天一起打掃，好嗎？

情境 2

Bill : Oh, boy! That's too bad.

Carl : What's the matter, Bill?

Bill : Tina finally would like to go to cinema with me tonight. But the boss asked me to finish the paper today, which means, I have to work late today!

Carl : Oh! **What a tragedy!**

比爾：噢，天啊！這真是太糟了。

卡爾：怎麼啦，比爾？

比爾：蒂娜今晚終於想要和我一起去看電影。但是老闆要我今天就把報告完成。這就代表我今天晚上得加班啦！

卡爾：噢。真是悲劇啊！

情境 3

Amy : **What a fine day today!**

Jim : Yes, it is. Would you like to have a walk in the park with me?

Amy : I'd love to. I love the fresh air and the nice view in the park.

Jim : Great. Let's go.

艾咪：今天天氣真好啊！

吉姆：是的，天氣很晴朗。 妳想不想和我去公園散個步？

艾咪：我很樂意。我喜歡公園裡新鮮的空氣和美麗的景色。

吉姆：太棒了。我們走吧。

情境 4

Maggie : **How fast time flies!** We are going to graduate this July.
　　Ann : You are right. I still remember the first day I went to this school.
Maggie : We were freshmen at that time, but now we are busy finding jobs.
　　Ann : But we really had a great time here.

　瑪姬：時間過得真快呀！我們七月就要畢業了。
　　安：妳說得沒錯。我還記得來學校的第一天呢。
　瑪姬：我們那時候是新生，但是現在卻都忙著找工作了。
　　安：不過我們在這裡真的過得很快樂。

情境 5

　Bill : It is raining heavily outside. We can't play football today, Mike.
Mike : **How disappointing!**
　Bill : But we can watch films at home in such a bad day.
Mike : Good idea!

　比爾：外面雨下得很大。我們今天不能踢足球了，麥克。
　麥克：真掃興！
　比爾：但是在這樣的壞天氣，我們可以在家看電影。
　麥克：好主意！

03 文法句型翻譯練習
Sentence Patterns Exercise

請運用上面學到的句型，試著寫出完整的英文句子吧！

01. 這朵花多麼漂亮啊！

---

02. 我們等你等了好久了！

---

03. 她唱得多麼好呀！

---

04. 多麼好的景色啊！

05. 她們看起來多麼高興呀！

04 延伸句型加分學習
Learning Plus!

such a / an...　如此……

　　such a / an... 表示「如此……」也是強調用法之一。such 修飾單數名詞時，放於不定冠詞 a (an) 之前，若名詞前有 one（一個）、no（沒有）、any（任何的）、some（一些的）、all（所有的）、many（許多的）等修飾時，such 放在這些修飾詞之後。例如：

She is such a beautiful woman.（她是一位如此美麗的女人。）
Don't be such a crybaby.（別動不動就哭。）

翻譯練習正確答案：

01. How beautiful this flower is!

02. What a long time we have been waiting for you!

03. How well she sings!

04. What a nice view it is!

05. How happy they look!

Level 2 可以開始簡單英語會話囉！（程度分級：高中第一～二冊）

15 你介意讓我先上廁所嗎？
Do you mind if I use the restroom first?

句型 **Do / Would you mind...?**

01 文法句型常用情境說明
Sentence Patterns Introduction

Do / Would you mind...? 意思是「你介意……嗎？」用來表示委婉的請求，或希望得到對方的許可，後接動名詞或 if（是否）子句。其中 would 比 do 語氣更委婉、更表禮貌用法。熟人之間說話時，可用 do 代替 would 。

02 文法句型示範情境會話
Dialogue Practice

情境 1

John : **Would you mind if I open the window?** It's very hot in the classroom.
Jack : Fine by me. It does not bother me at all.
John : Thank you.

約翰：你介意我打開窗戶嗎 ？教室裡太熱了。
傑克：我無所謂。這一點都不困擾我。
約翰：謝謝你。

情境 2

Teacher : **Would you mind giving your parents a message for me?**
Student : Of course not, sir. What do you want to say to my parents?
Teacher : Please tell your parents that I will visit your house tonight, O.K.?
Student : No problem, sir.

教師： 你介意幫我帶個口信給你父母嗎？
學生： 當然不，先生。您想和我父母説什麼？
教師： 請告訴你父母我今晚會去你家拜訪，好嗎？
學生： 沒問題，先生。

情境 3

Susan： **Would you mind helping me?**
Daniel： I'd be glad to. What do you want me to do?
Susan： Help me to hang up this picture.
Daniel： No problem. Hand me the hammer over, please.
Susan： Here you are!

蘇珊： 你能幫我個忙嗎？
丹尼爾： 我很樂意。妳想要我做什麼？
蘇珊： 幫我掛這幅畫。
丹尼爾： 沒問題。請把錘子遞給我。
蘇珊： 拿去。

情境 4

　　Wife： **Would you mind giving me a lift to the shopping mall?**
Husband： But I have to go to work now. We are not on the same way. You can take a taxi.
　　Wife： That's fine. Honey, bye.
Husband： Bye, sweet heart.

妻子： 你介意順道載我去購物中心嗎？
丈夫： 但是我現在必須去上班。我們不順路。妳可以搭計程車。
妻子： 沒關係。親愛的，再見。
丈夫： 再見，甜心。

情境 5

John： Hi, **do you mind if I sit with you?**
Mary： Of course not. I am alone.
John： Oh, thank you. Is this your first time here?
Mary： Yes, this is my very first time to Paris.
John： Really? So do you like this city?

Mary：Like it? No, I love it! It's like my dream finally comes true.

約翰：嗨，妳介意我坐在妳旁邊嗎？
瑪麗：當然不會。我一個人（坐）。
約翰：喔，謝謝妳。這是妳第一次到這裡嗎？
瑪麗：是的，這是我第一次來巴黎。
約翰：真的嗎？那妳喜歡這個城市嗎？
瑪麗：喜歡？不，我愛死了！對我來說這就像美夢成真一樣。

03 文法句型翻譯練習
Sentence Patterns Exercise

請運用上面學到的句型，試著寫出完整的英文句子吧！

01. 你介意我在這裡抽菸嗎？

_____

02. 你介意我跟你借點錢嗎？

_____

03. 你介意我問你一些私人問題嗎？

_____

04. 你介意把電視關掉嗎？

_____

翻譯練習正確答案：

01. Would / Do you mind if I smoke here?

02. Would / Do you mind if I borrow some money from you?

03. Would / Do you mind if I ask you some personal questions?

04. Would / Do you mind turning off the TV?

16 這場比賽不只令人屏息還令人非常難忘！

This game is not only breath-taking but also unforgettable.

句型 **not only... but also...**

01 文法句型常用情境說明
Sentence Patterns Introduction

- 1. not only... but also... 意指「不但……而且……」，為對等連接詞，用於連接兩個表示並列關係的形容詞、名詞、副詞甚至是動詞，並著重強調後者，其中的 also 可省略。例如：

  Mary is not only beautiful but (also) considerate.
  （瑪麗不但漂亮，而且還很體貼。）

- 2. not only... but also... 若連接兩個主詞，動詞需與最接近的主詞要保持一致。例如：

  Not only you but also I am in Class 201.（不只你還有我都在 201 班。）

- 3. 若連接兩個句子，句首若為 not only ，後面的句子要用倒裝句。例如：

  Not only should you set up a goal but also (you should) study hard.
  （你不只該立定志向，還應該要努力用功。）

02 文法句型示範情境會話
Dialogue Practice

情境 1

Peter： What do you think of David?
Frank： **He is not only weak but also vain.**

Peter : Oh, really? I thought he is an honest and generous guy.
Frank : Err... You know little about him.

　彼得： 你覺得大衛怎麼樣？
法蘭克： 他既軟弱又愛慕虛榮。
　彼得： 噢，真的嗎？我還以為他是一個誠實又慷慨的人呢。
法蘭克： 哦……你對他瞭解太少了。

情境 2

　　Jessie : Professor, **I heard that you can speak not only English but also French.** Is that true?
Professor : Yeah, I used to live in France.
　　Jessie : I love France very much. Can you tell me something about your life in France?
Professor : Yes, of course.

　潔西： 教授，我聽說您不但會說英語，還會說法語。是真的嗎？
　教授： 是的，我以前曾經住在法國。
　潔西： 我非常喜歡法國。您能跟我說些您在法國生活的事嗎？
　教授： 好呀，當然可以。

情境 3

Joy : I saw your new teacher yesterday. She is very pretty.
Lily : **She is not only beautiful but also very knowledgeable about classical music.**
Joy : You're so lucky.

喬伊： 我昨天看到了妳們的新老師。她非常漂亮。
莉莉： 是的，她不僅漂亮，而且對古典音樂的知識相當豐富。
喬伊： 妳們真是太幸運了。

情境 4

　Tina : Who is this lovely little girl, Emily?
Emily : She is my niece.
　Tina : Oh, she is so adorable. How old is she?
Emily : She is three years old now. You know what? **She can not only read but also write.**

Tina： She is so amazing.

蒂娜：艾蜜莉，這個可愛的小女孩是誰？
艾蜜莉：她是我的侄女。
蒂娜：噢，她真是太可愛了。她幾歲了？
艾蜜莉：她三歲了。妳知道嗎？她不但會讀還會寫。
蒂娜：她真是令人驚訝。

03 文法句型翻譯練習
Sentence Patterns Exercise

請運用上面學到的句型，試著寫出完整的英文句子吧！

01. 這孩子既健康又充滿活力。

_____

02. 我不僅懂英語，也懂法語。

_____

03. 氣體不僅改變形狀，而且改變體積。

_____

04. 莎士比亞不僅是一位劇作家，而且是一位演員。

_____

05. 我不僅喜歡打籃球，還喜歡打網球。

_____

翻譯練習正確答案：

01. The child is not only healthy but also full of energy.

02. I know not only English but also French.

03. A gas changes not only in shape but also in volume.

04. Shakespeare is not only a play writer but also an actor.

05. I like playing not only basketball but also tennis.

Level 2 可以開始簡單英語會話囉！（程度分級：高中第一～二冊）

17 瞭解世界趨勢對於學生來說相當重要。

It's very important for students to know the current trend of the world.

句型 It is + adj. + of / for sb. + to do...

01 文法句型常用情境說明
Sentence Patterns Introduction

　　It is + adj. + of / for sb. + to do... 表示「（對）某人來說……」，是非常常見的句型。其中的 it 是虛主詞，後面的動詞不定式才是真正的主詞。另外，此句型中用 of 還是 for，取決於其前的形容詞，若形容詞表示的是人的品質、性格，例如：kind（仁慈的）、nice（好心的）、clever（聰明的）、right（正直的）等，需用 of；若形容詞只是對動作的一般性描述，例如：difficult（困難的）、dangerous（危險的）、important（重要的）等，則用 for。

02 文法句型示範情境會話
Dialogue Practice

情境 1

Helen : **It's kind of you to explain this question to me,** Emma. I understand it very well now.

Emma : No problem. I am glad that you understand it now.

Helen : Thank you very much.

Emma : Not at all.

　　海倫：艾瑪，妳人真好，能解釋這個問題給我聽。我現在已經很清楚了。

　　艾瑪：沒什麼啦。我很高興妳現在懂了。

　　海倫：非常謝謝妳。

　　艾瑪：不客氣。

情境 2

Mother : Oh, my! What are you doing, Jack? **Don't you know it's dangerous for children to play with fire?**
Son : Mom, I am not a child anymore.
Mother : No, you are always a child for me, honey. So don't you ever play with fire again, O.K.?
Son : I'm sorry, Mom. I won't do that again.
Mother : Good boy.

媽媽：噢，我的天！你在做什麼，傑克？你不知道小孩子玩火很危險的嗎？
彼得：媽媽，我已經不是小孩子了。
媽媽：不，親愛的，在我眼中你一直是個孩子。所以下次不要再玩火了好嗎？
彼得：我很抱歉，媽媽。我不會再做了。
媽媽：好孩子。

情境 3

Teacher : **It's important for you to study hard.** I believe that you know it well. Just keep up the good work.
Student : Sure! I'll do my best.

老師：要用功，這對你很重要。我相信你很清楚。繼續保持你的好表現！
學生：一定會！我會盡全力。

情境 4

Alex : Where is my wallet? Did you see my wallet, Bella?
Bella : No, I didn't. What is in your wallet?
Alex : My ID, driving license, credit cards and some money. Today is really not my day. Those are very important things to me.
Bella : **It is very careless of you to lose your wallet.**

亞歷克斯：我的皮夾去哪了？妳看到我的皮夾了嗎，貝拉？
貝拉：沒有，你皮夾裡有什麼東西？
亞歷克斯：我的身份證，駕照，信用卡，還有一些錢。我今天真倒楣。那些東西對我來說很重要。
貝拉：你把錢包弄丟了，真是太粗心了。

情境 5

Alice：Jane, would you tell me how to improve my English?
Jane：I think it is important for you to practice English in your daily life. It is said that practice makes perfect. So just practice more.
Alice：**Wow, it is very kind of you to tell me that.** Thank you.
Jane：It is not a big deal.

愛麗絲：珍，妳能告訴我該怎麼讓我的英文進步嗎？
　　珍：我想對妳來説，在日常生活中練習英語是非常重要的。話説熟能生巧嘛。所以就多練習吧。
愛麗絲：哇，妳人真好，能告訴我這些。謝謝妳。
　　珍：小事一件。

03 文法句型翻譯練習
Sentence Patterns Exercise

請運用上面學到的句型，試著寫出完整的英文句子吧！

01. 你能幫助我，真好。

_____

02. 對我們來說獨自完成這項工作很困難。

_____

03. 廣泛的閱讀對於我們來說是很重要的。

_____

04. 他們拒絕採納這個提議是不明智的。

_____

05. 你為我們考慮這麼多，真是太好了。

_____

04 延伸句型加分學習
Learning Plus!

> **V-ing + is + adj...　做某事是…**

- 1. V-ing + is + adj. 句型中 V-ing 是動名詞做主詞，視為單數名詞，後面接形容詞作修飾，例如：

  Learning English is an important thing for us.
  （學習英語對我們來說是重要的。）
  Smoking is bad for our health.（吸菸對我們的健康有害。）

- 2. 有時為了保持句子通順，不頭重腳輕，通常用虛主詞 it 代替主詞，而把真正主詞放在後面。例如：

  It's a waste of time arguing about it.（爭論這件事是浪費時間。）

翻譯練習正確答案：

01. It's very kind of you to help me.

02. It's difficult for us to finish the job all by ourselves.

03. It's important for us to read extensively.

04. It's unwise of them to turn down the proposal.

05. It's kind of you to think so much for us.

Level 2 可以開始簡單英語會話囉！（程度分級：高中第一～二冊）

18 那達爾不認為這次發球有出界。
Nadal doesn't think that this serve is outside.

句型 **Sb. do / does not think / suppose / believe that...**

01 文法句型常用情境說明
Sentence Patterns Introduction

Sb. do / does not think / suppose / believe that... 意指「某人不覺得 / 不認為 / 不相信……」。此句型用來表示某人的觀點或者想法，其後接關係代名詞 that 所引導的名詞子句。

02 文法句型示範情境會話
Dialogue Practice

情境 1

Sam： Do you believe that there are aliens in other planets?
Tom： Actually, I do. **I don't think that earth is the only habitable planet.**
Sam： I think so.

山姆： 你認為其它的星球上存在著外星人嗎？
湯姆： 事實上，我相信。我不認為地球是唯一有生物棲息的星球。
山姆： 我也這麼認為。

情境 2

David： Eric, which team do you think will win the World Cup FIFA 2014?
Eric： **I think Brazil will be the champion.** It has won the World Cup for many times.

David： That's true. But I don't agree with you. **I think Argentina may win the game.** They have performed and coordinated very well this year.

Eric： Nobody knows the result untill the end of the game.

David： You are right. Nothing is impossible.

大衛： 艾瑞克，你覺得 2014 年的世界盃足球賽哪隻隊伍會贏？

艾瑞克： 我認為巴西隊會是冠軍。他們已經贏得了好幾次世界盃冠軍了。

大衛： 你說得沒錯。但我和你意見不同。我認為阿根廷有可能贏得比賽。他們在今年的比賽中一直打得不錯，調度得也不錯。

艾瑞克： 到比賽結束為止，沒有人能知道結果。

大衛： 你說得對。沒有不可能的事。

情境 3

Daughter： Dad, I want to buy a car of my own.

Father： Sweet heart, **I don't think that you need one.**

Daughter： Why not? Dad, I don't want go to work by bike every day.

Father： **But I think it is very good for your health.**

女兒： 爸爸，我想買輛屬於自己的車。

爸爸： 甜心，我不認為妳有必要買車。

女兒： 為什麼？ 爸爸，我不想每天騎腳踏車上班。

爸爸： 但我認為那樣對妳身體很好。

情境 4

Bella： Ah, it's hard to find a job nowadays.

Sarah： I can't agree more. But the government has taken some actions to improve the situation.

Bella： **I don't suppose that the situation will improve.** There are so many graduators each year, but jobs are few and limited.

Sarah： It's really true.

貝拉： 哦，現在找工作還真難。

莎拉： 我非常同意。但是政府已經採取一些行動來改善這種情形。

貝拉： 我不認為形勢將會得到改善。每年有這麼多的畢業生，但工作很少而且有限。

莎拉： 確實如此。

03 文法句型翻譯練習
Sentence Patterns Exercise

請運用上面學到的句型，試著寫出完整的英文句子吧！

01. 她不相信我說的話。

_____

02. 我不認為現在還是交通尖峰時間。

_____

03. 很多人不相信空氣有重量。

_____

04. 我不認為她們能準時抵達。

_____

05. 我不認為你知道那件事。

_____

_____

翻譯練習正確答案：

01. She does not believe what I said.

02. I don't suppose that it is still the rush hour.

03. Many people do not believe that air has weight.

04. I don't think that they can arrive on time.

05. I don't suppose that you know this information.

Level 2 可以開始簡單英語會話囉！（程度分級：高中第一～二冊）

19 貝拉該是時候決定她未來的職業。

It's time for Bella to decide her career.

句型 It's time (for sb.) to do sth.

---

01 文法句型常用情境說明
Sentence Patterns Introduction

It's time (for sb.) to do sth. 意為「該是做某事的時候了」，介系詞 for 可接所指稱的對象，用以表示其後的所表示的動作就是這個 sb. 所做的。

02 文法句型示範情境會話
Dialogue Practice

情境 1

Mother : **It's time to get up, baby!**
   Son : Mom, I'm very tired. I want to sleep for a little bit longer.
Mother : You will be late for school!
   Son : Mom, I don't feel well today. I don't want to go to school.
Mother : Let me see, baby. Oh, you have a little fever. You should rest at home. I will call your teacher.
   Son : Thank you, Mom.

媽媽：該起床了，寶貝！
兒子：媽媽，我覺得好累，我想多睡一下。
媽媽：你上學會遲到！
兒子：媽媽，我今天感覺不舒服。我不想去上學。
媽媽：讓我看看，寶貝。噢，你有點發燒。你應該在家裡休息。我會打電話給你的老師。
兒子：謝謝妳，媽。

情境 2

Nurse： **It's time to take medicine,** Jason.
Jason： Err..., this kind of medicine tastes very bitter. I don't want to take it.
Nurse： It's bad for your illness, Jason. Take the medicine, and then I will give you chocolate, O.K.?
Jason： That'll be great. Thank you.

護士： 該吃藥了，傑森。
傑森： 呃……，這種藥吃起來很苦。我不想吃。
護士： 傑森，這樣對你病情不好。 你先吃藥，然後我會給你巧克力，好不好？
傑森： 太棒了。謝謝妳。

情境 3

Mom： **It is time to have breakfast,** my son!
Son： Sorry, Mom. I'm afraid I have no time. I have to hurry, or I will be late for school.
Mom： It's bad for your health to skip your breakfast.
Son： I really have no time. Goodbye, Mom!

媽媽： 兒子，該吃早飯了！
兒子： 抱歉，媽媽。我恐怕沒時間吃早飯了。我得快點，否則上學要遲到了。
媽媽： 不吃早餐對你身體不好。
兒子： 我真的沒時間了。再見，媽媽。

情境 4

Bill： Spring comes. Trees are green and flowers bloom. **It's time to go for an outing.**
Jack： Yeah! That sounds great. I want to join your spring outing.
Bill： O.K. Let's plan for it.

比爾： 春天來了。樹木綠了，花兒開了。該是時候去郊遊了。
傑克： 是的！聽起來真棒。我想加入你的春遊行列。
比爾： 好的，讓我們來計畫一下吧。

情境 5

Vicky : **Jessie, it's time to have dinner.** Do you want to go with me?
Jessie : Sure. Where do you want to go?
Vicky : There is a new restaurant near our school. Let's go and have a try.
Jessie : O.K. Let's go.

薇琪：潔西，該吃晚飯了。妳要跟我一起去嗎？
潔西：當然。妳想去哪裡？
薇琪：我們學校附近有一家新餐館。我們去試試吧。
潔西：好，走吧。

03 文法句型翻譯練習
Sentence Patterns Exercise

請運用上面學到的句型，試著寫出完整的英文句子吧！

01. 現在是你該去睡覺的時候了。

_____

02. 現在該登機了。

_____

03. 是時候休息了。

_____

04. 現在是我們該動身的時候了。

_____

05. 是我們採取行動的時候了。

_____

04 延伸句型加分學習
Learning Plus!

It's (high / about) time that... 該是……的時候了

　　It's (high / about) time that... 此句型中為表示應做而未做的假設語氣，更暗示現在若不做某事的話就有點太遲了。由關係代名詞 that 所引導的子句需要用假設語氣，也就是以過去式動詞來表示對現在的假設。

　　It is time (that) we had classes.（是我們該上課的時候了。）
　　It is high time that we started.（ 我們該出發了。）

翻譯練習正確答案：

01. It is time for you to go to bed.

02. It's time to get on board.

03. It is time to have a rest.

04. It is time for us to start off.

05. It is time for us to take actions.

Level 2　可以開始簡單英語會話囉！（程度分級：高中第一～二冊）

20 曾雅妮是如此努力以致於她連續109週在女子高爾夫球選手中排名第一。

Yani Tseng works so hard that she was ranked number 1 in the Women's Golf Rankings for 109 consecutive weeks.

句型　**so... that...**

01 文法句型常用情境說明
Sentence Patterns Introduction

- 1. so... that... 意思為「如此……以致於……」，由 so 引導形容詞或副詞，用以形容由 that 引導的子句，並表示兩者之間的因果關係。例如：

Mary is so beautiful that all the boys in her school love her.
（瑪麗是如此的漂亮，以致於她學校裡的所有男孩都愛她。）

- 2. so... that... 也可為 so that...，連接兩個子句，直接表示兩個子句間的因果關係。

02 文法句型示範情境會話
Dialogue Practice

情境 1

Wife：Dear, can you give me a hand?
Husband：Yes, of course. What's it?
Wife：**Let's move the bed so that I can sweep the floor.**
Husband：No problem.

妻子： 親愛的，你能幫我一個忙嗎？
丈夫： 當然可以呀 。什麼事？
妻子： 我們把床移動一下，這樣我就可以掃地了。
丈夫： 沒問題。

情境 2

Bob： Tracy, have you changed your phone number? I have called you for many times, but you never answered.

Tracy： Yes, I did, and my new number is 537578.

Bob： Wait. **I want to find something to write it down so that I can remember it.**

鮑伯： 崔西，妳換號碼了嗎？我打了幾次電話給妳都沒人接。
崔西： 是的，我換號碼了。我的新號碼是 537578.
鮑伯： 噢，等等，我想找張紙記才好記住。

情境 3

Sales： May I help you?
Customer： Yes, please. I want to buy a dress for myself.
Sales： Dresses are over there. This way, please.
Customer： The blue one looks good. Can I try it on?
Sales： Sure.
Customer： Oh, it's too small for me. Do you have a larger one?
Sales： I'm sorry. This is the largest one in our store.
Customer： Ah, that's too bad. **I think I must lose some weight so that I can get in the dress.**

店員： 我能為您服務嗎？
顧客： 是的，我想幫自己買件洋裝。
店員： 洋裝都在那裡。這邊請。
顧客： 那件藍色的看起來不錯，我可以試穿嗎？
店員： 當然可以。
顧客： 噢，這對我來說太小了。有大一點的嗎？
店員： 很抱歉，這是我們店裡最大的了。
顧客： 噢，真糟糕。我想我得減肥，才能穿得下這件洋裝。

情境 4

Teacher：**Carl, please read louder so that all the students can hear you.**
Student：Yes, sir.
Teacher：Good, please continue.

老師：卡爾，請你唸大聲點，這樣一來所有同學才能夠聽見。
學生：好的，老師。
老師：很好，請繼續。

情境 5

Jim：Excuse me. Could you tell me how to get to the Legislative Yuan? I'm a stranger here.
Joe：Certainly. Just go straight down this street. Turn right at the fist traffic light and keep on going till the second traffic light. And then turn left.
Jim：It sounds a little bit complicate.
Joe：That's fine. **I will write it down for you so that you will not get lost.**
Jim：Thank you very much.
Joe：You are welcome.

吉姆：不好意思。你能告訴我怎麼去立法院嗎？我是外地人。
　喬：當然。你只要沿著這條街一直走下去。在第一個紅綠燈右轉，一直走到第二個紅綠燈然後左轉。
吉姆：聽起來有點複雜。
　喬：沒關係。我幫你寫下來，這樣你就不會迷路了。
吉姆：非常感謝你。
　喬：不客氣。

03 文法句型翻譯練習
Sentence Patterns Exercise

請運用上面學到的句型，試著寫出完整的英文句子吧！

01. 努力用功，以便以後你可以找個好工作。

_____

02. 請把窗戶打開，這樣我們才可以呼吸些新鮮的空氣。

_____

03. 她們沒搭到車，所以上課遲到了。

_____

04. 演講者說話很大聲，以致於所有的人都能聽得清楚。

_____

05. 為了今年能更進步，我每天花了更多時間學英語。

_____

翻譯練習正確答案：

01. Study hard so that you can find a good job in the future.

02. Please open the window so that we can have some fresh air.

03. They missed the bus so that they were late for class.

04. The speaker spoke so loudly that everyone could hear him clearly.

05. I spend more time learning English every day so that I can make greater progress this year.

21 起床，否則你開學第一天就要遲到了！

Get up, or you will be late on the first day to school.

句型 or / otherwise...

01 文法句型常用情境說明
Sentence Patterns Introduction

在祈使句後面加上 or / otherwise...，意為「否則、要不然……」。是連接兩個句子的對等連接詞，前面需加上逗號。otherwise 是一種陳述語氣，陳述如果不做某事，結果會怎樣……。而 or 就是帶有警告威脅之類的語氣。

02 文法句型示範情境會話
Dialogue Practice

情境 1

Wife : **Hurry up, or we will miss the train.**
Husband : Don't worry, sweet heart. We still have thirty minutes left. It is enough for us to get there.

妻子：快點，否則我們要錯過火車了。
丈夫：不用擔心，甜心。我們還有 30 分鐘。這時間足夠我們到那裡。

情境 2

Tracy : Why are you still playing the computer, Tina? You will have an exam tomorrow. **Prepare for it now, or you will fail the exam.**
Tina : Just for another ten minutes, O.K.?
Tracy : **No, shut off the computer right now, or I will tell Dad.**

Tina : Please don't tell dad, dear sister. I am shutting it off now.
Tracy : Good.

崔西：蒂娜，妳為什麼還在玩電腦？妳明天要考試。現在快準備吧，否則妳會被當的。
蒂娜：我再玩 10 分鐘，好嗎？
崔西：不行，現在馬上關掉電腦，否則我就告訴爸爸。
蒂娜：拜託不要告訴爸爸，親愛的姐姐。我馬上把電腦關掉。
崔西：很好。

情境 3

Bob : Hey, Tom. I didn't see you in the meeting yesterday.
Tom : **I was sick yesterday, otherwise I would have attended the meeting.**
Bob : What a pity!
Tom : It is O.K. My colleague took notes for me.

鮑伯：嗨，湯姆。昨天開會我怎麼沒看到你呀。
湯姆：我昨天生病了，否則我會去參加會議。
鮑伯：那太可惜了！
湯姆：沒關係。我同事有幫我記筆記。

情境 4

Manager : Nick, why did you make the same mistake again? Don't you know any mistake could ruin the business?
Nick : Sorry, sir. I will be more careful next time.
Manager : **Work harder or you are about to be fired.**
Nick : Err, I promise I won't do it next time.
Manager : Please keep what you said in mind.

經理：尼克，你為什麼又犯同樣的錯誤了？你不知道任何失誤都可能毀了這筆生意嗎？
尼克：抱歉，長官。我下次會更小心的。
經理：你要更努力，否則就準備被炒魷魚。
尼克：嗯，我保證下次不會了。
經理：請把你說的話牢記在心。

03 文法句型翻譯練習
Sentence Patterns Exercise

請運用上面學到的句型，試著寫出完整的英文句子吧！

01. 穿上外套，要不然你會感冒的。

_____

02. 我們得快點，要不然就沒座位了。

_____

03. 把握機會，要不然你會後悔的。

_____

04. 不許動，否則我開槍。

_____

05. 我們必須同心協力，否則就會失敗。

_____

翻譯練習正確答案：

01. Put on your coat, or you'll catch a cold.

02. We'll have to hurry, otherwise we may not get a seat.

03. Seize the chance, otherwise you'll regret it.

04. Freeze, or I'll shoot.

05. We must pull together, or we will fail.

Day18

Level 3 看到阿豆仔也不用怕！（程度分級：高中第三～六冊）

22 你每天水喝得越多，你就會越健康。

The more water you drink every day, the healthier you will be.

句型 the ＋比較級，the ＋比較級

01 文法句型常用情境說明
Sentence Patterns Introduction

the ＋比較級，the ＋比較級，意為「越……，就越……」，表示一方的程度隨著另一方的變化而變化，其中的兩個 the 都是副詞，而不是冠詞。第一個「the ＋比較級」為條件用法，第二個「the ＋比較級」才是句子強調的部份。整句話表示隨著第一個「the ＋比較級」改變，第二個「the ＋比較級」也隨著改變，強調兩者之間的連動關係。

02 文法句型示範情境會話
Dialogue Practice

情境 1

Writer：When should I hand in the files?
Editor：**The sooner you hand in the files, the better it would be.**
Writer：I will try my best to make it as early as possible. But when is the deadline?
Editor：The end of the month.
Writer：O.K. I get it.

作者：我應該什麼時候交稿？
編輯：你越快交稿，當然越好呀。
作者：我會盡力儘早交稿。但是截止日期是什麼時候呢？

22
你每天水喝得越多，你就會越健康。

編輯： 這個月底。
作者： 好的。我知道了。

情境 2

Carl : Did you read the newspaper today?
David : Not yet. What is it?
Carl : A director was sent to the prison for corruption and bribery.
David : He already had so much. Why did he still do that?
Carl : **Don't you know the more you have, the more you want?**
David : I can't agree more.

卡爾： 你看了今天的報紙了嗎？
大衛： 還沒。怎麼了？
卡爾： 一位局長由於貪污受賄進監獄了。
大衛： 他已經擁有那麼多了。為什麼還那麼做呢？
卡爾： 你不知道擁有的越多，想要的也越多嗎？
大衛： 你說的真好。

情境 3

Husband : Darling, when should we start off tomorrow?
Wife : **The earlier, the better.**
Husband : But I am not sure if I can get up so early.
Wife : Don't worry, honey. I will wake you up.
Husband : Thank you, darling.

丈夫： 親愛的，我們明天要什麼時候出發？
妻子： 越早越好。
丈夫： 但是我不確定我能不能那麼早起。
妻子： 別擔心，親愛的。我會叫你起床的。
丈夫： 謝謝妳，親愛的。

情境 4

Emily : I heard that you are learning piano, Catherine.
Catherine : Yes, I am. I have learned piano for a month, but I still can't play very well.
Emily : Don't give up, Catherine. You just need more practice. **The more you practice, the better you could play.**

Catherine：Thank you very much for encouraging me.

　Emily：Don't mention it.

艾蜜莉：凱薩琳，我聽說妳現在正在學鋼琴。

凱薩琳：沒錯。我已經學一個月了，但還是彈得不是很好。

艾蜜莉：不要放棄，凱薩琳。妳只是需要多練習。妳練得越多，就彈得越好。

凱薩琳：非常謝謝妳鼓勵我。

艾蜜莉：不客氣。

03 文法句型翻譯練習
Sentence Patterns Exercise

請運用上面學到的句型，試著寫出完整的英文句子吧！

01. 這本書我越讀越喜歡。

---

02. 你出發得越早，回來得就越早。

---

03. 你越努力，進步就越快。

---

04. 你練習得越多，理解得就越透徹。

翻譯練習正確答案：

01. The more I read the book, the more I like it.

02. The earlier you start off, the sooner you'll be back.

03. The harder you work, the more progress you'll make.

04. The more you practice, the more thoroughly you can understand.

Level 3　看到阿豆仔也不用怕！（程度分級：高中第三～六冊）

23 我恐怕無法去看女神卡卡的臺北演唱會了。

I'm afraid I can't go to Lady Gaga's concert in Taipei.

句型　**I'm afraid (that) ...**

---

01 文法句型常用情境說明
Sentence Patterns Introduction

I'm afraid (that) ... 意指「我恐怕……」，以關係代名詞 that 引導一個名詞子句，表示以較婉轉的語氣提出異議或拒絕對方請求。關係代名詞 that 引導的名詞子句當受詞，或句中主詞非 that 子句時，均可省略 that。

02 文法句型示範情境會話
Dialogue Practice

情境 1

Jim：Tomorrow will be your birthday. Will your parents come to visit you, Bill?

Bill：Err... **I 'm afraid that they might have forgot it.**

Jim：I don't think so. Maybe they want to give you a surprise.

Bill：I hope so.

吉姆：明天是你的生日。你父母會來看你嗎，比爾？

比爾：嗯……我恐怕他們可能已經忘記我生日了。

吉姆：我不那麼認為。也許他們是想給你一個驚喜吧。

比爾：希望如此。

情境 2

Jessie：Can you help me to solve this math question, Cindy?

Cindy：I am sorry. **I' m afraid I can't help you.** I'm not good at math.
Jessie：That's fine. I will ask someone else for help. Thank you anyway.
Cindy：Don't mention it.

潔西：妳能幫我解這題數學嗎，辛蒂？
辛蒂：很抱歉。恐怕我幫不了妳。我不擅長數學。
潔西：沒關係。我找其他人幫忙好了。還是謝謝妳。
辛蒂：不客氣。

情境 3

Bruce：**I'm afraid I must say goodbye now.** I will miss you all.
Boys：We will, too. Don't forget to write to us.
Bruce：O.K. Goodbye, guys.
Boys：Goodbye, Bruce.

布魯斯：恐怕現在我得和你們說再見了。我會想念你們所有人的。
男孩們：我們也是，不要忘了寫信給我們。
布魯斯：沒問題。大家再見。
男孩們：再見，布魯斯。

情境 4

Student：Good morning, Professor Liu.
Teacher：Good morning.
Student：May I ask you a question, sir?
Teacher：Of course you can.
Student：I wonder if I pass the exam.
Teacher：**I'm afraid you didn't.**

學生：劉教授，早安。
老師：早安。
學生：老師，我能問個問題嗎？
老師：當然可以。
學生：我想知道我這次考試是不是及格了。
老師：恐怕你沒有及格。

03 文法句型翻譯練習
Sentence Patterns Exercise

請運用上面學到的句型,試著寫出完整的英文句子吧!

01. 恐怕我現在得離開了。

_____

02. 恐怕我不能和你一起去。

_____

03. 恐怕我們幫不了你。

_____

04. 恐怕我不同意你的觀點。

_____

05. 我恐怕他沒有足夠的時間。

_____

翻譯練習正確答案:

01. I'm afraid (that) I have to leave now.

02. I'm afraid (that) I couldn't go with you.

03. We are afraid (that) we can't help you.

04. I'm afraid (that) I can't agree with you.

05. I'm afraid (that) he doesn't have enough time.

Day19

24 羅傑・費德勒就是那個打破多項世界網球紀錄的人。

It is Roger Federer who broke many world records of tennis.

句型 **It is / was... that / who...**

01 文法句型常用情境說明
Sentence Patterns Introduction

It is / was... that / who... 此強調句句型常用來強調句子中的某一部分，要加以強調的主詞、動詞、或受詞就放在 be 動詞後面，再接關係代名詞。在這個句型中，以虛主詞 it 代替被強調的成分，並以關係代名詞引導的形容詞子句，去修飾先行詞所強調的部份。如果被強調的部份是表示人的主詞，關係代名詞需用 who 或 that。如果是其他不是表示人的部份，關係代名詞則一律使用 that。

02 文法句型示範情境會話
Dialogue Practice

情境 1

Ricky：Mary, I heard you are going to get married next week. Is it true?
Mary：What? Who told you this?
Ricky：**It is Wendy who is spreading the news.**
Mary：She is just gossiping. I will have a talk with her.

瑞奇：瑪麗，我聽說妳下星期要結婚了。是真的嗎？
瑪麗：什麼？誰告訴你的？
瑞奇：是溫蒂在散布這個消息。
瑪麗：她只是在八卦。我會跟她好好談談。

情境 2

Julie： Who is that hot girl? She is very pretty.
Kate： The girl in red skirt? It is Catherine.
Julie： Catherine? Is she Ricky's ex-girlfriend?
Kate： Yes. **It is she who broke up with Ricky a few days ago.**

茱麗：那個辣妹是誰呀？她真漂亮。
凱特：那個穿紅裙子的女孩？那是凱薩琳。
茱麗：凱薩琳？她是瑞奇的前女友？
凱特：是的。就是她前幾天和瑞奇分手。

情境 3

　Teacher： Can anybody tell me who broke this window?
Class leader： **It is Jack who broke the window.**
　Teacher： O.K. Please ask him to come to my office after school.
Class leader： Yes, sir.

老師：誰能告訴我是誰把窗戶打破了？
班長：是傑克把窗戶打破的。
老師：很好。請叫他放學後到我辦公室來。
班長：好的，老師。

情境 4

　Tina： Who makes the decisions in your family, George?
George： Most of the time, **it is my mom who makes the decision.** But some important decisions are made by my dad.
　Tina： My dad makes the final decision in my family.
George： That's not strange at all.

蒂娜：喬治，你們家是誰做決定？
喬治：大部分是我媽做決定。但是有些重要的事是我爸決定。
蒂娜：我家是我爸做最終的決定。
喬治：這一點也不奇怪。

---

03 文法句型翻譯練習
Sentence Patterns Exercise

請運用上面學到的句型，試著寫出完整的英文句子吧！

01. 我是去年夏天學會游泳的。

_____

02. 她們是三點鐘回來的。

_____

03. 是他問話的方式讓我很心煩。

_____

04. 他們的會議是明天要開。

_____

05. 那個老太太就是在銀行前面被搶劫的。

_____

翻譯練習正確答案：

01. It was last summer that I learned to swim.

02. It was three o'clock that they came back.

03. It was the way he asked that really made me upset.

04. It is tomorrow that they will have a meeting.

05. It was in front of the bank that the old lady was robbed.

25 這很明顯是裁判誤判了。

It is obvious that the judge made a mistake.

句型 **It is obvious / clear that...**

01 文法句型常用情境說明
Sentence Patterns Introduction

It is obvious / clear that... 意思為「很明顯 / 清楚……」，此句型中 it 是虛主詞，用來代替由 that 引導的名詞子句。這個句型也是強調句的一種，用來強調後面名詞子句的「很明顯 / 清楚……」的含意。

02 文法句型示範情境會話
Dialogue Practice

情境 1

Eric : Oh, that's too bad. We failed again, Philip.
Philip : **It is obvious that we must try something else.**
Eric : I can't agree more. I don't want to fail once again.
Philip : Let's discuss with others.
Eric : O.K. Let's go.

艾瑞克：噢，真糟糕。我們又失敗了，菲力普。
菲力普：很顯然我們必須試試其他方法。
艾瑞克：我非常同意。我不想再失敗了。
菲力普：讓我們和其他人討論一下吧。
艾瑞克：好的。走吧。

情境 2

Wife : It smells really bad, honey. Can't you give up smoking? **It is obvious that smoking is harmful to health.**

Husband : Darling, I want to quit smoking, too. But it is really hard.
　　Wife : I can help you.
Husband : Thank you, darling.

　妻子：真是太難聞了，親愛的。你就不能戒菸嗎？很明顯吸菸是有害健康的。
　丈夫：親愛的，我也想戒煙。可是真的太難了。
　妻子：我可以幫你。
　丈夫：親愛的，謝謝妳。

情境 3

Husband : **It is clear that our daughter wants to learn dancing.**
　　　　　Why don't you agree?
　　Wife : I think studying is the most important thing for her as a student.
Husband : She can have some hobbies for fun.
　　Wife : That's true. But she must study hard first.
Husband : I think she can have hobbies and studies at the same time.
　　Wife : I can't agree no matter how.
Husband : You are too stubborn.

　丈夫：很明顯我們的女兒想學跳舞。為什麼妳不同意呢？
　妻子：我認為她身為學生，念書才是最重要的事。
　丈夫：她可以有自己的休閒興趣。
　妻子：是這樣沒錯。但是她還是應該先好好念書。
　丈夫：我認為她可以同時擁有學習和娛樂。
　妻子：不管怎樣，我就是不同意。
　丈夫：妳太固執了。

情境 4

Susan : I guess that doctor is the killer in the movie.
　Paul : No, no, no, you're wrong. **It is obvious that the young girl is the**
　　　　killer.
Susan : Oh, really?
　Paul : Of course. I bet that it is her.
Susan : O.K. Let's wait for the ending.

蘇珊：我猜那個醫生是這部電影當中的殺手。
保羅：不、不、不，妳錯了。很明顯，那個年輕女孩是殺手。
蘇珊：噢，真的嗎？
保羅：當然。我敢斷定就是她。
蘇珊：好吧。讓我們等著看結局吧。

情境 5

Ben : Oh, my god. Where is my mobile phone? Did you see my mobile phone, Ann?
Ann : Yes, I think it is in your yellow bag.
Ben : Oh, thank you very much. I can't live without it.
Ann : **It's clear that nowadays mobile phones play a very important role in our daily life.**
Ben : I can't agree more.

班：噢，我的天。我的手機在哪裡？妳有看到我的手機嗎，安？
安：嗯，我想它在你黃色包包裡。
班：噢，太感謝妳了。沒有它我活不了。
安：很明顯，手機在我們現在的日常生活中扮演著很重要的角色。
班：我非常同意。

03 文法句型翻譯練習
Sentence Patterns Exercise

請運用上面學到的句型，試著寫出完整的英文句子吧！

01. 很明顯，她在臺上非常緊張。

---

02. 很明顯，月球上沒有生物。

---

03. 很明顯他在說謊。

---

04. 很明顯，他是我們班上最好的學生。

05. 新來的業務很顯然地不能勝任他的工作。

04 延伸句型加分學習
Learning Plus!

It seems / seemed (that) 看起來好像……

- 1. 此句型由虛主詞 it 代替由 that 引導的名詞子句當主詞置於句首，用以強調「看起來好像……」。又或者可以用 as if 代替 that。

- 2. 如果與事實不相符合，則用過去式動詞表示虛擬語氣。例如：

  It seems (that) he was late for the train.
  看起來他好像趕不上火車了。

- 3. It is / was said (reported / hoped) that...「據說 / 據報導 / 據悉……」由虛主詞 it 代替由 that 引導的名詞子句。

  It is said that the food in this supermarket is cheaper.
  據說超市的食物更便宜。

翻譯練習正確答案：

01. It is obvious that she was terribly nervous on the stage.

02. It is clear that there is no life on the moon.

03. It is clear that he is lying.

04. It is obvious that he is the best student in our class.

05. It is obvious that the new salesman is incompetent with his job.

Level 3 看到阿豆仔也不用怕！（程度分級：高中第三～六冊）

26 這部電影實在太精彩了，所以大家都在討論它。

This is such a good movie that everyone is talking about it.

句型 **such... that...**

---

01 文法句型常用情境說明
Sentence Patterns Introduction

- 1. so / such... that... 的意思是「如此……所以……」常用來表示兩者間的因果關係。由 so 修飾形容詞或副詞，或以 such 修飾名詞，可強調與其後 that 子句間的關係。

  Jane loves movies so much that she goes to the movies more than three times every week.（珍是如此地喜歡電影，所以她每週看三次以上的電影。）

- 2. 在 such... that... 句型中，such 修飾名詞，但名詞前 many（很多，可數）、much（很多，不可數）、(a) few（一些，可數）、(a) little（一些，不可數）等形容詞時，要使用副詞 so 來修飾，因此要用「so... that...」而不能用「such... that...」。

  It is such a cute kitty that everyone loves it.
  （牠是這樣可愛的一隻貓咪，所以人人都愛牠。）

02 文法句型示範情境會話
Dialogue Practice

情境 1

Vivian： I have seen the National Geographic Channel, **in which people speak English so fast that I could hardly understand.** There are so many new words for me.

Betty： Don't worry. You can try to learn more about the topic.

薇薇安：我已經看了國家地理頻道了，裡面的人英文説得太快了，所以我幾乎聽不
　　　　懂。而且對我來説有好多不認識的單字。
　　貝蒂：不要擔心。妳可以試著多了解其主題。

情境 2

Jimmy : What do you think of Dr. Smith?
Catherine : You mean your neighbor, Dr. Smith?
Jimmy : Yes.
Catherine : He has made a donation of fifty hundred thousand dollars to
　　　　　　the Childcare Foundation. **He is such a selfless man that**
　　　　　　everybody respects him.

　吉米：妳覺得史密斯醫生怎麼樣？
凱薩琳：你是説你的鄰居史密斯醫生嗎？
　吉米：是的。
凱薩琳：他剛捐給兒童關懷基金會一筆 50 萬的捐款。他是如此無私的人，所以
　　　　大家都尊敬他。

情境 3

Donna : **Jessie, I am so nervous that I'm afraid I can say nothing in**
　　　　front of the interviewer.
Jessie : Take it easy. Believe in yourself, Donna.
Donna : Thank you, Jessie. I feel better now.

　唐娜：潔西，我好緊張，所以我怕我在面試官面前會什麼也説不出來。
　潔西：放輕鬆。對自己要有信心，唐娜。
　唐娜：謝謝妳，潔西。我現在感覺好多了。

情境 4

Tina : Jack, can you give me a hand? **This is such a heavy desk that I**
　　　　can't move it.
Jack : No problem. It is really too heavy for a girl to move.
Tina : Thank you so much.
Jack : You're welcome.

　蒂娜：傑克，你能幫我一下嗎？這個桌子是如此的重，所以我搬不動它。
　傑克：沒問題。對一個女孩子來説，這個桌子的確太重了。

蒂娜：真的很謝謝你。
傑克：不客氣。

03 文法句型翻譯練習
Sentence Patterns Exercise

請運用上面學到的句型，試著寫出完整的英文句子吧！

01. 那幅畫是那樣好看，所以大家都喜歡它。

02. 有這麼多的事要做，所以大家都覺得厭煩了。

03. 這電影很有趣，所以我看了兩次。

04. 他年紀太小了，所以不能照顧自己。

05. 她進步得如此多，所以老師們對她感到很滿意。

翻譯練習正確答案：

01. The picture is so beautiful that everyone likes it.

02. There was so much work to do that everybody got bored.

03. It was such an interesting film that I have seen it twice.

04. He is so young that he can't take care of himself.

05. She has made such great progress that the teachers are very pleased with her.

Day21

27 你最好趁夏天來之前開始減肥。

You had better begin to lose weight
before summer comes.

句型 You had / You'd + better (not)…

---

01 文法句型常用情境說明
Sentence Patterns Introduction

- 1. You had better (not)... / You'd better (not) ... 是指「你最好做 / 不做……」，後接原形動詞。
- 2. 句中的 had better 是固定片語用法，不隨時式做變化，否定句就直接在後面加 not，用 had better not 後接原形動詞來表示否定。
- 3. 此句型用來表示對別人的勸告、建議或一種願望。

02 文法句型示範情境會話
Dialogue Practice

情境 1

Ken : What's wrong with you, Tim? You look pale.
Tim : I have a stomachache.
Ken : **You'd better go to see a doctor.**
Tim : I will go after work.
Ken : **I think you'd better go now.**
Tim : Then, can you help me to ask for a day off?
Ken : No problem.

　肯： 你怎麼了，提姆？你看起來臉色好蒼白。
提姆： 我胃痛。
　肯： 你最好去看醫生。
提姆： 我下班後再去。
　肯： 我想你最好現在就去。

提姆： 那你可以幫我請假嗎？
　肯： 沒問題。

情境 2

Joy : Kate, I find you are a little chubbier than before.
Kate : Really? Oh, that's too bad.
Joy : Summer is coming. **You'd better watch your diet, Kate.**
Kate : I need to exercise more from now on.

喬伊： 凱特，我覺得妳比以前胖了點。
凱特： 真的嗎？噢，太糟糕了。
喬伊： 夏天要來了，妳最好注意妳的飲食。
凱特： 我從現在起要多運動了！

情境 3

Mother : It is cold outside. **You'd better put on more clothes .**
Son : Thank you, Mom. But I have worn a lot.
Mother : Anyway, take care of yourself.
Son : O.K. Mom.

媽媽： 外面很冷。你最好多穿點衣服。
兒子： 謝謝媽。但是我已經穿很多了。
媽媽： 總之要照顧自己，兒子。
兒子： 好的，媽媽。

情境 4

Steven : Excuse me, could you please tell me how to get to the Museum?
Passer-by : It's far from here. **You'd better go by taxi.**
Steven : O.K. Thank you.
Passer-by : Not at all.

史蒂芬： 不好意思，你能告訴我怎麼去博物館嗎？
　路人： 博物館離這裡很遠。你最好搭計程車去。
史蒂芬： 好的，謝謝。
　路人： 不客氣。

情境 5

Mike： **You'd better prepare for the examination, Matt.**
Matt： I don't think the exam will be very difficult for me.
Mike： **You'd better change your attitude, or you will fail.**
Matt： Maybe you're right. I have been too lazy lately.

麥克：你最好為考試做做準備，麥特。
麥特：我覺得這次考試對我來說不會很難。
麥克：你最好改變這種態度，不然你會被當掉。
麥特：也許你說得對。最近我一直太懶散了。

03 文法句型翻譯練習
Sentence Patterns Exercise

請運用上面學到的句型，試著寫出完整的英文句子吧！

01. 已經晚了。你該回家了。

_____

02. 你最好早點睡覺，要不然你明天會上學遲到。

_____

03. 你仔細考慮一下。

_____

04. 你最好安靜點。

_____

05. 你最好不要錯過末班公車。

_____

04 延伸句型加分學習
Learning Plus!

be (not) supposed to... 應該……

- 1. be supposed to... 其後接原形動詞。當主詞是「人」時，意為「應該……」、「被期望……」，用來表示勸告、建議、義務、責任等，相當於助動詞 should（應該）。例如：

  You are supposed to support your parents.（你應該撫養你的父母。）

- 2. be supposed to... 的主詞是「物」時，表示「本應……；本該……」，表示「某事本應該發生而沒有發生」。例如：

  The bus was supposed to arrive half an hour ago.
  （公共汽車本應在半小時之前到達。）

- 3. 當 be supposed to... 後面接「have ＋過去分詞」時，表示「應該已經做某事，卻沒做……」。如：

  He is supposed to have arrived an hour ago.（他應該一小時前就到了。）

- 4. be supposed to... 也可以以虛主詞 it 當主詞，其後接以 that 引導的名詞子句，表示「某事應該……」。例如：

  It is supposed that we should all love our country.
  （我們都應該要愛我們的國家。）

翻譯練習正確答案：

01. It's late. You'd better go home.

02. You'd better go to bed earlier or you will be late for school tomorrow.

03. You'd better think it over.

04. You'd better be quiet.

05. You'd better not miss the last bus.

Day21

28 就算要排隊等一個小時 我也要買到這間店的甜甜圈。

Even though I have to wait for an hour,
I still want to buy donuts from this shop.

句型 **Even though; Even if...**

---

01 文法句型常用情境說明
Sentence Patterns Introduction

- 1. Even though 與 Even if 均為連接詞，意思為「雖然」、「即使」。Even if 所連接的子句為推想的條件，因此需用假設語氣，以現在式動詞代替未來式。例如：

  Even if it rains, the carnival will not be canceled.
  （即使下雨，嘉年華會不會被取消。）→未必會下雨，但怎樣都不會取消

- 2. Even if 的句型中含有強烈的假定性，所引導的是把握不大或者假設的事情；而 even though 引出的則是確定的既成事實。

  Even though it rained, the carnival was not canceled.
  （雖然下雨，嘉年華會也沒有被取消。）→確定有下雨，且確定沒有取消。

02 文法句型示範情境會話
Dialogue Practice

情境 1

　　Emily：It rains heavily outside. Will your brother come?
Catherine：**He will come on time even though it rains.**

艾蜜莉：外面雨下很大。妳哥哥會來嗎？
凱薩琳：即使下雨，他還是會準時來的。

情境 2

Carl : What's the result? Did you win the soccer game yesterday, David?

David : **We lost the game even though we tried our best.**

Carl : Oh, what a pity. Don't be sad. Keep going!

David : Thanks.

卡爾：結果怎麼樣？你們昨天足球賽贏了嗎，大衛？

大衛：雖然我們盡力了，我們還是輸了。

卡爾：哦，太可惜了。別難過。繼續加油。

大衛：謝謝。

情境 3

Sam : I don't like Sophia.

Tracy : Why not? She is such a good girl.

Sam : **She always sticks to what she thinks is right, even though she is wrong.**

Tracy : Yes, she is little bit stubborn. But she is still a good girl.

山姆：我不喜歡蘇菲亞。

崔西：為什麼不？她是那麼好的一個女孩。

山姆：她總是堅持她認為對的事，即使那根本是錯的。

崔西：是的，她是有點固執。但她還是個好女孩。

情境 4

Simon : Tomorrow will be Bob's birthday. Did he invite you to his party?

Frank : **No, even if I was invited, I wouldn't go.**

Simon : Hmm..., I don't want to go, neither.

西蒙：明天是鮑伯的生日。他有邀請你去他的派對嗎？

法蘭克：沒有，即使我受邀了，我也不會去。

西蒙：嗯……，我也不想去。

情境 5

Betty : Look at this photo. The people look so happy in it. Where did you take this photo?

Susan : I took this photo in the mountains. **People there are always smiling even if they are very poor.**

Betty : Woo, I like these simple, optimistic, and kind-hearted people.

貝蒂：噢，看這張照片。裡面的人看起來很幸福。妳在哪裡拍這張照片的？
蘇珊：我在山裡照的。住在那裡的人總是一直保持笑容。即使他們很窮。
貝蒂：哇，我喜歡這些純樸、樂觀、又善良的人們。

03 文法句型翻譯練習
Sentence Patterns Exercise

請運用上面學到的句型，試著寫出完整的英文句子吧！

01. 即使你不會成功，他們也會支持你。

_____

02. 即使明天下雨，我們也絕不改變計畫。

_____

03. 雖然工作艱苦，我還是很喜歡。

_____

04. 即使我們在工作中取得了好成績，也不應該驕傲。

_____

05. 雖然他知道這個秘密，但他不會洩漏出去。

_____

翻譯練習正確答案：

01. They will stand by you even if you don't succeed.

02. Even if it rains tomorrow, we won't change our plan.

03. Even though it's hard work, I enjoy it a lot.

04. Even if we achieve great success in our work, we should not be proud.

05. Even though he knows the secret, he won't let it out.

Level 3　看到阿豆仔也不用怕！（程度分級：高中第三〜六冊）

29　我媽要我打掃房間。
My mother had me clean the room.

句型　have ＋ O ＋原形 V（主動時）/ P.P.（被動時）...

01 文法句型常用情境說明
Sentence Patterns Introduction

• 1. 動詞 have 可為使役動詞，表命令、要求或指使之意，其後接原形動詞，常用句型為「have ＋人＋原形動詞」，意思為「讓某人做某事」。

• 2. 比起另一個使役動詞 make，have 的用法較為委婉、客氣，而 make 則通常帶有「逼使、強迫」的硬性含意。例如：

Our teacher made us clean the toilet.（我們老師叫我們去掃廁所。）

• 3. 若要表示被動，如「讓某人 / 某事被……」，則在使役動詞 have 及 make 句型中，受詞後面的動詞要使用過去分詞。例如：

The police had the thief arrested.
（警方讓那個小偷被逮捕了。→警方逮捕了小偷。）

02 文法句型示範情境會話
Dialogue Practice

情境 1

Ricky：Why can't you play basketball with us?

Nick：**My mother had me clean the room. I need to have my room cleaned** before she comes back.

瑞奇：你為什麼不能跟我們一起打籃球呢？

尼克：我媽要我打掃房間。我得在她回來之前把房間打掃好。

情境 2

Gary： Mr. Chen, **would you have someone fix the faucet?** It's been leaking for two days.

Mr. Chen： OK. OK. **I'll have it fixed today.**

蓋瑞： 陳先生，你能不能找人把水龍頭修一下？已經漏水兩天了。

陳先生： 好的好的。我今天會把它修好。

情境 3

Carl： This work is an urgent. It needs to be done by five o'clock today.

Helen： **In that case, I'll have the team work on it right now.**

卡爾： 這項工作是急件。要在今天 5 點之前做好。

海倫： 那樣的話，我會讓大家現在馬上就開始做這件事。

情境 4

Jennifer： Hey, Tom. What's new?

Tom： I'm thinking to job-hop. **My boss always has me work overtime without giving me overtime pay.**

珍妮佛： 嘿，湯姆。有什麼新鮮事嗎？

湯姆： 我打算要換工作了。我老闆老是要我加班，卻不給加班費。

情境 5

Mark： Cindy is not at home now. Do you want to leave her a message?

Catherine： Yes. Please tell her that Catherine had called.

Mark： OK. **I'll let her know and have her call you back.**

Catherine： Thank you.

馬克： 辛蒂現在不在家。你要留言給她嗎？

凱瑟琳： 好，請告訴她凱瑟琳有打來。

馬克： 沒問題。我會讓她知道並叫她回電。

凱瑟琳： 謝謝你。

03 文法句型翻譯練習
Sentence Patterns Exercise

請運用上面學到的句型，試著寫出完整的英文句子吧！

01. 我的上司派我到機場去接布朗先生。

_____

02. 瑪莉要珍妮在她出門時幫她照顧孩子們。

_____

03. 灰姑娘的繼母要她做所有的家事。

_____

04. 你可以找人來幫我搬這些書嗎？

_____

05. 媽媽要我在晚飯後洗碗。

_____

翻譯練習正確答案：

01. My supervisor had me pick up Mr. Brown at the airport.

02. Mary had Jennie babysit her kids for her while she was away.

03. Cinderella's stepmother had her do all the housework.

04. Could you have someone carry these books for me?

05. Mom had me do the dishes after dinner.

Day22

30 不管發生什麼事，我都一定會支持我的家人。

No matter what happens, I will support my family.

句型 **no matter ＋疑問詞 ...**

01 文法句型常用情境說明
Sentence Patterns Introduction

No matter 意為「不管、無論……」，連接詞，其後接疑問詞 what（什麼）、which（哪一個）、who（誰）、whom（誰→受詞）、where（哪裡）、whose（誰的）、when（何時）、how（如何），由這些關係代名詞引導的副詞子句，作為強調的部分。例如：

No matter where you go, I will go with you.
（無論你去哪裡，我都跟你去。）
No matter whose bag it is, we should give it back.
（無論這是誰的袋子，我們都應該要還回去。）
No matter how bad the weather is, we are going to Kaohsiung.
（無論天氣有多糟，我們都會去高雄。）

02 文法句型示範情境會話
Dialogue Practice

情境 1

Wendy : I think Mr. Bruce doesn't like me.
　Mary : Why do you say so?
Wendy : **No matter how hard I try, he always picks my fault with my work.**
　Mary : Hmm..., I suppose that he just has a high expectation on you.
Wendy : Oh, really? I hope so.

溫蒂：我想布魯斯先生不喜歡我。
瑪麗：為什麼這麼說呢？
溫蒂：無論我多麼努力，他總是挑剔我的工作。
瑪麗：嗯……我認為他只是對妳期望太高了。
溫蒂：哦，真的嗎？希望如此呀。

情境 2

Wife : Honey, thank you for helping me get through all these.
Husband : Oh, sweet heart. **No matter what happens, you know I will always be there for you.**
Wife : Thank you very much. I will always love you, honey.
Husband : So will I.

妻子：親愛的，謝謝你陪著我度過了這一切。
丈夫：噢，甜心。無論發生什麼事，妳知道我都會在你身邊陪妳的。
妻子：真謝謝你。我會永遠愛你，親愛的。
丈夫：我也是。

情境 3

Daughter : Dad, I am going to lose my mind. **Things just don't go right, no matter how hard I try.**
Dad : Life is no plain sailing. **So just be yourself and keep on going no matter what happens.** You know I always have faith in you.

女兒：爸爸，我真的快要崩潰了。不管我怎麼努力，事情總是不順利。
爸爸：人生的道路並非總是一帆風順。所以不管發生什麼，只要做好妳自己，繼續前進就可以了。妳知道我一直對妳很有信心。

情境 4

Blair : **Don't trust Alice, no matter what she says.** She is a liar.
Joy : A liar? Why do you say that?
Blair : She has lied to me for several times. Whenever I forgive her, she lies again.
Joy : Oh, I see.

布萊爾：不管愛麗絲說什麼，都不要相信她。她是個騙子。
喬伊：騙子？為什麼你這麼說呢？

布萊爾：她已經跟我說了好幾次謊。每當我原諒她，她就又說謊了。
喬伊：哦，我知道了。

03 文法句型翻譯練習
Sentence Patterns Exercise

請運用上面學到的句型，試著寫出完整的英文句子吧！

01. 不管事情會變怎樣，我們都應當盡最大努力。

_____

02. 不管你是誰，你都無權那麼做。

_____

03. 不管你做什麼，千萬不要失去自我。

_____

04. 不論你在哪裡，都得遵守法律。

_____

05. 不管要花多長時間，都要堅持下去。

_____

翻譯練習正確答案：

01. No matter what will turn out, we should do our best.

02. No matter who you are, you have no right to do that.

03. No matter what you do, never lose yourself.

04. No matter where you are, you must obey the law.

05. No matter how long it takes, just hang in there.

單字陷阱．
一字多義使用篇

文法陷阱．
文法觀念辨析篇

第三階段：Day 23~30

40 個不能不閃的文法陷阱

文法陷阱．
文法使用差異篇

單字陷阱．
類義單字辨析篇

01 ago vs. before

01 文法使用錯誤範例
Sample of Wrong Grammar

> A: Kate, come here quickly. This is your favorite TV show. I'm sure you don't want to miss it.
> 凱特，快過來。這是妳最喜歡的電視節目，我想妳一定不想錯過。
>
> B: Never mind. I have watched it two days ago（✗）→ before（○）
> 沒關係，我兩天前就看過了。

02 文法誤用詳細解析
Grammar Analysis

ago 和 before 當作副詞均表「在⋯⋯（時間）之前」，但兩者的內涵及用法都有相當明顯的區別；另外，before 可當作介系詞或連接詞使用，ago 則否。詳見說明：

（1-1）ago 用來表示從現在推往過去的某一個「時間點」，通常與「過去式」連用，不與完成式連用，並且不可單獨使用，通常置於表時間的詞之後。例如：

This accident just happened 5 minutes ago.（這場意外就發生在五分鐘之前。）
過去簡單式 + ago → 表示過去單一時間點

（1-2）然而當 ago 用於表示推測的句子，或配合上下文脈絡用來加強語氣，使句子更生動呈現「早已經」的意思時，口語上也有與完成式連用的情形。例如：

You might have heard this song years ago.（你可能好幾年前就聽過這首歌。）
過去完成式 + ago → 加強語氣

（2-1）before 則是表示從過去某一個時間點往前推算，或者泛指過去（沒有搭配明確的時間點），通常與「過去完成式」或「未來完成式」連用。例如：

Tommy said that he had already finished his project 2 days before.
（湯米說他兩天前就已經完成了這個專案。）→ 從過去（兩天前）往前推算。

（2-2）若是事件發生在過去，但沒有特定的時間點，則可單獨使用 before，不須連接時間副詞，用來泛指「過去／從前」的時態，例如：

Have I met you before?（我以前見過你嗎？）→ 泛指以前，沒有特定時間點。

03 文法使用誤用辨析
Grammar Error vs. Correct

01. 你以前看過貓熊嗎？
    ❌ Have you ever seen a panda ago?
    ⭕ **Have you ever seen a panda before?**

02. 佩妮會在十點之前回來。
    ❌ Penny will come back ten o'clock ago.
    ⭕ **Penny will come back before ten o'clock.**

03. 愛琳娜說她跟丹尼五年前就已經結婚了。
    ❌ Elena said that she had married Danny five years ago.
    ⭕ **Elena said that she had married Danny five years before.**

04. 布朗先生以前在這所學校教英語。
    ❌ Mr. Brown has taught English in this school ago.
    ⭕ **Mr. Brown has taught English in this school before.**

05. 瑪麗的奶奶三年前就去世了。
    ❌ Mary's grandma died three years before.
    ⭕ **Mary's grandma died three years ago.**

06. 其實我很早以前就認識那個人了。
    ❌ Actually, I heard of that man long a time before.
    ⭕ **Actually, I have known that man long time ago.**

04 文法陷阱辨析練習
Grammar Practice

請選出題目選項中正確的用法。

01. He asked me whether I had been to Paris _____.
Ⓐ ago   Ⓑ before   Ⓒ after

02. The young man told us that he had become a journalist and worked in a leading newspapers 2 years _____.
Ⓐ after   Ⓑ ago   Ⓒ before

03. The old man _____ here ten years before I was born.
Ⓐ has been   Ⓑ having been   Ⓒ have been

04. I hope I'll finish my homework _____.
Ⓐ ten o'clock before   Ⓑ ten o'clock ago   Ⓒ before ten o'clock

05. Jamie has never been late _____.
Ⓐ after   Ⓑ ago   Ⓒ before

06. Lisa, there is a letter for you. It arrived a few days _____.
Ⓐ before   Ⓑ ago   Ⓒ after

07. I _____ such beautiful scenery before I arrived in Hawaii.
Ⓐ never saw   Ⓑ had never seen   Ⓒ has never seen

答案及題目中譯：

01. Ⓑ	他問我以前有沒有去過巴黎。
02. Ⓒ	那位年輕人告訴我們，他在兩年前成了一位記者，並且任職於一家具領導性的報社。
03. Ⓐ	在我出生前十年，這位老先生就在這裡了。
04. Ⓒ	我希望在十點以前我可以完成我的作業。
05. Ⓒ	潔米以前從來沒有遲到過。
06. Ⓑ	麗莎，那邊有一封妳的信。幾天前就已經寄到了。
07. Ⓑ	在我來到夏威夷之前，我從來沒有看過這麼美麗的景色。

02 any vs. some

01 文法使用錯誤範例
Sample of Wrong Grammar

A: Did you take some(✕) pictures when you spent your holiday in New York? → any(○)
你在紐約度假時有拍任何照片嗎？

B: Yes, I took some. Here they are.
有啊，我拍了。在這裡。

02 文法誤用詳細解析
Grammar Analysis

some, any 這兩個形容詞都可以用來修飾可數名詞與不可數名詞，表示「一些」的概念，但兩者的用法不同，請見以下說明：

（1）some 常用在肯定句中，意為「一些」，可修飾可數名詞的複數形態，例如：some desks（一些桌子）；也可用來修飾不可數名詞，例如：some ink（一些墨水）。

（2）any 則常用在否定和疑問句，意為「任何」，可以用來修飾可數名詞或不可數名詞，常用於疑問句和否定句，例如：
There are not any apples left.（沒有剩下任何蘋果了。）

（3）上述範例 A 為疑問句，一般疑問句常用 any，不用 some，除非是如 (4) 所示的例外，在 if 假設句中也常用 any 或 anything。例如：

If anything goes wrong, just let me know.（若出任何狀況，就要讓我知道。）
There are few, if any, mistakes in the book.（書中即便有錯，也錯得不多。）

但也可見 if 句型中用 some。例如：

Please call me if you need some / any help.（若需一些／任何協助，請打給我。）

（4）除上述一般情況以外，還需要注意以下幾種特殊情況：

（4-1）建議、反問和請求的疑問句中，或期望得到肯定回答時，多用 some 例如：
　　　 What about some orange juice?（要不要喝點柳橙汁？）
　　　 → 期望對方喝柳橙汁。

（4-2）當 any 表示「任何」時，為強調語法，可以用於肯定句中。例如：
　　　 Any student can use this map.（強調：任何學生都可以使用這張地圖。）
　　　 A : Juice, tea or coffee?（要果汁、茶還是咖啡？）
　　　 B : Any will do.（任何一個都可以。）→ 表「隨便」之意。

（4-3）遇到含有否定意義的動詞，形容詞、副詞、介詞時要用 any，而不用 some，
　　　 如：deny（拒絕）、prevent（防止）、unwise（不睿智的）、unaware（沒
　　　 察覺到的）、hardly（幾乎不地）、seldom;（不常地）、without（沒有）、
　　　 against（與……對立）等。

（4-4）否定句如要表達完全否定，用 any。要表達部分否定，則用 some。例如：
　　　 I don't need any help.（我不需要任何幫助。）→ 完全否定。
　　　 Some files are not on my desk.（有些檔案不在我桌上。）
　　　 → 部分否定，只有一部分不在我桌上。

03 文法使用誤用辨析
Grammar Error vs. Correct

01. 你要不要來點咖啡？
　　 ❌ Would you like any coffee?
　　 ⭕ **Would you like some coffee?**

---

02. 那邊有很多小孩子在跟我打招呼，但是他們中間有幾個我不認識。
　　 ❌ There are plenty of children saying hello to me, but I don't know any of them.
　　 ⭕ **There are plenty of children saying hello to me, but I don't know some of them.**

---

03. 他不是一個誠實的人，因為他否認我曾幫過他任何忙。
　　 ❌ He is not an honest person, because he denied I had offered him some help.
　　 ⭕ **He is not an honest person, because he denied I had offered him any help.**

04. 由於工作太繁忙，我幾乎沒有時間出去旅遊了。

　　☒ I have hardly some time to travel because of the busy work.

　　☑ **I have hardly** any **time to travel because of the busy work.**

---

05. 傑克被他的老闆毫不猶豫地開除了，因為他老是犯錯。

　　☒ Jake was fired by his boss without some hesitation, because he had always made mistakes.

　　☑ **Jake was fired by his boss without** any **hesitation, because he had always made mistakes.**

---

06. 瑪麗在學校有一些朋友，但是在辦公室裡沒有朋友。

　　☒ Mary has some friends at school, but she doesn't have some in the office.

　　☑ **Mary has some friends at school, but she doesn't have** any **in the office.**

04 文法陷阱辨析練習
Grammar Practice

請選出題目選項中正確的用法。

01. Tom is a cleaver boy and he can answer the teacher's questions without _____ difficulty, but Linda answers those questions with _____ difficulty.

　　Ⓐ any; some　　　　Ⓑ any; any　　　　Ⓒ some; any

02. She's too young to do _____ work.

　　Ⓐ some　　　　Ⓑ much　　　　Ⓒ any

03. _____ staff of the company can use this printer.

　　Ⓐ Much　　　　Ⓑ Some　　　　Ⓒ Any

04. A: Do you _____ water in the barrel?
　　 B: No, I don't have _____ left.

　　Ⓐ some; any　　　　Ⓑ any; any　　　　Ⓒ some; some

05. A: There were many people in your brother's birthday party.
Do you know them all?
B: No. I don't know _____ one of them.

A some   **B** the   **C** any

06. The expression on Sid's face told everyone that it was unwise to ask him _____ questions.

A some   **B** any   **C** much

07. He said, "I'll try my best to prevent _____ loss."

A any   **B** much   **C** some

08. Would you please give me _____ red ink?

A much   **B** some   **C** any

09. A: Are there _____ convenience stores near here?
B: No, there are _____ any convenience stores near here.

A some; not   **B** any; no   **C** any; not

答案及題目中譯：

01. **A**	湯姆是個聰明的男孩，他可以毫無困難地回答老師的問題，但是琳達回答問題卻有一些困難。	
02. **C**	她太年輕，沒能力做任何工作。	
03. **C**	公司裡的任何員工都可以使用這台印表機。	
04. **B**	A：你桶裡還有水嗎？ B：沒有了，我一點水都不剩了。	
05. **C**	A：你哥哥生日派對上有好多人，你全部都認識嗎？ B：不，我一個人都不認識。	
06. **B**	席德的表情告訴大家，問他任何問題都是不睿智的。	
07. **A**	他說：「我會盡全力去避免任何損失。」	
08. **B**	你可以給我一些紅墨水嗎？	
09. **C**	A：附近有任何一家便利商店嗎？ B：沒有，這附近一家便利商店都沒有。	

Trap 1 單字陷阱・類義單字辨析篇

03 asleep vs. sleepy

---

01 文法使用錯誤範例
Sample of Wrong Grammar

A: Linda, why do you look so asleep（✗）？ → sleepy（○）
琳達，為何妳看起來那麼睏？

B: Because I didn't fall sleepy（✗）until 23:30 last night. → asleep（○）
因為我昨晚到 23:30 才睡著。

02 文法誤用詳細解析
Grammar Analysis

asleep 與 sleepy 均為「sleep」的形容詞，兩者在用法上有所區別，請見以下說明：

（1）asleep 一般當主詞補語，指「睡著的」，強調狀態，指處於睡著的狀態，側重動作的結果。不能單獨放在名詞前作前位定語，但有時卻可放在名詞後作後置定語。需要注意的是，「睡得很熟；睡得很香」常用「fast / sound asleep」表示，而不說「very asleep」。

「be asleep」是指「睡著」的狀態，意為「睡著的」；如果表示「入睡」的意味，要用「fall asleep」，意為「剛剛入睡」，指「剛睡著」這動作。

（2）sleepy 常指人昏昏欲睡，或沉睡時的寂靜狀態，可當作補語，意為「睏倦的；想睡覺的」。片語 feel sleepy 表示「昏昏欲睡的、想睡覺的」。

　　範例中，A 所說的「Why do you look so asleep?」想要表達的意思是「你為什麼看起來這麼睏？」此處的「睏」指的是「睏倦的」，如上所述，asleep 應改為 sleepy；B 想要表達的意思是「23：30 才睡著」，此處的「睡著」是指「剛剛入睡」，如上所述，fall sleepy 應改為 fall asleep。因此整個例句正確的說法應為：

A: Linda, why do you look so sleepy?
B: Because I didn't fall asleep until 23:30 last night.

03 文法使用誤用辨析
Grammar Error vs. Correct

01. 我爺爺睡著了。
　　❌ My grandpa has fallen sleepy.
　　⭕ **My grandpa has fallen asleep.**

02. 我很累，想睡覺了。
　　❌ I'm very tired and I feel asleep.
　　⭕ **I'm very tired and I feel sleepy.**

03. 莉莉還在睡覺嗎？
　　❌ Is Lily still sleepy?
　　⭕ **Is Lily still asleep?**

04. 那位正在睡覺的女孩是佩妮的好朋友。
　　❌ The girl sleepy is Penny's good friend.
　　⭕ **The girl asleep is Penny's good friend.**

05. 電話響起時，傑瑞剛睡著。
　　❌ Jerry was asleep when the phone rang.
　　⭕ **Jerry fell asleep when the phone rang.**

06. 嬰兒在搖籃裡睡得很香。
　　❌ The baby was sound sleepy in the cradle.
　　⭕ **The baby was sound asleep in the cradle.**

04 文法陷阱辨析練習
Grammar Practice

請選出題目選項中正確的用法。

01. Jim has begun to feel _____.
　　Ⓐ slept　　　　　Ⓑ sleepy　　　　　Ⓒ asleep

02. He was so tired that he _____ on the sofa.
　　Ⓐ fell asleep　　　Ⓑ fall asleep　　　Ⓒ fell sleepy

03. You will be _____ asleep by the time we get home.
　Ⓐ sounded　　　　Ⓑ very　　　　Ⓒ fast

04. The cool weather made him _____.
　Ⓐ asleep　　　　Ⓑ sleep　　　　Ⓒ sleepy

05. The _____ dog's name is Tito.
　Ⓐ sleep　　　　Ⓑ asleep　　　　Ⓒ sleepy

06. Lucy_____for two hours.
　Ⓐ have been asleep　Ⓑ has been asleep　Ⓒ has fallen sleepy

07. Tina, are you _____? You can have a rest.
　Ⓐ asleep　　　　Ⓑ sleep　　　　Ⓒ sleepy

08. I had a sleepless night yesterday, so I _____ today.
　Ⓐ feeling sleepy　　Ⓑ feel sleepy　　Ⓒ feel asleep

09. When Nicole came home last night, her roommates were all _____.
　Ⓐ sleepy　　　　Ⓑ sleep　　　　Ⓒ asleep

10. Danny was _____; I couldn't wake him up.
　Ⓐ fast asleep　　Ⓑ very asleep　　Ⓒ fast sleep

答案及題目中譯：

01. Ⓑ	吉姆開始想睡覺了。
02. Ⓐ	他累到在沙發上睡著了。
03. Ⓒ	當我們到家時，你應該已經睡得很熟了。
04. Ⓒ	涼爽的天氣讓他昏昏欲睡。
05. Ⓒ	那隻懶洋洋的狗名字叫做提托。
06. Ⓑ	露西已經睡了兩個小時了。
07. Ⓒ	蒂娜，妳想睡覺嗎？妳可以休息一下啊！
08. Ⓑ	我昨天晚上失眠了。所以我今天覺得很睏。
09. Ⓒ	妮可昨天到家的時候，她的室友已經全部睡著了。
10. Ⓐ	丹尼睡得很熟。我沒辦法叫醒他。

04 bring vs. take vs. carry

01 文法使用錯誤範例
Sample of Wrong Grammar

A: Jenny, come and stay with us during the winter holidays.
珍妮，寒假期間到我們這裡來住吧。

B: Wonderful! Can I take(✗) a friend of mine? → bring(○)
太好了！我可以帶一個朋友過去嗎？

02 文法誤用詳細解析
Grammar Analysis

　　Bring、take、carry 都是含有「帶、拿」意思的動詞，但三者用法有所區別。請見以下說明：

（1）bring 意為「帶來；拿來」，表示將人或物「帶到／拿到自己（說話者）所在的位置」。

（2）take 意為「帶走；拿走」，常與 away 搭配，表示將人或物「拿開／帶離自己（說話者）所在的位置」。

（3）carry 意為「拿、提、扛、搬、攜帶」，較常指「用手或身體搬運」的意思，不強調動作的方向。

　　範例中，「帶一個朋友過去」指的是「說話者自己帶人到對方所在的位置」，如上所述可知，句中的 take 應改為 bring，因此正確的說法應為：

Can I bring a friend of mine?

03 文法使用誤用辨析
Grammar Error vs. Correct

01. 露西，出門的時候記得帶傘。

　　☒ Lucy, rememberto bring your umbrella when you go out.

　　☑ **Lucy, remember to carry an umbrella with you when you go out.**

---

02. 拉娜，請把那本字典拿過來。

　　☒ Lana, take the dictionary over here.

　　☑ **Lana, bring the dictionary over here.**

---

03. 她需要有人幫她提行李。

　　☒ She needs somebody to help her bring the luggage.

　　☑ **She needs somebody to help her carry the luggage.**

---

04. 下次來拜訪時，我會幫你帶一些好吃的巧克力過來。

　　☒ When I call on you next time, I'll take some delicious chocolates to you.

　　☑ **Next timeI call on you , I'll bring you some delicious chocolates.**

---

05. 你發高燒了，讓我帶你去醫院。

　　☒ You're having a high fever, let me bring you to hospital.

　　☑ **You're having a high fever, let me take you to the hospital.**

---

06. 這束花的味道很難聞，請把它拿開。

　　☒ The bouquet smells awful, please bring it away.

　　☑ **The bouquet smells awful, please take it away.**

04 文法陷阱辨析練習
Grammar Practice

請選出題目選項中正確的用法。

01. Please _____ my book to me tomorrow.

　　Ⓐ carry　　　　　　　Ⓑ take　　　　　　　Ⓒ bring

02. The mother _____ her baby in her arms.

　　Ⓐ took　　　　　　　Ⓑ carried　　　　　　Ⓒ brought

03. I forgot to _____ my purse with me when I left home.
　A carry　　　　　　**B** bring　　　　　　**C** take

04. _____ that cup of coffee away, please.
　A Bring　　　　　　**B** Take　　　　　　**C** Carry

05. Please _____ the box to another room. I need more space to work.
　A take　　　　　　**B** carry　　　　　　**C** bring

06. Don't forget to _____ me your resume tomorrow.
　A carry　　　　　　**B** take　　　　　　**C** bring

07. Kate _____ us to the boss's office.
　A took　　　　　　**B** carried　　　　　　**C** brought

08. A licensed taxi is allowed to _____ 5 passengers.
　A carry　　　　　　**B** bring　　　　　　**C** take

09. Excuse me. Could you help me _____ the box? It's so heavy.
　A bring　　　　　　**B** carry　　　　　　**C** take

10. Judy, please _____ this bag away and _____ me mine.
　A take; take　　　　　**B** bring; bring　　　　　**C** take; bring

答案及題目中譯：

01. **C**	明天請把書帶來給我。
02. **B**	那位母親將她的小孩抱在懷裡。
03. **C**	我出門的時候忘記帶皮夾了。
04. **B**	請把那杯咖啡拿走，謝謝。
05. **A**	請把那個箱子拿到別的房間。我需要多一點空間工作。
06. **C**	明天別忘了把你的履歷帶來。
07. **A**	凱特帶我們去老闆的辦公室。
08. **A**	領有執照的計程車可以載五位乘客。
09. **B**	不好意思。你可以幫我拿這個箱子嗎？它好重啊。
10. **C**	茱蒂，請把這個包包拿走，並且把我的包包拿過來。

Day23

05 hope vs. wish

01 文法使用錯誤範例
Sample of Wrong Grammar

A: Will it rain tomorrow?
明天會下雨嗎？

B: I wish（✕）not. I'll visit my grandma tomorrow. → hope（○）
希望不會，我明天要去看我外婆。

02 文法誤用詳細解析
Grammar Analysis

hope 與 wish 都表示「希望」，但兩者在用法上有所區別，不能隨意替換。

（1）hope 作動詞，表示可以實現或能達到的「希望、願望」，後面若接 that 引導受詞子句，該從屬子句的動詞應該用未來簡單式或現在簡單式。

（2）wish 作動詞，表示無法實現或難以實現的「希望、願望」，wish 後面若接 that 引導受詞子句，該子句中的動詞要用虛擬語氣（過去式或過去完成式）。

（3）作動詞時，兩者相同之處為：a) 都可以接不定式作受詞；b) 都能與介詞 for 連用；c) 都可以與過去完成式連用，表示本來想做而沒有做成；d) 都可以用於句型「It is / was to be...that」中，如「It is hoped / wished that...」。

（4）需要注意的是，wish 之後可以跟含有動詞不定式的複合受詞連用，如「I wish you to stay here.」意為「想要、希望」，相當於「would like / want」；wish 還可用於句型「wish sb. sth.」中，即 wish 後面可接雙受詞，表示好的「祝願」，而 hope 沒有這兩種用法；此外，在回答問句時，如果表示希望某事「不會」發生時，應用「I hope not.」，而不用 wish，且 not 不可以放在 hope 之前。

範例中，B 表示不希望下雨，如上所述，回答問句時應用 hope，而不用 wish，因此正確的說法應為：

I hope not. I'll visit my grandma tomorrow.

03 文法使用誤用辨析
Grammar Error vs. Correct

01. 湯姆，祝你成功。
　　☒ Tom, I hope you success.
　　☐ Tom, I wish you success.

02. 我真希望你昨晚有參加那場派對。
　　☒ I really hope that you could have joined the party last night.
　　☐ I really wish that you could have joined the party last night.

03. A：火車會準時嗎？　　　　B：我希望會。
　　☒ A: Will the train be punctual?　B: I wish so.
　　☐ A: Will the train be punctual?　B: I hope so.

04. 但願我是一隻蝴蝶。
　　☒ I hope I were a butterfly.
　　☐ I wish I were a butterfly.

05. 我希望蘇珊明天能夠早點來。
　　☒ I hope Susan to come earlier tomorrow.
　　☐ I hope that Susan will come earlier tomorrow.

06. 我真希望我能早點認識他。
　　☒ I wish that I know him before.
　　☐ I wish that I knew him earlier.

04 文法陷阱辨析練習
Grammar Practice

請選出題目選項中正確的用法。

01. I _____ my friends could go with me.
　　Ⓐ wish　　　　　　Ⓑ hope　　　　　　Ⓒ hopes

02. I _____ you will like the gift.
　　Ⓐ wish　　　　　　Ⓑ hope　　　　　　Ⓒ want

03. I wish I _____ the coat yesterday.
   A have bought   **B** buy   **C** had bought

04. I _____ you a pleasant journey.
   A hope   **B** wish   **C** wish to

05. A: Will the weather be fine tomorrow? B: _____.
   A I hope so   **B** I hope it so   **C** I hope

06. Jan, I _____ you a happy New Year.
   A wish   **B** hope   **C** wishes

07. I _____ you were here.
   A hope   **B** wish   **C** wish to

08. Jim is the best. I hope that Jim _____ the game.
   A will win   **B** to win   **C** had won

09. We _____ each other the best of luck in the exam.
   A wishes   **B** hope   **C** wish

10. I wish I _____ fly like a bird.
   A could   **B** can   **C** must

答案及題目中譯：

01. **A**	真希望當時我的朋友能跟我去。
02. **B**	希望你喜歡這份禮物。
03. **C**	真希望昨天我有買下那件外套。
04. **B**	祝你玩得愉快。
05. **A**	A：明天天氣會很好嗎？ B：希望如此。
06. **A**	珍，我祝妳新年快樂。
07. **B**	我真希望你在這裡。
08. **A**	吉姆是最棒的。我希望他會贏得比賽。
09. **C**	我們祝福彼此都能通過考試。
10. **A**	我真希望能像隻小鳥一樣的飛翔。

Trap 1 單字陷阱・類義單字辨析篇

06 everyday vs. every day

---

01 文法使用錯誤範例
Sample of Wrong Grammar

A: How do you go to school everyday(✕)? → every day(○)
你每天怎麼去學校？

B: By bike.
騎自行車。

02 文法誤用詳細解析
Grammar Analysis

（1）everyday 意為「日常的、每日的、普遍的」，是形容詞，後面可以直接加跟名詞，如："everyday English" 譯為「日常英語」，"everyday clothes" 譯為「便服」。

（2）every day 是常用片語，意為「每天、天天」，一般作副詞使用，放在句首或句尾，用來修飾整個句子。有時為了加強語氣，常在 every 和 day 之間加上 single。

範例中，A 強調的是「每天」，作副詞，用來修飾整個句子，因此正確的說法應為：

How do you go to school every day?

03 文法使用誤用辨析
Grammar Error vs. Correct

01. 網路已成為我們日常生活非常重要的一部分。
   ✕ The Internet has become a very important part of our every day life.
   ○ **The Internet has become a very important part of our everyday life.**

02. 艾瑪每天搭公車去學校。
　　❌ Emma goes to school by bus everyday.
　　⭕ **Emma goes to school by bus every day.**

03. 我並不是每天都見到傑瑞。
　　❌ I don't see Jerry everyday.
　　⭕ **I don't see Jerry every day.**

04. 這些日常英語對我們學習英語有很大的幫助。
　　❌ The every day English is very helpful for our English study.
　　⭕ **The everyday English is very helpful for our English study.**

05. 我們每天都講英語以促進英語學習。
　　❌ We speak English everyday to help improve our English.
　　⭕ **We speak English every day to help us improve our English.**

06. 這是一件很平常的小事。
　　❌ This is an every day trifle.
　　⭕ **It is an everyday trifle.**

04 文法陷阱辨析練習
Grammar Practice

請選出題目選項中正確的用法。

01. Lily bought an _____ dress yesterday.
　　🅐 everyday　　　　　🅑 every day　　　　　🅒 every-day

02. Lisa wears _____ clothes to work.
　　🅐 every day　　　　　🅑 every days　　　　　🅒 everyday

03. I go to school on foot _____.
　　🅐 everyday　　　　　🅑 every day　　　　　🅒 every-day

04. Jenny comes to see me _____.
　　🅐 every single days　　🅑 everyday　　　　　🅒 every single day

05. I need a small dictionary for _____.
　　🅐 everyday use　　　　🅑 every day use　　　　🅒 every-day use

06. My Dad does morning exercises _____.
   A everyday   **B** every days   **C** every day

07. Traffic accidents are _____ occurrences.
   A everyday   **B** every days   **C** every-day

08. Music is a part of _____ life.
   A every day   **B** every days   **C** everyday

09. Lucy studies very hard, and she gets up early _____.
   A everyday   **B** every days   **C** every day

10. Chocolate is my favorite food, and I eat one piece _____.
   A everyday   **B** every day   **C** every-day

答案及題目中譯：

01. **A**	莉莉昨天買了一件家居服。	
02. **C**	莉莎穿便服去上班。	
03. **B**	我每天走路上學。	
04. **C**	珍妮每天都會來看我。	
05. **A**	我需要一本小字典做日常之用。	
06. **C**	我爸每天做晨間運動。	
07. **A**	車禍事故天天都在發生。	
08. **C**	音樂是日常生活的一部分。	
09. **C**	露西很用功，而且每天都很早起。	
10. **B**	巧克力是我最喜歡的食物，我每天都吃一塊。	

Day24

07 fit vs. suit

01 文法使用錯誤範例
Sample of Wrong Grammar

A: This dress doesn't fit(✕) me. Do you have other styles? → suit(○)
這件洋裝不適合我穿，還有其他的款式嗎？

B: Yes. There is another style. You can try it on.
有，這裡有另外一個款式，妳可以試穿一下。

02 文法誤用詳細解析
Grammar Analysis

fit 與 suit 作為動詞，都有表示「適合」之意，但是兩者在具體意思上有所區別。

fit 表示形狀、尺寸、大小的適合、吻合，如「合身」，或「與……相稱」；suit 表示顏色、款式、風格等與人的氣質、身材或皮膚的相配、滴合，同時還可表示合乎需要、口味、條件、地位等。

範例中 A 說的 style 是指「款式、式樣」，因此如上所述，句中應用 suit，正確的說法應為：

This dress doesn't suit me. Do you have other styles?

需要注意的是，兩者在表示「使……適合」時，fit 常與 for 連用；suit 常與 to 連用。

03 文法使用誤用辨析
Grammar Error vs. Correct

01. 山姆認為這份工作不適合他。
    ✕ Sam thinks that this job doesn't fit him.
    ○ **Sam thinks that this job doesn't suit him.**

02. 媽媽昨天給我買的新大衣很合身。

　　☒ The coat mom bought me yesterday suits me perfectly.

　　☑ **The coat mom bought me yesterday fits me perfectly.**

---

03. 這道菜不合我胃口。

　　☒ The dish doesn't fit my taste.

　　☑ **The dish doesn't suit my taste.**

---

04. 她的經驗很適合這份工作，所以她在工作上表現得很出色。

　　☒ Her experience suits her for the job, so she can do the job very well.

　　☑ **Her experience fits her for the job, so she can do the job very well.**

---

05. 紅色很適合你。

　　☒ Red fits you very well.

　　☑ **Red suits you very well.**

04 文法陷阱辨析練習
Grammar Practice

請選出題目選項中正確的用法。

01. The key doesn't _____ the lock.

　　Ⓐ suit　　　　　　　Ⓑ fit　　　　　　　Ⓒ fitting

02. The trousers _____ me well, but the color doesn't _____ my shoes.

　　Ⓐ suits, fits　　　　Ⓑ fit, suits　　　　Ⓒ fit, suit

03. I think that haircut _____ Tina very well.

　　Ⓐ fits　　　　　　　Ⓑ suits　　　　　　　Ⓒ fit

04. That style of the dress doesn't _____ your stature.

　　Ⓐ suit　　　　　　　Ⓑ suit for　　　　　　Ⓒ fit

05. This coat doesn't _____ me. Do you have a smaller size?

　　Ⓐ suit　　　　　　　Ⓑ fit　　　　　　　Ⓒ fit to

06. My shirt _____ for me before until I washed it yesterday.
   A fitted   **B** suited   **C** fit

07. These shoes _____ me very well.
   A suit   **B** fit   **C** suits

08. Does the coat you bought yesterday _____ you?
   A fit   **B** suit to   **C** suited

09. The blue scarf _____ her disposition very well.
   A suits for   **B** fits   **C** suits

10. This song is well _____ to the occasion.
   A fitted   **B** fit   **C** suited

答案及題目中譯：

01. **B**	這把鑰匙跟鎖孔不合。
02. **C**	這件褲子很合身，但是顏色跟我的鞋子不搭。
03. **B**	我覺得這髮型很適合蒂娜。
04. **A**	那件衣服的款式跟你的身份不太搭。
05. **B**	這件外套我穿不合身。有尺寸小一點的嗎？
06. **A**	這件襯衫在我昨天洗它之前都還很合身的。
07. **B**	這些鞋子很合我的腳。
08. **A**	你昨天買的外套合身嗎？
09. **C**	這條藍色的圍巾跟她的個性很配。
10. **C**	這首歌很適合這個場合。

Day24

08 hear vs. listen to

01 文法使用錯誤範例
Sample of Wrong Grammar

A: I can't listen to(✕) your voice clearly. → hear(○)
我聽不清楚你的聲音。

B: Sorry. We seem to have a bad connection.
不好意思，我們的收訊好像不太正常。

02 文法誤用詳細解析
Grammar Analysis

hear 與 listen to 都有「聽」的意思，但是兩者有所區別，請見以下說明：

（1）hear 強調耳朵能聽見，有「聽見、聽說、聽取」等意思，指聲音傳進了耳中，即使你不集中注意力也聽得見，一般不用於進行式。

（2）listen 強調的是「留神傾聽」的動作，一般會接 to ＋受詞，表示集中注意力認真聆聽。

此外，要注意當父母、長官等以上對下責問子女、部屬「聽到我（叫你）沒有？」時通常用 Do you hear me? 而非 Do you listen to me?

另外，Are you listening (to me)? 表「你有沒有在聽我說（的內容）？」

03 文法使用誤用辨析
Grammar Error vs. Correct

01. 她的聽覺不太好。
　　✗ She can't listen very well.
　　○ She can't **hear** very well.

02. 蘇珊喜歡聽流行音樂。
　　✖ Susan is fond of hearing pop music.
　　⭕ Susan is fond of **listening to** pop music.

03. 我仔細聽，但還是沒有聽見老師說的話。
　　✖ I heard the teacher carefully, but I didn't listen to her words.
　　⭕ I **listened to** the teacher carefully, but I didn't **hear** her words.

04. 我花了一個晚上聽朋友借給我的唱片。
　　✖ I spent the whole night hearing the record borrowed from my friend.
　　⭕ I spent the whole night **listening to** the record borrowed from my friend.

05. 你能聽到我的聲音嗎？
　　✖ Can you listen to me?
　　⭕ Can you **hear** me?

06. 他聽到他的背後有腳步聲。
　　✖ He listened footsteps behind him.
　　⭕ He **heard** footsteps behind him.

04 文法陷阱辨析練習
Grammar Practice

請選出題目選項中正確的用法。

01. Please _____ me. I have something need to let you know.
　　A listen　　　　　　**B** hear　　　　　　**C** listen to

02. Can you _____ somebody coming?
　　A hear　　　　　　**B** listen to　　　　　**C** hear to

03. She _____ his story carefully.
　　A listened　　　　　**B** heard　　　　　　**C** listened to

04. Jim could _____ a dog barking last night.
　　A listen to　　　　　**B** hear　　　　　　**C** listen

05. Didn't you _____ what the boss said?
Ⓐ hear   Ⓑ listen   Ⓒ hear to

06. She _____ a strange noise suddenly.
Ⓐ listened   Ⓑ heard   Ⓒ listened to

07. Please _____ the radio carefully.
Ⓐ listen to   Ⓑ hear   Ⓒ listen

08. I'm very glad to _____ your voice.
Ⓐ listen   Ⓑ hear   Ⓒ listen to

09. I didn't really _____ what they were saying carefully.
Ⓐ listen   Ⓑ hear   Ⓒ listen to

10. I _____ the twins talking in the next room.
Ⓐ listened   Ⓑ heard to   Ⓒ heard

答案及題目中譯：

01. Ⓒ	請聽我説。我有事情必須讓妳知道。
02. Ⓐ	你聽得見有人正往這裡來嗎？
03. Ⓒ	她很仔細在傾聽他的故事。
04. Ⓑ	吉姆昨天晚上聽到一隻狗在叫。
05. Ⓐ	你沒聽見老闆説的話嗎？
06. Ⓑ	她突然聽見一陣奇怪的吵鬧聲。
07. Ⓐ	請仔細聽收音機。
08. Ⓑ	我很高興聽見你的聲音。
09. Ⓒ	我其實沒有很認真在聽他們説話。
10. Ⓒ	我聽到隔壁間那對雙胞胎在説話。

Day24

09 speak vs. say vs. talk vs. tell

01 文法使用錯誤範例
Sample of Wrong Grammar

A: Did you speak(✕) anything about the travel plan to your mom?
→ talk(○)
你有跟你媽媽說什麼有關旅遊計畫的事嗎？

B: No. I spoke(✕) nothing. → said(○)
不，我什麼都沒說。

02 文法誤用詳細解析
Grammar Analysis

speak, say, talk, tell 都含有「說」的意思，但四者的含義和用法有所區別，請見以下說明：

（1）speak 為「談論；發言；講……語言；提起」之意，強調的是「說」的動作，而非說話內容。speak to sb. 意為「跟某人講話」。此外，speak 常用在意指說哪一種語言上。例如：

My mom can't speak English at all.（我媽媽完全不會說英文。）

（2）say 為「說」的意思，強調說的內容，故常用在後接說話內容的句子。用言語表達自己的思想，受詞通常為名詞、代名詞或子句。例如：

My sister said that she doesn't want to go to work at night.
（我姐姐說她不想晚上去工作。）

Say goodbye to your teacher.（跟你的老師說再見。）

（3）talk 為「說話；談話；討論」的意思，主要是表達與什麼人說話或談論什麼事情。和介系詞 to, with 連用時，意為「與……交談」，和介系詞 about 或 of 連用時，意為「談論……內容」。例如：

I don't want to talk about my girlfriend.
（我不想要談論跟我女朋友有關的事情。）

另補充 talk 的常見片語：sweet talk 指「甜言蜜語」；nice talk 是「說得好」。

（4）tell 為「講；告訴」的意思，後面接「人」時，不必加 to；接「雙受詞」時，則可用 to 連接動詞，形成命令句 tell sb. (not) to do sth.，表示「囑咐或語氣較輕的命令」。例如：

Mom tells us to do our homework.（媽媽叫我們去做功課。）

此外，tell 還有以下常見用法：tell stories（說故事）；tell the truth（說實話）；tell lies（說謊）；tell fortune（算命）；You're telling me.（還要你說啊！／我早就知道了。）

03 文法使用誤用辨析
Grammar Error vs. Correct

01. 他說法文。
　　☒ He says French.
　　☑ **He speaks French.**

02. 我們必須談一談。
　　☒ We need to speak.
　　☑ **We need to talk.**

03. 請告訴我實情。
　　☒ Please talk me the truth.
　　☑ **Please tell me the truth.**

04. 請用英文說。
　　☒ Please speak it in English.
　　☑ **Please say it in English.**

05. 他們正在談論他們的巴黎之旅。
　　☒ They are talking their trip to Paris.
　　☑ **They are talking about their trip to Paris.**

06. 我不了解吉姆所說的。
　　✖ I don't understand what Jim spoke.
　　◯ I don't understand what Jim said.

04 文法陷阱辨析練習
Grammar Practice

請選出題目選項中正確的用法。

01. "Please help me carry the box," Tina _____ to me.
　　A told　　　　　　**B** talked　　　　　**C** said

02. Mr. Smith _____ at our class meeting yesterday.
　　A told　　　　　　**B** talked　　　　　**C** spoke

03. Mom _____ the interesting story to me.
　　A told　　　　　　**B** talked　　　　　**C** said

04. The teacher is _____ with Lily in the office.
　　A saying　　　　　**B** telling　　　　　**C** talking

05. Could you _____ me how to get to the museum?
　　A say　　　　　　**B** talk　　　　　　**C** tell

06. The old man _____ that he saw the little girl yesterday.
　　A says　　　　　　**B** talks　　　　　**C** tells

07. Excuse me, Mr. Brown, I can't _____ Russian.
　　Could you _____ me what has happened in English?
　　A talk; tell　　　　**B** speak; tell　　　**C** say; talk

08. The old man went out and_____ nothing.
　　A said　　　　　　**B** talked　　　　　**C** told

09. Her mom _____ her not to stay up late.
　　A said　　　　　　**B** talked　　　　　**C** told

10. Lisa, may I _____ to you?
　　A say　　　　　　**B** talk　　　　　　**C** speak

答案及題目中譯：

01. **C**	蒂娜對我説：「請幫我拿這個箱子。」
02. **C**	史密斯先生昨天在我們的班級會議上發表談話。
03. **A**	媽媽告訴我一個有趣的故事。
04. **C**	老師正和莉莉在辦公室內交談。
05. **C**	可以請你告訴我如何前往博物館嗎？
06. **A**	這位老先生説他昨天看到那位小女孩。
07. **B**	抱歉，布朗先生，我不懂俄語。可以請你用英文告訴我發生什麼事情了嗎？
08. **A**	這位老先生不發一語的走出去了。
09. **C**	她的媽媽告訴她不可以熬夜。
10. **B**	莉莎，我可以跟你談談嗎？

Day24

10 spend vs. cost

01 文法使用錯誤範例
Sample of Wrong Grammar

A: How much does this bike spend(✗)? → cost(○)
這輛自行車多少錢？

B: It spent(✗) me 3,000 dollars. → cost / took(○)
它花了我 3000 元。

02 文法誤用詳細解析
Grammar Analysis

spend 和 cost 均可表示「花費」，但兩者的用法及含義有相當明顯的區別，請見以下說明：

（1-1）spend 的主詞通常是人，受詞則可以是時間或錢。常用句型有以下幾式：

第一式，sb. spend time / money on sth. 意思是「某人在某一事物上花了多少時間 / 錢」。例如：

Mr.Willson spent lots of time on his wife.
（威爾森先生在他太太身上花了很多時間。）

第二式，sb. spend time / money (in) doing sth. 意思是「某人在做某事方面花多少時間 / 錢」。例如：

Mrs. Smith spends a lot of money in entertaining friends.
（史密斯太太在招待朋友這方面花了很多錢。）

（1-2）spend money for sth. 意思是「花錢買……」。其後不可接不定詞。例如：

I enjoy spending money for books.（我樂於花錢買書。）

（2-1）cost 的主詞通常是事或物，不能是人。cost 若不表示「花費」，而是表示客觀上地或被動地「耗費」，則也可用人作主詞，受詞通常是錢。例如：

This DVD player cost me two thousand dollars.
（這台 DVD 放映機花了我 2000 元。）

（2-2）cost 也可用來比喻付出代價（勞力、麻煩、精力、生命等）。例如：

This car accident cost him twenty thousand dollars.
（這次的交通事故花了他兩萬元。）

所以範例中的正確說法應為：It cost me 3,000 dollars.

03 文法使用誤用辨析
Grammar Error vs. Correct

01. 我花了三小時來修復這個。
　　☒ I cost three hours fixing this.
　　☑ **I spent three hours fixing this.**

02. 一台新電視要花一大筆錢。
　　☒ A new TV spends a lot of money.
　　☑ **A new TV costs a lot of money.**

03. 他在這項成果上花了很多時間。
　　☒ He spent much time in the achievement.
　　☑ **He spent much time on the achievement.**

04. 二十元就花在這頂帽子上。
　　☒ Twenty dollars was cost on the hat.
　　☑ **Twenty dollars was spent on the hat.**

05. 那場事故差點要了他的命。
　　☒ The accident almost spent him his life.
　　☑ **The accident almost cost him his life.**

06. 湯姆付出極大的努力來幫我。
　　☒ Tom cost great efforts to help me.
　　☑ **Tom spent great efforts to help me.**

04 文法陷阱辨析練習
Grammar Practice

請選出題目選項中正確的用法。

01. The coat _____ me lots of money.
 A spent　　　　　 **B** cost　　　　　 **C** was spent

02. Mr. Green _____ a lot of time helping Jim with his English yesterday.
 A spent　　　　　 **B** cost　　　　　 **C** was spent

03. They spent two years _____ this building.
 A in building　　　　 **B** to build　　　　 **C** on building

04. Finishing the work _____ him a lot of time.
 A spent　　　　　 **B** was cost　　　　 **C** cost

05. The mistake _____ the company one million dollars.
 A spent　　　　　 **B** was cost　　　　 **C** cost

06. I didn't buy the camera because it _____ too much.
 A spent　　　　　 **B** cost　　　　　 **C** was spent

07. Sam _____ much money on books.
 A spends　　　　 **B** costs　　　　 **C** is spent

答案及題目中譯：

01. **B**	這件外套花了我很多錢。	
02. **A**	格林先生昨天花了很多時間幫吉姆學英文。	
03. **A**	他們花了兩年蓋這幢建築物。	
04. **C**	完成這項工作花了他很多時間。	
05. **C**	這項錯誤讓公司損失了一百萬元。	
06. **B**	我沒有買那個相機，因為要花太多錢。	
07. **A**	山姆花很多錢在書上面。	

Day25

11 travel vs. trip

01 文法使用錯誤範例
Sample of Wrong Grammar

We took a travel(✗) to the mountains. → trip(○)
我們去山上玩了。

02 文法誤用詳細解析
Grammar Analysis

travel 與 trip 均可表示「旅行」，但兩者在用法上有所區別，請見以下說明：

（1-1）travel 可當作不可數名詞，為「旅行；旅遊；遊歷」之意，泛指一般的旅行，而非特指某次具體的旅行。常用來表達路途較遠或時間較長的旅遊。例如：

My parents usually plan two-week travel for me every summer.
（我父母通常每年夏天都為我安排兩個星期的旅遊。）

（1-2）travel 當作動詞時，意為「長途行走；旅行；遊歷」。例如：

The White family is travelling in UK.（懷特一家人在英國旅遊。）

（2）trip 可當可數名詞，是「旅行；旅程；出遊」的意思，多指短時間、短距離往返的旅行。take a trip to 則是指「去某地旅行」。business trip 則是「出差」。例如：

Roth took a business trip to Japan last month.（羅斯上個月去日本出差。）

（3）trip 當作動詞、名詞皆有「服用毒品而產生幻覺」的意思。例如：

He trips out on LSD.（他服用 LSD 迷幻藥而處於幻覺之中。）

（4）voyage 源自法文，本指「海上旅行」，現也用於航空、太空旅行等長途旅行；Bon voyage. 則為「一路順風」，適用於採行任何交通方式的旅程。例如：

Life is compared to a voyage.（人生好比一趟旅程。）

03 文法使用誤用辨析
Grammar Error vs. Correct

01. 我搭公車上班，路程要花一個小時。
- ☒ I go to work by bus, and the travel takes one hour.
- ☑ **I go to work by bus, and the trip takes one hour.**

02. 你父母旅行回來了嗎？
- ☒ Are your parents back from their many travels yet?
- ☑ **Are your parents back from their travels yet?**

03. 莉莉這趟旅行順利嗎？
- ☒ Did Lily have a good travel?
- ☑ **Did Lily have a good trip?**

04. 那個老人環遊了全世界。
- ☒ The old man tripped the whole world.
- ☑ **The old man traveled the whole world.**

05. 你對《馬可波羅遊記》有興趣嗎？
- ☒ Are you interested in *The Trips of Marco Polo*?
- ☑ **Are you interested in *The Travels of Marco Polo*?**

06. 我想去鄉下走走。
- ☒ I want to take a travel to the countryside.
- ☑ **I want to take a trip to the countryside.**

04 文法陷阱辨析練習
Grammar Practice

請選出題目選項中正確的用法。

01. Jim has gone off on his _____ again.
- Ⓐ travels
- Ⓑ a trip
- Ⓒ a travel

02. I go to school by bike, and the _____ takes half an hour.
- Ⓐ travels
- Ⓑ trip
- Ⓒ a travel

03. Jake is _____ in Paris.
  A tripping   **B** traveled   **C** traveling

04. Do you want to take a _____ to the suburb?
  A trip   **B** travel   **C** voyage

05. The manager has to make business _____ every now and then.
  A trips   **B** travels   **C** voyages

06. Lucy, do you like books of _____?
  A a travel   **B** trips   **C** travels

07. Mr. Smith came home after years of foreign _____.
  A travel   **B** trips   **C** trip

08. This is the best _____ of my life.
  A a travel   **B** trip   **C** travels

09. He works in a _____ agency.
  A travel   **B** trip   **C** travels

10. Jim, let's prepare for the _____.
  A travel   **B** trip   **C** travels

答案及題目中譯：

01. **A**	吉姆已再次出發去旅行了。	
02. **B**	我騎自行車去上學。路程要花半個小時。	
03. **C**	傑克正在巴黎旅遊。	
04. **A**	你想要去郊外走走嗎？	
05. **A**	這位經理必須時常出差。	
06. **C**	露西，妳喜歡旅遊書嗎？	
07. **A**	在多年的國外旅遊後，史密斯先生回到家了。	
08. **B**	這是一趟我人生中最棒的旅遊。	
09. **A**	他在旅行社工作。	
10. **B**	吉姆，我們來為旅行準備準備。	

12 wait vs. expect

01 文法使用錯誤範例
Sample of Wrong Grammar

A: Why is Jim standing at the school gate all the time?
吉姆為什麼一直站在校門口？

B: Because he is expecting（✗）for his mom. → waiting（○）
因為他在等他的媽媽。

02 文法誤用詳細解析
Grammar Analysis

wait 和 expect 都可以用來表示「等待」的意思，但是含義還是有明顯的區別：

（1）wait 是「等候」的意思，通常與介詞 for 合用，指在一個地方待著，沒有採取任何行動。主要是強調時間的流逝且含有耽誤的意思，有時候甚至有暗示某人來得太晚或某事發生得太遲的含義。例如：

Simon has been waiting for his wife for two hours.
（賽門已經等了他太太兩個小時了。）

（2）expect 有「期待；預料；指望；要求」的含意，通常當作及物動詞，後面不加介詞 for，主要是強調某事（可指好或不好的事）很可能會發生或到來，不強調時間的遲早，只表達一種心情。例如：

I expect to get an email from my friend that I made in summer camp last year.
（我期盼能收到去年在夏令營交到的朋友的來信。）

（3）此外，expect 尚有「懷孕、懷胎」之意，通常以進行式表達。例如：

My wife is expecting again.（我太太又懷孕了。）

所以範例中的正確說法應為：Because he is waiting for his mom.

03 文法使用誤用辨析
Grammar Error vs. Correct

01. 她在期待著她丈夫的信。
　　❌ She is waiting for a letter from her husband.
　　⭕ She is **expecting** a letter from her husband.

---

02. 我在等公車。
　　❌ I'm excepting the bus.
　　⭕ I'm **waiting** for the bus.

---

03. 她期盼著男朋友向她求婚。
　　❌ She is waiting a proposal from her boyfriend.
　　⭕ She is **expecting** a proposal from her boyfriend.

---

04. 我預計星期一回來。
　　❌ I wait to be back on Monday.
　　⭕ I **expect** to be back on Monday.

---

05. 媽媽，別對我期望太高。
　　❌ Mom, don't wait for too much of me.
　　⭕ Mom, don't **expect** too much of me.

---

06. 我已經等我的朋友半小時了。
　　❌ I've been expecting half an hour for my friend.
　　⭕ I've been **waiting** half an hour for my friend.

04 文法陷阱辨析練習
Grammar Practice

請選出題目選項中正確的用法。

01. We are _____ the rain stop before we begin to work.
　　Ⓐ waiting for　　　　Ⓑ expecting for　　　　Ⓒ expecting to

02. The teacher _____ us to be punctual.
　　Ⓐ expected for　　　　Ⓑ expected　　　　Ⓒ waited

03. What are you _____ for?
   A wait   B expecting   C waiting

04. I'll _____ you at 7:00.
   A wait   B expect   C expect for

05. He was _____ his girlfriend in the park.
   A waiting for   B expecting for   C waiting

06. He was _____ a telephone call from his girlfriend.
   A waiting for   B expecting for   C waiting

07. Jake _____ to fail the exam.
   A waited   B expect   C expected

08. Don't _____ too long before acting.
   A wait   B expect   C wait for

09. I _____ to go with you.
   A wait   B expect   C wait for

10. We don't _____ that Jim has done such a thing.
   A expect   B wait   C wait for

答案及題目中譯：

01. A	我們期盼著這場雨能在我們開工之前停下來。	
02. B	老師要求我們要準時。	
03. C	你在等什麼？	
04. B	我預計你七點能到。	
05. A	他在公園裡等他的女朋友。	
06. C	他在等他女朋友的來電。	
07. C	傑克預計這次考試會失敗。	
08. A	行動之前不要等太久。	
09. B	我期望能跟你一起去。	
10. A	我們沒有預期吉姆會做這樣的事。	

Trap 1 單字陷阱・類義單字辨析篇

13 **worth vs. worthy**

---

01 文法使用錯誤範例
Sample of Wrong Grammar

A: What do you think about this book?
你覺得這本書怎麼樣？

B: It'll be very helpful for you, so it's worth(✕) of buying. → worthy(○)
它對你的學習很有幫助，所以它值得你買。

02 文法誤用詳細解析
Grammar Analysis

worth 與 worthy 都可當作形容詞，都有「值得」的意思，但兩者在用法上有所區別，請見以下說明：

（1-1）句子的主詞是物質名詞時，worth 後面通常要加受詞，該受詞通常是名詞或者動名詞，例如：

The painting is worth ten thousand dollars.（這幅畫作價值萬元。）

（1-2）worth your while 這個片語的含義為「值得你（們）去做某事」，也可以寫做 "worth my while", "worth his while", "worth her while", "worth their while"，"worth our while" 等。例如：

It's worth your while to see the movie.（這是部值得你看的電影。）

（2-1）worthy 可與介系詞 of 連用，組成片語 be worthy of，後面可接名詞或動名詞的被動形式，例如：

This is worthy of being done.（這是件值得做的事。）

（2-2）worthy 也可與不定詞連用，此時 worthy 後面不可再用介詞 of，要直接用不定詞，且不定詞要用被動語態，例如：

This book is worthy to be read.（這本書值得一讀。）

所以範例中的正確說法應為：

It'll be very helpful for you, so it's worthy of buying.

03 文法使用誤用辨析
Grammar Error vs. Correct

01. 這個課題值得研究。
   ❌ This issue is worthy of studying.
   ⭕ **This issue is worthy of being studied.**

02. 這幅畫大約值十萬美元。
   ❌ This painting is worthy about $100,000.
   ⭕ **This painting is worth about $100,000.**

03. 這則新聞值得大家關注。
   ❌ The news is worth of attention.
   ⭕ **The news is worthy of attention.**

04. 購物之前先規畫一下對我們有益
   ❌ It's worthy our while making a plan before we go shopping.
   ⭕ **It's worth our while making a plan before we go shopping.**

05. 這是一本值得再看一遍的書。
   ❌ This book is worthy of to be read again.
   ⭕ **This book is worthy to be read again.**

06. 這座博物館有很多很棒的收藏品，值得參觀。
   ❌ There are lots of fine collections in this museum. It is worth to visit.
   ⭕ **There are lots of fine collections in this museum. It is worth visiting.**

04 文法陷阱辨析練習
Grammar Practice

請選出題目選項中正確的用法。

01. The records of Lady Gaga are _____, for her songs can make us happy.
A worth being bought　　**B** worthy of being bought　　**C** worth of buying

02. It will be worth your while _____ the meeting.
A to attend　　　　　　**B** attend　　　　　　　**C** to go

03. The suggesting is well _____ considering.
A worth of　　　　　　**B** worthy　　　　　　　**C** worth

04. The traffic accident is worthy _____ more attention.
A paying　　　　　　　**B** of to be paid　　　　**C** to be paid

05. Some findings of this report are _____ note.
A worth of　　　　　　**B** worth　　　　　　　**C** worthy

06. It is worth while _____ out that Mike's advice is well _____ consideration.
A pointing; worthy of　　**B** to be pointed; worth　　**C** pointing; worth of

07. This film is excellent. It is worth _____ again.
A to watch　　　　　　**B** watch　　　　　　　**C** watching

08. These cleaners are _____.
A worthy of respecting　　**B** worth being respected
C worthy of being respected

答案及題目中譯：

01. **B**	女神卡卡的唱片很值得買，因為聽她的歌讓我們很開心。	
02. **A**	參與這次會議將對你有益。	
03. **C**	這個提議很值得好好思考一下。	
04. **C**	交通事故值得我們多花些心思關注。	
05. **B**	這份報告裡的研究結果很值得註記。	
06. **A**	麥克這個建議很值得提出來好好考慮。	
07. **C**	這部電影很棒，值得再看一次。	
08. **C**	這些清潔人員很值得受人尊敬。	

14 occur vs. happen vs. take place

01 文法使用錯誤範例
Sample of Wrong Grammar

A: Jerry, can you show me the way to the Café?
傑瑞，你可以告訴我怎麼去那家咖啡廳嗎？

B: Sorry, I don't know. You can ask Tom, he occurred (✕) to know the place. → happened (○)
不好意思，我不知道怎麼去。你可以問問湯姆，他碰巧知道那個地方。

02 文法誤用詳細解析
Grammar Analysis

occur, happen 和 take place 三者都表示「發生」，都是不及物動詞，都不可以用於被動語態，但具體含義及用法都有明顯區別，請見以下說明：

（1）occur 是「出現；存在於；出現於」的意思，指單純的發生。句型 occur to sb./sth. 則有「某人突然想起……」。例如：

It occurred to him that he should go visit his grandparents more often.
（他突然想起他應該更常去探望他的祖父母。）

（2）happen 是「發生；碰巧」的意思，特別指那些偶然的或非預知的事件「發生」。主詞如果是「事」時，則有「偶然發生」之意；主詞為人時，則意指「某人碰巧……」。例如：

I happened to see one of my high school classmates two days ago.
（兩天前我碰巧遇見一位高中同學。）

（3）take place 是「發生；舉行；舉辦」的意思，一般指非偶然性事件，即按照計畫或安排而必然會發生的事情。例如：

When will the concert take place?（演唱會何時舉辦？）

所以範例中的正確說法應為：You can ask Tom, he happened to know the place.

03 文法使用誤用辨析
Grammar Error vs. Correct

01. 你的生日派對什麼時候舉行？
🅧 When will your birthday party happen?
🅞 **When will your birthday party take place?**

---

02. 那起交通事故發生在上個星期一。
🅧 The traffic accident was occurred last Monday.
🅞 **The traffic accident occurred last Monday.**

---

03. 他發生什麼意外了嗎？
🅧 Has anything occurred to him?
🅞 **Has anything happened to him?**

---

04. 會議將在下週六召開。
🅧 The meeting will be taken place next Saturday.
🅞 **The meeting will take place next Saturday.**

---

05. 我突然想起來我把雨傘忘在辦公室了。
🅧 It happened to me that I left my umbrella in the office.
🅞 **It occurred to me that I left my umbrella in the office.**

---

06. 我碰巧在回家的路上遇見莉莉。
🅧 I took place to meet Lily on my way home.
🅞 **I happened to meet Lily on my way home.**

04 文法陷阱辨析練習
Grammar Practice

請選出題目選項中正確的用法。

01. It _____ that I didn't know his name.
🅐 occurred　　　　🅑 happened　　　　🅒 took place

02. The basketball match will _____ next Monday.
   Ⓐ take place　　　　　Ⓑ happen　　　　　Ⓒ occur

03. It _____ to me that she didn't know how to go there.
   Ⓐ occurred　　　　　Ⓑ happened　　　　　Ⓒ took place

04. When did the accident _____?
   Ⓐ been occurred　　　Ⓑ happened　　　　　Ⓒ occur

05. Jake _____ to know the details of it.
   Ⓐ occurred　　　　　Ⓑ happened　　　　　Ⓒ took place

06. The Olympic Games of 2016 will _____ in Rio de Janeiro.
   Ⓐ take place　　　　　Ⓑ happen　　　　　Ⓒ occur

07. I'm sorry to tell you that something _____ to your grandma.
   Ⓐ occurred　　　　　Ⓑ happened　　　　　Ⓒ took place

08. It _____ that she comes home just now.
   Ⓐ happens　　　　　Ⓑ happened　　　　　Ⓒ has happened

09. The old man remembers everything exactly as if it _____ yesterday.
   Ⓐ was happening　　　Ⓑ happens　　　　　Ⓒ happened

答案及題目中譯：

01. Ⓐ	我突然想起我不知道他的名字。
02. Ⓐ	這場籃球對抗賽會在下週一舉行。
03. Ⓐ	我突然想起她不知道如何到那兒。
04. Ⓒ	意外何時發生的？
05. Ⓑ	傑克碰巧知道這件事的細節。
06. Ⓐ	奧林匹克運動會將於 2016 年在里約熱內盧舉行。
07. Ⓑ	很抱歉，我得告訴你，你的祖母發生事情了。
08. Ⓐ	她剛好現在到家。
09. Ⓒ	這位老人記得所有的事情，就好像這些事昨天才發生過一樣。

15 can vs. may vs. might

01 文法使用錯誤範例
Sample of Wrong Grammar

omeone is knocking at the door. May（✗）it be your mom? → Can（○）
有人在敲門。會不會是你媽媽？

02 文法誤用詳細解析
Grammar Analysis

　can, may, might 都有「可以；能」的涵義，通常用來表達請求或允許，多用於口語中，但三者在用法上還是有所區別，請見以下說明：

（1）can 有「能力；允許；可能性」的意思，代表對陳述的內容有 70% 的信心；用於否定句或疑問句時，則有「懷疑、猜測、驚異」的涵義。若有 100% 的信心，則用 must。例如：
　　Can you come and help me with my math?（你可以過來幫我加強數學嗎？）
　　The ground is wet. It must have rained last night.
　　（地是濕的。昨晚必定下過雨。）

（2）could 用於指涉可能性時，表示對陳述內容有大約 60% 的信心，例如：
　　It's a fine day. Joe could be enjoying the sun.（天氣很好，喬可能在享受陽光。）

（3）may 表示詢問或說明一件事可不可以做，且代表對陳述內容有大約 50% 的信心。例如：
　　May I use the bathroom?（我可以用一下洗手間嗎？）
　　Sure. Go ahead.（當然。去吧。）

（4）might 是 may 的過去式，用來表示過去可以做的事或可能發生的事，可能性較小，代表對這句話的內容的信心指數只有 30% 以下；用在疑問句中，則表示一種委婉、客氣的態度。例如：
　　My manager thought we might finish the project earlier.
　　（我們經理以為我們可以早一點完成這個專案。）

所以範例中的正確說法應為：Can it be your mom?

03 文法使用誤用辨析
Grammar Error vs. Correct

01. 你會說法文嗎？
   ☒ May you speak French?
   ☑ **Can you speak French?**

02. 他以為他可以完成這項任務。
   ☒ He thought he may finish the task.
   ☑ **He thought he might finish the task.**

03. 電話響了。會是湯姆打來的嗎？
   ☒ The telephone rings. Might it be Tom?
   ☑ **The telephone rings. Can it be Tom?**

04. 那可能是真的，也可能不是。
   ☒ It can or can not be true.
   ☑ **It may or may not be true.**

05. 我可以借這本書嗎？
   ☒ Might I borrow this book?
   ☑ **May I borrow this book?**

06. 那個女孩不可能是琳達，琳達已經去法國了。
   ☒ That girl might not be Linda. Linda has gone to France.
   ☑ **That girl can not be Linda. Linda has gone to France.**

04 文法陷阱辨析練習
Grammar Practice

請選出題目選項中正確的用法。

01. You _____ not buy a dog at an electronic store.
   Ⓐ might   Ⓑ can   Ⓒ may

02. I'm not sure. But she _____ be right.
   A might　　　　　　**B** can　　　　　　**C** may

03. It _____ not be a rabbit. It's a dog.
   A might　　　　　　**B** can　　　　　　**C** may

04. They hoped they _____ be there on time.
   A might　　　　　　**B** can　　　　　　**C** may

05. He got the first rank in the exam. He _____ have studied hard.
   A can　　　　　　**B** may　　　　　　**C** must

06. Come what _____, we'll stand by you.
   A might　　　　　　**B** may　　　　　　**C** can

07. There is a purse. _____ it be yours?
   A Can　　　　　　**B** May　　　　　　**C** Might

08. He _____ have killed himself, but the doctor saved him.
   A might　　　　　　**B** may　　　　　　**C** can

09. _____ I help you, sir?
   A Might　　　　　　**B** Would　　　　　　**C** May

答案及題目中譯：

01. **B**	你不可能在電器行買到一隻狗。
02. **C**	我不太確定。但她也許是對的。
03. **B**	牠不可能是一隻兔子。牠是一隻狗。
04. **A**	他們本來希望可以準時抵達的。
05. **C**	他考第一名。他必定很用功。
06. **B**	無論發生什麼事，我們都會支持你。
07. **A**	那裡有一個皮包。會是你的嗎？
08. **A**	他原本可能送命的，但這位醫生救了他。
09. **C**	需要我幫忙嗎，先生？

Trap 1 單字陷阱・類義單字辨析篇

16 maybe vs. may be

01 文法使用錯誤範例
Sample of Wrong Grammar

A: Mom, I can't find my purse.
媽媽，我找不到我的錢包。

B: May be (✗) you put it on the desk. → Maybe (○)
你可能把它放在桌上了。

02 文法誤用詳細解析
Grammar Analysis

maybe 與 may be 均有「可能；也許」的意思，但兩者的用法及含義有所區別。請見以下說明：

（1）maybe 是副詞，意思是「也許；可能」，與 perhaps 用法類似，常位於句首。
例如：

Maybe I'll go to America to get my Master degree next year.
（也許明年我會去美國攻讀碩士學位。）

（2）may be 為情態動詞 may + 原形動詞 be，意思是「也許是；可能是」。例如：

He may be a nice guy.（他也許是個好人。）

所以範例中的正確說法應為：Maybe you put it on the desk.

03 文法使用誤用辨析
Grammar Error vs. Correct

01. 他搞不好是個騙子。
　　✗ He maybe a swindler.
　　○ He may be a swindler.

02. 他也許會約你出去。

☒ May be he'll ask you out.

◎ **Maybe he'll ask you out.**

03. 蘇珊可能今晚會來。

☒ May be Susan will come tonight.

◎ **Maybe Susan will come tonight.**

04. 他可能是一位老師。

☒ He maybe a teacher.

◎ **He may be a teacher.**

05. 也許你忘了拿鑰匙了。

☒ May be you forgot to take the key.

◎ **Maybe you forgot to take the key.**

06. 那可能是一隻小狗。

☒ It maybe a puppy.

◎ **It may be a puppy.**

04 文法陷阱辨析練習
Grammar Practice

請選出題目選項中正確的用法。

01. _____ he can tell you the truth.

Ⓐ May   Ⓑ Maybe   Ⓒ May be

02. The man _____ a soldier.

Ⓐ may   Ⓑ maybe   Ⓒ may be

03. _____ the little girl is five years old.

Ⓐ May   Ⓑ Maybe   Ⓒ May be

04. She _____ right.

Ⓐ may be   Ⓑ maybe   Ⓒ may

05. _____ she will go to school this afternoon.
　A May　　　　　　**B** May be　　　　　　**C** Maybe

06. She _____ at home.
　A may be　　　　　**B** maybe　　　　　　**C** may

07. _____ the lady over there is her mother.
　A May　　　　　　**B** Maybe　　　　　　**C** May be

08. You can ask the teacher for answer. He _____ in his office.
　A may be　　　　　**B** maybe　　　　　　**C** may

09. _____ you will have another chance next time.
　A May　　　　　　**B** May be　　　　　　**C** Maybe

10. Your mobile phone _____ in that box.
　A may be　　　　　**B** maybe　　　　　　**C** may

答案及題目中譯：

01. **B**	他也許可以告訴你事實真相。
02. **C**	那男人也許是一位軍人。
03. **B**	這小女孩或許是五歲。
04. **A**	她也許是對的。
05. **C**	今天下午她可能會去學校。
06. **A**	她也許在家。
07. **B**	也許在那裡的女士是她的媽媽。
08. **A**	你可以去跟老師問答案。他可能在他的辦公室裡。
09. **C**	也許你下次會再有一次機會。
10. **A**	你的手機可能在那個盒子裡。

17 during vs. while vs. when

01 文法使用錯誤範例
Sample of Wrong Grammar

A: Why are you so depressed?
為什麼你如此沮喪？

B: While(✗) I got to the station, the train had left. → When(○)
當我到達車站的時候，火車已經開走了。

02 文法誤用詳細解析
Grammar Analysis

during, when, while 均表示「在……的時候」，但在用法上有所區別。說明如下：

（1）during 意為「在……期間；在……的某個時候」，用在已知的時期、節日或表示時間觀念的名詞之前，其後通常接 the, this, that, these, those, my, your, his……等詞，既可指某個動作在某個時期裡連續不斷地進行，也可以指某個動作在這段時期裡的某個時間發生。例如：

I didn't pay attention during the class.（上課的時候我不專心。）

（2）when 意為「在……時候；當……時；在……期間」，既指時間點，也可指一段時間，引導的時間子句中的動詞可以是非持續性動詞，也可以是持續性動詞，子句的動作和主句的動作可以同時，也可以是先後發生，主句用過去進行式時，子句則用一般過去式。例如：

I was watching television when my father came home.
（我爸爸回家時我正在看電視。）→ come 是非持續性動詞

She didn't show up when he kept waiting for her last night.
（昨晚他一直等她時，她並未現身。）→ wait 是持續性動詞

（3）while 意為「當……的時候；與……同時」，引導的子句中的動詞必須是延續性動詞，強調主句和子句兩個動作同時發生。例如：

We must strike while the iron is hot.（打鐵必須趁熱。）

此外，while 也有「……而……」的轉折語用法，例如：
I like coffee, while he likes tea.（我愛咖啡，而他愛茶。）

03 文法使用誤用辨析
Grammar Error vs. Correct

01. 湯姆長得很壯碩，而他的弟弟卻很瘦弱。
　　☒ Tom is strong when his brother is weak.
　　☑ **Tom is strong while his brother is weak.**

02. 表演期間，請不要站起來。
　　☒ Please don't stand up when the performance.
　　☑ **Please don't stand up during the performance.**

03. 老師進來的時候，我們正在討論問題。
　　☒ While the teacher came in, we were discussing the questions.
　　☑ **When the teacher came in, we were discussing the questions.**

04. 他在上課中打瞌睡。
　　☒ He dozed off while the class.
　　☑ **He dozed off during the class.**

05. 我正在寫作業，燈突然熄了。
　　☒ I was doing my homework, while suddenly the light went out.
　　☑ **I was doing my homework, when suddenly the light went out.**

06. 當媽媽在煮飯時，我在看電視。
　　☒ When Mom was making dinner, I watched TV.
　　☑ **While Mom was making dinner, I watched TV.**

04 文法陷阱辨析練習
Grammar Practice

請選出題目選項中正確的用法。

01. I'll stay at home _____ the last four days.
   A during　　　　　　**B** when　　　　　　**C** while

02. _____ I came in, my brother was sitting in the sofa.
   A During　　　　　　**B** When　　　　　　**C** While

03. I was dancing _____ she was singing.
   A during　　　　　　**B** when　　　　　　**C** while

04. I only saw him once _____ my stay in Paris.
   A during　　　　　　**B** when　　　　　　**C** while

05. Please call me _____ you finished your work.
   A during　　　　　　**B** when　　　　　　**C** while

06. Anna is tall _____ her sister is short.
   A during　　　　　　**B** when　　　　　　**C** while

07. I was doing the housework _____ the phone rang.
   A during　　　　　　**B** when　　　　　　**C** while

08. He is very good at English _____ his brother is absolutely hopeless.
   A during　　　　　　**B** when　　　　　　**C** while

答案及題目中譯：

01. **A**	最後這四天我會待在家。	
02. **B**	我進來的時候，我弟弟正坐在沙發上。	
03. **C**	她在唱歌時，我正在跳舞。	
04. **A**	我待在巴黎時只見過他一次。	
05. **B**	當你完成工作時，請打電話給我。	
06. **C**	安娜很高，而她的姐姐很矮。	
07. **B**	電話響的時候，我正在做功課。	
08. **C**	他對英文很擅長，而他的弟弟卻無藥可救。	

18 prefer vs. rather

---

01 文法使用錯誤範例
Sample of Wrong Grammar

A: Which sport do you like, playing basketball or football?
你喜歡哪項運動，打籃球還是踢足球？

B: I prefer(✗) play basketball than football. → would rather(○)
我喜歡打籃球勝過踢足球。

02 文法誤用詳細解析
Grammar Analysis

　　prefer 與 rather 都有「寧願；更……」的意思，但兩者用法有明顯區別。請見以下說明：

（1）prefer 後面可以接名詞、動名詞或不定詞，句型的呈現方式有以下幾種：
　　　a) prefer + V-ing + to + V-ing
　　　b) prefer + n. + to + n.
　　　c) prefer + to + V + (rather) than + (to) + V →第二個 to 常省略

　　　例如：
　　　a) I prefer cooking to eating.（我比較愛煮，不愛吃。）
　　　b) She prefers long coats to jackets.（比起夾克她更喜歡長外套。）
　　　c.) He prefers to listening to music rather than reading books.
　　　　（他寧可聽音樂也不願看書。）

（2）rather 通常與 would 以及 than 連用，構成 would rather...than 的結構，意為「寧願……而不願……」，表示主觀願望，即在兩者之中選擇其一。would rather 單獨使用時，意為「寧願；寧可；更；最好」，後接原形動詞，其否定形式是 would rather not do sth.；rather 只與 than 連用時，表示客觀事實，意為「是……而不是……；與其……不如……」，它連接的並列成分可以是名詞、代名詞、形容詞、介詞（片語）、動名詞、分詞、不定詞、動詞等。例如：

I'd rather find out what's wrong than criticize. (我寧願找出問題，也不願批評。)

所以範例中的正確說法應為：I would rather play basketball than play football.

03 文法使用誤用辨析
Grammar Error vs. Correct

01. 我寧願待在家裡也不要出去。
　　☒ I prefer staying at home to go out.
　　☑ **I prefer staying at home to going out.**

02. 她寧願死也不願投降。
　　☒ She would rather die to surrender.
　　☑ **She would rather die than surrender.**

03. 當我還是個小女孩時，我喜歡黑色勝過白色。
　　☒ I had would rather black than white when I was a little girl.
　　☑ **I would like rather black than white when I was a little girl.**

04. 比起跳舞，露西更喜歡唱歌。
　　☒ Lucy enjoys singing rather than dance.
　　☑ **Lucy enjoys singing rather than dancing.**

05. 他喜歡打籃球勝過游泳。
　　☒ He prefers to playing soccer rather than swim.
　　☑ **He prefers to play soccer rather than swim.**

06. 那個小男孩不願意去上學。
　　☒ That little boy would rather not to go to school.
　　☑ **That little boy would rather not go to school.**

04 文法陷阱辨析練習
Grammar Practice

請選出題目選項中正確的用法。

01. A: Do you like swimming?
   B: Yes, but I prefer _____.
   A skate   **B** to skating   **C** skating

02. She'd rather _____ in the countryside.
   A to working   **B** work   **C** working

03. Joe prefers swimming to _____ football.
   A playing   **B** play   **C** have would rather

04. I _____ walk there than take a bus.
   A had would rather   **B** would rather   **C** played

05. He is a teacher _____ an actor.
   A rather than   **B** would rather   **C** prefer

06. Kate preferred to stay at home rather than _____ to see a film.
   A going   **B** to go   **C** gone

07. The students preferred writing a term paper _____ taking an exam.
   A of   **B** to   **C** in

08. I would rather have noodles than _____ hamburgers.
   A to have   **B** having   **C** X

答案及題目中譯：

01. **C** 　A：你喜歡游泳嗎？　　B：是的，但我更喜歡溜冰。

02. **B** 　她寧可在鄉下工作。

03. **A** 　比起足球，喬更喜歡游泳。

04. **B** 　比起搭公車，我寧可走路去那裡。

05. **A** 　與其說他是個演員，不如說他是一位老師。

06. **B** 　凱特寧願待在家裡，也不願出去看電影。

07. **B** 　學生們寧可寫一篇學期報告，也不願考試。

08. **C** 　比起漢堡，我更喜歡吃麵。

Trap 2 單字陷阱・一字多義使用篇

01 think 的用法

---

01 文法使用錯誤範例
Sample of Wrong Grammar

A: What can I do for you?
有什麼需要我幫忙的嗎？

B: Yes. I want to know what this is. I can't think about(✗) its name.
→ of(○)
是的，我想知道這東西是什麼。我突然想不起它的名稱。

02 文法誤用詳細解析
Grammar Analysis

think 作為動詞，其過去式和過去分詞均為 thought，有「思考、想、認為、想起、打算」之意。例如：

I think Germany will be the winner.（我認為德國將會獲得冠軍。）

think 後面可接介詞構成不同意思的介詞片語，這裡主要介紹 think of, think about, think over 三個容易混淆的介詞片語。

（1）think of 與 think about 最容易混淆，在表示「考慮」或「對……有某種看法」時，兩者可以通用。例如：

What do you think of / about that hat?（你認為那頂帽子怎麼樣？）

需要注意的是，在這種情況下如果出現「think highly of … 認為……很好」、「think badly / ill of… 認為……不好」等片語時，of 不可改為 about。另外，在下列情況中兩者也不可以通用：

a) 當表示「想要、打算、想出、想到、關心、想起、記得」時，一般用 think of，而不用 think about。如：

He's thinking of cheating.（他打算要作弊。）

範例中「I can't think of its name.」是指「想不起該物品的名稱」，此時「想起」應用 think of。→ I can't think of it's name.

b) 當表示「回想過去的事情、考慮某事／某計畫是否可行」時，一般有 think about，而不用 think of。例如：

I'll never think about that thing.（我不會再想那件事。）

（2）think over 意為「仔細考慮；重新考慮」，比 think of 與 think about 更深入與慎重。如：

Think it over, and we'll find a way to solve this problem.
（仔細考慮一下，我們會找到辦法來解決這個問題的。）

03 文法使用誤用辨析
Grammar Error vs. Correct

01. 琳達聽到那首歌的時候，想起了她的一個朋友。
   ☒ Linda thought about one of her friends when she heard that song.
   ☑ **Linda thought of one of her friends when she heard that song.**

02. 他說，他需要幾天時間來仔細考慮這件事情。
   ☒ He said he needed several days to think this matter.
   ☑ **He said he needed several days to think this matter over.**

03. 我明天再給你答覆，因為我需要考慮一下這個計畫，看看是否可行。
   ☒ I'll give you my answer tomorrow, because I need to think of the plan and see if it is practicable.
   ☑ **I'll give you my answer tomorrow, because I need to think about the plan and see if it is practicable.**

04. 凱特，妳打算和傑克去旅遊嗎？
   ☒ Kate, are you thinking about taking a trip with Jake?
   ☑ **Kate, are you thinking of taking a trip with Jake?**

05. 不要因為他犯過一次小錯誤，就對他產生壞印象。
   ☒ Don't think ill about him just because he made a mistake last time.
   ☑ **Don't think ill of him just because he made a mistake last time.**

06. 我從來不認為自己是那樣的人。

☓ I never thought over myself in that way.

○ **I never thought of myself in that way.**

04 文法陷阱辨析練習
Grammar Practice

請選出題目選項中正確的用法。

01. I can _____ I have met Carol at least three times this morning.
🅱 think about   🅲 think over   🅳 think of

02. Jimmy is forward to help others, and he is always _____ others.
🅱 thinking of   🅲 thinking over   🅳 thinking to

03. My dad is thinking _____ buying a new car.
🅱 for   🅲 over   🅳 about

04. I'm _____ going to the cinema this weekend.
🅱 thinking of   🅲 thinking over   🅳 thinking

05. Can you _____ an idea for me? I'm brain dead.
🅱 think of   🅲 think about   🅳 think over

06. Ada often _____ what her mother said.
🅱 thought of   🅲 thought over   🅳 thought

答案及題目中譯：

01. 🅳	我記得今天早上跟凱洛至少碰過三次面了。	
02. 🅱	吉米不只熱心助人，而且總是會為人著想。	
03. 🅳	我爸在考慮要買一部新車。	
04. 🅱	我打算這個週末去看電影。	
05. 🅱	你可以幫我想個主意嗎？我腦袋打結了。	
06. 🅲	艾達經常都會考慮到她媽媽的看法。	

02 time 的用法

01 文法使用錯誤範例
Sample of Wrong Grammar

A: What is the central idea of this article?
這篇文章的中心思想是什麼？

B: Its central idea is that time has changed(✗) and women can do anything men can do. → as the times changing(○)
它的中心思想是，隨著時代的變遷，女人可以做男人能做的任何事。

02 文法誤用詳細解析
Grammar Analysis

　　time 的本意為「時間」，是一個抽象的不可數名詞，我們常說的「光陰似箭」即可譯為 "How time flies!"，詢問時間時有兩種說法，分別為 "What time is it?" 以及 "What's the time?"。

time 作此意解時，還有以下兩種常用句型：

（1）It's time (for sb.) to do sth.（某人）是時候做某事了。

　　在使用該句型時需要注意的是：It is time 後面如果接「that 子句」時，子句要用過去式，因為是假設語氣，若要指與現在事實相反，則用過去式。

（2）I have no time to do sth.（我沒有時間做某事。）

　　除基本意思外，time 還可表示「一段時光」或「歷史時期、時代」。作「一段時光」時，是一個具有具體意義的可數名詞；作「歷史時期、時代、境況」講時，必須用複數形式 times 來表示。

範例中，「時代的變遷」之中的 time 應該用其複數形式 times。因此正確的說法應為：

Its central idea is that as the times changing, women can do anything men can.

03 文法使用誤用辨析
Grammar Error vs. Correct

01. 我們該下班了。
   ☒ It's time that we get off work.
   ☑ **It's time that we got off work.**

02. 我沒有時間吃早餐，因為上學要遲到了。
   ☒ I have not times to have breakfast because I'll be late for school.
   ☑ **I have no time to have breakfast because I'll be late for school.**

03. 你在莉莉的生日派對上玩得開心嗎？
   ☒ Did you have good time at Lily's birthday party?
   ☑ **Did you have a good time at Lily's birthday party?**

04. 這個方法節省了時間，所以我才能迅速地完成任務。
   ☒ This method saves a lot of times, so I can finish the task quickly.
   ☑ **This method saves a lot of time, so I can finish the task quickly.**

05. 吉姆和他的家人在那個小島上度過了一段美好的時光。
   ☒ Jim and his family have wonderful time on the island.
   ☑ **Jim and his family had a wonderful time on the island.**

06. 生命中總有些時候，我們必須作出正確的抉擇來實現我們的夢想。
   ☒ There is time in our lives when we have to make the right choices to realize our dreams.
   ☑ **There are times in our lives when we have to make good choices to realize our dreams.**

04 文法陷阱辨析練習
Grammar Practice

請選出題目選項中正確的用法。

01. If there is no competitive pressure, we should _____ at school.
   A had a happy time　　**B** have a happy time　　**C** have had a happy time

02. It's time that we _____ lunch.
   A have　　　　　　**B** to have　　　　　**C** had

03. I _____ answering the question.
   A have a difficult time　**B** has difficult time　**C** have difficult time

04. In _____ the lifetime of humans was extremely short.
   A ancient times　　**B** the ancient times　　**C** the ancient time

05. Rita _____ finding her pencil.
   A had hard time　　**B** have a hard time　　**C** had a hard time

06. You do not need to envy his good body. It's time for you _____ exercise.
   A must do　　　　**B** to do　　　　　**C** will do

07. My friends and I spent our holiday in Hawaii, and we _____.
   A had a wonderful time　**B** had wonderful time　**C** had wonderful times

---

答案及題目中譯：

01. **B**	如果不是有競爭壓力，我們應該會有段愉快的求學時光。
02. **C**	我們該吃午餐了。
03. **A**	回答問題讓我很痛苦。
04. **A**	古時候人類的壽命很短。
05. **C**	麗塔找她的鉛筆找了很久。
06. **B**	你不用羨慕他的好身材。你該運動了。
07. **A**	我和我朋友到夏威夷去度假，我們過了愉快的時光。

03 help 的用法

01 文法使用錯誤範例
Sample of Wrong Grammar

A: Can you help me to(✕) my French? → with(○)
你能幫助我學法語嗎？

B: Yes. Of course.
當然可以。

02 文法誤用詳細解析
Grammar Analysis

help 作動詞，意為「幫助、協助、援助、促進、促使」。該詞有以下幾種句型，所表達的意思也有所區別。

（1）help sb. (to) do sth. 意為「幫助某人做某事」，to 現在一般都會省略；help sb. with sth. 意為「在某方面幫助某人」，with 是介詞，後面接名詞；help (to) do sth. 意為「有助於做某事」；help oneself (to) 意為「自用（食物等）」；help sb. out 意為「幫助某人克服困難、渡過難關、解決問題、完成工作」。

範例中，A 所要表達的意思是「在法語學習方面得到幫助」，應該使用句型 help sb. with sth.，因此正確的說法應為：

Can you help me with my French?

（2）另外，help 與 can't 連用時的特殊用法有

a) can't help + V-ing 意為「情不自禁做某事」

b) can't help but + V 意為「不得不做某事」，加強記憶：but 是對等連接詞，前後要接同性質的詞，故前後的 help 和 V 均用原形。例如：
We can't help laughing. = We can't help but laugh.（我們忍不住笑出來。）

03 文法使用誤用辨析
Grammar Error vs. Correct

01. 這本書有助於提高我的英語水準。
　　⊠ This book helps with improving my English.
　　☑ **This book helps improve my English.**

02. 她忍不住哭了。
　　⊠ She couldn't help to cry.
　　☑ **She couldn't help crying.**

03. 朋友就是在我們處於困境的時候幫我們渡過難關的人。
　　⊠ Friends are the people who always help us when we're in trouble.
　　☑ **Friends are the people who always help us out when we're in trouble.**

04. 你可以幫我做報告嗎？
　　⊠ Can you help me my report?
　　☑ **Can you help me with my report.**

05. 為了生活，我不得不做這份工作。
　　⊠ For a living, I can't help do the job.
　　☑ **For a living, I can't help but do the job.**

06. 請隨意吃點蛋糕。
　　⊠ Help to eat the cake.
　　☑ **Help yourself to the cake.**

04 文法陷阱辨析練習
Grammar Practice

請選出題目選項中正確的用法。

01. Jo helped me _____ my English.
　　🅐 to　　　　　　　　🅑 with　　　　　　　🅒 of

02. I can't help you _____ the box.
　　🅐 carry　　　　　　🅑 to carrying　　　　🅒 carried

03. Please ＿＿＿＿＿＿ some beer.
　　Ⓐ help yourself　　Ⓑ help to　　Ⓒ help yourself to

04. Rita can't help ＿＿＿＿＿＿ by his enthusiasm.
　　Ⓐ be impressed　　Ⓑ to be impressed　　Ⓒ being impressed

05. Danny ＿＿＿＿＿＿ with money when I'm in trouble.
　　Ⓐ helped me out　　Ⓑ helped me in　　Ⓒ help me out

06. Lana, can you help ＿＿＿＿＿＿ this patient to the hospital?
　　Ⓐ sending　　Ⓑ send　　Ⓒ sent

07. I'll help you＿＿＿＿＿＿ the housework.
　　Ⓐ with　　Ⓑ to　　Ⓒ of

08. I can't help but ＿＿＿＿＿＿ every day.
　　Ⓐ going to work　　Ⓑ to work　　Ⓒ go to work

09. His speech helps us ＿＿＿＿＿＿ the policy.
　　Ⓐ understand　　Ⓑ understanding　　Ⓒ with understand

10. Sorry, I know nothing about this, so I can't ＿＿＿＿＿＿.
　　Ⓐ help you to do　　Ⓑ help you　　Ⓒ help you with

答案及題目中譯：

01. Ⓑ	喬幫我學英文。
02. Ⓐ	我沒辦法幫你搬這個箱子。
03. Ⓒ	請自己隨意喝點啤酒。
04. Ⓒ	麗塔無法不對他的熱情留下深刻印象。
05. Ⓐ	當我有困難時，丹尼用金錢助我度過了難關。
06. Ⓑ	拉娜，妳可以幫忙把這位病人送進醫院嗎？
07. Ⓐ	我會幫你做家事。
08. Ⓒ	我不得不每天去工作。
09. Ⓐ	他的演講有助於我們了解這項政策。
10. Ⓑ	抱歉，我對這個一點都不了解，所以沒辦法幫你解決問題。

Trap 2 單字陷阱・一字多義使用篇

04 hurt 的用法

01 文法使用錯誤範例
Sample of Wrong Grammar

A: Lucy, what's wrong with you?
露西，你怎麼了？

B: Mom, my stomach is hurt(✗). → hurts(○)
媽媽，我肚子痛。

02 文法誤用詳細解析
Grammar Analysis

hurt 可作動詞，也可作形容詞。

（1）作動詞時，可兼作及物動詞與不及物動詞，意為「刺痛、傷害、（使）痛心、（使）傷感情、危害、損害、受傷」，表示精神上或肉體上的「創傷」，即「使人的肉體受傷而疼痛」或「傷了某人的自尊心或感情」之意，作不及物動詞時表示「痛」。另外，過去分詞只作主詞補語，不作形容詞用。例如：

Be careful, you could end up getting hurt. → 過去分詞 hurt 當主詞補語
（小心，最後你可能傷到自己。）

（2）作形容詞時，意為「（身體上或感情上）受傷害的、受委屈的」，與 be 一起構成主詞補語。

I am hurt.（我感到受傷。）

所以範例中的 welcome（形容詞）即指「被允許的；可隨意使用⋯⋯的」，不必改為被動式 be welcomed to⋯。但此句的 welcome 亦可用動詞形式表達，也就是 You are welcomed to...，表示「你」是被歡迎去使用我的電話的。

範例中，B 所要表達的是「肚子痛」，如上所述，表示「痛」一般用動詞 hurt，因此正確的說法應為：Mom, my stomach hurts.

03 文法使用誤用辨析
Grammar Error vs. Correct

01. 湯姆從樓梯摔下來，受傷了。
- ❌ Tom is hurt himself when he fell down the stairs.
- ⭕ Tom **hurt** himself when he fell down the stairs.

---

02. 佩妮沒有被邀請去露西的生日派對，她感到十分難過。
- ❌ Penny deeply hurt because she had not been invited to Lucy's birthday party.
- ⭕ Penny **was deeply hurt** because she had not been invited to Lucy's birthday party.

---

03. 他傷害了拉娜的感情。
- ❌ He is hurt Lana's feelings.
- ⭕ He **hurt** Lana's feelings.

---

04. 他吼我時，我感到很受傷。
- ❌ I feel hurting when he yelled at me.
- ⭕ I feel **hurt** when he yelled at me.

---

05. 我的手打籃球的時候受傷了。
- ❌ My hand is hurt when I was playing basketball.
- ⭕ My hand **hurt** when I was playing basketball.

04 文法陷阱辨析練習
Grammar Practice

請選出題目選項中正確的用法。

01. _____ you badly hurt?
- Ⓐ Have
- Ⓑ Did
- Ⓒ Are

02. My feet _____.
- Ⓐ hurt
- Ⓑ hurts
- Ⓒ is hurt

03. It won't _____ you to miss lunch for once.
- Ⓐ to hurt
- Ⓑ hurt
- Ⓒ be hurt

04. Many passengers were _____ when a truck and a bus collided.
　　A hurt 　　　　　　　**B** to hurt 　　　　　　**C** hurting

05. The ball _____ him in the chest.
　　A hurting 　　　　　　**B** to hurt 　　　　　　**C** hurt

06. She _____ my feelings yesterday.
　　A hurts 　　　　　　　**B** was hurt 　　　　　**C** hurt

07. She _____ because Jerry didn't invite her.
　　A hurts 　　　　　　　**B** was hurt 　　　　　**C** hurt

08. The driver _____ himself badly in the traffic accident
　　A hurt 　　　　　　　　**B** was hurt 　　　　　**C** hurts

09. He _____ when he heard what his mom said.
　　A hurts 　　　　　　　**B** hurt 　　　　　　　**C** was hurt

10. Don't be afraid. The rabbit won't _____ you.
　　A hurt 　　　　　　　　**B** to hurt 　　　　　**C** be hurt

答案及題目中譯：

01. **C**	你傷得很嚴重嗎？
02. **A**	我的腳好痛。
03. **B**	你只不過是少吃一次午餐，不會怎樣的啦。
04. **A**	卡車和巴士相撞時，許多乘客都受傷了。
05. **C**	球打到他的胸口上，使他受了傷。
06. **C**	她昨天傷了我的心。
07. **B**	因為傑瑞沒邀請她，使她受到打擊。
08. **A**	司機在車禍中受重傷。
09. **C**	他媽媽說的話讓他很受傷。
10. **A**	別怕，這兔子不會傷害你的。

Trap 2 單字陷阱・一字多義使用篇

05 mind 的用法

01 文法使用錯誤範例
Sample of Wrong Grammar

A: Do you mind **I smoke**(✗) here? → my smoking(○)
你介意我在這兒抽煙嗎？

B: I'm sorry, but I do.
抱歉，我介意。

02 文法誤用詳細解析
Grammar Analysis

　　mind 作為動詞有「介意、在乎」之意，既可當不及物動詞，也可當及物動詞，請見以下說明：

（1）作不及物動詞時，一般用於 Do / Would you mind if ＋子句這一句型，表示詢問對方「是否介意（說話人）做某事」。例如：「你介意我打開門嗎？」可譯為 "Do you mind if I open the door?"（你介意我打開門嗎？）

　　　針對這一問句有「同意」與「反對」兩種不同的回答。表示「同意」時，答語要用否定形式，可直接用 No 來回答，也可以用 Not at all. / Certainly not. 等其他形式來回答；表示「反對」時，答語要用肯定形式，但是在用 yes 等詞語回答之前一般用 I'm sorry / afraid... 等，以緩和語氣。

（2）作及物動詞時，後面通常接名詞、代名詞、V-ing、複合句、子句等，例如，上面的例子「你介意我打開門嗎？」也可以這麼說 "Would you mind my opening the door?"

　　　需要注意的是，Do / Would you mind doing sth.? 是表示麻煩他人做某事，可譯為「可否請您……？」開頭常用 would 表示請教對方的意願，do 較少用，答語與上述作不及物動詞時情況相同。

　　範例中，Do you mind I smoke here? 是一個錯誤的句子，如上所述，如果句中的 mind 作不及物動詞，則應該 mind 後面加 if；如果 mind 作及物動詞，則 I smoke 應改為 my smoking。因此以上兩種皆為正確的說法：

Do you mind if I smoke here? / Do you mind my smoking here?

03 文法使用誤用辨析
Grammar Error vs. Correct

01. A: 你介意我在這裡踢足球嗎？　B: 不，毫不介意。
　　☒ A: Would you mind my play football here?
　　　 B: No, not at all.
　　☑ **A: Would you mind my playing football here?**
　　　 B: No, not at all.

02. 請不要亂扔垃圾好嗎？
　　☒ Would you mind not to littering?
　　☑ **Would you mind not littering?**

03. 你介意我把收音機的音量調大一點嗎？
　　☒ Do you mind I turn up the radio a bit?
　　☑ **Do you mind if I turn up the radio a bit?**

04. A: 你介意洗這些盤子嗎？　B: 沒問題，我馬上去洗。
　　☒ A: Would you mind washing the plates?
　　　 B: Yes, no problem. I'll do it right away.
　　☑ **A: Would you mind washing the plates?**
　　　 B: Not at all. / Of course not. I'll do it right away.

05. A：你介意我說話聲音大一點嗎？　B：是的，我準備睡覺了。
　　☒ A: Do you mind if I speaking loudly?
　　　 B: No. I'm ready to go to bed.
　　☑ **A: Do you mind if I speak loudly?**
　　　 B: Yes, I do. I'm ready to go to bed.

06. 我晚一點去拜訪你好嗎？
　　🅧 Do you mind to visit you later?
　　🅞 **Do you mind if I visit you later?**

04 文法陷阱辨析練習
Grammar Practice

請選出題目選項中正確的用法。

01. A: Lucy, I can't hear you clearly, would you mind _____ more loudly?
　　B: Sorry. I'll speak loudly.
　　🅐 speak　　　　　　🅑 speaking　　　　　🅒 to speak

02. Do you mind _____?
　　🅐 if I turn the light on　🅑 I turn the light on　🅒 if I turning the light on

03. A: Would you mind _____ the dictionary?
　　B: _____ Here you are.
　　🅐 passing; Yes, I do.　🅑 to pass; Certainly not.　🅒 passing; Certainly not.

04. Would you mind _____ all the time?
　　🅐 not swear　　　　🅑 not to swear　　　🅒 not swearing

05. A: Do you mind _____ this book away?
　　B: I'm sorry, _____. Because I'll read it later.
　　🅐 I take; but I do　🅑 if I take; of course not　🅒 if I take; but I do

06. Would you mind _____ the car? I'm very tired.
　　🅐 driving　　　　　🅑 drive　　　　　　🅒 to drive

07. Would you mind _____ over here, David? Grandpa is sleeping now.
　　🅐 no reading　　　　🅑 not read　　　　🅒 not reading

08. Excuse me, would you mind _____ my car here?
　　🅐 my parking　　　　🅑 I parking　　　　🅒 my park

09. A: Lisa, would you mind _____ your bike away? I'm sweeping now.
    B: _____. I'll do it in a minute.

    A moving; Yes　　　　　**B** move; No　　　　　**C** moving; No

10. Mrs. Brown, would you mind _____ this sentence again?

    A to explain　　　　　**B** explaining　　　　　**C** explained

答案及題目中譯：

---

01. **B**　A：露西，我聽不清楚妳的聲音，妳可以再大聲點嗎？
　　　　　B：抱歉，我會說大聲一點。

---

02. **A**　你介意我開燈嗎？

---

03. **C**　A：你介意把字典傳過來嗎？
　　　　　B：當然不會。字典給你。

---

04. **C**　你可以不要整天都在罵人嗎？

---

05. **C**　A：你介意我把這本書拿走嗎？
　　　　　B：很抱歉，我介意，因為我等一下要看。

---

06. **A**　由你開車好嗎？因為我好累。

---

07. **C**　大衛，你可以不要在這裡看書嗎？爺爺正在睡覺。

---

08. **A**　不好意思，你介意我把車停在這裡嗎？

---

09. **C**　A：莉莎，妳可以把腳踏車移開嗎？我正在打掃。
　　　　　B：好的，我馬上移。

---

10. **B**　布朗太太，妳可不可以把這個句子再解釋一遍？

---

06 welcome 的用法

---

01 文法使用錯誤範例
Sample of Wrong Grammar

A: You are welcome(✕) to use my phone. → welcome / welcomed(○)
   我的電話你儘管用。

B: Thank you very much.
   非常謝謝你。

02 文法誤用詳細解析
Grammar Analysis

　　welcome 有很多種詞性，在句子中可當作感歎詞、名詞、動詞、形容詞……等，這裡先介紹較常見的動詞以及形容詞用法，請見以下說明：

（1）welcome 作動詞時為及物動詞，用來表達「歡迎（某人或某物）」。例如：

Let's welcome our special guests from Shanghai.
（讓我們歡迎來自上海的貴賓們。）

（2）welcome 作形容詞時，則用來表達「受歡迎的；令人喜歡的」。可解釋為「被允許的；可隨意使用……的」，表示樂於讓某人做某事。值得注意的是 welcome 當作形容詞時，需與被動語態中的動詞用法分清楚，例如：

Leonardo DiCaprio is a welcome super star all over the world.
（李奧納多狄卡皮歐是全世界都歡迎的超級巨星。）→ 形容詞用法

Fast food is always welcomed by teenagers.
（速食總是受到青少年的歡迎。）→ 被動語態動詞用法

所以範例中的 welcome（形容詞）即指「被允許的；可隨意使用……」，不必改為被動式 be welcomed to...。但此句的 welcome 亦可用動詞形式表達，也就是 You are welcomed to...，表示「你」是被歡迎去使用我的電話的。

03 文法使用誤用辨析
Grammar Error vs. Correct

01. 讓我們歡迎我們的新同事。
    ❌ Let's welcome to our new colleagues.
    ⭕ Let's **welcome our new colleagues.**

02. 我去拜訪莉莉父母的時候，得到了他們衷心地歡迎。
    ❌ I was heartily welcome by Lily's parents when I visited them.
    ⭕ **I was heartily welcomed by Lily's parents when I visited them.**

03. 歡迎你隨時來看我。
    ❌ You're welcomed to visit me anytime.
    ⭕ **You're welcome to visit me anytime.**

04. 大家熱烈歡迎吉姆回到公司。
    ❌ Jim was warmly welcome back to the company.
    ⭕ **Jim was warmly welcomed back to the company.**

05. 任何想來這裡來學習的人都是受歡迎的。
    ❌ Anyone who wants to come here to study will be welcomed.
    ⭕ **Anyone who wants to come here to study will be welcome.**

06. 他提出了一個極受歡迎的建議。
    ❌ He came up with a most welcomed suggestion.
    ⭕ **He came up with a most welcome suggestion.**

04 文法陷阱辨析練習
Grammar Practice

請選出題目選項中正確的用法。

01. There were more than 50 students lined up to _____ those visiting leaders this afternoon.
    🅐 welcome to　　🅑 welcoming　　🅒 welcome

02. Jerry's marriage was not _____ by his family.
    🅐 welcomed　　🅑 welcome　　🅒 to welcome

03. You are _____ to use my bike.
A welcoming **B** welcome **C** to welcome

04. We _____ the students from the station to the school yesterday.
A welcome **B** welcome to **C** welcomed

05. A: Thanks for your cake. It's very delicious.
    B: _____
A You're welcome. **B** You're welcoming. **C** You're welcomed to.

06. Tony is a _____ guest for my family.
A welcomed **B** welcome **C** welcoming

07. Nate doesn't _____ Jack.
A welcoming **B** welcome **C** welcomed

08. There is a _____ sign in the picture.
A welcoming **B** welcomed **C** welcome

09. It's a pleasure to _____ you to my home.
A welcome **B** welcomed **C** welcoming

答案及題目中譯：

01. **C**	這天下午超過 50 位學生排隊歡迎前來參訪的領袖們。
02. **A**	傑瑞的婚姻沒有得到他家人的認同。
03. **B**	歡迎你隨時使用我的自行車。
04. **C**	我們昨天從車站到學校一路迎接我們的學生。
05. **A**	A：謝謝你的蛋糕。非常美味。　B：不客氣。
06. **B**	東尼是我們家隨時都歡迎的客人。
07. **B**	奈德不歡迎傑克。
08. **C**	圖片裡有一個歡迎的標誌。
09. **A**	迎接你來到我們家是我的榮幸。

Day27

01 動詞＋動名詞 vs. 動詞＋不定詞

01 動詞＋動名詞 vs. 動詞＋不定詞

01 文法使用錯誤範例
Sample of Wrong Grammar

A: Please stop **to cry**(✗) and tell me what happened. → crying(○)
不要哭了，告訴我發生了什麼事。

B: I got dumped by my boyfriend.
我被我的男朋友給甩了。

02 文法誤用詳細解析
Grammar Analysis

　　在英語中，有很多動詞或片語後面既可以接動名詞又可以接不定詞，後面所接形式不同，句子的意思也不同，這些字詞或片語又可以分為以下幾種情況：

（1）動詞 forget, remember, regret 等接不定詞，意為「……將要做某事」；接動名詞則為「……做過某事」。例如：

I forgot to post the mail.（我忘了去寄信。）

I forgot posting the mail.（我忘了寄過信了。）

（2）動詞 mean 接不定詞，意為「打算做、想要做」，表示一種意圖；接動名詞，意為「意味著、意思是」，表示解釋。動詞 try 接不定詞，意為「設法做、盡力做」，表示一種決心；接動名詞，意為「試著做」，表示嘗試。例如：

He tried hard to convince me of his innocence.（他極力使我相信他的清白。）

I try knocking at his door.（我試著敲他的門。）

（3）動詞 want, need, require 接不定詞，意為「想、要做……」，是用被動形式表示被動意義；接動名詞，意為「必須、該……」，是用主動形式表示被動意義。需要注意的是，若 need, require, want 後接動詞成為句子主詞所做的動作，則只能用不定詞，不能用動名詞。例如：

The patient needs looking after.（這位病患需要照顧。）→被動意義

（4）動詞 stop 和動詞片語 go on 後也可以接動名詞或不定詞。stop 接不定詞，意為「停下來去做……」，即要去做另外一件事；接動名詞，意為停止做正在做的事。go on 接不定詞，表示「做完正在做的事之後，繼續做另一件事」；接動名詞，即繼續做原來就在做的同一件事。

範例中，A 所要表達的意思是「不要再哭了」，如上所述，停止做正在做的事應該用 stop doing sth. 因此正確的説法為：

Please stop crying and tell me what happened.

（5）此外，can't help 後接不定詞，意為「不能幫忙做某事」；接動名詞當作受詞，意為「不能幫忙做某事」；接動名詞，意為「禁不住去做某事」。be used to 接不定詞，意為「被用來做什麼」；接動名詞，意為「習慣於」。look forward to 接動名詞，意為「期望做某事」。

I'm used to leading a metropolitan life in Taipei.（我習慣過台北的都市生活。）

I looking forward to seeing you.（我期待見到您。）

03 文法使用誤用辨析
Grammar Error vs. Correct

01. 我忘記把鑰匙給你了。
    ⊠ I forgot giving you the key.
    ⊙ **I forgot to give you the key.**

02. 我的小狗每天都需要洗澡。
    ⊠ My dog needs to wash every day.
    ⊙ **My dog needs washing every day.**

03. 這部電影很感人，她情不自禁地哭了起來。
    ⊠ The movie was very moving that she couldn't help to cry.
    ⊙ **The movie was very moving that she couldn't help crying.**

04. 喝完一杯咖啡後，湯姆繼續對他的朋友講那個有趣的故事。

☒ After a cup of coffee, Tom went on telling his friends that interesting story.

🔵 **After a cup of coffee, Tom went on to tell his friends that interesting story.**

05. 明天我會想辦法買到那本書。

☒ I'll try getting the book tomorrow.

🔵 **I'll try to get the book tomorrow.**

06. 我想，他的意思是要點披薩，不要點沙拉。

☒ I think he meant ordering pizza rather than salad.

🔵 **I think he meant to order pizza rather than salad.**

04 文法陷阱辨析練習
Grammar Practice

請選出題目選項中正確的用法。

01. I remembered _____ the CD to Linda, but she said I didn't.
   A give   **B** giving   **C** to give

02. He forgot _____ me the money yesterday, so he paid just now.
   A to pay   **B** paying   **C** pay

03. Kate didn't mean _____ you. You should forgive her.
   A hurting   **B** to hurt   **C** to be hurt

04. We stopped _____ a rest after jogging for a long time.
   A having   **B** had   **C** to have

05. Sorry, I'm very busy now, so I can't help _____ the boxes.
   A carrying   **B** carried   **C** to carry

06. Nicole, you can't go on _____ this way. You should begin a new life.
   A living   **B** to live   **C** lived

07. I need _____ my pot plant or it will dry out.
   A watering   **B** to be watered   **C** to water

08. I tried _____ the text without your help.
　　A to reciting　　　　**B** reciting　　　　**C** recited

09. Don't worry. You'll be used to _____ here soon.
　　A living　　　　**B** to live　　　　**C** lived

10. I'm looking forward to _____ from you soon.
　　A heard　　　　**B** to hear　　　　**C** hearing

答案及題目中譯：

01. **B**	我記得我將 CD 給琳達了，她卻說我沒給她。
02. **A**	昨天他忘了付錢給我，所以剛剛付了。
03. **B**	凱特不是故意要傷害你的，你就原諒她吧。
04. **C**	慢跑了一陣之後，我們停下來稍作休息。
05. **C**	抱歉，我現在很忙，所以沒辦法幫忙搬這些箱子。
06. **A**	妮可，妳不能繼續這樣生活下去，妳必須換個新的生活方式。
07. **C**	我必須幫我的盆栽澆水，不然它會乾掉。
08. **B**	我試著在沒有你的協助下背完文章。
09. **A**	別擔心，你很快就會適應這裡的生活了。
10. **C**	我期待很快就會有你的消息。

Trap 3 文法陷阱‧文法觀念辨析篇

02 過去簡單式vs. 過去完成式

01 文法使用錯誤範例
Sample of Wrong Grammar

A: Have you watched(✕) the basketball match yesterday?
→ Did... watch(○)
你昨天看籃球比賽了嗎？

B: Yes, I did. It was great!
是的，我看了。很精彩！

02 文法誤用詳細解析
Grammar Analysis

一般過去時與過去完成式都表示發生在過去的事情，但兩者有明顯的區別：

（1）一般過去式表示過去某個時間裡發生的動作或狀態，即陳述過去的事實，常和表示過去的時間副詞（ago, last, just now, yesterday）連用。

（2）過去完成式表示在過去某一時間或動作之前已發生或完成的動作或狀態。可以用介詞片語或時間副詞（when, as soon as）子句來銜接先後發生的兩件事。

需要注意的是：

a) 敘述歷史事實，可不用過去完成式，而只用一般過去式。
Confucius traveled all around the countries.（孔子周遊列國。）

b) 兩個動作如按順序發生又不強調先後，或用 then, and, but, so 等連接詞時，通常用一般過去式。
He was quite happy then, but an accident stroke him down.
（那時他蠻快樂的，但一件意外事故將他擊垮。）

c) 在過去不同時間發生的兩個動作中，發生在先的，用過去完成式，發生在後的，用一般過去式。
Grandma had slept when / after / before I came home late last night.

（昨晚我晚歸的時候 / 之後 / 之前，祖母已經睡了。）

d) 表示意向的動詞，如 hope, wish, expect, think, intend, mean, suppose 等，用過去完成式表示過去未曾實現的願望、打算、想法或意圖時，意為「原本……、未能……」。例如：

I suppose you have already known the truth.（我以為你已經知道真相了。）

範例中，「你昨天看籃球賽了嗎？」是陳述過去的事實，且有具體的過去時間狀語 yesterday，應用一般過去時來陳述，所以正確的說法應為：

Did you **watch** the basketball match yesterday?

03 文法使用誤用辨析
Grammar Error vs. Correct

01. 吉姆走進辦公室向老師問好。
    ☒ Jim had entered the office and had said hello to the teacher.
    ☐ **Jim entered the office and said hello to the teacher.**

02. 我到他家以前，他已經出去了。
    ☒ He went out before I got to his home.
    ☐ **He had gone out before I got to his home.**

03. 那時露西希望莉莉能來參加她的生日派對，但是莉莉沒有來。
    ☒ Lucy hoped that Lily would come to her birthday party, but Lily didn't.
    ☐ **Lucy had hoped that Lily would come to her birthday party, but Lily didn't.**

04. 完成他的工作之後，他就回家了。
    ☒ After he finished his work, he went home.
    ☐ **After he had finished his work, he went home.**

05. 在我朋友吃完晚餐之前，我就離開餐廳了。
    ☒ I left the restaurant before my friends finished dinner.
    ☐ **I had left the restaurant before my friends finished dinner.**

06. 當公車來的時候，我在車站已等了 30 分鐘。
    ☒ I was at the bus station for 30 minutes when a bus came.
    ☐ **I had been at the bus station for 30 minutes when a bus came.**

04 文法陷阱辨析練習
Grammar Practice

請選出題目選項中正確的用法。

01. He _____ his dictionary, so I lent him mine.
   Ⓐ lose　　　　　Ⓑ lost　　　　　Ⓒ had lost

02. The thieves _____ when the police arrived.
   Ⓐ had run away　　Ⓑ ran away　　Ⓒ run away

03. We _____ that Lisa would come to visit us.
   Ⓐ hoped　　　　Ⓑ hope　　　　Ⓒ had hoped

04. He _____ around but saw nothing.
   Ⓐ looked　　　　Ⓑ had looked　　Ⓒ looks

05. Luna said she _____ born in 1990.
   Ⓐ had been　　　Ⓑ X　　　　　Ⓒ was

06. The postman told me that my package _____.
   Ⓐ did not arrive　　Ⓑ has not arrived　　Ⓒ had not arrived

07. Tina _____ the housework before she went out shopping.
   Ⓐ did　　　　　Ⓑ was doing　　Ⓒ had done

答案及題目中譯：

01. Ⓑ 他的字典弄丟了，所以我把我的借給他。

02. Ⓐ 那些小偷在警察到達之前就溜了。

03. Ⓒ 我們本來希望莉莎會來看我們的。

04. Ⓐ 他到處觀望，但什麼也沒看到。

05. Ⓒ 露娜說她是 1990 年出生的。

06. Ⓒ 郵差告訴我我的包裹還沒送到。

07. Ⓒ 蒂娜出去逛街前已經做完家事了。

03 慣用被動式的句子

01 文法使用錯誤範例
Sample of Wrong Grammar

My daughter had just been returned(✕). → returned(○)
我女兒剛剛到家。

02 文法誤用詳細解析
Grammar Analysis

英文中慣用被動方式呈現的動詞有以下幾類：

（1）這類動詞以來往動詞居多，但與其說是慣用被動式，到不如說式過去分詞當形容詞用。上述範例即用 be + p.p. 表達，但要注意的事，這類句型用簡單式即可，不需要用到完成式。類似例子還有：

He is gone.（他走了。／他過世了。）

（2）dress, marry, retire, close, read 全都慣用過去分詞當形容詞，特別的是：

dress 慣用被動式或反身受詞：He is dressed in white. = He dressed himself in white.（他身穿白色衣服。）若用主動是則意指幫別人穿衣服：She dressed her daughter in red.（她給女兒穿紅色衣服。）

marry 慣用過去分詞形容一個人的婚姻狀態：He is married.（他已婚。）未婚的話，則可用 unmarried。

（3）表情緒的動詞，常用過去分詞形式修飾人的主詞，如：ashamed, bored, excited, interested, surprised, tired, touched, confused, embarrassed, frightened 等等，譯為該主詞「感到……」。然而，這類動詞的現在分詞則可用來修飾事物或人，譯為該主詞是「令人感到……的」。

We were deeply touched by Ang Lee's movie.（我們深受李安的電影感動。）

It is a touching story.（這是個令人感動的故事。）

03 文法使用誤用辨析
Grammar Error vs. Correct

01. 他精通中國古典文學。
- ✗ He is deeply readed in Chinese Classics.
- ✓ **He is deeply read in Chinese Classics.**

---

02. 主題樂園關門了。
- ✗ The theme park closed.
- ✓ **The theme park is closed.**

---

03. 老萊子是父母的開心果。
- ✗ Lao Lai-zi is amused to his parents.
- ✓ **Lao Lai-zi is amusing to his parents.**

---

04. 他胃不舒服。
- ✗ He suffered from an upsetting stomach.
- ✓ **He suffered from an upset stomach.**

---

05. 她下個月退休。
- ✗ She retired next month.
- ✓ **She is retired next month.**

---

06. 萬里長城令人驚嘆。
- ✗ **The Great Wall is amazed.**
- ✓ **The Great Wall is amazing.**

04 文法陷阱辨析練習
Grammar Practice

請選出題目選項中正確的用法。

01. It _____ that he is married.
- **A** said
- **B** says
- **C** is said

02. He _____ for apparent reason that his health was failing.
- **A** is resigned
- **B** resign
- **C** is resigning

03. The patient needs _____ after.
A look　　　　　**B** looking　　　　　**C** looked

04. Lisa will do anything to get _____.
A notice　　　　　**B** noticing　　　　　**C** noticed

05. I _____ three years ago.
A had graduated　　**B** graduated　　　　**C** graduate

06. I saw him _____ by a scoundrel last night.
A beat　　　　　**B** beated　　　　　**C** beaten

07. He has _____ to metropolitan lifestyle.
A been using　　　**B** got used　　　　**C** used

08. The decision _____ on whether you support me or not.
A depending　　　**B** is depended　　　**C** depends

09. The trip sounds _____.
A interesting　　　**B** interested　　　**C** interest

10. He is _____ in classic music.
A reading　　　　**B** readed　　　　**C** read

答案及題目中譯：

01. **C**	聽說他已經結婚了。
02. **A**	他辭職顯然是因為健康出問題。
03. **B**	這個病人需要被照顧。
04. **C**	為了引人注意，麗莎會做出任何事情。
05. **B**	我三年前畢業。
06. **C**	我看見他昨晚被一個流氓揍。
07. **B**	他已逐漸習慣都市的生活模式。
08. **C**	這項決定要看你是否支持我而定。
09. **A**	這趟旅遊聽起來很有趣。
10. **C**	他精通古典樂。

04 形容詞的詞序問題

01 文法使用錯誤範例
Sample of Wrong Grammar

A: Why are you so happy?
你為什麼這麼開心呢？

B: Because my mom bought me a new green beautiful silk dress（✗）
yesterday. → beautiful new green silk dress（○）
因為我媽媽昨天買了一件又新又漂亮的綠色絲質洋裝給我。

02 文法誤用詳細解析
Grammar Analysis

（1）在英語中，當名詞有多個形容詞修飾時，其順序為：（冠詞｜序數｜基數｜性質＋大小＋形狀＋新舊＋顏色＋出處＋材料）＋名詞。例如：

a new yellow leather bag（一個新的黃色皮包）

（2）「冠詞」包括：the, our, this, whose, some, plenty of 等。「出處」指一個國家或地區的詞，例如：Italian, French 等。「材料」的形容詞，例如：leather, glass, silk 等。例句如下：

This is a beautiful small round old yellow French wood study.
（這是一間精美小巧圓形的舊式黃色法國木質書房。）

所以範例中的正確說法應為：Because my mom bought me a beautiful new green silk dress yesterday.

03 文法使用誤用辨析
Grammar Error vs. Correct

01. 蒂娜的爸爸送給她一款精美的紅色德國手機作為生日禮物。
   ☒ Tina's dad gave her a Germany nice red phone as a birthday gift.
   ☑ **Tina's dad gave her a nice red Germany phone as a birthday gift.**

02. 這個新的小型棕色皮質手提包怎麼樣？
   ☒ What about this new little brown leather handbag?
   ☑ **What about this little new brown leather handbag?**

03. 艾倫買了一件昂貴的俄國黑色毛皮大衣。
   ☒ Allen bought an expensive Russian black fur coat.
   ☑ **Allen bought an expensive black Russian fur coat.**

04. 這張圖片上有一隻美麗的中國白孔雀。
   ☒ There is a beautiful Chinese white peacock in the picture.
   ☑ **There is a beautiful white Chinese peacock in the picture.**

05. 蘇珊非常喜歡這個精巧袖珍的日本娃娃。
   ☒ Susan likes this little fine Japanese doll very much.
   ☑ **Susan likes this fine little Japanese doll very much.**

06. 我穿著一件短的黑色棉質 T 恤。
   ☒ I am dressed in a black short cotton T-shirt.
   ☑ **I am dressed in a short black cotton T-shirt.**

04 文法陷阱辨析練習
Grammar Practice

請選出題目選項中正確的用法。

01. The _____ girl is very smart.
   Ⓐ tall pretty foreign　　　Ⓑ foreign pretty tall　　　Ⓒ pretty tall foreign

02. Mike has a _____ car.
   Ⓐ large foreign white　　　Ⓑ large white foreign　　　Ⓒ white large foreign

03. That _____ boy is Jerry's brother.
   Ⓐ handsome little French　　　Ⓑ French little handsome
   Ⓒ French handsome little

04. A: Is that your English teacher?
   B: No. My English teacher is a _____ lady.
   Ⓐ tall charming American　　　Ⓑ charming tall American
   Ⓒ charming American tall

05. My mom bought a _____ scarf.
   Ⓐ grey nice silk　　　Ⓑ nice grey silk　　　Ⓒ nice silk grey

06. He was singing a _____ song for her.
   Ⓐ lovely old Spanish　　　Ⓑ old lovely Spanish　　　Ⓒ old Spanish lovely

07. That _____ shopping bag is really cool.
   Ⓐ large plastic blue　　　Ⓑ large blue plastic　　　Ⓒ blue large plastic

08. The _____ house smells as if it hasn't been lived in for years.
   Ⓐ short grey wooden　　　Ⓑ grey wooden short　　　Ⓒ wooden grey short

答案及題目中譯：

01. Ⓒ	這位漂亮高駣的外國女孩很聰明。	
02. Ⓑ	麥可有一輛大型的白色進口車。	
03. Ⓐ	那位俊俏的法國小男孩是傑瑞的弟弟。	
04. Ⓑ	A：那位是你的英文老師嗎？ B：不，我的老師是一位迷人高駣的美國女士。	
05. Ⓑ	我媽媽買了一條很好的灰色絲質圍巾。	
06. Ⓐ	他當時正在唱一首可愛的西班牙老歌給她聽。	
07. Ⓑ	那個大型的藍色塑膠購物袋非常酷。	
08. Ⓒ	那幢矮小的木造灰色房子聞起來像是已經很多年沒人住了。	

05 間接問句的用法

01 文法使用錯誤範例
Sample of Wrong Grammar

A: Excuse me. Can you tell me where is the nearest bus station(✕)?
不好意思，您能否告訴我最近的公車站在哪裡？

B: I don't know where is the bus station(✕). Sorry that I can't help you.
我不知道公車站在哪兒耶。抱歉幫不上忙。
→ where the (nearest) bus station is(○)

02 文法誤用詳細解析
Grammar Analysis

直接問句和間接問句在句子中的呈現方式是不同的，請見以下說明：

通常疑問句都是由直述句當中的主詞和動詞倒裝而形成的，例如：He is a student. 必須將主詞和動詞倒裝成為 Is he a student? 才能成為疑問句。將問句併入另一個問句中，就成為間接問句。在間接問句的句型中，附屬的間接問句就成為句子中的「名詞子句」，整個子句也就成為主要子句中動詞的受詞，所以必須以一般句子結構出現，亦即「主詞＋動詞……」。例如：

Can anyone tell me where my purse is?（有誰能告訴我我的皮包在哪兒？）

Do you know where you leave your handbag?（你記得你把手提包留在哪兒嗎？）

若是直接問句中沒有疑問詞（who, where, where），而是以 be 動詞或助動詞（will, do, can...）為首的 yes / no 疑問句，此類疑問句當做間接問句使用時，就可以疑問詞 whether 或是 if 連接兩個句子。例如：

Nobody knows whether / if Mike will come today.（沒人知道麥可今天會不會來。）

所以範例中的正確說法應為：Can you tell me where the nearst bus station is?
I don't know where the bus station is.

03 文法使用誤用辨析
Grammar Error vs. Correct

01. 你知道現在幾點嗎？
- ☒ Do you know what time is it?
- ☑ **Do you know what time it is?**

02. 你能告訴我意外是怎麼發生的嗎？
- ☒ Can you tell me how did the accident happen?
- ☑ **Can you tell me how the accident happened?**

03. 你記得他的電話號碼幾號嗎？
- ☒ Do you remember what is his phone number?
- ☑ **Do you remember what his phone number is?**

04. 請讓我知道你住在哪裡。
- ☒ Please let me know where do you live.
- ☑ **Please let me know where you live.**

05. 我不會告訴你他是誰。
- ☒ I won't tell you who is he.
- ☑ **I won't tell you who he is.**

06. 能不能請您告訴我可以在哪裡找到這個男人？
- ☒ Would you please tell me where can I find this man?
- ☑ **Would you please tell me where I can find this man?**

04 文法陷阱辨析練習
Grammar Practice

請選出題目選項中正確的用法。

01. I can't remember when _____ Mr. Lee.
- Ⓐ I saw
- Ⓑ did I see
- Ⓒ I did see

02. Don't tell my mother where _____. I'm hiding from her now.
- Ⓐ I am
- Ⓑ am I
- Ⓒ me

03. Does anyone know how _____ the truth?
   A did he find out   **B** is he finding out   **C** he found out

04. I don't know _____ come to the office today.
   A will Mr. Smith   **B** Mr. Smith will   **C** whether Mr. Smith will

05. None of them knows when _____ the new semester _____.
   A X; begin   **B** will; begin   **C** if; begins

06. Can anyone tell me why _____?
   A is he here   **B** he here is   **C** he is here

07. The man will never forget what _____ his father _____ him.
   A did; tell   **B** X; told   **C** is; telling

08. Do you know _____ Jessica was invited to the party?
   A if   **B** who   **C** did

09. It is surprised that nobody knows how _____.
   A old is Grandpa   **B** old Grandpa is   **C** is Grandpa old

10. Even his parents don't know _____ now.
   A where is he   **B** he is where   **C** where he is

答案及題目中譯：

01. **A**	我不記得我什麼時候看過李先生。	
02. **A**	別告訴我媽媽我在哪。我正在躲她。	
03. **C**	有誰知道他是怎麼發現真相的嗎？	
04. **C**	我不知道史密斯先生今天會不會進辦公室。	
05. **A**	沒有人知道學校這學期什麼時候開學。	
06. **C**	有誰可以告訴我為什麼他會在這兒嗎？	
07. **B**	那個男人沒有辦法忘記他父親跟他說過的話。	
08. **A**	你知道潔西卡有沒有被邀請來參加這場宴會嗎？	
09. **B**	沒有人知道爺爺幾歲，這真令人驚訝。	
10. **C**	連他的父母都不知道他現在在哪裡。	

Trap 4 文法陷阱・文法使用差異篇

01 have been to vs. have gone to

01 文法使用錯誤範例
Sample of Wrong Grammar

A: Where is Mr. Smith?
史密斯先生在哪裡？

B: He has been(✗) to New York. → gone(○)
他去紐約了。

02 文法誤用詳細解析
Grammar Analysis

have been to 與 have gone to 後均可接地點，但是在用法與所表達的意思上有很大區別。

（1）have been to 意為「曾經去過某地」，表示現在已不在那裡了，強調「最近的經歷」。可以用任何人稱，通常可與表示次數的副詞連用。如 once, twice 等，表示「去過某地幾次」，也可和 just, never, ever 等詞連用。

（2）have gone to 意為「已經到某地去」，表示還沒回來，強調說話時，人不在現場，也可以理解為「動作的完成」，強調人已離開說話現場。

範例中，B 所要表達的意思是「去紐約了」，如上所述，因此正確的說法應為：

He has gone to New York.

需要注意的是，兩者在遇到 here, there, home, abroad 這四個地點副詞時，要刪掉 to。

03 文法使用誤用辨析
Grammar Error vs. Correct

01. 他們已經到新加坡去了。
- ⊠ They have been to Singapore.
- ⊙ They **have gone to Singapore.**

02. 我去過那個博物館兩次。
- ⊠ I have gone to the museum twice.
- ⊙ **I have been to the museum twice.**

03. 傑克和他女朋友看電影去了。
- ⊠ Jake has been to the cinema with his girlfriend.
- ⊙ **Jake has gone to the cinema with his girlfriend.**

04. 佩妮不在這裡，她去超級市場了。
- ⊠ Penny isn't here. She has been to the supermarket.
- ⊙ **Penny isn't here. She has gone to the supermarket.**

05. 我從沒有去過日本。
- ⊠ I have never gone to Japan.
- ⊙ **I have never been to Japan.**

06. 你以前來過這裡嗎？
- ⊠ Have you been to here before?
- ⊙ **Have you been here before?**

04 文法陷阱辨析練習
Grammar Practice

請選出題目選項中正確的用法。

01. A: How long have you _____ Taiwan? B: For about 2 months.
- Ⓐ been
- Ⓑ gone to
- Ⓒ been to

02. Sophie has _____ to Italy three times.
- Ⓐ gone
- Ⓑ been
- Ⓒ went

03. The children have _____ to swim in the swimming pool.

    A been   **B** went   **C** gone

04. Tina has been _____ here twice.
    A to   **B** of   **C** X

05. He has _____ to visit his aunt.
    A went   **B** gone   **C** been

06. How many times have you _____ to Hawaii?
    A been   **B** went   **C** gone

07. Lisa has _____ to the garden. I want to go, too.
    A went   **B** gone   **C** been

08. Barry doesn't want to see you, so he has _____ to another country.
    A gone   **B** been   **C** went

09. David likes traveling, but he has never _____ abroad.
    A been   **B** been to   **C** gone

10. She has never _____ to Paris.
    A went   **B** gone   **C** been

答案及題目中譯：

01. **A**   A：你在台灣待多久了？   B：大約兩個月。

02. **B**   蘇菲去過義大利三次了。

03. **C**   孩子們已經去游泳池游泳了。

04. **C**   蒂娜來過這裡兩次。

05. **B**   他去找他阿姨了。

06. **A**   你去過夏威夷幾次？

07. **B**   莉莎已經去花園了，我也想去。

08. **A**   貝瑞不想見妳，所以他出國去了。

09. **A**   大衛喜歡旅行，但是他從未出國過。

10. **C**   她從未去過巴黎。

02 neither...nor vs. either...or

01 文法使用錯誤範例
Sample of Wrong Grammar

A: Jim, why don't you taste the food?
吉姆，為什麼不嚐嚐這些食物？

B: Because I like either butter or (✗) cheese, and the food has some butter and cheese in it. → neither... nor (○)
因為我既不喜歡奶油也不喜歡起司，而這個食物裡面兩者都有。

02 文法誤用詳細解析
Grammar Analysis

either 與 neither 都可當作連接詞，...either... 當作連接詞時可與 or 構成片語 either...or，意為「若非……就是……」，表示兩者任擇其一，不能作否定句的主詞；neither 作連詞時可與 nor 構成片語，neither...nor 意為「既非……也非……」，表示兩者都否定。這兩個片語常用來連接兩個並列成分，但應注意以下幾點：

（1）動詞的單複數形式必須和最靠近的一個主詞保持一致，人稱代名詞作主詞也一樣，即採用「就近原則」（動詞與靠近的名詞、代名詞在「人稱、數」上保持一致）。

（2）在表示一個人沒有做某事，另一個人也沒做同一類事時，可用 neither 或 nor 進行簡略回答，其結構為：Neither / Nor ＋助動詞 / 助動詞 / be 動詞＋主詞。

範例中，B 所表達的意思是「既不喜歡奶油也不喜歡起司」，表示「既不……也不……」應用 neither...nor，因此正確的說法應為：

Because I like neither butter nor cheese.

03 文法使用誤用辨析
Grammar Error vs. Correct

01. 你可以選擇一樣，果汁或湯。
- ⊠ You can have neither fruit juice nor soup.
- ⊙ **You can have either fruit juice or soup.**

02. 我不喜歡這個房間，既不寬敞又不明亮。
- ⊠ I don't like this room because it is either spacious or bright.
- ⊙ **I don't like this room because it is neither spacious nor bright.**

03. A: 大衛不是步行去上學的。　　　　　　B: 我也不是。
- ⊠ A: David doesn't go to school on foot.　B: So do I.
- ⊙ **A: David doesn't go to school on foot.**　**B: Nor do I.**

04. 不是我，就是你錯了。
- ⊠ Either I or you is wrong.
- ⊙ **Either I or you are wrong.**

05. 傑克和我都不喜歡游泳。
- ⊠ Neither Jake nor I likes swimming.
- ⊙ **Neither Jake nor I like swimming.**

06. 珍妮不能準時到那裡，我也不能。
- ⊠ Jenny can't get there on time, or can I.
- ⊙ **Jenny can't get there on time, nor can I.**

04 文法陷阱辨析練習
Grammar Practice

請選出題目選項中正確的用法。

01. It's neither cold _____ hot today.
- Ⓐ nor
- Ⓑ or
- Ⓒ and

02. You can_____ write _____ make a phone call to answer the questions.
- Ⓐ either / nor
- Ⓑ neither / or
- Ⓒ either / or

03. Either you or I _____ mad.
Ⓐ is　　　　　　　　Ⓑ am　　　　　　　　Ⓒ are

04. Neither I nor Jim _____ a student.
Ⓐ is　　　　　　　　Ⓑ am　　　　　　　　Ⓒ are

05. A: He didn't finish the work yesterday.
　　B: _____ did I.
Ⓐ Or　　　　　　　Ⓑ So　　　　　　　Ⓒ Neither

06. I can _____write _____ speak French.
Ⓐ either / nor　　　Ⓑ neither / nor　　　Ⓒ neither / or

07. _____ either you or I going there tomorrow?
Ⓐ Is　　　　　　　Ⓑ Are　　　　　　　Ⓒ Am

08. When Joy is happy, she _____ sings _____ dances.
Ⓐ either / nor　　　Ⓑ neither / or　　　Ⓒ either / or

09. A: I don't like sports.
　　B: _____ do I.
Ⓐ Or　　　　　　　Ⓑ So　　　　　　　Ⓒ Nor

答案及題目中譯：

01. Ⓐ	今天天氣不冷也不熱。	
02. Ⓒ	你可以用寫的或打電話來回答這些問題。	
03. Ⓑ	不是你，就是我瘋了。	
04. Ⓐ	我跟吉姆都不是學生。	
05. Ⓒ	A：他昨天沒完成工作。　B：我也沒有。	
06. Ⓑ	我不會寫，也不會說法文。	
07. Ⓑ	明天要去那裡的是你還是我？	
08. Ⓒ	喬伊高興的時候不是唱歌就是跳舞	
09. Ⓒ	A：我不喜歡運動。　B：我也不喜歡。	

Day29

03 other vs. the other vs. another

01 文法使用錯誤範例
Sample of Wrong Grammar

A: How many kids do you have?
   你有幾個小孩？

B: I have two kids. One is ten and another(✕) is eight. → the other(○)
   我有兩個小孩，一個十歲，另一個八歲。

02 文法誤用詳細解析
Grammar Analysis

other, the other 以及 another 都可作不定代名詞，但三者在含義及用法上有所區別。

（1）other 可作形容詞或代名詞，做形容詞時意為「別的，其他」，其複數形式為 others，在句中可作主語、受詞。

（2）the other 指總數為二時的「另外一個」，經常與 one 搭配，其複數形式為 the others，特指某一範圍內的「其他的（人或物）」，此時的 other 作代名詞。

（3）another 也可作形容詞或代名詞，泛指同類事物中的三者或三者以上的「另一個」，只能用於三個或更多的人或物，前面不能加任何冠詞，後面也不能加 s。

　範例中，「有兩個小孩，一個十歲，一個八歲」，如上所述，指兩者中的一個應用 the other，句中的 another 只能用於三個或更多的人或物，因此正確的說法應為：

One is ten and the other is eight.（一個十歲，另一個八歲。）

　簡言之：兩者→ one…, the other…；一個 + 多個 → one…, the others…；三者 → one…, another…, the other…；三者以上 → one…, another…, the others…。

03 文法使用誤用辨析
Grammar Error vs. Correct

01. 我不喜歡黑色，這件你還有其他的顏色嗎？
　　☒ I don't like black. Do you have this of the other colors?
　　☑ **I don't like black. Do you have this of other colors?**

---

02. 我們還需要多加幾張桌子。
　　☒ We need other few desks.
　　☑ **We need another few desks.**

---

03. 這裡有三位老師，一位教英文、一位教數學、一位教歷史。
　　☒ There are three teachers. The other teaches English, other teaches Math and another teaches history.
　　☑ **There are three teachers. One teaches English, another teaches math and the other teaches history.**

---

04. 請把另一隻手也伸過來。
　　☒ Give me another hand, please.
　　☑ **Give me the other hand, please.**

---

05. 這個不適合你，試試另一個吧。
　　☒ This one doesn't fit you. Try the other one.
　　☑ **This one doesn't fit you. Try another one.**

---

06. 約翰比班上其他學生都聰明。
　　☒ John is cleverer than the other in his class.
　　☑ **John is cleverer than the others in his class.**

---

07. A：你是大笨蛋。　B：你也是！
　　☒ A: You are a stupid fool.　B: You are the other!
　　☑ **A: You are a stupid fool.　B: You are another!**

04 文法陷阱辨析練習
Grammar Practice

請選出題目選項中正確的用法。

01. Jim, why are you the only one here?
Where are _____ of your group gone?
A other　　　　　**B** the others　　　　　**C** the other

02. Let's think of _____ ways.
A other　　　　　**B** the others　　　　　**C** the other

03. The project will be finished in _____ three months.
A other　　　　　**B** the others　　　　　**C** another

04. I have two hats. One is black and _____ is grey.
A other　　　　　**B** the others　　　　　**C** the other

05. The old man has three sons. _____ is a doctor, _____ is a teacher, _____ is an engineer.
A One / one / another　　　　　**B** Another / another / the other
C One / another / the other

06. It is hard to tell the twin sisters _____ from _____.
A one / the other　　　　　**B** the other / one　　　　　**C** another / the other

07. Tina is more careful than _____ members in the company.
A other　　　　　**B** the others　　　　　**C** the other

08. This coat is too big. I'll try on _____.
A other　　　　　**B** the others　　　　　**C** another

答案及題目中譯：

01. **B** 吉姆，為什麼只有你一個人在這裡？其他人呢？

02. **A** 讓我們想想看有沒別的辦法吧。

03. **C** 再追加三個月這項計畫就能完成。

04. **C** 我有兩頂帽子，一頂是黑色的，另一頂是灰色的。

05. **C** 老人有三個兒子。一位是醫生，一位是老師，另一位是工程師。

06. **A** 這對雙胞胎很難辨識誰是誰。

07. **C** 蒂娜比公司其他員工都要細心。

08. **C** 這件外套太大了，我要試穿另外一件。

Day29

04 shameful vs. ashamed

01 文法使用錯誤範例
Sample of Wrong Grammar

A: Your ashamed(✗) behavior makes us embarrassed. → shameful(○)
你丟臉的行為讓我們很尷尬。

B: I'm sorry for that.
我很抱歉。

02 文法誤用詳細解析
Grammar Analysis

　　shameful 與 ashamed 均為動詞 shame 的形容詞形式，含有「羞愧的」之意，但兩者在具體含義及用法上有所區別。

（1）shameful 意為「可恥的；丟臉的」，指人或人的行為本身不光彩、不道德，是客觀評價，表示事物本身是「可恥的」，既可作補語也可做形容詞，作補語時，主詞常指物。而範例中，「你的丟臉的行為」是指人本身的行為不光彩、不道德，形容此行為應該用 shameful，因此正確的說法應為：

Your shameful behavior makes us embarrassed.

（2）ashamed 意為「感到羞愧的；覺得慚愧的」，指主詞本身感到慚愧、羞恥，是主觀感覺，用於人，常做補語，一般用於 sb. be ashamed of 句型中。例如：

He is ashamed of having cheated in the exam.（他為考試作弊感到羞愧。）

03 文法使用誤用辨析
Grammar Error vs. Correct

01. 偷東西是可恥的行為。
　　❌ Stealing is an ashamed behavior.
　　⭕ **Stealing is a shameful behavior.**

02. 他媽媽為他感到羞恥。
　　❌ His mom felt shameful of him.
　　⭕ **His mom felt ashamed of him.**

03. 我不認為誠實地承認創新，有什麼可恥之處。
　　❌ I don't see anything ashamed about honestly admitting to innovation.
　　⭕ **I don't see anything shameful about honestly admitting to innovation.**

04. 她應該為她說這種謊而感到羞恥。
　　❌ She should be shameful of herself for telling such a lie.
　　⭕ **She should be ashamed of herself for telling such a lie.**

05. 這種想法是可恥的。
　　❌ It's an ashamed thought.
　　⭕ **It's a shameful thought.**

06. 這並不可恥。
　　❌ It's nothing to be shameful of.
　　⭕ **It's nothing to be ashamed of.**

04 文法陷阱辨析練習
Grammar Practice

請選出題目選項中正確的用法。

01. The criminal is _____ of himself for having done that.
　　Ⓐ shamed　　　　　Ⓑ ashamed　　　　　Ⓒ shameful

02. Robbing is a (an) _____ behavior.
　　Ⓐ ashamed　　　　　Ⓑ shameful　　　　　Ⓒ shame

03. Students should not be _____ of asking questions in class.
　　Ⓐ ashamed　　　　　Ⓑ shameful　　　　　Ⓒ shame

04. You shouldn't have done that. What you've done is _____.
   A ashamed of   **B** ashamed   **C** shameful

05. How could you do that? You should be _____ of yourself.
   A ashamed   **B** shameful   **C** shamed

06. That man doesn't think it's _____ to be a beggar.
   A ashamed   **B** shameful   **C** shame

07. Lily was _____ of her rudeness.
   A shame   **B** ashamed   **C** shameful

08. The poor boy was not _____ of his low origin.
   A shame   **B** ashamed   **C** shameful

09. Tom played a (an) _____ role in the farce.
   A shame   **B** ashamed of   **C** shameful

10. Luna was _____ being unable to answer the question.
   A ashamed of   **B** shameful   **C** shame

答案及題目中譯：

01. **B**	這犯人對自己做了那種事感到很羞愧。
02. **B**	搶劫是一種可恥的行為。
03. **A**	學生不應該為了在課堂上發問而感到羞恥。
04. **C**	你不該做那種事的，你應該為此感到羞愧。
05. **A**	你怎能做那種事？你該為自己的行為感到慚愧。
06. **B**	那個人不認為當乞丐很羞恥。
07. **B**	莉莉對自己的無禮感到很羞愧。
08. **B**	這個窮孩子並不以自己出身低微為恥。
09. **C**	湯姆在這齣笑劇中扮演一個丟人的角色。
10. **A**	露娜對自己沒辦法回答這個問題而感到羞愧。

Trap 4 文法陷阱・文法使用差異篇

05 sometime vs. sometimes vs. some time vs. some times

01 文法使用錯誤範例
Sample of Wrong Grammar

A: How do you go to school every day?
你每天怎麼去學校？

B: On foot，but some times(✗) by bike. → sometimes(○)
步行，不過有時候會騎腳踏車。

02 文法誤用詳細解析
Grammar Analysis

sometime, sometimes, some time, some times 都表時間，但意思及用法有別。

（1）sometime 是個時間副詞，意為「（過去或將來的）某一時刻；在某時期」，多置於句子後半。也可指「任何時候」，同 anytime；當形容詞則指「以前的」。

I met her sometimes last year.（我在去年某時遇見她。）
Come over sometimes you feel like it.（你任何時候想來就來。）
Cecile was a sometimes actress.（瑟西爾以前當過演員。）

（2）sometimes 是個頻率副詞，表「有時、偶爾」，近似 at times，occasionally, from time to time，可置於句首，也可以放 be 動詞後，或者放在動詞前。例如：

Old people are sometimes forgetful.（老人有時多忘事。）

（3）some time 意為「一段時間、一些時間」。

I took some time to clean up my room.（我花了些時間打掃房間。）

（4）some times 意為「好幾次、……次」，這裡的 time 當作次數。

Scientists have warned the risk of tsunami some times.
（科學家已數度警告有海嘯的危險。）

範例中，B 所表達的意思是「有時騎車去上學」，如上所述，表示「有時」要用 sometimes，而句中的 some times 表示的是次數，因此正確的說法應為：

On foot, but sometimes by bike.

03 文法使用誤用辨析
Grammar Error vs. Correct

01. 這可能會花你一些時間。
   ❌ This may take you sometime.
   ⭕ **This may take you some time.**

02. 那場交通事故發生在去年的某個時期。
   ❌ The traffic accident happened sometimes last year.
   ⭕ **The traffic accident happened sometime last year.**

03. 有時候，我喜歡一個人旅遊。
   ❌ Sometimes, I like traveling alone.
   ⭕ **Sometimes, I like traveling alone.**

04. 我去過那兒幾次。
   ❌ I have been there sometimes.
   ⭕ **I have been there some times.**

05. 你任何時候都可以過來這兒借書。
   ❌ You can come and borrow the book some time.
   ⭕ **You can come and borrow the book sometime.**

06. 我媽媽有時候脾氣很暴躁。
   ❌ My mom is some times very hot-tempered.
   ⭕ **My mom is sometimes very hot-tempered.**

04 文法陷阱辨析練習
Grammar Practice

請選出題目選項中正確的用法。

01. I saw John _____ last month.
    A sometime   **B** some time   **C** sometimes

02. Lucy _____ writes to me.
    A sometime   **B** some time   **C** sometimes

03. Sam, a _____ lecturer of English of the college, is now the headmaster.
    A some time   **B** sometime   **C** sometimes

04. Jim's house is _____ larger than Jan's.
    A sometime   **B** some time   **C** some times

05. My grandparents will stay here for _____.
    A sometime   **B** some time   **C** sometimes

06. Rita will be back _____ in May.
    A some times   **B** some time   **C** sometime

07. _____ the teacher wonders if Ann is clever.
    A Sometimes   **B** Some time   **C** Some times

08. All of us have studied math for _____.
    A sometime   **B** some time   **C** sometimes

答案及題目中譯：

01. **A**	我上個月某時看過約翰。
02. **C**	露西有時候會寫信給我。
03. **B**	山姆以前是這所大學的英文講師，現在已經升為校長了。
04. **C**	吉姆的房子比珍的大了幾倍。
05. **B**	我父母會在這裡住一段時間。
06. **C**	麗塔五月某日會回來。
07. **A**	有時候，老師會忍不住想，安到底算不算聰明。
08. **B**	我們所有人都學過數學一段時間了。

06 one 的指示代名詞

---

01 文法使用錯誤範例
Sample of Wrong Grammar

A:　Who has a pen?
　　誰有筆？

B:　I have it(✗) → one(○)
　　我這裡有一枝。

A:　Who has a pen?
　　這枝筆是誰的？

B:　I have one(✗) → it(○)
　　是我的。

02 文法誤用詳細解析
Grammar Analysis

one 可作代名詞，在不同的場合用法也有所不同。

（1）one 作不定代名詞時，意為「任何人、誰都……」，當人稱代名詞時，意為「個人、某人」；為避免重複，one 可以代替前面剛提到過的同一類人或物，前面不加任何限定詞，其複數形式為 ones。

I need a cup. Can you lend me one?（我需要杯子。你能借我一個嗎？）

（2）不定冠詞 a/an 不可直接和 one 連用，但 one 與形容詞連用時，該形容詞前面常接 a, the, this, that, next, last, my, her 等限定詞，例如：a single one, the beautiful one。

（3）one 只能代替可數名詞，遇到不可數名詞，應該用 that 或 it，that 用來指同類事物，it 則指同一事物。例如：This area is short of water; you can only get it far away from here.（這地區缺水，你只能從很遠的地方取得水。）

（4）one 通常不用在名詞所有格和形容詞性的所有格代名詞（如 mine, his, hers, its, ours, yours, theirs, whose）之後，也不用在 own 和 both 之後。

（5）one 不可以替代句中的不定詞或子句等充當主詞或受詞，也不可以替代上文全句的內容或部分內容，而 it 可以。

　　左側範例中，以 a pen 問，沒有指定哪一枝筆，故要用不定代名詞 one 回答。右側範例中，以 the pen 詢問，the 為定冠詞，故要用 it 回答，因為 it 可以代表特定或指定的人事物。

03 文法使用誤用辨析
Grammar Error vs. Correct

01. 露西的書放在左邊，莉莉的書放在右邊。
    - ☒ Lucy's books are kept left and Lily's ones are kept right.
    - ☑ **Lucy's books are kept left, while Lily's are kept right.**

02. 我覺得這部電影不如我們上次看的那部好。
    - ☒ I think this film is not so good as one we saw last time.
    - ☑ **I think this film is not so good as the one we saw last time.**

03. 老師告訴我們，學習英文與學習中文一樣重要。
    - ☒ The teacher tells us that the study of English is as important as Chinese.
    - ☑ **The teacher tells us that the study of English is as important as that of Chinese.**

04. 我的外套是黑色的，她的是白色的。
    - ☒ My coat is black, her one is white.
    - ☑ **My coat is black, hers is white.**

05. 這裡有洋裝嗎？我要一條棉質的。
    - ☒ Are there any dresses? I need cotton one.
    - ☑ **Are there any dresses? I need a cotton one.**

06. 這台電腦是你借的，還是你自己的？
    - ☒ Do you borrow the computer or is it your own one?
    - ☑ **Do you borrow the computer or is it your own?**

04 文法陷阱辨析練習
Grammar Practice

請選出題目選項中正確的用法。

01. I have a new hat and several old _____.
　　A one　　　　　　　**B** ones　　　　　　**C** the ones

02. John is _____ to solve all the problems.
　　A the one　　　　　　**B** ones　　　　　　**C** the ones

03. This room and _____ upstairs are being decorated.
　　A one　　　　　　　**B** ones　　　　　　**C** the one

04. I need a cell phone; I think I must buy _____.
　　A ones　　　　　　　**B** one　　　　　　**C** the one

05. There were a few old people and some younger _____ in the hall.
　　A X　　　　　　　　**B** one　　　　　　**C** ones

06. _____ mus tlove his country.
　　A The ones　　　　　**B** One　　　　　　**C** The one

07. Mr. Brown is the teacher, _____ who is loved by his students.
　　A the ones　　　　　**B** the one　　　　**C** one

08. A: Have an orange, please.
　　B: No, thanks. I've just had _____.
　　A the ones　　　　　**B** one　　　　　　**C** the one

答案及題目中譯：

01. **B** 我有一頂新的和幾頂舊的帽子。	
02. **A** 約翰就是那個能解決所有困難的人。	
03. **C** 這間房間和樓上那幾間都正在裝潢。	
04. **B** 我沒有手機，我想我得買一支了。	
05. **C** 有幾位老人和一些年輕人在大廳裡。	
06. **B** 每個人都必須愛自己的國家。	
07. **C** 布朗先生就是一位相當受到自己學生愛戴的老師。	
08. **B** A：吃顆柳橙吧！　B：謝謝，不用了。我剛剛才吃完一顆。	

Trap 4 文法陷阱・文法使用差異篇

07 **so vs. such**

---

01 文法使用錯誤範例
Sample of Wrong Grammar

A: Who is this? She is so（✗）a beautiful girl. → such（○）
她這位是誰？她真是一個美麗的女孩。

B: Her name is Judy, my best friend.
她叫茱蒂，是我最好的朋友。

02 文法誤用詳細解析
Grammar Analysis

so 與 such 均有「如此、這麼、那麼」之意，可以進行同義改寫，但在用法有別。

（1）so 為副詞，表「如此、這樣」，後面常接形容詞或副詞。即：so ＋ adj. ｜ a / an ＋單數名詞；so ＋ adj. / adv. ＋ that ＋子句。

（2）such 為形容詞，表「如此的、這樣的」，修飾名詞，可接可數名詞或不可數名詞，其常用句型結構有：such ＋ adj. ＋ n.；such a / an ＋ adj. ＋單數可數名詞；such ＋ n. ＋ that ＋子句。例如：

She is so smart and kind that we all like her.
（她那麼聰明和善良，所以我們都喜歡她。）
It is such delicious food that I can eat it up all by myself.
（這食物這麼美味，我自己一個人就可以把它吃完。）

需要注意的是，只有 such 後面可接複數名詞或不可數名詞，但是如果名詞前有 few, many, little, much 等形容詞時，就必須用 so，而不能用 such；不過 a lot of 例外，只能用 such 搭配。

範例中，A 所要表達的意思為「她一個如此美麗的女孩」，girl 為單數名詞，如上所述，應為 so ＋ adj. ＋ a/an ＋單數名詞，或 such a / an ＋ adj. ＋單數可數名詞，因此正確的說法應為：

She is so beautiful a girl. 或 She is such a beautiful girl.

03 文法使用誤用辨析
Grammar Error vs. Correct

01. 他是一個如此聰明的孩子。
    ❌ He is such clever a child.
    ⭕ **He is such a clever child.**

02. 這是一件多麼漂亮的外套。
    ❌ It's so a nice coat.
    ⭕ **It's so nice a coat.**

03. 露西是如此可愛的一個女孩，以致每個人都喜歡她。
    ❌ Lucy is so a lovely girl that everyone likes her.
    ⭕ **Lucy is such a lovely girl that everyone likes her.**

04. 這部電影如此精彩，以致於我想再看一次。
    ❌ This film is such wonderful that I want to watch it again.
    ⭕ **This film is so wonderful that I want to watch it again.**

05. 這類事情不應該再發生了。
    ❌ So kind of things should not happen again.
    ⭕ **Such kind of things should not happen again.**

06. 安靜一點！不要這麼吵！
    ❌ Be quiet! Don't make such much noise!
    ⭕ **Be quiet! Don't make so much noise!**

04 文法陷阱辨析練習
Grammar Practice

請選出題目選項中正確的用法。

01. It is _____ weather that we decide to go out for a picnic.
    🅐 such fine   🅑 so fine   🅒 fine such

02. There are _____ people in the cinema.
    🅐 few so   🅑 such few   🅒 so few

03. The teacher spoke _____ quickly that I couldn't follow him.
   A so　　　　　　　**B** such　　　　　　　**C** a so

04. He sings _____ well.
   A so　　　　　　　**B** so that　　　　　　**C** such

05. There are _____ clever students in the classroom.
   A a so　　　　　　**B** a such　　　　　　**C** such

06. It is _____.
   A such fine a day　**B** so a fine day　　**C** such a fine day

07. There are _____ books in the library.
   A so many　　　　**B** such many　　　　**C** many so

08. _____ people like his songs.
   A Such a lot of　　**B** So a lot of　　　**C** A lot of so

09. There is _____ milk in the bottle.
   A so little　　　　**B** such few　　　　**C** much so

10. It is _____ delicious food that all the kids want to taste it.
   A so　　　　　　　**B** such　　　　　　　**C** such a

答案及題目中譯：

01. **A**	天氣這麼好，所以我們決定去野餐。	
02. **C**	電影院裡人好少。	
03. **A**	老師說話好快，我跟不上他。	
04. **A**	他唱得真好。	
05. **C**	這個教室裡有這麼聰明的一群學生。	
06. **C**	天氣真好。	
07. **A**	圖書館裡好多書喔。	
08. **A**	有這麼多人喜歡他的歌。	
09. **A**	瓶子裡的牛奶好少。	
10. **B**	這食物美味極了，所有小孩都想嚐看看。	

08 what vs. which

01 文法使用錯誤範例
Sample of Wrong Grammar

A: What's that under the sofa?
沙發下面那是什麼？

B: It's a puppy what(✗) I found on the street. → which(○)
它是我在路上撿到的小狗。

02 文法誤用詳細解析
Grammar Analysis

which 和 what 兩者都是疑問詞，分別有不同的用法和涵義：

（1）what 用作疑問詞時意為「什麼」，可以用於選擇範圍較大或不明確的場合；which 用作疑問詞時意為「哪一個」，可以用於選擇範圍較小或較明確的場合，但是，若指人，即使選擇的範圍不明確，也可用 which。例如：

What kind of movis do you like?（你喜歡哪一類電影？）
Which movie do you like? Harry Potter or The Lord of the Rings?
（你喜歡哪一部電影，哈利波特或是魔戒？）

（2）what 可用在關係子句中，但不能有先行詞。而 which 可以修飾表事物的先行詞，在關係子句當做主詞、受詞或者形容詞。例如：

This is what I want.（這就是我要的東西。）
This is the room which I study in.（這就是我讀書的房間。）

所以範例中的正確說法應為：It's a puppy which I found on the street.

03 文法使用誤用辨析
Grammar Error vs. Correct

01. 你想喝點什麼？
   - ☒ Which do you want to drink?
   - ☑ **What do you want to drink?**

02. 去博物館最近的路是哪一條？
   - ☒ What is the nearest way to the museum?
   - ☑ **Which is the nearest way to the museum?**

03. 瑪麗有一條裙子，那條裙子很漂亮。
   - ☒ Mary has a skirt, what is very nice.
   - ☑ **Mary has a skirt, which is very nice.**

04. 這本書是關於什麼的？
   - ☒ Which is this book about?
   - ☑ **What is this book about?**

05. 書桌上的哪一本書是你的？
   - ☒ What book is yours on the desk?
   - ☑ **Which book is yours on the desk?**

06. 她正在讀一本關於音樂的書。
   - ☒ She is reading a book, what is about music.
   - ☑ **She is reading a book, which is about music.**

04 文法陷阱辨析練習
Grammar Practice

請選出題目選項中正確的用法。

01. _____ subject do you like?
   - **A** What
   - **B** Which
   - **C** That

02. _____ subject do you like, English or Chinese?
   - **A** What
   - **B** Which
   - **C** That

03. _____ are you talking about?
   - **A** That
   - **B** Which
   - **C** What

04. This is the hat _____ I bought yesterday.
    A which   **B** what   **C** That

05. _____ of you knows the answer?
    A That   **B** Which   **C** What

06. _____ else have you bought in your trip to Japan?
    A What   **B** Which   **C** That

07. This is the book _____ I want.
    A that   **B** what   **C** which

08. There are many teachers in the office. _____ is your English teacher?
    A What   **B** Which   **C** That

09. He was reading a book, _____ he had borrowed from the library.
    A that   **B** what   **C** which

10. You look tired. _____ is your dream?
    A What   **B** Which   **C** That

答案及題目中譯：

01. **A**	你喜歡什麼科目？
02. **B**	你喜歡哪一個科目，英文還是中文？
03. **C**	你在說什麼？
04. **A**	這是我昨天買的那頂帽子。
05. **B**	你們當中有誰知道答案？
06. **A**	你去日本旅行還買了什麼？
07. **C**	這是我所喜歡的一本書。
08. **B**	辦公室裡有很多老師。哪一位是你的英文老師。
09. **C**	他正在讀一本書。是他從圖書館借回來的那一本。
10. **A**	你看起來很累。你夢到什麼了？

Trap 4 文法陷阱・文法使用差異篇

09 whether vs. if

01 文法使用錯誤範例
Sample of Wrong Grammar

A: Lily, please tell me if(✗) or not he will come to my party.
→ whether(○)
莉莉，請告訴我他是否能來參加我的派對。

B: I have no idea.
我不知道。

02 文法誤用詳細解析
Grammar Analysis

whether 與 if 均可表示「是否」。一般用 if 引導合定的從屬句時。以下幾種情況下，則須用 whether，請見說明：

（1）以「是否」為句子的開頭時，例如：

Whether we can stay in my cousin's place depends on her mood.
我們是否能待在我表姊家，全看她的心情決定。

（2）whether 作為主詞補語；或是前面的名詞子句的同位語時。

（3）whether 在不定詞之前或在介系詞之後。

（4）whether 與 if 都可與 or not 連用，但緊接著 or not 時僅能用 whether，例如：

We don't know if/whether the news is true or not.
（我們不知道這新聞是否是事實。）

而在範例中，與 or not 緊連著用時，不能用 if，改用 whether。

所以範例中的正確說法應為：

Lily, please tell me whether or not he will come to my party.

03 文法使用誤用辨析
Grammar Error vs. Correct

01. 他不知道是不是該去那裡。
    ☒ He doesn't know if to go there.
    ☐ **He doesn't know** whether **to go there.**

---

02. 湯姆很擔心他是否會遲到。
    ☒ Tom is worried about if he will be late.
    ☐ **Tom is worried about** whether **he will be late.**

---

03. 我們是否能準時參加會議必須依交通狀況而定。
    ☒ If we can attend the meeting on time depends on the traffic.
    ☐ Whether **we can attend the meeting on time depends on the traffic.**

---

04. 我不在乎明天是否不會下雨。
    ☒ I don't care whether it won't rain tomorrow.
    ☐ **I don't care** if **it won't rain tomorrow.**

---

05. 你必須回答我你是否愛她的這個問題。
    ☒ You have to answer my question if you love her.
    ☐ **You have to answer my question** whether **you love her.**

---

06. 問題是我是否應該告訴她這個消息。
    ☒ The question is if I should tell her the news.
    ☐ **The question is** whether **I should tell her the news.**

04 文法陷阱辨析練習
Grammar Practice

請選出題目選項中正確的用法。

01. The mother didn't know _____ to laugh or to cry.
    Ⓐ if　　　　　　　Ⓑ whether　　　　　　Ⓒ X

02. You haven't answer my question _____ you get the book or not.
    Ⓐ if　　　　　　　Ⓑ X　　　　　　Ⓒ whether

03. I don't know _____ it isn't right.
A whether / if　　　　**B** whether　　　　**C** if

04. They're discussing _____ they should go on working.
A whether　　　　**B** X　　　　**C** if

05. _____ it is true, I will believe it.
A If　　　　**B** Whether　　　　**C** X

06. Ted, I shall go, _____ you come with me or stay at home.
A whether / if　　　　**B** whether　　　　**C** if

07. I don't know _____ it won't be sunny tomorrow.
A if　　　　**B** whether　　　　**C** whether / if

08. I'll tell you _____ or not I can come.
A if　　　　**B** whether　　　　**C** X

09. _____ it is sunny or rainy, I shall go there.
A If　　　　**B** X　　　　**C** Whether

10. _____ you ask Jim, he will help you carry the box.
A X　　　　**B** Whether　　　　**C** If

答案及題目中譯：

01.	**B**	這位母親不知道該笑還是該哭。
02.	**C**	你還沒有回答我你是否已經拿到書。
03.	**A**	我不知道它是否是不正確的。
04.	**A**	他們在討論是否該繼續工作。
05.	**B**	不管是不是事實我都相信。
06.	**A**	泰德，不管你跟我走或是留在家，我都得走了。
07.	**A**	我不知道明天是否會是晴天。
08.	**B**	我來或不來都會告訴你。
09.	**C**	不管是晴天或雨天我都會去那兒。
10.	**C**	假如你要求吉姆，他會幫你提箱子。

10 could vs. would

01 文法使用錯誤範例
Sample of Wrong Grammar

A: Jim failed in his English exam again.
吉姆又沒有通過英語考試。

B: How would(✗) he be so stupid? → could(○)
他怎麼會這麼笨？

02 文法誤用詳細解析
Grammar Analysis

could 與 would 均為情態動詞，兩者在用法上有所區別，請見以下說明：

（1）could 表能力時，意思是「能；會」，用來表達過去的習慣能力；表達可能性時，意思是「可能」；表示驚異、不信等情緒，常用於疑問句或否定句中；而表達與事實相反的情況，則常用於假設語氣。例如：

I could speak English well since I was a high school student.
（當我還是個高中生時，我的英文說得很好。）

How could she be so elegant?（她怎麼能夠這麼優雅。）

I could get the job if I had a second chance.
（如果還有第二次機會的話，我就可以得到那份工作了。）

（2）would 通常用於提出提議或邀請，委婉地表示自己的意見；如果要表示請求對方做一件麻煩的事情，通常會採用 would you mind ＋ V-ing 的句型，這樣的表達語氣較為客氣。例如：

Would you mind turning down the radio?（你介意將收音機關小聲一點嗎？）

所以範例中的正確說法應為：How could he be so stupid?

03 文法使用誤用辨析
Grammar Error vs. Correct

01. 他怎麼這麼無禮？
 ✗ How would he be so rude?
 ○ **How could he be so rude?**

02. 想不想要來一杯咖啡？
 ✗ Could you like a cup of coffee?
 ○ **Would you like a cup of coffee?**

03. 可以將尺遞給我嗎？
 ✗ Could you mind passing me the ruler?
 ○ **Would you mind passing me the ruler?**

04. 他無法回答你的問題。
 ✗ He wouldn't answer your question.
 ○ **He couldn't answer your question.**

05. 如果你願意的話，明天我可以過來。
 ✗ I can come tomorrow if you like.
 ○ **I could come tomorrow if you like.**

06. 露西能夠早上六點起床。
 ✗ Lucy would get up at 6:00.
 ○ **Lucy could get up at 6:00.**

04 文法陷阱辨析練習
Grammar Practice

請選出題目選項中正確的用法。

01. The young man _____ look at the problem a little differently.
 🅐 is 　　　　　　🅑 would 　　　　　　🅒 can

02. She _____ be delighted, if you went to see him.
 🅐 would 　　　　　　🅑 will 　　　　　　🅒 can

03. She _____ go to the airport that day.
Ⓐ wouldn't   Ⓑ would   Ⓒ couldn't

04. _____ you mind opening the window?
Ⓐ Would   Ⓑ Could   Ⓒ Can

05. My grandpa _____ go to bed strictly at 22:00.
Ⓐ could   Ⓑ would   Ⓒ will

06. How _____ she be so beautiful?
Ⓐ could   Ⓑ would   Ⓒ can

07. John _____ have enough money for a new computer.
Ⓐ wouldn't   Ⓑ would   Ⓒ couldn't

08. You _____ pass the exam if you studied hard.
Ⓐ will   Ⓑ can   Ⓒ could

09. _____ I speak to Mr. Smith, please?
Ⓐ Could   Ⓑ Would   Ⓒ Will

10. _____ you like to buy a hat?
Ⓐ Could   Ⓑ Would   Ⓒ Can

答案及題目中譯：

01. Ⓑ 這位年輕人會以稍微不同的角度面對這個問題。
02. Ⓐ 如果你去看他的話，她會很開心。
03. Ⓒ 那一天她沒有辦法去機場。
04. Ⓐ 你介意開個窗嗎？
05. Ⓑ 我爺爺準時晚上十點鐘上床睡覺。
06. Ⓐ 她怎麼會這麼美麗？
07. Ⓒ 約翰不可能有足夠的錢買新電腦。
08. Ⓒ 如果你用功的話，你一定可以通過考試。
09. Ⓐ 請問，我可以和史密斯先生說一下話嗎？
10. Ⓑ 你想要買一頂帽子嗎？

11 than 在比較級句型中的用法

01 文法使用錯誤範例
Sample of Wrong Grammar

A: Is it okay that we have our class reunion party at your place?
同學會在你的住處舉辦好嗎？

B: I'm afraid that my apartment is too small for the party.
Let's ask Jeff. His apartment is much bigger than me(✗). → mine(○)
我的公寓要辦同學會恐怕太小了。
我們去問傑夫吧。他的公寓比我的大得多了。

02 文法誤用詳細解析
Grammar Analysis

以 than 比較兩者時，要注意前後兩者必須是相同性質的事或物。也就是說人要跟人比、事要跟事比、物要跟物比。後兩者常用到所有格代名詞，如 mine、yours。

My desk is messier than yours. (yours = your desk)（我的桌子比你的亂。）

I'm taller than you.（我比你高。）

My brother can run faster than I do.（我的弟弟可以跑得比我快。）

除了 than 之外，同級比較用的連接詞 as...as 也應注意相同情形。例如：

My brother's English is not as good as yours. (yours = your English)
（我哥哥的英文不像你的英文那麼好。）

所以範例中的正確說法應為：His apartment is much bigger than mine.

03 文法使用誤用辨析
Grammar Error vs. Correct

01. 台北的房子比台南的房子貴。
　　☒ Houses in Taipei are more expensive than Tainan.
　　☑ **Houses in Taipei are more expensive than those in Tainan.**

02. 你奶奶做的櫻桃派嚐起來比我媽媽做的好吃。
　　☒ Your grandma's cherry pie tastes better than my mother.
　　☑ **Your grandma's cherry pie tastes better than my mother's.**

03. 我的學校比你的要遠。
　　☒ My school is farther than you.
　　☑ **My school is farther than yours.**

04. 今天的天氣比昨天熱。
　　☒ It is hotter than yesterday.
　　☑ **It is hotter than it was yesterday.**

05. 他說故事比你精采。
　　☒ He tells better stories than yours.
　　☑ **He tells better stories than you do.**

06. 台灣人比日本人友善。
　　☒ Taiwanese are more friendly than Japan.
　　☑ **Taiwanese are more friendly than Japanese.**

04 文法陷阱辨析練習
Grammar Practice

請選出題目選項中正確的用法。

01. He looks thinner than _____.
　　Ⓐ yesterday　　　　Ⓑ he did yesterday　　　Ⓒ he was yesterday

02. The public order in Taiwan is better than _____.
　　Ⓐ in Thailand　　　Ⓑ Thailand　　　　　Ⓒ it is in Thailand

03. The blue skirt looks prettier than _____.
　　Ⓐ the pink　　　　Ⓑ pink skirt　　　　Ⓒ the pink one

04. Things in the department store are more expensive than _____.
    A the night market　　**B** in the night market　　**C** those in the night market

05. Math homework is more difficult than _____.
    A science　　**B** science homework　　**C** science one

06. Traffic in the city is heavier than _____.
    A countryside　　**B** that in the countryside　　**C** countryside's

07. The weather is more changeable in London than _____.
    A Taipei　　**B** in Taipei　　**C** Taipei's

08. Life in the past was not as convenient as _____.
    A nowadays　　**B** it is nowadays　　**C** in nowadays

09. Your dress looks more formal than _____.
    A her　　**B** hers　　**C** she

10. Quitting smoking is not as easy as _____.
    A quitting coffee　　**B** coffee　　**C** quit coffee

答案及題目中譯：

01. **B** 他看起來比昨天還瘦。

02. **C** 台灣的公共秩序比泰國還好一些。

03. **C** 藍色的裙子看起來比粉紅色的更漂亮。

04. **C** 百貨公司的商品比夜市中的商品要來的貴。

05. **B** 數學的作業比科學的還要難。

06. **B** 城市中的交通比起鄉下要來的更繁忙。

07. **B** 倫敦的天氣比台北更多變。

08. **B** 從前的生活不像現代這麼方便。

09. **B** 妳的洋裝看起來比她的更為正式。

10. **A** 戒菸不像戒咖啡這麼簡單。

圖解式英文文法
30 天攻略本

作　　　者	朱懿婷 Gillian
審　　　定	羅展明
封 面 設 計	高鍾琪
內 頁 構 成	華漢電腦排版有限公司
發　行　人	周瑞德
總　編　輯	高致婕
執　行　編　輯	陳欣慧
校　　對	徐瑞璞、劉俞青
印　　製	世和印製企業有限公司
初　　版	2014 年 7 月
定　　價	新台幣 399 元
出　　版	力得文化
電　　話	（02）2351-2007
傳　　真	（02）2351-0887
地　　址	100 台北市中正區福州街 1 號 10 樓之 2
E　m　a　i　l	best.books.service@gmail.com
港澳地區總經銷	泛華發行代理有限公司
地　　址	香港筲箕灣東旺道 3 號星島新聞集團大廈 3 樓
電　　話	（852）2798-2323
傳　　真	（852）2796-5471

國家圖書館出版品預行編目（CIP）資料

圖解式英文文法 30 天攻略本／朱懿婷 Gillian 著 .
-- 初版 . -- 臺北市：力得文化，2014.07
面；　公分 . -- (Leader；001)
ISBN：978-986-90759-0-9 （精裝）
1. 英語　2. 語法
805.16　　　　　　　　　　　　　103010696

力得文化
Leader Culture

Lead your way, be your own leader!

力得文化
Leader Culture

Lead your way, be your own leader!